MW01438774

Paul James Thompson

Published by Paul James Thompson on Amazon KDP

Copyright 2018 © Paul Thompson

Please remember to leave a review for my book at your favorite retailer

License notes

Thank you for purchasing my book. This book remains the copyrighted property of the author, and may not be redistributed to others for commercial or non-commercial purposes. If you enjoyed this book, please encourage your friends to order their own copy from their favorite authorized retailer. Thank you for your support.

This story and characters are original and any similarities or resemblance to any other existing stories and characters is purely accidental or coincidental.

Chapter 1

Joss slumped forward on the table in front of him. Another cigarette burned down between his fingertips as he stared into space. He barely flinched as the embers began to singe his numb flesh. He took one last drag before discarding the butt on top of the heaped ashtray; the overwhelming swell of anger and sorrow still refused to subside. He'd tried to force himself to doze off more than once while waiting. There was still just enough adrenalin pumping through his veins to keep him awake, despite feeling exhausted.

The small, cramped room would have been peaceful if not for the repetitive sound of the large ventilation turbine that took up the entire west wall. Although the noise wasn't especially loud, it seemed to gnaw into his brain, deeper with each turn. Back when Joss was a detective he'd often used this room for interrogations. He'd leave perps to stew for as long as it took before they finally cracked, sometimes the full 24 hours he was legally allowed to detain them. Now it was his turn to wait it out.

The refreshing sound of the door sliding open snapped him from his trance. Three FRA agents entered the room; one stopped beside the door and the other two in front of him at the other side of the table. The first was the bulky guard that had been posted outside for as long as he'd been waiting. He wasn't sure how long he'd been there, but it was long enough to lose track of time. There weren't any clocks in any of the interrogation rooms and the screen on the wrist tablet integrated into his armor had been smashed in the fight.

He stared at the feds through bloodshot eyes; the bruises and scratches on his face stung as his expression switched from vacant to that of a frustrated scowl. The last thing he needed was a grilling from the feds.

"Good morning, Sergeant Akura," started the bald man in front of him. His pompous, self-serving demeanor was clear the instant he entered the room. "I am Inquisitor Darahk, Fusion Response Agency. You've already met Lieutenant Rosair."

Joss remembered the woman from earlier that morning, not to mention the fact she was moments too late when he really could have used the backup. Darahk's name also sounded familiar, although they'd never met. He'd heard his Father talk about him numerous times in the past. He knew they'd both fought in the Suu'vitan Military during the war. They weren't overly fond of one another if he remembered correctly, not that his Father liked anybody working for the Agency.

Joss had had his fair share of run-ins with the FRA throughout his short complicated career. They used their badge as an all-access pass to interfere in everyone else's business. He had no love for the feds either, but that didn't mean he'd forgotten how to play nice.

He cleared his throat and tried to hold back the full extent of vexation in his tone. "I've been detained here for hours! Couldn't you have waited for the damn report?"

"I assure you, we got here as soon as we could," replied Darahk.

The unrelenting lines of seriousness on his angular face and his overall body language portrayed him as a man of procedure and protocol. Joss couldn't help but notice how pristine his uniform looked. He seemed to move in such a way as not to crease it. *One stiff-looking, old bastard,* he thought.

"We have some questions to ask you about this morning's incident," said Darahk. "Let me start by saying…"

Joss shook his head and raised a lazy, yet firm finger, making Darahk pause mid- sentence. "You've got questions?!" He barked. "Nobody's told me shit since your grunts picked me up".

"Sergeant Akura, please…."

Joss wasn't finished. "And what's with the ape guarding the fucking door? If he tells me to 'please, sit down' one more time I'm going to ram that cannon up his ass! He even followed me to the pisser!"

He'd tried to leave the room several times while he'd been waiting and the guard only let him past that once, under close supervision. Joss had used the awkward opportunity to push for more information but the guard's lips had remained tightly sealed. Joss watched as Darahk looked over at the large FRA trooper, who shuffled around uncomfortably. He wore the emblem for the Commissar's guard, likely assigned to this post under orders directly from the man himself, rather than the Inquisitor.

Joss glanced to his right as Rosair stepped forward. The Lieutenant had a particular look he recognized, the look of a field agent that really couldn't be bothered with this bullshit part of the job. Her body language suggested that she had something better to do, or at least she thought so.

Rosair got straight to the point. "Our intel showed that you might have come into contact with certain elements, of a sensitive nature," she said. "We had orders to keep you confined until we could question you."

There was something that intrigued him about her. She had a small O'sar tattoo on the side of her neck, but her skin was darker like that of a Suu'vitan. Joss pondered over her origin while he decided how to respond. *Likely a half-breed who'd taken the right of passage to show her respect for the old traditions,* he thought.

Since the end of the war, the surrounding clans had mixed with the Suu'vitan population. The younger individuals with O'sar roots did their best to display an interest in their heritage, even though they lived like any other city dweller.

"Finally!" Joss bellowed after a fatigued delay. "Would it have killed him to tell me that when I got here!? Just what kind of 'sensitive elements' are we talking about?"

"All in good time, Sergeant," Darahk muttered, before producing a small interface chip that hung from his belt on a chain.

Darahk approached the table as Rosair pulled out the chair to save her commanding officer the trouble. The inquisitor lowered himself down into the seat before inserting the device into the console. A small holo-emitter in the center of the table came to life, projecting a series of images in the space between them.

Joss watched the Inquisitor re-adjust his uniform. He seemed to look uncomfortable in the seated position.

Darahk cleared his throat. "It's important that we hear your account of events beforehand. The sooner you start cooperating, the sooner you'll get answers." Darahk leaned forward, bringing his hands together an inch away from his face. "Tell us everything that happened, from the top."

Joss looked back at them while toying with his cigarette packet "Ok!" he said after a pause. "... Anything to get things moving." He grabbed the last smoke from the pack.

"These weren't your usual scumbags," said Joss, while playing with his lighter. "They were equipped for close combat and were heavily armored...they could fight too..." He kept them waiting for a couple of seconds more while he lit the cigarette. "These guys were pros..."

....

Earlier that morning...

"Come on Walter! What the fuck?!" Shouted Joss. It was the second time this week he'd been late for his shift and updating his code clearance had slipped his mind. Joss finally resorted to pounding on the door with his fist after ringing the buzzer repeatedly for ten seconds. It wouldn't have been so bad if it hadn't been for the pissing rain and a chilling wind that was unusual for this time of year.

Walt was probably watching him on the monitors and had decided to teach him a lesson. He had sat through more than one rant about the importance of punctuality and being prepared for the job, not that the old man wasn't a bit of a hypocrite. Joss sighed and turned to look over the city. From the quiet outer rim the view of the Porta Orbis city center looked spectacular. The metropolis glowed like the illuminated beacon of light it was actually believed to be. The rain gave it a misty haze, making it appear warmer in comparison to his current location. Joss pulled his cloak up around his face and blew off the stream of water running from his helmet down to the end of his nose. Suddenly, the door slid open and Joss entered with a start.

Walter looked over casually from his station and the column of monitors in the center of the room. He was pouring something from a hip flask into his morning coffee.

"You mean old bastard. It's blowing a gale out there," barked Joss, hanging up his drenched over garment. Beneath it he wore the standard issue LEX uniform complete with body armor. He did his best to shake off any excess rainwater and wandered over to his station.

The outpost was a small cylindrical building, relatively poky inside, but with work stations for four or five officers. LEX was short-staffed with barely enough enforcers to meet the two-guard minimum required for each outpost. Most of the equipment around this particular station was outdated, all except the shiny new gildecycle sitting on the dispatch ramp.

"Morning, lad," said Walt, not fazed by the bitching of his young partner. He was almost twice Joss' age. He looked like he'd been handsome in his youth and sported a well-crafted mustache. The sweeper had gone gray with age to match his hair, which could still be described as a 'full head', despite the receding hairline.

"Started barely an hour ago and he's drinking already," said Joss, dropping into his chair beside him. A deck of cards sat on the console beside a hot cup of coffee, mixed with whatever concoction Walter had made on his days off.

Walt came from a place called Intake, a settlement north of Porta Orbis. It lay in ruin these days like many other towns outside the city since the declaration of peace. The old man's accent sounded pre-war, with a sort of unrefined harshness, different from that of the average city dweller.

After the war, the thousands left homeless fled to the safer, more stable city interior. It had grown to become a swelling metropolis over the last twenty years, a multicultural hub. The younger generation had developed a more modern sounding dialect in the diverse environment.

Walter raised his cup in front of Joss' face before tapping it on the side. "This stuff'll warm ya' bones," he hummed, raising his bushy eyebrows before gulping down a mouthful.

"I hope it's better than your last batch," said Joss, cautiously slurping the liquid back. It burnt as it went down and he was about to make a face when he noticed that Walt still maintained eye contact, eagerly awaiting feedback. Joss gave a reassuring nod of his head and had one more sip before placing the cup down again.

Apparently satisfied with the result, Walt picked up the cards and started to shuffle them. "So, how's the street's looking?"

"Dead! Nobody's dumb enough to be out in this shit." Joss had patrolled the area for the last hour on route to the outpost, his usual routine.

With a passing thought, Joss activated the upper part of his armor to retract his helmet. The layers came apart with a smooth sliding sound and shifted back to fit inside the collar section of his carapace. "Did you catch the news feed this morning?" He said. "There's been another raid, on government labs this time. They blew up a whole damn block!"

"Ah…the infamous Effigy," muttered Walter, while proceeding to deal the worn out deck of cards. "Or at least that's who's getting the blame. The FRA have branded him and his sheep 'The New Terrorist threat'."

"Last thing I heard this guy was some sort of political activist. Looks like he's taking things to the next level." Joss picked up his hand and looked between his cards and the old man.

Walt was a few years younger than Joss' father and a passing acquaintance during harder times. He had been barely a man when he'd fought in the home guard against the unorthodox renegades. After that he'd joined LEX Enforcement and was part of a special unit set up to take down related splinter groups, participating in key raids that brought down the Brood, one of the most notorious.

"First it was all that shit with the Brood and now this Freak. You'll always get people who listen to these nut jobs, and then look what happens…" Walter started to rant. "The war's been over for 20 years and there's still those hell-bent on plunging back into chaos, ranting on about invasion and government conspiracy. Problem is that kind of preachin' attracts all sorts of other lunatics. At least the Brood were just thugs that couldn't change with the times. This guy feeds on people's fear, using it to control them."

This morning it was obvious Walt had got into the home brew a little early. He'd been a great cop in his day according to the other vets around the station, and had even agreed to stay on an extra five years due to the lack of new recruits. During the time they were posted together, he'd confessed to Joss more than once that he was ready to turn in his badge, and was more than happy to spend his remaining time working the graveyard shift.

Joss took another card from the deck and the small talk continued. " News says he has over a thousand followers".

"Mostly outsiders I'd bet…" said Walt, taking a card, " and those too young to remember the real shit storm."

Joss studied the old man as he savored his next sip. Walter loved this kind of debate. The last 20 years had been the most peaceful time in Walter's life, or that's at least the way he told it. When the treaty was signed uniting the O'sar and Suu'vitan people, it was an end to an ongoing conflict lasting for almost half a century. O'sar raiding parties were a weekly occurrence along the outskirts where Walt had grown up. The old cop had seen his share of action and was happy to live out the rest of his days in the peace that he helped fight for.

Walt rearranged his cards, delicately moving them around between his fingers. "An old buddy down at central mentioned something about the FRA launching their own investigation".

"That so? I've hardly heard anything from downtown since my transfer." Joss took another card and shuffled them around in his hands before he realized he'd given Walt an opening. He could feel his partner's stare burning into the side of his head.

"Still nothing on how long they're going to keep you here?" Walt asked. The question hung in the air for a second before Joss answered.

"Not a peep. The Chief won't even take my calls. All I know is that they've got some rookie working my cases." Joss could see Walt shake his head through his peripherals. The subject of his dismissal from the homicide department wasn't something he liked talking about. He was going to leave it at that before deciding to add one last statement. Joss took another sip of the concoction. "As far as I'm concerned they can kiss my ass."

Walt glared at him. "It's that kind of attitude that got you busted to patrol in the first place! With all the shit that's been going down recently they could use you where the action is!"

"Then who else would they find to put up with your crap? If they want to let some wet nose fuck up all I worked for that's their problem." It wasn't the first time they'd had this particular argument and Joss struggled for something to say that might stop it dead before they really got into it.

Before Joss could say another word, Walt invaded his peripherals again, this time with a shaky, insinuating finger.

"You act like you don't give a shit, but the truth is you expected all this to blow over eventually, and it's the fact that it hasn't that really pisses you off." Walt leaned in with a stiff glare and a serious frown that demanded a reaction. "You're going to have to fight for this one, my boy. I've told you this before. You ask your father too, he'll tell yer' better than anyone…"

Joss rubbed his forehead with two fingers. "…Here we go…"

"You don't get what you want just handed to you! You've got to act! March right in there…" Walt dictated.

Joss turned sharply, meeting Walt's eyes and cutting him off mid sentence, "Come on!" he snapped, "It's too early for a damn lecture. Not everyone here's been drinking all morning!"

There was silence, before Joss spoke again. "…We're supposed to be playing cards." He knew Walt often thought of Joss like the son he never had as well as his partner. He sometimes found it hard to balance the scales with certain subjects.=

The two men backed down almost simultaneously and went back to their hands. Walt had hit that particular nerve before.

"I take it you two still aren't talking?" He said, in a softer tone. "Hell, I never listened to my old man either, we were just as bad as each other."

Joss kept looking at his hand. "Take a card."

Walt took another from the deck and rummaged around for the right words. "I was always too damn stubborn to make the call after we came to blows. You know I never got chance to put things right before…."

Joss cut him off, but this time in a calmer tone. "And you never forgave yourself. This *ain't* the first time I've heard this one either." Joss said, catching himself using intermittent words of pre-war slang he'd adopted over the months they'd worked together.

"Well, if I've said it before that means it's important. You can hold onto a grudge for too long, you know."

Joss looked at the old man as he took his third card. The crotchety bastard had also become somewhat of a father figure to Joss more recently, but with that common understanding you'd get from a close friend or brother. He'd not spoken to his brother for even longer that his father and Walt had acted as a great substitute for both of them. The comparison triggered further thoughts of his brother Reagan. He'd been away in the badlands for exactly three years now. The realization that they'd be reunited in a few hours suddenly hit him, despite the fact he'd been expecting it.

He thought it was about time he told Walt that he was due to return. He'd avoided family gossip for as long as possible because of the situation with his father, The Lord Prefect.

"Look, our paths are bound to cross sooner or later. My brother got back to the city yesterday evening."

Walt stopped short of his next sip. "He's back already?" he said, raising his eyebrows, looking surprised, "I'd assumed he still had another year, since you hadn't mentioned anything. Why the big secret?"

Joss threw a frown Walt's way, with a crooked smile to back it up. "Because I knew you'd start with this family values crap again."

"You really have been cooped up here with me too long," Walt muttered, knocking back another gulp.

"I was going to ask if you minded me catching a few winks in the back. I'm planning to head over to the temple as soon as my shift's up."

"Be my guest, kid," chuckled Walt. "You lads have got a lot of catching up to do. I bet he's got some stories to tell you! All kinds of vermin roaming the Terran badlands."

Almost instantly after the comment, Walt leaned forward and switched to his game face. "Now, then. You ready?" Walt laid out his cards on the table. "Beat that, kid!"

There it was, a full set. Walter always seemed to win. If he'd been playing against anyone else he'd have suspected a fixed deck, but he knew that foul play just wasn't in the old boy's nature. He was about to lift his cup for another slurp when…

…The Alarm sounded! Every screen showing the relevant surveillance points lit up on the center column, streaming the footage in real time. In the center, there was a map of their sector and the specific location where the security system had been triggered.

"Let's see what we've got here," Joss said, standing from his chair. He noticed a blur of motion past one of the surveillance feeds. "Punch it up on the main screen."

Walt pressed a few buttons on the console and read out the details. "It's a break-in at a warehouse two blocks away! Three guards down. The surveillance drones are tracking the perps."

"Looks like they're heading right for us," said Joss, already by the door. With a thought, his armor powered up in less than a second and he drew his weapon. "Sync the feed to my wrist tablet."

"Way ahead of you. I'll take the bike and head them off before the wall."

Joss grabbed an extra clip from the weapons rack by the door.

Walt hopped around a railing to the glidecycle on a down ramp behind the console. He fired up the pulse manifolds and hit the control to open the hanger door. "You cut through the back streets in case they split up". He held back for a second and tipped the peak of his helmet before jetting off through the exit.

Joss had already hit the flooded streets at his fastest sprint. He could hear Walt's voice loud and clear over the COM system integrated into his helmet. The rain had slowed to a light shower, but the downpour had left huge puddles making the alley slick under foot. He could hear gunfire not too far away, presumably the perps taking shots at the drones. They were closer than he thought.

"I'll meet you behind the power station. Don't move on them until I get there." Joss shouted through the microphone.

"Yeah, yeah," said Walt, cutting him off, "Keep movin' and stay on the line."

Joss followed the path laid out by the automated drones, which were in hot pursuit. The rush of adrenaline reminded him of what he'd been missing since his reassignment. He bounded down the street like he had unlimited energy to burn. In the excitement, he realized he'd forgotten to call it in. "This is Akura 187 in pursuit of five suspects, maybe more. Requesting backup".

He bolted over a fallen section of wall, then down a staircase that hugged tight to a cliff around the side of an abandoned high-rise. He was coming up on the last block before the perimeter wall surrounding the city. A lot of the buildings around the edge had been deserted after the war. There simply weren't enough enforcers in the city to monitor and maintain every section of the wall, and sections weakened by artillery had gone unrepaired. These breaches left nearby buildings vulnerable to intrusion from undesirables. Nobody wanted to be out on the perimeter.

Despite the current state of the neighborhood, Joss had found his station to be boring rather than dangerous. Aside from the occasional intoxicated hoodlum or vandals smashing up old storefronts, the night shift was usually quiet. Not tonight.

Joss pushed back his thoughts as he leapt down some stairs to the lower level, before hopping over a railing he noticed at the last minute. The next obstacle was a half collapsed archway; he darted through hastily before he laid eyes on the perpetrators. He paused and watched them over the rooftops, two buildings separating hunter and prey; just in time to see them split up down two newer looking gangways. Both passages looked to be heading in the same direction.

The drones followed closely behind, sticking with the larger group, leaving a lone straggler free to escape. If Joss lost sight of the fifth man, there was no way they were going to catch him before he got outside the wall. *Presuming that's where they're heading,* he thought.

Joss ran back and forth along the edge of the building, scanning the area for a quick way across. Porta Orbis had been destroyed and rebuilt so much over the years that parts of the city looked like they had grown naturally rather than been constructed. It was as if different mismatched sections had evolved together to form a complex maze of stone and meta-coral. Joss clambered over the first rooftop before leaping to the next. He only just made it over the gap, managing to grab hold of some hanging cable and pull himself onto the gangway. He stumbled slightly before steadying himself and accelerating to a full sprint.

He could see the perp's shadow flicker for a moment around every turn as he closed in. He was at full pelt and just made it around the next corner in time to see the figure disappear into one of the buildings. It was one of the neighboring structures connected to what looked like a power station.

He peered around from the edge of a wall before cautiously heading inside. The interior would have been pitch-black if not for the light of the moon peeking through the partially caved in rooftop. He was pretty sure the perp hadn't seen him coming and decided against using his shoulder lamp. There was just enough light for him to notice a staircase towards the back of the ground floor.

Suddenly, he heard a clang on the metal staircase! Then a shot! It missed him, but not by much. He reacted with a thought that activated his lamp, dazzling the crook. Before he could return fire, he disappeared down the stairwell.

"Shots fired. I'm moving in toward the lower levels. Walter, what's your location?!'

On an alternate route, Walter flew down a wider passage that had have been an old road at one time. Carcasses of old vehicles ran down one side of the flooded street. He hit the throttle hard, leaving two even walls of spray behind him. The drones had mapped all possible exits limited to their programmed city schematic. They were heading toward a dead end as far as he could tell, but any unauthorized breach wouldn't be visible on the map.

…

Walt recognized the structure ahead. He was coming up on an old coralite power station once used to power the old city defense turrets. Any of the old plasma cannons that weren't destroyed in the war were rendered nonfunctional. They were built into the structure and too difficult to deconstruct fully. The turrets and their stations still managed to look imposing despite their redundancy. Whenever he'd heard people complain that they were eyesores, he told them that they were there to serve as a reminder of how bad things used to be.

He dismounted and drew his sidearm. "I've tracked the drones to the southwest corner of the building. They've entered through a breach into an under passage," he whispered.

Walter edged toward a gaping hole in the side of the building. It was dark inside and the display on his wrist tablet was flickering with interference. He moved in cautiously.

"I can't see shit. Must be the walls in here fucking up the transmission." Walt edged further inside. He thought he saw movement in the shadows and squinted to try and make out the shape in the distance. He increased his pace down the corridor, careful to keep as close to any cover that he could.

Walt could hear Joss over the COM but responding could give away his position.

"Walt! I'm closing on your location. You wait for me, damn it!"

The old man had his shoulder lamp on now, moving toward a wider part of the corridor. It was an intersection that seemed to split off into three. Suddenly, he heard the sound of heavy footsteps.

Walt's eyes widened before he dove left, barely dodging one of the drones as it flew smoldering past him, crashing to the ground. The second flew by his face, sparks flying. He managed to duck beneath it, half dazzled by the sparks and smoke.

His eyes adjusted just in time to see the large figure lunge toward him. The last thing he saw was the large claw in the flickering light of his shoulder lamp as he tried to raise his weapon.

Joss had reached the bottom of the staircase when he heard his partner scream.

"Walt!" Joss yelled, with no response.

The scream was followed instantly by two shots from a LEX issue revolver and the sound of the rounds deflecting from a metal surface.

Joss double-timed it through the sub lever corridor. This part of the building still had power and he felt himself slow for a moment, feeling exposed in the saturating light: *No time for hesitation*, he thought before pushing on. He had to move faster.

As Joss got closer to the end of the passage he could just make out a figure lying on the ground. He clasped his revolver as he skidded to a halt. He took a second to check for danger before zoning in on Walt, slumped against a wall.

The old man clutched the large wound across his abdomen, but that wasn't enough to stop the bleeding. A dark red puddle covered the ground around him and more blood bubbled from Walt's mouth each time he spluttered for breath.

"Fuck!" shouted Joss. "Why didn't you wait you stubborn bastard?!"

Walt gargled another mouthful of blood while trying to talk.

Joss snapped the compact med-kit from his belt. The sense of conflicting decisions made him grit his teeth. He could see them running down the hall toward daylight, getting farther away with each step while his partner clung to life.

"Officer down! I need a medic fast. Where the hell's my backup?!" screamed Joss, with a frantic edge to his voice. He knew he had to remain calm, but suddenly he had a thought. *I've been on the bench too long, losing my edge... Bullshit!* He forced any inkling of doubt from his mind. He sprayed the foam field bandage across Walt's stomach. It was the best he could do for now.

Joss battled the urge to continue the pursuit, lifting his head to see them making their escape. Once outside the wall any criminal was considered beyond jurisdiction without special orders. All of a sudden an unfamiliar voice sounded of the intercom. Not the LEX strike team he expected.

"We have agents closing in, minutes from your location," said the calm voice, "the perpetrators are high priority. You're ordered to continue the pursuit."

Joss's glance switched franticly between Walt and the attackers getting away.

Walt had also received the transmission and understood the order. He reached out grabbing Joss's arm, meeting his eyes. "Get em', kid. Go!" He spluttered.

Joss jumped up, drawing his weapon once again! That was all he needed to hear. He forced any thoughts of hesitation out of his mind and took off after them. There was a tattered sheet hanging over the makeshift entrance. The morning sun flickering through as it blew in the wind. He fired two warning shots though the rag before swiping it aside.

He dropped down a couple of meters and he was on the outside of the outer wall. He glanced back to the wall that stood 100 feet high in this section, with a steep gravel slope running down another 50. He could see the perps heading for the ruins of the old city. He felt unsteady on the loose ground, sliding a few feet before finding his footing. Once he'd found his balance, he picked back up to full speed down hill until it started to level off. He watched as the first of the perps reached the ruins and moved out of sight.

With every stride he got closer, but if he didn't do something quickly he'd risk losing them in the maze of old town. He stopped with a skid and a cloud of dust as he noticed a boulder that would provide adequate cover and a suitable place to take a shot. Joss crouched down and tried to gauge the distance.

His hands were shaking. He took a deep breath, and then let it out slowly. Two more of the perps were almost in cover, with the last of them a good distance behind. He had one chance at a shot before the straggler moved out of sight.

His heart rate began to slow down. His hands were steady now. He rested his gun arm on the boulder and held his revolver with both hands. One more deep breath in as he took aim, then out slowly as he took the shot.

The sound of the shot bounced around the valley. The split second felt like an eternity before the slug hit the target in the back of the head. Joss saw a burst of red mist a moment before hearing the thud. The force sent the perp spiraling into a heap on the hard dirt. Joss was already up and closing on the location. He dodged between limited cover before reaching the ruins. The skeletal frame of the old buildings loomed overhead. The setting was silent again, except for the gentle whistle of the wind.

He approached the body of what appeared to be a male physique at first glance, although the face was covered with a mask and helmet. A pool of dark blood surrounded the head, but Joss checked the vitals anyway while he surveyed the area. A few feet away he noticed a case the guy had been carrying, it lay busted open on the ground.

He looked around for any sign of the others. *They could have gone in any one of the buildings,* he thought. There was a slim chance that they would have passed up the opportunity to escape.

He turned his attention back to the case and a few of the items that had spilled out onto ground. The strange tech looked unfamiliar to him, yet he felt drawn toward one of the larger items. The circular device seemed to sparkle significantly in the morning sun.

He was reaching over the body to grab it when he felt the ground shake around him. He barely had time look up before a huge figure charged out of the shadows in his direction.

Joss' eyes fixed on the weapon the beast carried before the actual perp; a giant claw- like gauntlet, complete with the remnants of Walt's blood dripping from the talons. He just about managed to stand and raise his revolver as the monster brought the claw down. The motion was faster than he expected from a combatant of that size. The claw sliced through his weapon, turning it to scrap. His left hand held the device, but not for long…

Immediately, another one came at him from the side with both feet!

Joss felt the full weight of his attacker crush into his face and ribs. He fell through the air, smashing through the remains of an old wall.

He managed to turn himself over before realizing he no longer had the device. His vision was blurred for a moment before he was able to focus on both of them, and now a third came into view from the cover of the shadows.

Joss scanned the three figures that stood looking at him. The large, clawed beast stood panting like a wild animal. The monster stood over half a meter taller than the other two. It wore armor that looked pieced together randomly, different from the style of weapon it wielded. The claw looked newer and far more advanced, some kind of High Grade Fusion tech or HGF.

The one who'd kicked him had retrieved the case and the rest of the items while Joss composed himself. He wondered about the larger item for a moment before deciding to concentrate more on the immediate threat before him. They'd caught him off guard before and he was lucky he was still breathing.

This second attacker barely looked human. It crouched on an angle; its feet grabbing the steel beam like they were hands. The attacker looked muscular and strong and had an almost animal agility to the way it moved. It also wore strange, bulky armor, yet it didn't seem to encumber its movements, similar to coral-formed tech, but somehow different to any other HGF battle suit. Its face was covered with bandages around wild eyes that glared at him without blinking.

The third one moved a few steps closer and displayed the body language of the one giving the orders. The leader snatched the case from the one with the bandages. It was difficult to really confirm the sex or race of any of them, especially the leader. They were all so heavily armored and disguised. The leader wore a cloak around its angular shoulders and sported armor that looked of a far higher quality than the other two. The craftsmanship more closely resembled the weapon the giant carried.

Joss estimated that his backup should be arriving anytime and wondered about the other perps who might be close. If they attacked him all at once, his chances of survival were slim.

The third spoke, in a distorted, almost mechanical voice. "Finish him off. Make it quick."

Joss snapped out of the daze he was in. If this was going to be the end, he was going to hurt them bad before he stopped breathing. He spat out a mouthful of blood and drew his blade.

He was back on his feet again as the clawed beast charged him. Joss threw his weight into the fight, parrying a strike from the huge claw. Joss deflected and drew back; *such inhuman strength*, he thought, and proceeded to duck and dance around his opponent.

The beast lunged at him again, this time missing him completely. Instead the talons made contact with the ground knocking the beast off balance.

Joss jumped in with a kick, knocking it back against the wall. Kicking the thing was like sparring with a tree coated with iron.

It growled through its grizzly mask expelling a foul spray of dark drool, then came at Joss again. This time the claw made contact with his blade at just the right point, slicing it in three pieces, barely missing his hand and only inches from his face.

It grabbed Joss by the throat with its free hand, lifting him a meter from the ground. The beast squeezed hard.

Joss struggled and kicked his legs trying to break free, but had nothing left.

His vision started to fade to black when he heard something…muffled through fatigue at first then becoming clear… the sharp whip of a high velocity bullet tearing through the air and hitting metal.

The beast's grip weakened immediately after…then another bullet made contact. It made the thing convulse and scream in agony before sending Joss flying through the air once again.

Joss looked up from the ground in time to see the third round hit. The clawed arm exploded from the shoulder joint with a splash of dark blood and smoke. The claw dropped to the ground in front of him with a metallic thud.

Joss watched the beast take off into the ruins along with the others. In the distance, Joss could hear the sound of an FRA hopper closing in on his location. "About time," he whispered to himself before slumping on the ground.

He surveyed the crime scene around him and noticed something glisten in the corner of his vision. He shifted over a few feet and got to one knee. It was the circular device. The center looked like sort of an iris, like a mechanical eye, with a dark reflective center like glass.

He leaned toward the item. As he got closer, it seemed to almost pull at his finger like a magnet. All of a sudden two small parts at the edge flicked open and a bolt of energy made contact with his hand. He overpowered his instinct to jump back and grabbed it.

The sound of the hopper overhead broke his concentration and he looked up to see a squad of FRA agents closing in across the ground. When he looked back at the device it was lifeless once again. He quickly hid it away in the storage compartment under the wrist plate of his armor.

The adrenalin started to subside as two feds marched over and helped him to his feet. He allowed himself to lower his guard and instantly remembered his partner.

Joss shook off the agents heavy hands, feeling smothered all of a sudden. "I'm fine. Where's Walt?!"

Joss stumbled as fast as he could over to the hopper, ignoring a female lieutenant who stood by the entrance. He could see Walt lying on the stretcher aboard the transport. The two medics stepped back from his dead body as they saw him approach.

"I'm sorry. There was nothing we could do. The wound was too severe and he'd lost too much blood," said the FRA medic.

Joss felt struck with a numbing paralysis with news of his friend's death. He'd known the wound was likely fatal, but had refused to believe it at the time. Walt was gone and the bastards had gotten away.

The voice that gave him the order to pursue came via a Federal transmission. There was no sign of any other LEX personnel. He made the quick assumption that whatever it was he'd recovered, it was probably important to the FRA. The politics involved with withholding evidence from the feds washed over him before he quickly shrugged it off. If he handed it over, he was going to lose the only lead he had.

Chapter 2

Darahk waited until he was sure Joss was finished before he spoke," What do you know about the Effigy?"

Joss stared at the Inquisitor for a moment and thought back to his conversation with Walt. " Just what I've seen on the broadcast. You think this guy's behind it?"

Darahk sat back in his chair and searched for the correct response. He could see the obvious frustration on the LEX cop's tired face.

Joss swallowed the lump in his throat and gritted his teeth behind his lips." Ok…Let's say he was. What was he after?"

Darahk spoke up, "The warehouse they hit was a storage facility. The items they stole were components for concept tech, did you come into contact with anything resembling that description, any unfamiliar tech at all?"

Joss knew the response Darahk was looking for, but something told him that giving the Inquisitor everything wasn't the right move. It was the only bargaining chip he had, not to mention a viable lead.

The Inquisitor cleared his throat and asked the question again.

This time Joss managed to process the question and fabricated the appropriate answer. His eyes shifted from vacant space to make eye contact with the Inquisitor. "They snatched the case before I had chance to look." There was a pause. The old Fed was going to have to give him more than that. "Are we talking about weapons here?"

Darahk sat back in his chair but maintained an intrusive look, saying nothing.

Joss continued, "These guys were killing without a second thought. They would've killed me if it wasn't for your sniper."

Joss noticed a change in their expression as the two agents turned to look at one another. It was only a glimpse of surprise, but enough to give them away.

The Lieutenant entered in a few commands to her wrist tablet, adding a few images to the holographic display between them. Pictures from the FRA wanted list.

Darahk opened the palms of his hands leaving only his fingertips touching. "Could you I.D the individual that you say took the shot?"

Rosair stepped forward. "These are surveillance stills of suspects under investigation. We believe the Effigy could be tied to these attacks, and that one or more of these perpetrators were involved."

Joss' gaze switched between the two feds. Their demeanors were black and white. Darahk had obviously worked hard to get where he was with the agency and had built his career by playing by their rules. He just sat there like a rock, almost comfortable with the current level of control of the situation.

The Lieutenant's body language was the total opposite, and suggested a sort of urgency. She had patiently waited her turn like a good subordinate and had jumped straight in given the slightest opportunity. He could hear the edge to her voice. It was clear to him that they were working more than one angle, deliberately or not. She was after the perpetrators, maybe one of them in particular. She seemed to be invested in this case personally, and it was starting to show. Joss stared her right in the eyes and she stared right back. Whatever she wanted, she wanted it bad.

"Well?" barked Rosair.

Joss squinted through tired eyes at the low quality images. Three of them were total strangers, but the last one caught his eye. The image was blurred from the motion of the shot and the lighting wasn't great, yet there was something familiar that reminded him of the guy he fought. There was something animal in the hunch of the stance.

As Joss searched for an answer, he became aware that the images weren't the only things that were blurry. He cycled back through their conversation, forcing his mind through the clouds of fatigue, when he remembered that they'd avoided his question about the tech completely.

It was clear that they weren't going to share anything they had. He hated being on this side of the table. He knew the drill and the game went both ways. What did they even know exactly? They seemed totally baffled by the existence of this apparent sniper, and if it wasn't them who saved his ass this morning who the fuck was this mysterious third party?

"Are you saying it wasn't one of your guys? You were on the scene minutes after it happened," Joss said and looked at them waiting for an answer. There was a long pause and no answer before Joss decided to continue. "My attention was focused on the bastard squeezing the life out of me!"

Joss had been trying not to raise his voice, but he was finding it hard. The Fed's blank expressions and tight, reluctant lips were starting to rub him the wrong way. "She was there running the team. Just who the hell were we supposed to be chasing? What are you really after?!"

Darahk paused for second and cleared he throat again. " I can tell you that whoever it was who supposedly saved you, it wasn't one of ours. It could have been one of *their* guys with lousy aim for all we know. In any case, you're lucky to be alive."

Joss stared up at the ceiling then over to the ventilation fan which had started to buzz louder and more annoyingly. In a split second he fantasized about drawing his pistol and unloaded an entire clip at the thing just to enjoy the gob-smacked expressions on the agents' faces.

Darahk leaned forward with the facial expression of a schoolteacher who'd caught you daydreaming.

"I ask again, Sergeant," Darahk said, in a commanding tone, "Do you recognize any of the assailants in these pictures?"

Joss took a deep breath. "They were all well-disguised. Aside from the two I fought, I only got a glimpse of one of the others. He looked like the one giving the orders."

Rosair leaned toward him. "So you can't confirm any discerning markings or features? Not even gender or race. How did he look to you? Come on, Akura!" Her face was as serious as ever. She froze the one image of the animal figure in front of him, singling it out from the others.

Joss wasn't the only one getting frustrated. He looked up calmly. The image in front of him definitely resembled the one he fought. There was a dark image of the face that accompanied the action shot. There was something primal in the creature's brow and shoulders. The character intrigued him, and he obviously wasn't the only one. This is what she wanted!

The more the feds pushed for details without reprisal the more he gathered that he'd likely get nothing he could use from the exchange. *Maybe I'll call their bluff before I show them my full hand,* he thought.

"Like I said, they were disguised, heavily armored," said Joss. "What about the one I clipped? If you like we can all go downstairs and check out the corpse together."

Darahk pushed back from the table. "The body's already been moved to FRA HQ We're taking over the investigation. If there's nothing else, I'd say we're done here." He started to get up from his chair.

"What?!" He barked. That was it. Joss felt enraged despite his expectations. He knew the feds wouldn't give him much, but to remove him from the case completely? Now, he was pissed.

"That perp was my kill, for fuck's sake! What about that gauntlet the other guy was slinging? The HGF?" Joss had seen a lot of illegal tech in his time, and your average street punk didn't use that kind of weapon.

"The item has been sent to our labs. Illegal High Grade Fusion weapons are a federal concern," said Darahk, as he stood up straight in front of him. He appeared to puff out his chest in a display of authority.

Joss was starting to believe every story he'd heard about the guy. Darahk was a pompous ass with a superiority complex. "That bastard almost killed me, you bald fuck! You can't just shut me out!"

Darahk turned back to face him with a scowl, displaying extreme distaste for the subordinate's petty and insulting statement. "It was your incompetence that led them to escape. If we need you for any further questioning, we'll contact your superiors."

"You've not heard the last of this, Darahk!" shouted Joss.

"This case is no longer within LEX jurisdiction. That will be all!" Darahk pulled the interface with a sharp tug, and it snapped free of the console.

The Lieutenant glared at him with a moderately smug look. She turned to follow her boss out of the room. The ape at the door waited for them to leave before he followed them out.

As the door slid closed it took all he had not to shout out and roar as loud as he could. Joss stood with his palms face down on the table trying to calm down. He was almost there when the fan started rattling again, as if to mock him. He felt the heat bubble up through his neck and his face swelled red. He gritted his teeth together and tried to contain the frenzy, but it was no good. His spun around, smashing the full ashtray hurtling at the wall. Cigarette butts went flying around the room as it smashed against the cage covering the hardware.

....

Darahk hastily marched through LEX HQ. He noticed another LEX officer throw him a dirty look as they passed. It annoyed him intensely that these grunts refused to understand their place in the city. Not that he thought the job they did wasn't needed. A city needed lawmen, but that's where it ended.

Anything beyond general law enforcement was above their pay grade and to be reported to the FRA, especially illegal fusion tech. The FRA bridged the gap between the Enforcement hierarchy and the Patronas Order. This had become the way of things after the war and 20 years of peace had been the result. As far as he was concerned, it was a perfect system, and he was in charge of monitoring it closely.

Rosair quickened her pace to catch up with the Inquisitor. "'Akura': A hard name to live up to. I'm familiar with his father's reputation."

Darahk frowned at her. He'd noticed that she'd been waiting for an opportunity to say something. "His reputation as a war hero, no doubt, not the notorious troublemaker that I have come to know over the years. It seems his son shares the same disrespect for authority."

Even though he'd fought side by side with the old Prefect back in the day, that didn't mean he liked him. After the treaty was signed, the FRA was formed. Its primary function was to monitor Meta-fusion production and those who wielded such technology. The Patronas Order had scriptures dating back hundreds of years, internal laws that restricted them to that specific set of rules. Different chapters' practices varied from interpretations, but even with their subtle differences they all agreed on the practices they had deemed 'orthodox methods'.

During the time of war the rules were bent, even broken toward the end, and that was to put it mildly. After the war ended, the scriptures were modified through careful scrutiny to suit the new alliance and were now federal law. It was the FRA's job to make sure everyone stayed on the straight and narrow.

Rosair continued, "Unusual for the son of a Paladin not to follow in his Father's footsteps, especially a warrior held in such high regard."

"Joshlen Akura was an orphan taken in by the prefect after the war. The new laws in place after the treaty was signed meant he couldn't be trained in the arts. His blood origin was unknown. His family ties to the Order meant the FRA was out of the question. LEX Branch was his only option if he wanted to make a difference on any sort of level."

"Not exactly living up to daddy's expectations," she said with an arrogant tone, "that explains the obsessive tendencies, not to mention his defiant attitude toward the Agency."

Darahk hit a few buttons on his wrist before Rosair's own tablet lit up after receiving the data. "Check out his file," he said.

A miniaturized holographic display appeared in front of her. She browsed over the data as they approached the main lobby.

The hectic atmosphere seemed to spill in as the two doors slid open in front them. Morning sunshine poured in from windows around the top of the room. The bright light accentuating the dust kicked up from all the activity on the ground level.

The busy sounds of the place echoed around the high walls. No less than 80 people all seemed to be talking or shouting at once in a slur of incomprehensible gibberish. A large rectangular workstation stood a few steps higher in the center with more desks around the edges of the room; almost all were in use, some with a lineup.

Above the main entrance was the LEX insignia. The emblem was split into two halves in the shape of a shield. On one side was the familiar symbol of the city, a small technical design of a lotus flower against a white background. The other side was black with a smaller white diagonal stripe across it; the mark of the government and part of the FRA insignia. The design was supposed to represent what the organization stood to protect and the powers they answered to. Across the top was another rectangular stripe reading L.E.X. (Law Enforcement 10) for the ten LEX outposts around the city.

The Agents passed at least 50 LEX officers going about their daily routine before entering a side corridor that led toward the aerial landing pad.

Darahk gave the Lieutenant adequate time to summarize the date before he continued. "He was the youngest cadet ever to make detective. Assigned to homicide a year out of the academy, and later given command of the Chief's special task force. After that initial short burst of success it was pretty much downhill."

Rosair scanned the document. "It says the Commissar personally terminated his contract. 'Acted beyond jurisdictional limitations while jeopardizing an FRA investigation'," she looked at Darahk, "He blew one of our long-term ops! I don't remember hearing about this."

"We're talking one major fuck up," continued Darahk, once out of earshot from any of the LEX cops, "He gunned down an informant we'd been working for years, not to mention injuring operatives that were working undercover when he stormed the place."

"He's lucky to be still wearing a badge," said Rosair with a discerning expression. Any admiration for the aforementioned credentials seemed non-existent.

"Take a look at that arrest record. His captain used special privileges to keep him on the payroll. He was a hell of a cop, apparently."

The double paneled security door opened through to the exterior. Rosair powered down the tablet as they walked onto the landing pad. The pilot fired up the primary manifolds on the hopper as he saw them approaching.

The guard, who'd been walking behind them jogged past before jumping onto the rig.

Rosair stopped to address Darahk before they got too close to the loud sound of the charging engines. "No matter how good he used to be, he still managed to let that son of a bitch escape. We were so close this time."

Darahk raised his voice to shout over the secondary manifolds as they surged to life in the background. "We'll get another chance. Re-establish contact with the source as soon as we get back to HQ."

...

The Agents had been too preoccupied with their conversation to notice the cloaked figure watching them as they left the building.

Lord Akura listened as they passed by an intersection leading to a small waiting room. The Prefect stood to watch the hopper take off, as a thick puff a smoke curled around his hooded face.

"Darahk..." he muttered to himself, stroking the distinguished sideburns. The thick hair covered everything but his pronounced chin and the two inches of face below his piercing amber eyes. His skin was a shade darker than olive, with a serious brow that looked weathered by experience rather than fatigue.

He turned to exit the room, tucking his arms inside his robe. As he marched back toward the lobby, he thought about the history between Darahk and himself. He looked forward to their inevitable confrontation in the near future; the thought brought a conspiring grin to his determined face.

Chapter 3

The Secretary jumped up from behind her desk outside Chief Flint's office. "Hey! You can't just..."

Joss barged past before she could finish her sentence. The automatic doors only just opened in time for Joss to walk through, completely ignoring the young woman.

Flint didn't even have to look up to see which of her grunts was standing in front of her. She traded the pen in her hand for the smoldering stogie sitting in the ashtray before making eye contact. "What do you want, Sergeant? You've already been debriefed."

"I want to be assigned to the case!" Joss yelled at his commanding officer.

Flint was a tough, middle-aged, black woman with chiseled features, accentuated by her small square glasses. She stood up slowly from behind her desk before pulling down sharply on her suit to straighten it out. It looked at least a size too small. Flint took a long toke on her stogie between sentences. "I signed over all the paperwork to the FRA an hour ago."

She glared down at the man almost half her age. She was as tall as Joss and certainly heavier, looking solid and moving like an old dinosaur. She'd been the first woman to rise to the rank of captain at central and had held the position for nearly a decade.

"Is there anything else?" she said, responding to Joss' attitude with a stony expression. She almost laughed at his attempt at a threatening demeanor: *Not even on his best day*, she thought.

Joss felt the effect of the stare down. "Come on!" shouted Joss, "I was on the scene. It was on my watch."

Flint cleared her throat. "I don't like this any more than you do. My orders come straight from the top! I..."

Joss cut her off. "They killed one of ours! You know this is bullshit!"

Flint's brow tightened to match her lips. She removed the cigar from her mouth and aimed a finger at Joss. "Watch your mouth, kid. You're not even a homicide detective anymore. It's not even your problem. I can keep you up to date with..."

"...With what?" he interrupted again, " If they give you anything it'll be crap. There's more to this than they're telling us. Who knows what they're keeping in those warehouses?"

Joss waited for a response but Flint just stood there, turning around slightly to face the large window looking out across the city. The sun was high in the sky now and the smoke danced in the sunlight as she exhaled.

Flint had always credited Joss for his abilities, but he'd acted insubordinately more times than she could count, and the last time he'd paid for it. She wasn't his mother, *but maybe the closest thing to one in that screwed up mind of his,* she thought. She decided to give him one last chance to back off.

Joss could sense she was giving him the opportunity to walk away before anything else happened. He considered it for a second before remembering how she'd been ignoring his calls. *Well, not this time*, he thought. This time they were face to face! "If you're going to submit to bullshit politics rather than actually do anything about this.

I'll take it to the Commissar myself!" said Joss, crossing his arms and waiting for her reaction.

"You'll do no such thing! "Flint stared at Joss over her glasses, lowering her gaze to meet his eyes, "You undermine me or this precinct, and I'll have your balls on display as a warning to the next smart-mouthed punk that walks through that door!"

She stubbed the cigar out in the ashtray and lowered herself back down into a seated position. The chair creaked under the strain. "I'm taking you off the action roster for the time being." She said, picking up her pen to continue the work she was doing. "Should give you time to get some perspective."

"You're suspending me?!" said Joss, simmering back down to reality, "Chief, you can't… Those punks were running around with HGFs I've never seen before."

"It's not a suspension. You just lost your partner. I know you two were close. I'm willing to write this little tantrum up as the result of extreme stress due to circumstances," Flint said.

"I don't need time off! I need this case!" demanded Joss, staring back at his long-suffering Captain. Flint was standing her ground and there wasn't a force on the planet that could make her budge. He realized all of a sudden that she wasn't telling him the whole story either. He'd seen it before. *The Commissar*, he thought.

"The Commissar?! That old bastard…He's gotten to you too," Joss stated, looking through red eyes.

"I'll be blunt. The Commissar wants to keep you out of this no matter what. You have a bad habit of interfering in matters that don't concern you, and it's pissing a lot of people off."

She produced another cigar from her desk drawer and cradled it, waiting for him to leave. "Three weeks leave. Attend the festivities. I don't want to see you anywhere near this case, or my precinct. Is that clear?"

Joss straightened his body respectfully, trying his best to hold back the attitude. "Yes Ma'am!..." But he couldn't resist. "Crystal, Ma'am."

She spun around in her chair a quarter of the way around to enjoy the view once more, about to light the stogie. "You're dismissed, Sergeant. Get your sorry ass cleaned up and check your badge at the desk."

Chapter 4

Joss took the elevator down to his designated shower room and equipment repository. The room was separated down the middle by eight maintenance alcoves. There were another eight lined up each side, running the length of the wall. The room was dimly lit; all except the brightly illuminated shower room at the far end. Joss walked over to his assigned booth. Every Enforcer had their alcove. As well as using it to store their gear, it had everything they needed to perform routine maintenance on their armor and weapons. While been posted on the outskirts of town he'd been storing them at his domicile and had let the upkeep slide a little, if he was totally honest with himself.

He stepped inside the cramped area that measured roughly four meters square. There was a small, uncomfortable looking metal chair in the center surrounded by an array of mechanics. He dropped himself on the seat with a groan; it felt like every single muscle and joint ached after the morning's activities.

Fortunately, Joss only had to think to activate the alcove. It ran a quick scan to verify the user and the machine came to life. The arms moved around his shoulders, accompanied by an almost melodic orchestra of metal shifts and sounds. Piece by piece they started to remove his armor, starting from his upper arms and torso.

He reached forward to place his arms down on the designated rests beside him. The vambrace sections around his elbows separated from each of the gauntlets covering his wrists and hands. The armored plate split in half, folding back in layers just enough so that he could free his arms. Joss finally got the chance to stretch out as the large piece around his sternum was lifted over his shoulders.

Back when he was a detective, he wasn't restricted to the standard issue uniform and equipment. He'd used a sleek, more compact body armor; just as strong but much less clunky. The revolver was the only personal touch permitted for standard duty, although limited to standard ammunition and zero upgrades.

He stood up and the armor folded away neatly inside the alcove, leaving only the gauntlets, utility harness and sidearm accessible. The guys in the tech department had redesigned them about a year ago so that you could access any of the storage compartments while the rest of the armor remained stored away. With the old model, you'd only realize you'd left something in one of the compartments once the ten-minute maintenance cycle had started.

Joss disposed of his dusty, bloodstained uniform down the laundry chute on his way to the shower room. He glanced at the clock in passing. He had a little less than an hour before shift change, just enough time to enjoy a hot shower without any company.

The hot jets soothed his cramping muscles as he braced himself with one hand against the cold tiled wall. The swirling motion of the water down the drain helped him to relax; the frustration and tiredness seemed to wash away along with the blood and filth. Still, he couldn't shake the lingering feeling that he had unfinished business to attend to: He tilted his head back to wash his face, forcing it to the back of his mind, if only to enjoy the moment before he started the busy day ahead of him. He hadn't seen Reagan in three years.

Joss wondered if his brother would be the same. His Father had always told them that the trials changed a man. The savageness of the badlands was an experience that would stay with you. Joss had only ever been a few miles outside the wall and only a handful of times. This last one had proven to be almost more savage than he could handle.

He couldn't take his eyes off his gauntlet while he dried up and changed into his street clothes. Without further hesitation, he hit the panel to open the gauntlet. The compartment slid apart to reveal the iris. He inspected the foreign device as he threw on his jacket. It seemed beaten up, but the details looked more like general wear and tear, rather than actual damage. It definitely wasn't concept technology.

As he stared at the iris more closely, he felt a strange mesmerizing sensation, like it was sucking him in. Suddenly, he heard someone shout his name. He snapped out of his trance and threw the item in his pocket.

It was Jarvis, a rookie he'd met briefly before his transfer. "Sorry to hear about Walt she said, "I heard Wings took over the case."

'Wings' was the nickname that LEX had given to the FRA. The gold wing against the black shield with a white stripe striking through it was the emblem on their uniforms, but that wasn't the main reason. The feds swanned around with a kind of deluded angel complex, like it was their sole responsibility to protect everyone in the city. They always acted like they were a level above everyone else, especially LEX cops. The best thing about it was that they'd been calling them 'Wings' for years to their faces, and they still hadn't realized that it was meant derogatorily. It made for a great inside joke.

Another agent spoke up across the room; Joss couldn't remember his name at first. He was an older man in his late 20s, similar to Joss. He had a bald head and goatee.

Joss scanned back over his mental files. These last few months working on the outskirts had dulled his abilities. *Singleton,* he thought suddenly, *that was his name.*

"Word is they were after some Fed killer," said Singleton, "I overheard them talking to the Chief. You didn't hear that from me."

Joss raised his eyebrows. "That a fact?!" A few pieces started to fall into place. He thought about the Lieutenant, and the fact that her concentration seemed to be elsewhere. She was after a murderer. He wondered how that connected with the robbery and the tech, or if they were even related at all.

"Cheers for the intel," he said. One piece of evidence; a few scattered clues to go on. It wasn't much, but enough to whet his appetite.

He turned to a panel on the outside of the alcove and pressed his hand against it. It took a second to scan his palm before the cove began to close up. He dug around inside his left inside pocket before pulling out a crumpled cigarette. "No wonder they were so pissed," Joss muttered to himself as he headed up the stairs to the main lobby.

He sparked up as he walked passed the no smoking sign by the front desk. The gesture felt liberating despite the pettiness. At this point he was past caring. He slid his badge from his belt and barely looked as he threw it to the guy stationed at the desk.

The action surprised the man and he only just caught it, dropping the paperwork he was holding in one hand.

"Pass that on to the chief from me," Joss yelled across the room and casually waltzed through the main entrance.

The light of the day felt harsh on his face at first, his tired eyes taking a moment to adjust. The center of the metropolis was packed with people enjoying the autumn sun as it beamed through the staggered high rises. He'd always loved the sound of the busy streets around the bustling center, at least until the recent changes.

Joss cringed before turning to his right to see the huge view screen power up. These broadcast stations were another new addition to the city. Joss liked to catch up on the news as much as the next guy, but these particular broadcast had become known for their false and phony propaganda pieces. The abrasive sound of bellowing speakers destroyed the noisy tranquility.

They were funded by the Commissar's office with the intention of force-feeding ruthlessly biased information to the public. He'd noticed the number of broadcasts increased leading up to the festivities. With the Initiation Ceremony approaching, the Patronas Order was dominating public interest and the Commissar couldn't have that.

The image of the Commissar appeared on the screen. He did his best to ignore whatever public announcement he was making. A few words like 'the Effigy' and 'terrorist' stood out in the overly politically correct statement. It wasn't until the Commissar mentioned the strength of relations with the Patronas Order that Joss decided to look up, deciding to stop and give the screen his full attention.

It showed a public meeting between Commissar and an Order Patriarch Glasrail. *Glasrail of all people,* he thought. Reiko Glasrail was a council member in the Patronas Order and the leader of the largest of the O'sar chapters. It was widely known that she despised public interaction and had no love for the FRA. After the treaty, she was outspoken about her desire to adhere to old traditions and disapproved of the Commissar's rule over the city. She was one of the three Patriarchs out of twelve with an opposing vote against the Coalition.

Joss tried to see through the politics. What was Glasrail's angle? Was she looking to improve public relations by kissing the Commissar's ass? It sounded out of character for someone who prided herself and her Chapter on their self-sufficiency. The public had been quick to generalize, believing the entire Order shared Glasrail's arrogant view and opinion.

Lord Akura had expressed his distrust of Glasrail on several occasions. Their relationship on the council had often been turbulent, despite their mutual disapproval of the coalition. His Father had different reasons for his opinion against the Commissar's level of control, but at least it gave them common ground where they saw eye to eye.

Joss suddenly realized that this particular chain of thought was only adding to his fatigue. He'd spent the last year staying away from his father and anything Order-related, but something had changed since the fight that morning. The signals drawing him closer had become difficult to ignore. The Patronas Templum was the place he'd been deliberately trying to avoid; yet now that he was actually heading there, he felt nothing but an overwhelming feeling of anticipation.

He saw the sky train pull into the station ahead of him and the subject of politics quickly vanished from his mind, replaced by thoughts of his brother. "Another wonderful morning," he whispered to himself, picking up his pace to a steady jog to make sure he caught the train.

Chapter 5

Sapian dropped six meters before grabbing the bottom strut of an old steel ladder, hoping it wouldn't give way. It moaned and rattled as he swung over to the other side of the tunnel. He backed against the wall to make way for the other five. There was just enough light from the surface to illuminate the old maintenance shaft. It got darker through the middle section, with just a flicker of light to aim for at the bottom. The Stranger leading them had gone down ahead. 'Stranger' had become his alias since he'd neglected to give a name when they first met to plan the job.

    One of the others slid down a hanging cable head first, passing him without a sound. Not all of them were as agile or silent. The hulking beast, now minus an arm, had been struggling to keep up as they made their way through the old city. He watched as the large figure jumped from one intersection to the next with a thud. Guys in this line of work didn't make a habit of asking for help.

    Sapian usually worked alone and this debut team venture hadn't exactly run smoothly. He looked through his ragged facial garment at the last man peeping over the platform at the top before he cautiously made his way down the ladder. '*All accounted for,*' thought Sapian. He looked down at the shaft again to see the Stranger staring back at him through the optics on his strange helmet. The light shimmered off the Stranger's unusual armor, leading him to wonder what it was made from or where he got it. Sapian threw up his hand to signal 'ok' before continuing his descent.

    Once he could see the ground, he zeroed in on a clear spot. He gauged the distance, dropping the rest of the way down the shaft, before landing softly in a crouched position beside the beast. The monster lurched around with a start to look at him, only for a second before continuing down the corridor.

    No one had said a word since the fight with the cop, so he thought it best to follow suit and keep his mouth shut. He looked around at the masked faces of the group, suddenly thinking to tighten the bandages disguising his own face. After he'd made sure everything was concealed, he followed after them.

He took this opportunity to examine the motley crew as they walked down the old passage. The beast's severed arm added to his already grizzled appearance. He smelled unnatural, like death walking. The deranged-looking mask appeared to be fused to his face with parts of his armor surgically attached. That, combined with his sheer size, was enough to strike fear into some of the toughest criminals.

Sapian remained alert, always consciously aware of his situation. Venturing deep into the city's underbelly with such undesirables wasn't without its dangers, but at least it was safe from the law. Even with most of the buildings on the surface destroyed, parts of the lower levels still looked intact and had power. He'd heard rumors of small settlements existing down here, but nobody was using this particular passage. It was obvious the Stranger had planned this escape route out beforehand and seemed to known exactly where he was going.

At the end of the passage, they came to a large sealed door complete with control panel. The Stranger walked over to a terminal that looked like it hadn't been used for over a decade, possibly even broken. Without saying a word, he reached out from under his cloak with an arm exposing that beautiful armor again. Two thin, metal, snake-like probes extended from beneath the armor plates and made contact with the circuit board. Sapian leaned around to try and see more, but the Stranger seemed to operate with speed and discretion with almost every action.

Sapian pondered on that thought while he waited. The ragged cloak was the only thing tying him in to the current environment, everything else about the Stranger looked out of place, and that wasn't all. The scent he got from him was like nothing he'd smelt before. He wasn't even sure if the Stranger was male. It was obvious this guy was from out of town. Way, way out of town. His methods were covert, precise and efficiently determined, which Sapian found intriguing.

After a few seconds, the doors ground open to reveal what looked like an elevator. The leader stood aside while the others entered. Two of the men seemed to stick close together, like maybe they knew each other. The Stranger let them in first. Sapian had noticed that they'd seemed a little shaken by the death of the other guy and thought they might have been a trio. He entered after them, crouching down between the two. The beast was the last to step inside, making a point to eyeball the Stranger as he passed. The doors closed and the platform started to move. It seemed to move backwards rather than up or down.

The silence was broken suddenly as the beast erupted, letting out a furious roar as if he couldn't hold it back any longer. "What the hell was that!?" he screamed, "We were supposed to wreck the place and get out! Nobody said anything about stealing any tech."

Sapian saw the two beside him look at each other, still no words. The Stranger remained with his back to them and didn't budge.

The Stranger spoke without turning to face the brute. "I didn't expect it to be an issue. I was led to believe you could handle a simple night watchman," he said calmly with a deliberately condescending tone, "He was half your size and carrying a toothpick".

"Screw that! I had him until the F.R.A showed up!" he barked, edging closer to the Stranger, who still had his back to him.

Sapian noticed the beast's eyes shift to the case that was strapped around the Stranger's shoulder.

"I'm betting whatever's in that case is worth something. Something more than...I don't know... A new fucking arm!" The monster's voice rumbled, echoing around the small space! The tension was rising quickly, about to hit the roof!.

The one to the left of him stepped forward, drawing a blade. "I think he's holding out on us."

The Stranger still had his back to them, even though the beast was standing less than a meter away.

Sapian's eyes shot to the right as the other man drew his pistol. Sapian's knuckles remained planted on the floor. He wasn't overjoyed at the prospect of a scrap in close quarters, never mind a shoot out. He tried to maintain a neutral stance but was ready for anything.

The Stranger spoke, "You'd do best to withdraw. I've paid you all a considerable amount and I'd hate for you to come to any further harm."

The monster laughed, "Looks to me we got you outnumbered." He flicked out a blade from a compartment on his remaining arm, "Let's see what's in that case!"

The stalemate turned to action faster than anyone could blink. The monster lunged forward at a surprising speed. The Stranger reacted with such fluidity he made his opponent look slow, stepping to the side before grabbing the arm he had left. With one sharp tug and a twist the arm snapped, sending the knife flying. The brute let out an agonizing roar before the Stranger spun him around, an opponent twice his weight, driving his head into the hard steel wall with a smash.

It was time for the other two to make their move; Sapian reacted as he saw the pistol aim in his direction. He went for the gun, disarming the culprit with his foot, while simultaneously landing a clawed swipe across the jaw. The attacker let out a surprisingly feminine yelp as he tore the woman's lower mandible clean off, spraying the wall with blood. The body fell in a heap against the wall.

The last of the turncoats rushed at the Stranger, bringing his blade down hard. He'd seen the attack coming a mile off, dodging the blow with an angelic pirouette before producing a blade out of nowhere, swiftly slicing off the attacker's head. The headless body continued on its trajectory, smacking full sprint into the doors. It flailed for a second on the ground, twitching a few times before death finally caught up with it.

The carriage came to a halt and the doors opened. The two of them stood there. Sapian examined the scene. The body of the beast hung out of the wall, smoldering and lifeless. Sapian still held the pistol, in an intentionally non-threatening manner. He'd seen enough in the preceding seconds to confirm the extent of the Stranger's combat skill.

The Stranger shook the blood from his blade with a sharp flicking motion before it disappeared beneath the dusty cloak. The mask stared at Sapian, seemingly registering the submissive gesture. The fight was over.

It was Sapian's turn to break the silence, not that he really knew what to say. He said the first thing that came into his head, "You just can't get good help these days." His tone couldn't have been more deadpan.

"It appears that you are proof of the contrary," said the mask. It sounded uniquely distorted, but not so much that you couldn't tell that the wearer was well-spoken. "I am in your debt. Expect to hear from me."

The cloak whipped around as he turned, taking off down another passage leading toward daylight. He was out of sight in seconds.

Sapian glanced at the cheap hardware in his hand before threw the pistol to the ground with the rest of the trash. The scent of death in the confined space was almost overwhelming.

"Lucky, fucking me," he said out loud. He was the only one left breathing.

Chapter 6

An unwelcome chime woke Joss from his deep snooze. The nap had alleviated the exhaustion somewhat, but the aches and bruises were something else entirely. He stretched out his neck until it cracked, stiff from leaning against the window of the carriage.

"Next stop 'Templum Patrona'," shouted the attendant who walked down the center of the train.

Joss rubbed his eyes and took in the view; he'd not travelled this way in years. The winding track had been constructed by architects and engineers trained by the Paladin. They schooled them in the arts of meta-coral manipulation, limited to their technological creativity, rather than weapons. It was truly a work of art the way it twisted inside and around the lush mountains. The rainfall was a lot heavier at this altitude. The landscape looked totally different from the rockier terrain around the city.

The train entered the last tunnel before their destination, taking a short time to pass through the mountain before he saw it: The Templum Patrona, training grounds the Patronas Order. The scenery on route was breathtaking but it barely prepared you for the sight of the awesome structure. Towers and walkways grew up around it, leading to different balconies and lookout points. The clouds seemed to break for it deliberately, allowing the morning sun to enhance the sight further. The building got thinner toward the top before fanning out like the petals of a large flower, particularly a lotus flower.

Joss got off the train and walked up the stairs to the grand entrance. The staircase was long and steep and he couldn't help counting every step, just as he'd done as a child. There were 103, just as he'd expected, the same as before. The tenderfoot disciples called them the 100 steps and that inaccuracy had always bothered him, more than the fact that there were an extra three in the first place. There were pros and cons to an obsessive-compulsive mind.

The initial sight of this place had always amazed him. The closer you got, the more you felt the flourishing life force within this seemingly inanimate structure. He'd had no reason to visit the temple for the longest time, but rediscovering its beauty made him wonder why he'd ever stayed away for so long. Aesthetically flawless, the meta-coral structure was appealing on a subconscious level. It seemed to call out to you with the promise of an open perspective. Despite the familiar sensation, something was different this time. Something felt askew and conflicted when crossing the threshold, like something within was resisting.

The huge doors were three times his height and formed from optimum-grade meta-coral, 10 inches thick. No conventional weapons could penetrate them. Only a Paladin could move them. These doors had actually been replacements for the originals that were destroyed in the war. After the treaty, it was decided that the new ones should display the insignia of each of the 12 chapters. They'd been here for as long as Joss remembered, open dawn until dusk, to anyone seeking counsel. Nostalgia washed over him reminding him of his childhood.

The main hall demanded his attention, drawing him toward the giant trunk of raw, naturally formed meta-coral stretching up through the center of the building. His father had told him that it was believed that temple had been constructed around it, and how it was thought to have been there for 1000 years. Two thick branches pushed up out of the ground, each roughly ten feet around. About 20 feet up, the branches twisted into one piece, resembling a DNA helix. It stretched up another 100, just below the top of the structure.

At the top there was a large hole in the center of the softly coned roof. Around it the manipulated coral formed what resembled a lotus flower around the opening. The moonlight would shine down through the opening, creating an illuminating shimmer that lit up the main hall.

The aura of the place was like no other. It was a haven of tranquility, swelling with history and culture. Three old prefects floated on their shields 20 meters in the air. The masters were in a deep state of meditation, maintaining a steady magnetic field between their bodies and the coral structure surrounding them. Levitation for such an extended period of time was a talent not easily come by.

He came back to reality as a Paladin approached him. He mistook the old man for a Prefect before he noticed the amulet around his neck.

"Good morning, my boy." said Patriarch Victus, "May the wisdom of the Order guide you." Every chapter Patriarch wore the sacred emblem of their chapter around their neck, a shimmering, meta-coral heirloom passed down from one patriarch to the next. He looked like he was in his late 70s, and held a large staff, moving with the strength and vitality of a younger man. "Are you here seeking counsel?"

The Patriarch was the leader of his Father's chapter. A modest man with all the wisdom you'd expect from a Paladin with his experience. Over his years meeting various Patriarchs, he'd found some of the others sharing the same rank had become somewhat grandiose in their position. Not Patriarch Victus. His Father had always expressed his admiration for his superior; an honorable man who could never be accused of forgetting his roots. Joss hadn't seen him in years.

Joss tipped his head with a look of constraint. "Not today, Patriarch," Joss said, suddenly feeling obliged to straighten himself up in the man's presence, "I'm here to see my brother. I have an appointment to see Reagan Akura."

The Patriarch squinted and a hand slid lower down on his staff. "Then you must be Joshlen. You've filled out since the last time I saw you." The Paladin led off in one direction.

Joss smiled with a more enthusiastic nod and set off to follow The Paladin.

"He's giving a lecture to the tenderfoot, in the east hall," stated Victus. He walked slowly down the corridor without a rush in the world.

As they circled the coral formation, he noticed some of the younger disciples and tenderfoot initiates gathered beneath it in the center. A female Paladin lectured them on the history of the great spiritual site. Joss knew the tale well, but he couldn't resist listening to it again as he wandered by.

The woman's voice echoed melodically around the building. "Suu'vitan and O'sar ancestors alike would travel over vast distances to reach these lands, drawn to this very site by the coral's alluring energy. Centuries ago they believed it to have magical qualities, with little understanding of the science behind their symbiotic connection."

She paused to take in the site around her before continuing, "After years of meditating on this ground, they discovered that they could manipulate the physical structure of the coral with their minds. The first five Acolytes gave their lives to the construction of this place, spending years together in deep metabolic stasis. They slowly grew this structure around them, eventually becoming one with it. A monumental example to all those who follow the scriptures."

Hearing the lecture made Joss think back to his Father's teachings. He'd told them that the temple stood as a monument to show how far their people were willing to go to move forward. Their whole civilization was founded on the connection with this strange mineral. Their ancestors had used it for shelter when they had none, used it to power technology once they'd acquired the knowledge to create it. The Acolytes had inspired their entire civilization.

Before this place The O'sar and Suu'vitan were nothing but savages in comparison, rival tribes and clans fighting over the wastes. Any history predating the formation of the temple was a little foggy at best, difficult to distinguish facts and theory from folklore and mythology. After the place was constructed more and more people flocked to the area. Eventually, there were millions of them. Settlements were formed, then cities. Porta Orbis wasn't the first of them, but it had become the largest.

Over the years, the Suu'vitan clans, or chapters as they'd become know, became settled in a progressive, thriving environment. The O'sar tribes were more rooted in old traditions and believed that things were moving too quickly. O'sar elders told their people stories of the Progenitors and their self-destructive nature, and started to make comparisons to some of the Suu'vitan chapters. Somewhere along the way they'd developed such strongly conflicted views to go to war over: a war lasting over a 100 years. It took the return of the Acolytes to force them to see the error of their ways and the true evil that divided them.

The subject of whether they were actually the original five acolytes was a question Joss had always asked his father, to a somewhat unsatisfying answer. He'd told him that there couldn't have been any other explanation. They had endured such savagery with no end in sight, only to be brought back from the brink of destruction. He'd described the Acolyte's influence as nothing less that divine. The experience had left his father a more devout believer than ever, and he wasn't the only one. Their people had been enjoying an era of peace for the last two decades.

Joss continued to admire the architecture as Patriarch Victus led him down the east corridor. The windows of the place had been engineered to reflect the daylight inwards, like the main hall. The Patronas Templum was constructed long before the application of met-fusion to electrical technology and utilized the natural light and energy wherever it could.

"I've heard nothing but tidings of excellence on your brother's part," mentioned Victus, in an attempt to bring the boy back from his thoughts, "your Father must be very proud."

"I'm sure he is," Joss answered after a pause.

"Prefect Le'san's reports show remarkable achievements, far surpassing many of the other initiates. His combat methods are a true spectacle."

Joss smiled again, he felt like he should look more impressed but hearing Reagan's mentors gush over his talents wasn't exactly a recent thing. "It looks like I'm in for a treat."

"Here we are," said the Prefect, gesturing toward two tall glass doors.

Joss walked in, doing his best to be quiet while the students listened to his brother speak. Last time he'd seen his brother he was the learner, about to leave on a pilgrimage across dangerous territory. You could hear the change in his voice; a more confident edge that only comes with experience.

...

"The journey over the Terran badlands is one every tenderfoot must take," said Reagan. "The world beyond these walls is both violent and enduring. You must be well-prepared if you are to survive."

As Joss sat down, the door closed behind him. Reagan looked over to see his brother. Joss folded his arms in a gesture that said, 'Well, get on with it.' Reagan threw back a grin before turning back to his students.

"I would have met with death more than once if it were not for my extensive combat training, faith in my Preceptor, and skills in the art of Meta-coral alteration."

Reagan took a step back and gestured toward the apparatus behind him. To his right was a chunk of raw coral-alloy, standing the same height at Reagan and over a meter around. Another Paladin stood a few meters to his left by a weapons rack. He wore training garments and seemed to be waiting patiently to assist, with his arms behind his back. Reagan turned his attention to an armored dummy to the right of the Meta-coral, standing roughly at eye level.

"Each member of our species exists as two separate organisms combined. We live as a single entity through our symbiotic connection," said Reagan, walking toward the dummy. He stood a meter away now, holding up his right arm. "It is from the energy generated by this bond, from which a Paladin draws power…"

Before Reagan finished his sentence, a crackling bolt of energy materialized around his arm, startling a few of the disciples. Armor began to grow around Reagan's forearm taking no more than a second to form layer upon layer of armored plates covering his bare skin. Before saying another word, he shunted forward, suddenly striking the dummy in the center of the torso. The power from the punch ripped like a shockwave through the armor, sending a few pieces flying through the air. He withdrew as quickly as he attacked, reviewing the devastated armor around the area he hit.

The crowd began to whisper, grinning with excitement. There were even a few claps before Reagan turned to address them once again. He casually disposed of the robe covering his torso as he walked back toward center stage. Josh noticed how muscular and lean his brother's physique was and how it attracted the attention of two female initiates sitting in the front row.

Their father had always said that Reagan reminded him of his late wife and how he'd inherited her more polite, gentile nature. Joss had no frame of reference having never met Reagan's birth mother but recognized gentleness the old man certainly never had. This refined version of Reagan now resembled his father more closely, that same discipline and experience his recognized from the Lord Prefect.

Over his sculpted muscles you could see where the synthiant inhabited his body, as it was more pronounced beneath the shallow areas of flesh. Darkened areas ran around the pectoral muscles and abs. The thin appendages of the synthiant resembled a network of thick veins, but in a more mechanical pattern, like circuitry. At various points where the channels intersected, thin coral disks sat on the surface of his skin. Each exhibited a specific forge symbol from the optimum scriptures. Two larger disks were positioned over his shoulder blades leading to several small ones running down his spine. These were the primary forge tablets every Paladin had, and wore like medals.

Reagan pointed at the raw coral. "In its natural form, the meta-coral is essentially dead, an amalgam fossil in dormant stasis. Through sharing our life force with the synthiant, it grants us the power to alter the coral on a molecular scale…"

Reagan stood at ease, both hands out by his sides before continuing "…. letting us break it down structurally before absorbing it within." As he brought his hands together, bolts of energy started to shoot around his body with a series of cracks and flashes.

The coral disks seemed to turn to liquid and spread over his body. Some of the liquid pulled free from his body, moving around his torso above the surface of his skin.

Joss watched eagerly. He'd seen this sort of thing in the past, demonstrated by other Paladin, as well as his Father. It had always amazed him, but never as much as now. His brother wielded the meta-coral with a smooth, refined technique.

Once a tenderfoot's synthiant was harmonically attuned to survive the bonding, they could absorb Meta–coral within their body, storing it inside. The process required years of training and immense concentration. Once the meta-coral was part of them, it represented itself as these strange amulets when dormant, and could be forged into any manner of tools. The Patronas Order perfected these methods over centuries, learning to manipulate the coral to form armor and weapons. Their optimum-grade weapons were far superior to any other manufacturing process.

Reagan continued, "Once fused with the element in symbiosis, you can reassemble the atoms into any form the scriptures allow." There was a change in the sound of the energy. "Your Sacred carapace..."

In little more than a second, a spectacular suit of armor grew around his body, assembling the coral into a variety of plates and pieces. Each armored plate positioned itself automatically around his arms and torso before hardening and fitting in place. A few remaining pieces continued to circle his body, melodically. He moved forward a few paces before they found their location.

A few of the students leaned in to take a closer look while others at the back had stood up from behind their desks.

"This natural armor is synchronized to my every movement or action," Reagan said, wearing a proud smile as the students inspected the construct.

Joss examined the armor from across the room. The craftsmanship was immaculate. Paladin's armor varied from chapter to chapter and each individual. You could usually notice unique, aesthetic and ergonomic details brought forward by whoever forged it, especially if you knew them personally. Reagan's armor had a shimmer and sleekness that reflected his own personality.

Reagan held out his right arm. "A Paladin in the field needs a weapon," He continued and as the chatter of the crowd died down, "Your Vesica!"

The blade materialized from his hand, growing a meter and half in length in a split second. Close up, the weapon was covered in beautiful markings with a partition an inch wide through the center of the blade. The intricate details would have taken an engraver days to produce. Reagan could do it in a second using practiced alteration methods and a focused mind.

"A Paladin's lethal instrument of vanquish against the enemies of justice." Reagan brought the sword closer to inspect the form. "You can feel the energy channeling through you, bringing the coral to life."

With a quickstep and sharp turn, Reagan pirouetted, slicing the raw piece of coral behind him across the middle. He noticed the silence of the crowd as they watched. Reagan remained in a combat stance until the severed piece of coral slid free on its cross section, clattering to the floor by his feet.

Reagan waved over another young Paladin waiting to assist on the sidelines.

The Paladin grabbed a bladed staff from the weapons rack and moved toward the center of the stage.

Reagan casually formed a shield around his left arm as he watched him approach. "Formed with no imperfections, Optimum Grade Coral will stop any normal blade or bullet."

The assistant lifted the staff before striking down toward Reagan's head. Reagan stepped back and moved the shield up to block!

The crowd gasped and clapped as the blade shattered into several pieces.

Reagan bowed to his opponent and stood at ease. "You must sustain constant, symbiotic focus for this to be achieved. Stay true to the Optimum Scriptures to maintain harmonic balance."

There was a burst of excitement in the crowd before they realized the demonstration was over. They returned to silence respectfully for their teacher to say the words.

"Class dismissed," said Reagan with a grin.

"Impressive," commented Joss, with a comically smug expression. He moved in for a strong handshake that developed into more of a hug. "The triumphant Paladin returns! Looks like you've learnt a thing or two along the way."

"You look a lot more beat up than I remember," said Reagan, inspecting the bruises and cuts on Joss' face.

The two appeared similar in age. Joss didn't know exactly how old he was but had always suspected Reagan might have had a couple of years on him. He remembered nothing of his life before being taken in by the Akura. He couldn't have been older than three or four at the time.

He and Reagan had grown up together as best friends as well as brothers. It wasn't until Reagan had begun extensive Paladin training that their relationship was tested for the first time. Reagan had always been the responsible one; his youth spent looking out for his adopted brother whenever he inevitably got into trouble,

Joss stretched out his back, feeling stiff from the fight. "It's a long story."

"Can't wait to hear it! Let's grab a bite to eat," said Reagan, throwing an arm around Joss in a warm, brotherly gesture.

Chapter 7

Almost three years earlier...

They'd been walking for two days now and Reagan had barely spoken to his new master. This was the furthest he'd been from Porta Orbis and the comfort of his own bed. He'd been able to see a settlement on the horizon for a mile now, causing his imagination to run wild with thoughts of a warm bath and a hot meal.

It felt like it was taking forever to reach it, giving him chance to scrutinize as the town became more visible. The skies above were stormy and dark and as they'd gotten closer, he'd noticed an imposing silence surround them that gave him the creeps.

Reagan suddenly realized he'd been dawdling and had fallen behind. He jogged ahead a few paces to catch up with Prefect Le'san. "There's something about this place, something that makes me wonder why we'd want to visit it."

"He speaks!" said Le'san, flashing him a smile, "I was just starting to think it was going to be a long three years. What you sense is the history, the death. That is why there are no birds. Talon hates this place."

Reagan looked at the grumpy old hawk on his master's shoulder. It was sitting with its head tucked in as far as it could with its feathers puffed out. You could almost see worry in the thing's face, if a bird was capable of such an expression.

"Reprataas is the old Synthatech headquarters, responsible for 90% of the weapons and tech used toward the end of the war. Look around you, boy, what do you see?"

Reagan had noticed the discolored ground and lack of green vegetation for the last couple of miles. "There's nothing living here, but I only noticed when I started getting hungry. I haven't even seen anything we could eat, not a single rabbit or even a rat."

Le'san let out a laugh that seemed to surprise Reagan. "This is the part of your training I wanted to get out of the way first. My stomach's been rumbling so loud the thought of eating old Talon even crossed my mind. There is plenty of life around here, and you will be eating soon, just don't get your hopes up for anything as tasty as a rabbit."

Reagan laughed back, before wondering what he meant by that last statement. He'd never seen this side of The O'sar Prefect, only ever stern facial expressions, with little conversation not related directly to training, and never anything personal. Initially, seeing the old man laugh had lightened his mood, but now he was beginning to wonder.

"I though all the Synthatech factories were destroyed?" questioned Reagan

"They were, and there was only ever one place used for weapons manufacture. The others were depots constructed closer to the city to make them more readily available to both armies." Le'san walked over to the side of the trail. "Come and take a look at the ground you're walking on."

Reagan rushed over to where Le'san was squatting down, prying back one of the larger rocks. A subtle light seemed to be glowing from behind it, and as Reagan looked closer he could see a strange fungus attached to a sort of jagged crustacean. The texture reminded him of the meta-coral that stretched up through the center of the Templum Patrona, only with a slimier, wet-looking surface.

"Hold back this rock," said Le'san, as he drew his knife.

Reagan grabbed the rock without question and began to watch his master carve off some of the lighter, end parts of the mushrooms about an inch or two from the stem, depending on the length of the growth.

"You have to be careful not to cut too low otherwise you'll prematurely sterilize the coral," said Le'san.

"The coral?" asked Reagan, " like Meta-coral?"

"This is what the coral looks like in its infantile, living state. It's the one good thing to come out of the war," Le'san wiped off his blade on his tunic and stored the cuttings away in his satchel. " We were lucky to find the amount we need in one spot. You've really got to know where to look."

"Hold on," said Reagan, following after Le'san as he continued walking. "Is that dinner? We're going to eat the coral?"

"Oh, you're going to eat it alright, but I wouldn't exactly call it dinner. It doesn't taste great, but it has nutrients that far outweigh the enjoyment gained from a flavorful meal," said Le'san.

"I've never seen coral like this. Alive, I mean," said Reagan. He ran ahead and started picking up other rocks. He tried a few more before finding another patch of mushrooms. As he went for a closer look, he stepped on one accidently. The thing seemed to deflate and recoil, sending a sudden burst of light beneath the ground, visible for a few meters, like a small bolt of lightning beneath the soil.

"I told you to be careful!" said Le'san, with a more serious tone, "this place might feel like death, but there is life here rarely found anywhere else."

"I'm sorry, master," said Reagan sheepishly, stepping back a few steps. He looked at the patch again as it appeared to be pulsing. As he looked around the area again he noticed something he'd missed before. The discoloration across the dark rocky plane was actually small pulses of light. It was more obvious now, as the light faded.

"It's ok. The coral will survive. It's just that it's become such a precious commodity since the chapters united. This is why I brought you here. You have been taught that the coral is everywhere, even in the soil and the ground we walk on. The soil you see on the ground is made up of around 70% fungal mass, both living and dead. Where the Temple stands and the surrounding area is one of the largest dead deposits we know of."

"I guess it made sense to build Porta Orbis near the source of the building material, not to mention the closest water source…" said Reagan

Le'san continued… "but it wasn't until decades later that we found coral samples in their living state. Exploring the badlands was treacherous but not without reward."

"So this is what the coral looks like in its adolescence. Why can't we grow this in the city?"

"A question that has baffled the elders for generations. O'sar Shamans used to travel far and wide to find the most minute quantities of the coral in this state. We know, that when the coral dies, what's left behind is what we've come to know as meta-coral, the mineral and resource that our whole civilization has been built around. We are able to channel our symbiotic energy to alter the matter to suit the purpose, whether to create energy or physical items. We essentially bring some of that life back to it, but with limitations. We've never been able to make more."

"And this place. This is why Synthatech chose this place to develop their weapons?"

"It's possible. But before they came here we knew of this place, mapped it out decades earlier, it was nothing like it is now. The coral was amalgamic, like the deposit beneath the temple. O'sar clans visited the place to find material to form tools. Whatever Synthatech did here, for all the harm they did, they managed to bring life back to this place. After the factory was destroyed and the war was over, there were those who decided to build a settlement here to study the phenomenon."

Le'san pointed ahead of them toward a small settlement. "Your father and I thought it was necessary to bring you here for your Ver'du ritual."

"I'm going to get my Vesica!" said Reagan excitedly. He'd wondered when he was going to get his weapon, the sword of Paladin that he'd been training to wield since he could remember.

Le'san laughed again, this time louder. "You sound so enthusiastic. It is good to keep high spirits before something so mentally enduring."

Reagan's smile dropped and his complexion whitened. "What do you mean by that?"

"You'll see," cackled Le'san. "When I was your age it was considered a great privilege to go through the ritual, but the mushrooms were in short supply. These days they are in abundance; this location is truly a blessing from the Ancestors. You are lucky to be born in such a time."

They walked the next three miles in silence until they reached the settlement, or what was left of it. Reagan had had time to think about their conversation and it was safe to say that his mind was no longer preoccupied with filling his belly.

The settlement seemed to have increased in size beyond expectations by the time they got to the first building. What remained of the old factory looked like a fallen titan, once living, makeshift shelters jutted out in every direction as if they were growing out of the parts of the structure. It looked like a nest of fallen spikes and spires that had come from the darkness above.

An aged O'sar man stood by what passed for the main entrance. He was shorter than Le'san by more than a foot, not to mention bald and skinny. He looked like he hadn't had a good meal in years. Reagan thought of the gross mushrooms he wasn't looking forward to eating. *Why would his Father subject him to this?* he thought, with a hint of despair.

The old man grinned at him with rotten teeth as they approached. " Welcome to paradise," he said, "my name is Quadro and I am lucky enough to call this magnificent place my home."

Reagan looked around at the crumbling building. It had started to rain as they'd gotten closer and he could hear the water dripping through the gaping holes in the structure. "Nice to meet you. My name is Reagan."

"We've met your boot already," chuckled the man. "you really must be more careful here, where the coral lives."

"The two of us spoke after the incident," said Le'san.

"You mean when I stomped on those mushrooms? asked Reagan, looking bewildered. "That was miles away, there's no way you could have seen that."

The old man looked at Le'san. "This one's a city dweller for sure, close-minded, even for a Suu'vitan."

Reagan frowned at the old geezer. "I've been trained by the best since I was a child…"

Le'san cut him off. "He's just trying to get under your skin, boy. You're not going to let this old fool bother you, are you?"

The old man let out a burst of laughter and gave Le'san a hardy slap on the arm. "He's a wise one, your Preceptor. You'd do best to heed his wisdom," he stated with sincerity, while ushering them forward, "come, there's a fire going in the main hall. A night like this is perfect for the ritual and we've yet to prepare the serum."

Reagan looked up at his master, who nodded at him to follow.

"Do as he asks, my boy. I'm going to find a drink from a place I know and I'll be with you shortly," said Le'san, giving Reagan a shove with his hand.

Reagan felt a brief feeling of panic before biting down on his lip and coming to his senses. The place around him was making him feel an unusual amount of fear, and fear was something he could control. It was something Le'san had always told him in their sessions at his father's house. Maybe that was the point of all the years of intimidation tactics.

"There's no rush. I'll be fine, master," he said confidently, and was about to take off after the old man when Le'san grabbed him.

"Don't forget these," he said, holding up the satchel of mushrooms.

Reagan grabbed them, and followed the old man, who'd decided not to wait for him..

Chapter 8

The two brothers wandered through the back streets of Porta Orbis, not far from the temple. This section of the city had always been a favorite hang out. It was half way between the temple and their Father's house, where they grew up. A variety of food stands and other stalls packed both sides of the long narrow alleyways. An almost overpowering array of smells and sounds made up the atmosphere that reminded the boys of their teenage years.

Joss had filled Reagan in on his morning's activities on the train ride down from the temple. They moseyed through the bustling streets with the welcome feeling of reminiscence.

"Sorry to hear about your friend," Reagan said, trying to lighten the situation. "We could have arranged to meet later. I thought I was the one off on the crusade."

Joss laughed. "Forget it. Besides, I've got work to do later. There's got to be someone who can tell me what this thing is." His mind was still on duty.

Reagan could see Joss was having trouble letting go of the load on his mind. Joss was a lot like their Father in that way, although he'd never admit it. Sometimes, Reagan could have sworn they were blood-related.

They approached a small food stand where a petite Eastern lady chopped up vegetables and threw them into a big pot. She had another one on the fire beside the stand, bubbling away.

Joss ordered the food, signaling with two fingers to the lady who was looking in their direction. Each small food stand specialized in one or two dishes. This one was known for noodle soup. Joss knew they'd be waiting a few minutes and wasted no time removing the iris from his pocket.

"What do you make of it?" said Joss, passing his brother the device. "It's been dead since I got it back to the station."

"What did you do to activate it before?" asked Reagan, as he started to examine it.

"I didn't do anything. I went to pick it up after the fight and sparks started flying. The feds were pretty vague on the specifics of what was actually stolen. They told me the place was used to store some kind of concept tech."

Reagan ran his fingers over the rough edges and scarring. "This thing's anything but brand new. This damage looks like it's been there a while."

His Paladin training made him sensitive to coral tech and often gave him a sense as to how things were put together or functioned. This particular item was different. "I'd say it's constructed from a coral alloy of some sort, but I get no reading from my synthiant."

"Could it be a weapon?" Joss asked. If it was, just being in possession of it was a federal crime, whether it was functional or not. "These guys were willing to kill for it."

"It might be tech left over from the war, maybe part of a weapon." Reagan passed it back to his brother.

Joss stashed the item back in his inside pocket. "There's a few guys I know who are nuts about this kind of thing."

Reagan hadn't forgotten what determination looked like on his brother's face. The fact that whatever Joss was about to do might be illegal or dangerous wouldn't be an issue once his mind was made up. This was yet another trait he shared with their father. It somehow always seemed to be his job to act as the voice of reason or at least the person to point out any underlying concerns. He must have taken after his mother. She'd died in the war.

"I shouldn't have to tell you what'll happen if they catch you with that. You'll get more than suspended!" Reagan noticed the woman walking over with their breakfast and lowered his voice. "It's obviously more important than they're letting on."

The lady carefully placed the two bowls of noodle soup in front of them. An aromatic vapor rose up from the broth that made Reagan feel like he was home. He smiled at her and they both said "thanks". They waited for her to get back to the stand before they continued.

Joss could see a familiar look of concern on Reagan's face. "Don't worry about my sources. I have people I can trust," he said, hunching forward.

Reagan was about to pinch up a fat wonton with his chopsticks when he paused. "Will you take it to father?"

Joss looked up and laughed as he slurped up the noodles. "That's not exactly the person I had in mind. I've done fine without the Prefect's intervention so far. I'm not about to run to him for help now."

Reagan nodded his head and proceeded to wind up his own noodles with the chopsticks. "What happened between you two anyway? When I asked about you yesterday he just grunted and changed the subject."

"That's an even longer story," barked Joss. "I'm sure he's told you his side of it."

His brother and Father had always butted heads; Reagan assumed it was down to their similar, stubborn attitude. It got worse when Reagan had started his Paladin training and Joss was denied entry to the Order. When Reagan had left for the badlands he sensed an aura of frustration surrounded his brother. He still hadn't managed to shake off the dark cloud that followed him.

"He told me you were kicked off homicide," said Reagan. "He didn't go into the details of why."

" 'What I did', had nothing to do with it!" Joss stopped eating. "He never disagreed with my actions. I even requested his presence to act in my defense!"

"Then what was it?" asked Reagan before taking another bite.

"When the day came for my hearing, the bastard didn't even show up!"

"The Order must have denied your request. They prefer to stay out of LEX Branch internal matters."

Joss nodded his head, forcing down another mouth full of noodles before he could continue. He pointed his chopsticks at Reagan. "I didn't request the Order. I requested him. He wasn't there for me and it wasn't the first time!"

Joss sat back in his chair, picking up an onion from his bowl with his fingers and throwing it into his mouth. "After the hearing, I went by the house. He barely even mentioned it. He told me he was busy with Order affairs. That's when I lost it." Joss rubbed his face with both hands before pushing away his bowl. "We haven't spoken since."

The two of them sat quietly for a few seconds and tucked into their breakfast, which had cooled down to the perfect temperature. Reagan chased a shrimp around in his bowl waiting for Joss to speak; he noticed that his brother looked exhausted.

"You know what he's like," said Joss. "The Order always comes first. I'm surprised he managed to drag himself away from work long enough to welcome you back."

Reagan looked off to the side and thought back to earlier in the morning. "I only saw him for a few minutes as we passed in the hallway."

When Reagan faced back toward his brother, Joss was eyeballing him, as if his last statement had just been confirmed. It had been three years and not even a hug or warm gesture. Reagan also believed his duty to the Patronas Order to be his primary responsibility, but he'd always thought that loyalty to his family fell into that category. Since he could remember, the Akura family had been part of the Order.

Gailan Akura was an old war hero who'd mastered the arts in harder times. He was never one to tiptoe around an issue or offer sympathy, even when it was needed. His hardship through the years had sculpted the Lord Prefect's legendary character, not always the most ideal father figure.

Joss always said that their father was consumed by his work, at the expense of everything else. Maybe all three of them were guilty of that. They knew only duty. Reagan had always put it down to the lack of a nurturing female element.

Joss let out a big sigh and put on a smile, as if to change the subject. "Can we talk about something else? It's been years and all we can do is bitch about dad. Tell me about the trials! I was hoping to hear tales of adventure and glory over my soup. I can't imagine spending that long with Prefect Le'san. I bet he made it hell."

Reagan shrugged with a grin. "Quite the contrary, actually. I couldn't have hoped for a better teacher. I'm grateful to father for getting him assigned to me."

"Are you kidding?!" said Joss, in shock. He started to laugh, remembering the situation. "I can remember the look on your face when he came to collect you. You were scared shitless!"

"Maybe at first, but over time, fear turned into respect. He taught me things I could have never learned from a Suu'vitan Preceptor."

Le'san was an O'sar brave back before the treaty. Now, they were all part of the new Patronas Order. Their Father had come to respect Le'san over the years since the war and when it came time for Reagan to head out over the wastes, he needed a Preceptor. Akura pulled strings on the council to get Le'san assigned to his son. An O'sar preceptor assigned to a Suu'vitan disciple had never been done before.

"He'll be dining with us at the house tonight. I was hoping that you'd come too," said Reagan.

"What!?" said Joss raising his eyebrows. "Have you been listening to anything I've said?"

"You have to be there! I've been looking forward to this since we set off home. There's so much I have to tell you."

Joss stood up from his stool. "I thought that's what we were doing now?"

"I've got to be getting back to the temple, and you look like you could use some sleep." Reagan reached for his satchel as he stood up.

"Hey, this one's on me," Joss said, pulling his own wallet from his jacket. He walked over to pay the lady, feeling Reagan's eyes burning into the back of his head as he walked around the table to the kiosk.

"Well?" Reagan asked again. There was only one answer he was willing to accept.

Joss looked back over to his brother. "…I knew this was coming. Does he know about this…that I'm coming?"

"I didn't think I needed his permission. I never gave it a second thought. You can't avoid each other forever. You're both just going to have to show a little civility. You can go first, be the 'better man', so to speak."

Reagan knew that Joss couldn't resist the temptation of getting one up on his father. Over the years he'd learned how to appeal to, or in this case manipulate his brother's competitive qualities.

"The second lecture I've had today and I've only just had breakfast!" shouted Joss, looking up into the sky.

"So that means you'll be there?" asked Reagan, fishing for a confirmation he knew Joss wouldn't go back on.

The two of them wandered back onto the busy street. They were heading in separate directions and it was time for Joss to make a decision.

"If I don't, I'll never hear the end of it." Joss folded his arms. "Just don't expect any hugs and kisses."

Reagan laughed, placing a hand on Joss' shoulder. "Look on the bright side. If the Order has files on that gizmo of yours, Father would have the clearance to access them. They might even tell you who'd want to steal it.

"A positive I.D. on any of them would be more than I've got. I'd even settle for the shooter."

"Whatever it is you're caught up in, it couldn't hurt to have this guy watching your back." said Reagan.

Joss started to walk back toward the closest sky train station. "I'm still not sure he wasn't trying to blow my damn head off."

Chapter 9

"Hey wake up!" shouted Williams, giving Burt a hard nudge in the ribs. The two of them had been on guard duty for the last eight hours. "Someone's coming."

Burt yawned as he sat up on the worn out mat he'd been using for a bed. "Is it him?"

"Could be…" said Williams, adjusting the focus on a mounted telescope in front of him. "Get the gun ready. Look for the signal."

The tripod sat on the partially collapsed section of the wall in the derelict tower block. The two men were positioned at the first checkpoint leading to their secret hideout, miles away from the city.

Burt squinted, looking off into the distance as he positioned the rifle. He could just make out a figure waltzing between the ruins of the old city. If it wasn't their master, it was somebody too naive to understand the risks of being exposed in such dangerous territory. He had the rifle set up now, looking through the sight. He could just make out the individual's cloak blowing in the wind. As it whipped back and forth, he noticed a weapon. Whoever the intruder was carried a high caliber rifle or heavy automatic.

They both waited, as the figure got closer, watched as he stopped and started to lift the weapon. Burt loaded a round, ready to fire! The figure seemed to look right at them before raising the weapon above his head and circling around once.

"There it is!" exclaimed Williams, with a sigh of relief. "Talk about leaving it to the last second!"

Burt picked up the radio from a box between them. "It's him. Move in."

From about a mile away, the Effigy looked toward the window where his men were positioned. He waited for them to signal with a mirror; three flashes for the all clear, before he continued to move forward. He'd trained them to believe that they could never be too cautious. Their base of operations had remained hidden to outsiders since he'd discovered the site more than a decade ago. Allowing the sanctuary to be compromised at this crucial time could be catastrophic.

The Effigy threw his gun back over his shoulder and picked up the pace. He could see Rayne and two men ride out from behind another building, each mounted on large ram-steeds. They had discovered the beasts roaming wild around the old ruins and developed methods of training them for transport. They were perfect for the harsh environment. They moved over the rough terrain with ease and speed and didn't spook as easily as other beasts of burden.

Rayne rode up to him holding to the reins to another steed for the Effigy. Each was male and had large tusk-like horns, curling around from the base of their skulls and out beneath their jaws. The animal that Rayne rode had horns that extended half a meter from its head. The Effigy had watched them fight in the wild during mating season and knew they were capable of doing some serious damage.

"I'm glad to see you made it back safely," said Rayne, leading the spare steed toward the Effigy. "I had ten of my best ready to aid you in battle."

"The time for battle will be upon us soon enough." The Effigy jumped up onto the young animal. He gave the reins a tug as it fidgeted around, adjusting to his weight. "This was something I had to do alone."

He set off riding and the others followed. Rayne was his third in command and knew when to expect an answer he wouldn't fully understand. Rayne had been the most suspicious out of all of them when they first met, a Suu'vitan outcast with a history of betrayal by those he loved and trusted. Now, he addressed him as if he was some kind of hero or savior, as did many of the others with him since the beginning.

Rayne had developed exceptional leadership skills of his own over the last decade and many of the younger disciples respected and looked up to him. He was no stranger to violence, and had learnt a variety of survival skills and combat techniques over the years that made him a force to be reckoned with.

The Effigy was silent while he mulled over the details of his business in the city. He had taken the first step in a chain of events he'd been preparing for, for well over a decade. It had been carefully planned and had played out almost exactly as he'd hoped. He'd watched as Joshlen Akura chased down the criminals that killed his friend. He'd been aware of roughly how long the FRA took to respond and how to properly evade them. He knew that it was his destiny to help this man and knew the importance of when and how he should. The Effigy had the luxury of viewing the events from a perspective outside of relative time. Rayne and the others would never fully understand this, but they trusted him and had faith in his wisdom.

They rode back to the base at a steady pace. The sun was up over the wastes, but the tall foothills shaded the path they were on. The morning air felt damp and cold and the sound of the wind bounced between the rocky hillsides as they entered the valley. Rayne's riders carried out one last perimeter check before they went any further.

The Effigy's vision shifted to the cliffside, around ten meters from where he knew the last checkpoint was. He could barely make out the small cavern in the rockface, but he knew they were there.

The three-man team looked down at their leader tracking their movements from the position above. One watched closely with a par of binoculars while another sat behind a large Gatling gun. The third seemed to be preparing food in a pot they had on the fire. The man tending to the pot took a second to radio through. "I've got positive I.D. at the entry checkpoint. Prepare to open the gate."

Rayne heard the chatter through his earpiece and signaled to the others to lower their guard. Two of the riders galloped ahead inside, passing a woman who walked out to meet them. She shouted to the Effigy as he rode towards the entrance, "I trust everything went to plan?" Jada asked.

"It went exactly as I knew it would, if not exactly as I had planned," said the Effigy. He didn't mean to sound cryptic, but with the knowledge he had this was the most honest answer.

Jada laughed, "Forever the enigma, whether the question or the answer." Sounding as if she'd expected such a response. She could usually interpret it as a positive or negative result. "…A success then?"

"Oh, a victory by any means!" said the Effigy, flashing a crooked smiled at her. He gave the beast a light kick and it accelerated toward the entrance. Artificial lamps lit up the cavern highlighting the ancient blast door at the end. With a loud groaning noise, the doors began to open. They scraped and creaked as if they'd been opened for the first time in 100 years.

Jada moved over to help the Effigy down from his steed. "Everyone is assembled in the amphitheater. They are ready to hear your words."

"Then I mustn't keep them waiting," said the Effigy.

Chapter 10

Almost three years earlier...

It must have been at least an hour since Quadro had given him the foul-tasting serum. It seemed like forever and still he felt nothing. Quadro had also decided he wasn't in the mood for chitchat, making things worse. Reagan found this strange because Quadro had done nothing but talk since they arrived. Yet, every time he'd tried to engage the peculiar man in any kind of conversation, he'd been shut down with grunts and brief snappy answers.

There was, however, another man that had just joined them from elsewhere in the complex. He was taller and leaner, and moved slowly, which told Reagan he was probably no spring chicken. He couldn't get a good look at his face beneath the hood and bushy beard, but noticed a shakiness to his hands when he'd removed his gloves to warm them by the fire. He'd not seen anyone his own age since he'd gotten there.

The second man had also showed up with mushrooms, turning them over to Quadro to prepare another batch. Reagan had been about to open a dialogue on the subject when Quadro beat him to it. The two of them spoke to each other in a strange O'sar dialect he didn't fully understand, but he gathered that they knew each other. Reagan had been schooled in the savage tongue for most of his life, but he found the dialect faster and more random than he was used too.

Reagan glared into the fire as the wrinkly old man stoked the flames. He suddenly noticed that Quadro was staring right at him, flashing him a grin through his awful teeth. He'd spooned out the leftover fungi from the broth and threw them on the fire. They popped and fizzled with a puff of colored smoke that caught him off guard, making him jump.

"The fire talks to you, yes?" He said, before bursting out laughing along with the other man.

It made Reagan feel a little uncomfortable all of a sudden, and he felt a chill run up his spine. The space around the fire seemed to swell before his eyes, enhanced by the sound of cackling laughter that echoed around him in sequence.

He took a long, deep breath, which felt like he was literally taking in the world around him. He could taste the smoke and moisture in the air and became hypersensitive to every sound and each drop of water. His palms had started to sweat and he felt damp, like he'd sat in something wet. He was surprised that he didn't feel warm, sitting so close to the fire.

"Am I supposed to feel cold?" he asked the two men.

Quadro had started to pack a pipe with something while he tended to the broth. He took his precious time to get it ready and lit it up before he answered. "You are supposed to feel vulnerable. This lesson starts with giving in, a challenge you're not so used to, I think."

"Where's the challenge if all I have to do is give up?" Reagan asked.

"I said 'giving in'," He answered, offering the pipe to Reagan.

"No, thank you," he said, "I always hated the smell of those things when my Father smoked them."

"I find it helps with the visions, the anxiety that some of the hallucinations can cause," said Quadro, giving the pipe to the other man along with his serum. "Your Paladin training focuses on learning to control, overcoming that which you struggle against. Suu'vitan Prefects don't teach you how to let go. That is what I meant by giving in, giving in to what you cannot control. This is the lesson that's been taught to O'sar braves for centuries, and a practice essential to understanding our history. All the more important now under Suu'vitan rule."

Reagan frowned at the statement, "Suu'vitan rule? We have an alliance. The chapters are united and the only authority the Order answers to is the Commissar, who is O'sar."

The tall man remained silent, but shook his head as if to disagree.

"O'sar Braves and Shamans never trained in a temple, and were in tribes, not chapters," continued Quadro, "They learnt from the land, lived as nomads. There's more to this world that than Porta Orbis and the Patronas Order. Prefects like Le'san are the only hope we have of preserving our culture."

Reagan was starting to feel isolated and uncomfortable, though he wasn't sure whether it was because of the fungi or the political discussion. Some could have argued it was a religious debate, but Reagan saw every Paladin or coral wielder as students of the same craft. This was common in initiates of his generation and this modern age, but maybe he was just in denial, ignorant of the spiritual routes of the art.

Suddenly, a churning feeling in his gut and a rush of adrenalin interrupted his train of thought. For a second, he thought he was going to throw up, then before he knew it he was on his feet with nobody around him. The fire he'd just been staring at for the last hour had gone out, leaving only a few smoldering embers.

"What the fuck is going on?" he said aloud, feeling his heartbeat through his fingertips.

He jumped around as he heard something behind him in the distance. "Quadro!" he shouted. I don't know what kind of trick you guys are playing, but…" He felt cold sweat running down his face and the chill up his back once again. This time it felt like a warning, like there was something coming. He looked around for a blade, anything he could use as a weapon.

He saw something dash past in his peripherals; wrenching his neck around in a panic to try and see what it was. The urge to investigate was overwhelming, despite his fears. He took off full sprint toward the movement, but there was nothing! "Prefect Le'san!" he shouted. He noticed the quivering sound in his voice and it made him feel embarrassed, before clearing his throat and trying to calm his nerves.

"It's just the serum…" he said to himself, taking a deep breath and closing his eyes. He squeezed them shut for several seconds before feeling compelled to open them, and when he did, the environment had changed again! The change in the lighting was the first thing he noticed. The brightness hurt his eyes so much that he couldn't hold back the vomit this time, dropping to one knee.

His eyes were closed again now, and he found himself praying to the Acolytes, asking that everything would be back to normal once he opened them again. *I guess deep down he was a spiritual man*, he caught himself thinking. He opened them again, and everything was the same as before, but this time he was ready for it. He felt his strength come back to him and forced himself to stand up and examine what he was actually seeing.

It looked like he was back where he started, except everything was newer. The gaping holes around the walls and roof were no longer there, and the place surged with energy. Where he'd sat around the fire was now a room with various workstations round the edges.

Reagan jumped when he heard an unfamiliar voice behind him.

"You made it through the first part without crashing," said the voice. It was the tall man from around the fire. His voice sounded as soft as a whisper, and his words were in a language he could understand.

Reagan looked at the man, his face still hidden and blurred, even though he was close enough to see him clearly. Reagan tried rubbing his eyes to no effect, "What is this place, and why are you here?"

"Your time here is short, Akura, don't waste it," said the man, ignoring his question. He lifted a heavy hand, pointing off down one of the corridors.

Reagan turned to face that direction. He could hear the sound again, this time louder. "Are you saying we should go this way?" When he got no response, he turned back to see the man had gone again. " Great," he muttered, "I guess there's only one thing to do then."

Reagan started walking down the corridor cautiously, but the further down he went the more he felt compelled to run. It was like jogging down a steep hill, and it was getting steeper. All of a sudden he let out a cry, realizing that he was now at full sprint and wasn't able to slow down!

He could see the large doors at the end as he accelerated, bursting through effortlessly into what looked like the central chamber. His legs seemed to give out momentarily, sending him tumbling across the ground. The noise was even louder and clearer now. It sounded like battle.

There was a large arched window ahead of him where he could see the outside. Before he knew it, he was staring out of it, hanging over the ledge at the highest part of the building. How had he gotten so high up while running downhill? The thought bothered him for a second before he felt his mind relax with the notion that he was exactly where he was supposed to be.

He could smell the air around him now; it was the smell of the storm in the skies around him and the blood below as the battle raged. He could sense the army below, rather than see it, a thousand warriors at least, O'sar and Suu'vitan united, against a common enemy. For whatever reason, he felt consciously passive in the face of the carnage.

For the first time since drinking the serum, he felt like he was gaining control of what he assumed were hallucinations. He remembered why he was here, why Le'san had brought him to this place—to get his Vesica!

His next thought was cut short when the room around him exploded, engulfed by a whirlwind of rock and dust as a projectile struck the outer wall of the structure. Reagan fell on his back hard, winding himself. He could sense the enemies coming but felt restrained somehow, struggling to muster up the strength to stand up.

The door at the other side of the room burst open and the enemy poured in. His first reaction was to go for his weapon, but he found nothing. His second was to size up the enemy. The instant his eyes met his attacker, everything seemed to slow down, as if in his favor. The hulking attacker charged at him through the smoke, something familiar about the shape, the silhouette.

Reagan rose up to take a stance, he was going to be ready. He drew back; ready to direct a front kick toward his opponent, but then he saw his face. It was Le'san! Reagan squinted to focus on his master. It was definitely him, but something was different. He looked younger, and more muscular. There was an element of savagery and fury to him that Reagan had never seen before.

Young Le'san was no more than two meters away from him now, moving a third of normal speed. Reagan was about to speak when he felt that same nauseous feeling again and the familiar chill up his spine. He was about to cry out when everything sped up so fast it was like being rushed by lightning. Reagan had already decided it was over as the blade came down. He could almost feel the edge slice into him when his eyes closed again.

Silence! He felt no pain and the sound of battle around him was gone. He opened his eyes again, with an overwhelming feeling of relief. He was around the smoldering fire, like before. It was dark and damp and he thought he was alone at first, until he heard sobbing from across the clearing.

It was too dark to make out who it was. The figure sounded like a man and had his back to him, crouched down on the ground. His attention seemed to be on something in front of him at his feet, maybe a person. The man wore a large ragged cloak and it was difficult to see around him.

Before he could stop himself, Reagan spoke, "Hey!" he shouted, suddenly feeling intrusive.

The man looked around at him. He could see now that he had long dark hair, and his face was badly disfigured, blackened and scorched.

"I mean you no harm," said Reagan, "Can I offer you some assistance?"

The man grunted back at him with an almost sarcastic chuckle. "Help from you?" he asked, with disgust, " I think you've done enough!" he said, and stood up to turn around.

As the figure turned to face Reagan, he picked up the thing in front of him, now obviously a body. Reagan stared at the dead warrior as the Stranger held him in his arms. The face was unrecognizable from the wounds. Blood and scorch marks blackened a good portion of his armor.

The man holding the body glared at him through the matted hair that partially covered his face. His eyes glowed yellow and seemed to burn into his soul. He was breathing heavily; slow breaths that sounded hauntingly wheezy through his burnt mouth.

Reagan took two steps forward before the dead warrior's arm fell from beneath his cloak. The armor was undamaged in this area and he could clearly make out the family emblem and rank. Reagan felt the nausea again, but this time with intense grief and disbelief. The dead man was his Father, hardly recognizable from the disfiguration.

Reagan ran toward them through the dying fire, kicking the embers flying in every direction. He was no more than a meter away when the man lunged forward throwing his father's lifeless body right at him. Reagan dug in his heels and braced for the impact. The body sent him crashing backwards through the trail of embers left on the ground.

Reagan sat hunched on the ground, staring at his father. He frantically wiped the blood from his face, hoping that he was somehow mistaken. He tried to force himself to believe that it wasn't real, but every sense told him otherwise. He was about to close his eyes again when the Stranger spoke.

"You're too late to save him. You're too late to save any of them," said the Stranger, drawing a blade from beneath his cloak. The blade was already stained with blood.

Reagan stared at the blood dripping from the blade, leading him to only one conclusion. His feelings of grief were replaced by fury. He could only see his enemy ahead. He pushed aside his father and climbed up on one knee. He clenched his fists tight before noticing a glimmer on the ground in front of him.

Where the fire had been before, just beneath the surface of the ground, a light flickered like the morning sun off the water. It made him blink and want to turn away, but his hand was drawn toward it. He reached forward to clear away the dirt when a bolt of energy shot out to meet his palm. He hesitated for a second before another bolt hit him, then another. He felt the energy surge throughout his body, the life through his heart. The blade materialized before his eyes, a blade curved like water to an elegant point, with a flawless double edge, razor sharp.

Reagan stood up, the blade held firmly in his hand. He looked over at the Stranger, standing at the ready, holding the blood-soaked weapon that resembled his own in size and shape. He was about to charge when the figure raised his sword as if to salute him. The air around him started to blow, whirling around the clearing, kicking up the dust and dirt so much that he could barely see the Stranger. Reagan tried to stand his ground through the gale, but he lost his balance. As he fell backwards into the vortex, he clutched his Vesica tightly and closed his eyes for the final time.

This time, he knew he'd be somewhere different and clenched his eyes shut for an extra few seconds before opening them. He was relieved to find himself sitting by the fire again, burning as furiously as ever. Quadro had finished boiling another pot of water and was serving the other man tea, as well as Le'san, who was now sitting next to them.

Reagan looked around the space and tried to assess if what he was seeing was real. The feeling of nausea was gone, replaced with a something new, a confidence he didn't have before. He looked around him for his father's body, and then felt overwhelming relief when it wasn't there. The next thing he looked for was his blade.

It was nowhere to be seen, but that didn't mean he didn't have it. He held out his hand and tried to summon it. The feeling was so real a moment ago, and he couldn't help feeling disappointed when nothing appeared. As he stood up slowly and took a step closer to the fire, the thought that he'd failed crossed his mind.

Le'san had noticed Reagan coming to his senses and stood up to greet him, "You look different, my boy. The effects of the coral are a lot to take in. What you see in the vision often takes time to decipher."

Quadro held out the teapot and offered him a cup, "Have some tea, boy."

Reagan was about to take the cup when something in the fire caught his eye. Without wasting another moment he grabbed the pot from old man and threw the contents on the fire! Steam and smoke flared up in their faces and all the men jumped up in surprise.

"Calm yourself, Akura! You still feel the effects of the serum," said the tall man, talking for the first time since the hallucination.

Le'san stepped forward, offering out a hand, "Listen to Piesus! He was there to help guide you through your vision."

Reagan pushed his master aside and raised his right forearm, constructing a gauntlet around his hand and wrist. The forge was crude and hastily formed, but it provided the protection he needed. He thrust his arm into the hot embers, digging around until he could feel the familiar sensation. A bolt of energy ripped around his gauntlet, and when he pulled out his hand the magnificent blade followed.

Reagan held the blade out in front of him, taking a moment to examine the weapon. The blade felt familiar, like a part of him no different to any other limb.

Le'san was silent at first, looking for Quadro's reaction before speaking, "He's his Father's son, that's for sure," he said.

Piesus didn't seem as excited as the others, instead taking a step back to look at the Vesica, still glowing from the heat, "A blade born of fire is the strongest and most furious…" he said, "…but carrying such a weapon always comes with a price."

Quadro's expression was also that of concern, "What else did you see, boy?" he asked, eagerly.

"Let the boy enjoy this moment, old man," said Le'san. "We have the next three years to discuss his vision. The images you see never make sense at first, even if you remember them. Impossible to make sense of them without further meditation."

"Le'san's right, regardless of what the future holds for the boy. It's a rare thing, a weapon created in this manner. We are privileged to have witnessed this display of energy," said Piesus, somberly.

Reagan heard the words, suddenly noticing that the tall man was staring right at him. He realized it was the first time he'd seen the old man's eyes. They were black, with only the reflection of what remained of the fire giving life to them.

Reagan knew exactly what he had seen and remembered every part quite vividly, even if he didn't yet understand the meaning. From the way Piesus was staring at him he knew that he must have seen it too, or at least felt some of whatever he was feeling. Who was the disfigured man in the vision and why had he murdered his father? It was the only question that stuck in his mind. It made him miss home, especially since he knew his trials were just beginning.

He'd felt like a young boy the past few days before coming here, eager and naive about each new experience he was presented with. Now, he felt different; a new energy within hungered for the next new experience. The quest for knowledge before him had never felt so invigorating.

Chapter 11

The Effigy composed himself in his living quarters. He had come to call this ancient place home; a safe haven. The room was humble and minimalistic in every way, in contrast with its spectacular view. He could see the interstellar Viaduct across the water, standing magnificently atop the mountain. Today, it was partially covered by the low clouds, standing over 1000 years strong. And, 1000 years ago, the ancestors would have stood in this very location, foolishly praying to forgotten gods. They prayed for salvation on their doomed planet, the looming threat of extinction ever- present.

    Twenty years ago, he had learned of this location and the tunnels that connected it to other ancient facilities as well as the Ark. He'd grown up calling the Viaduct the Lotus Ark. He'd heard storied from Suu'vitan priests about how the Progenitors used the structure as a means of space travel, leaving their flourishing world to create life elsewhere. He'd also heard stories from the O'sar elders about their ancestors who built the structure to banish the Progenitors, and whose negligence had destroyed their beautiful world. They were both correct to an extent, depending on your point of view, and yet both gravely mistaken. Twenty years ago, he had learned the truth and twenty years ago the war ended. The Effigy felt that he'd had a hand in the eventual resolve that lead to peace, and it was up to him to make sure things stayed that way.

    He took a deep breath and stepped through a large archway onto a grand balcony overlooking the amphitheater. The room was huge and echoed with the cheers of the crowd that gathered below. Sunlight poured through the skylights, partially covered by nature's reposition. Tarnished metals integrated with the natural rock and concrete: a marvel of engineering by an ancient civilization pre-dating meta-coral alteration.

    He approached the edge of the terrace, where Rayne stood, waiting patiently. The roar of the crowd got even louder as the Effigy came into view. He raised his arms high in the air and waited for the crowd to calm down. Their cries went on for a good ten seconds before there was silence. He looked down at their faces; people of all ages and race. Idealists and outcasts stood united, eagerly awaiting his words of wisdom.

"I am honored to stand before you! The defenders of truth," said the Effigy. His voice reverberated clearly around the room, a result of precise acoustics, "All of the pieces move into play. We stand together in great anticipation!"

He allowed the crowd one more round of applause on his behalf before he continued.

"We once wandered alone, our minds tormented, consumed by darkness. But it was only so long before we began to find others; others who shared the pain we felt within." He waved his arms and used grandiose gestures that enhanced his speech.

"As one became two, two became many. We arose united, bound by a curse that had become our duty." His cloak whipped around as he walked from one side of the balcony to the other. "After the war, we were cursed to live as outcasts. We watched from the cold as those we once knew rebuilt their lives."

"While our brethren rejoiced, our enemy lay dormant, unchallenged and forgotten, but not by us."

The crowd roared once again! The Effigy had found his first disciples beyond the walls of the city, spread thin across the wastes. He had rallied those who were desperate to spread the word to others under the illusion of security. They had no idea that the peace they had fought for was about to come to an end.

They'd all come to him different from who they were now. Through his teachings and training they had become something more. He had recruited soldiers and disavowed Paladin, even criminals and savages from the wastes. Those who knew how to fight and kill taught the others. The ones who knew how to scavenge and farm shared their knowledge. They had been trained to use weapons, and engage in hand-to-hand combat, espionage and guerilla tactics. They knew how to operate under a veil of secrecy, yet hide in plain sight.

Via their public demonstrations, some had come to call them idealists, while others called them terrorists. Whatever people thought, it didn't matter. Their true objective remained a secret, exactly as intended.

"With the day of retribution almost upon us, we are all that stands between our people and the enemy. We will show them once again that this is their world no longer. Their time has long since passed! We are ready to give our lives to defend it, as free Children of Orbis!"

"The Effigy's words!" shouted a man in the crowd, as they erupted with excitement and started to chant, "The Effigy's words!...The Effigy's words!..."

The Progenitors destroyed this world once, and in their absence it flourished. The Effigy wouldn't let them destroy it again. He had to destroy the Omega faction for good this time.

The Effigy turned and walked past Rayne toward the staircase leading back up to his chambers. At the bottom, stood Jada, leaning casually by the wall. He paused beside her and she reached out for his arm.

"They would follow you to their death if you commanded it," she said. Her face looked like it could have been beautiful at one time, but it had been burned badly around her neck and the bottom part of her face. She usually hid the scaring with her long flowing hair, but not from the Effigy. "You've come a long way from the man I met all those years ago."

The Effigy shrugged, walking past her and on up the stairs. She had been with him since the start of his crusade, or at least since he became the Effigy. She proceeded to test him, but only to his advantage. She was more than his second in command and loyal soldier. Her guidance made him see clarity and helped keep him on the path to retribution.

The two of them walked to the large opening where the Lotus Ark was now fully visible. The cloud had lifted and the daylight enhanced the spectacular sight.

"There are but a few crucial moves left to make, the rest is up to them. Even I can't be certain of the conclusion."

She clutched his hand with a gentle, but firm grip. "As should be the way of things. We must do what we can with the knowledge we have. That's all we can ever do."

The Effigy kept no secrets from Jada, and knew she had at least some understanding of his unique insight. She'd told him she often wondered how he kept from going insane. It was beyond a normal mind to be able to process information not grounded by normal temporal boundaries. They were born as linear beings with a linear perception of time. His knowledge transcended the fact, and his mind was anything but that of a normal man.

Those who followed him thought that he could see the future. The action taken earlier that morning was a significant step for him, to make the decision to intervene in an event that changed a man's destiny. The Effigy had understood it as a course of action that was meant to happen. It had been a long road that began with him losing everything he'd once known. If he'd given in to death all those years ago instead of embracing rebirth, Joss Akura would be dead.

"Will he be ready?" she asked the Effigy. The both knew of whom she spoke.

"He has been waiting for this day almost as long as I have, even if he doesn't know it yet." The Effigy looked out across the dark channel. "The next time we meet it'll be face to face".

"And what of the others?" she asked. She knew that recounting the plans ahead always motivated him and helped push any doubts or misconceptions from his mind.

He took her hand as they walked through the open door over to the edge of the cliff. To the left, they could see Porta Orbis in the distance. At night, the lights stood out against another wise jet-black landscape. To the right of them was the island where the Viaduct stood, roughly 800 feet above sea level. Jagged cliffs surrounded the ancient structure, making it impossible to climb. Between them and the Viaduct was the black channel. Many had tried to cross the water since the first settlers set up camp. None made it back from the treacherous waters around the island.

The Effigy felt the breeze from the water and they edged closer together. Their affection for one another was undeniable, yet secondary to their mission. "I will see them all again before the end. Everything is about to change forever."

Chapter 12

Sapian thought it best to get as far from the scene of the crime as possible. He leapt from the top of an old, familiar building. A jump he'd made countless times. He'd managed to get the precarious descent to his refuge down to an art. He dropped 30 meters, making light contact with the surrounding objects to slow him self down. In the split second of free-fall, he replayed the events of the morning in his head. The likelihood of the feds tracking him this far out of town was slim, but a wanted criminal could never be too careful. Another cop dead, not by his hands this time, but he was definitely an accomplice.

  He landed in a crouched position, evenly spreading out his body weight. Any shock his muscles and joints couldn't handle was absorbed by his sleek armored exoskeleton. The suit had been with him from the beginning. It had been designed especially for him and enhanced his every move or action. This much he knew, even if he couldn't remember how or why.

  As he moved silently through the mid-levels of a ruined parking lot, he was careful to check his 6:00 for anyone who might be following. He smelt the air as it blew through the open space; nothing but the musk of the uninhabited environment. Scent never lied.

  He stood at what passed for the main entrance, not that any trespasser would notice. Cables hung from the half-collapsed level above, supported by large crumbling pillars that disappeared into the endless dark below. The man-made cavern ahead was in near total darkness, but his animal eyes adjusted to assist him through every obstacle he'd carefully laid out in case of intruders. To him, each cable and platform was in precisely the right place.

He ran and leapt from the asphalt, grabbing the first cable that hung meters away over a sheer drop! He swung a further ten meters forward before letting go and landing on the next platform. It ran horizontal between two beams and was rigged to a pulley system activating a switch. He heard the trap door open and saw the light poke through from his hideout. He pushed off from the platform with his feet to grab the rope ahead, swinging up, behind and over through the open passage above. He stopped dead, bracing himself with both arms and legs between the narrow walls. The door closed beneath him and another opened in front. He jumped through, landing on the rug laid out in the center of his living space.

Sapian prided himself on the complexity of his security measures. He'd discovered the place a year ago, a big enough space for his junk with thick concrete walls impervious to external scans. Apparently, there were dark zones like this all over the wastes, buried beneath the remains of old buildings dating back to the pre-metacoral age. He'd ventured deeper to the lower levels on a number of occasions, finding artifacts from various sites, which now cluttered up every corner of his abode. He'd also found other machinery too big to carry, strange-wheeled transports along with the skeletal remains of beings he'd assumed were Progenitors. He had everything from tools and children's toys to old engine parts and pieces of furniture.

His presence triggered several lights around the main room that flickered on. Apart from a thin window at the top of the north wall about six feet wide and five inches tall there was no other natural light. There were two more rooms off to the side that remained dark. His control center took up the entire south wall. A large worn-out armchair sat in the front of an array of mismatched computers, old and new. Cables and wires seemed to run all over the place to various screens and different equipment.

Sapian walked over toward the chair, starting to unwrap the bandages from his face. It felt good to get them off. This was the only place where he felt comfortable without a mask or disguise. He discarded the rags on the ground and stared at his reflection in the main monitor screen. As well as dealing with being a wanted criminal, he was an ape of some kind, a fact that had baffled him as much as it disturbed anybody else. He considered himself intelligent and had the mannerisms of a human, but something instinctive inside of him felt primal and savage. He remembered very little from his past, but he somehow knew he hadn't always been this way.

He hopped onto the large chair and lit half a stogie that sat in an ashtray attached to the right armrest. He hit a few buttons on the makeshift console attached to the left arm and systems came to life. It took a few seconds to boot up before a large fat face appeared on the main screen.

"Ahh, Sapian," said the grotesque mug. He had a greasy residue around his fat lips and seemed to have no neck between his face and bulky shoulders. Two tubes ran up to his face, one up his left nostril with the other bent into his fat chin. "That little job you pulled has been all over the broadcast this morning."

Sapian pushed back in his chair. It reclined back with a creak. " Those lunatics you set me up with weren't exactly low profile." He took a big puff of the cigar and prepared to suffer through Zed's usual bullshit.

"I deal with unique clientele," he spluttered. "Ethically misunderstood individuals such as yourself." The screen zoomed out a little to reveal more of Zed's blubbery mass.

Zed looked off to the side, presumably another screen on his end. "Seems you've been making a big impression throughout the underground. A guy came to me asking for you specifically. Rumor is this guy's a major player."

Sapian paused for a second. "...The intel's for real? This last gig almost got me busted, not to mention killed!"

"Real as it comes! I've sent you an encrypted file with the time and a map to the location. Don't suppose you could tell old Zed what you're after?" he asked, rubbing his greasy chin with two fat fingers.

"Mind your damn business!" barked Sapian. It wasn't the first time Zed had tried to pry the details out of him. He'd already had to divulge more information than he'd felt comfortable with. Zed was his agent after all, even if that particular title did sound a little too professional for such a vile wretch.

Zed leaned forward, imposing his features on Sapian. "He sounded cryptic. He said he had what you were looking for."

Sapian was a federal criminal and wanted murderer. The first real thing he could remember was that specific incident where he violently killed three federal agents. He'd seen some ugly shit in his line of work, but that was the day everything had changed, and the fact that he remembered almost nothing prior to that had been driving him crazy. He couldn't remember the last time he had a decent night's sleep without the aid of liquor.

At one point, he even considered turning himself in, hoping to find some sort of truth about his origin or background before the slaughter. Better judgment prevailed and he'd decided to look for his own answers, rather than sitting behind bars. He'd been seeking answers in less than savory circles, taking on jobs and working his way up the corporate ladder of low lives. This latest proposal was definitely setting off a few warning bells, but something about it sounded like the closest thing to a lead he'd had.

Sapian scanned over the information that Zed had sent across. "So…Tomorrow night then? A little short notice don't you think? Sounds a little too good to be true!"

On the other end of the transmission, Zed sat back in his large enclosed seat/work station. He had all kinds of different sized tubes connected to various body parts. He looked naked, but his huge flabby gut and appendages hid any kind of undergarments he might be wearing. His workstation was a mess and the stench almost appeared visible, hanging in the air above him. From the collection of empty food containers around him, it looked like he rarely left that spot.

"He didn't like talking over the wireless system. This guy's smart. Any trace I ran was cut short, but as for the encryption code…." Zed waved a chubby digit in front of his smug face.

"So you peaked?" asked Sapian, looking pissed. He had difficulty trusting Zed, but unfortunately he was one of the more competent 'Agents' in the business.

"It's my business to protect my investment and the well-being of all my employees."

"Spare me the bullshit, would you?!" said Sapian, cutting him off. "What else did he tell you?"

"To come alone, of course. You will be careful?..." Zed said. His brow narrowed and the way the light hit his fat face made his black eyes look almost predatory for a brief moment, like a hungry shark.

"You're all heart," said Sapian, pointing an accusing finger at the fat bastard. "This guy better be for real."

Zed was about to say something else when Sapian ended the transmission. Dealing with that slippery bastard always made him feel like he was operating at the same level, like his filth managed to rub off on him over the transmission. He sat back and took the last drag of his stogie before killing it in the ashtray.

He flipped casually out of the chair and walked over to the thin window, peering out over the channel. He needed some air. He tried not to use his one and only escape route to enjoy the view, but after the morning he'd had, he needed to relax. He bounded over to one of the darker sections of his hideout and pulled on a heavy chain hanging from the ceiling. In an instant, he was pulled up a narrow tunnel to one of the higher levels. He pulled back a heavy cage door and walked out onto a concrete platform jutting out diagonally over a drop off. It was so high he couldn't see the ground below due to the layer of smog.

Sapian walked over to the edge and felt the strong wind wrap around him. Nobody could touch him here. He knew he could make it down if he really had to, maybe grappling the closest structure, 30 meters lower and 50 across. It would be impossible for any significant force to enter his lair through the small tunnel he'd set up as an escape route. First, they'd have to figure out how to open two doors from the wrong side, and even if they did, they'd have to come down one at a time, and that's after finding the place.

He inhaled and took in the view across the channel. 'The Lotus Ark' was what the city folk called the anomalous structure on the island. He'd heard various rumors about the ruins. Some said that no man could get close to it, that it emitted an aura that disrupted the synthiant inside them. The thought caused Sapian to touch the scars around his face, deep dark ruts that burrowed into his eye sockets. He had similar markings around his chest and spine.

Beyond the obvious visible aspects, he'd quickly determined that he wasn't like the rest of these people that surrounded him. Every Terran existed as a symbiotic being. They were two, born as one, never knowing anything different. He wasn't like them, yet some days he could sense another presence, something dark, lurking in his subconscious. He sometimes felt enhanced by this foreign entity, like it drove him to a certain extent, and yet other times it haunted his every thought. His unique biology was another question high up on the list of things to investigate.

He was about to turn away from the Ark when he thought he saw something sparkle in the distance. He blinked and wiped his eyes, quickly dismissing it as fatigue. He had enjoyed the view long enough. He had work to do.

Chapter 13

The wall surrounding Porta Orbis might have been constructed to defend their great city, but as far as Lucas was concerned it was shutting them off from the rest of the world. From the other side of the channel, the city at night glowed against the dark landscape, but in the daytime it looked almost lifeless.

Lucas clutched the case recovered from the raid. *A short walk on the beach in the morning, while the tide was out*, thought Lucas. It had become a routine of late. A devout instrument of the Omega faction wouldn't normally allow R&R to interfere with the mission, but 140 seconds to reflect on the previous part of the mission felt acceptable, before continuing to the next stage.

Lucas looked up at the towering Viaduct and the jagged cliff face leading to it. There was still enough power in the suit for a few more warp jumps. It was time to report to the overlord. The mission had not gone exactly to plan, but was still on schedule. Lucas squatted down and reached for the controls positioned above the right leg on the armor. A simple two-switch combination activated the displacement iris.

With a surge of green light, a ball of energy surrounded the armored figure and with a bright flash, there was nothing. While in the vortex, time seemed to move slower, but once on the other side it was like no time had passed at all. These few seconds felt a lot like dreaming with a lucid mind, before awakening at your destination. An instrument of Omega wouldn't rest before the mission was completed, but in these short moments waiting was unavoidable; just part of the job.

Lucas reappeared in another ball of green light, crouched on the ground 100 meters above. Looking up at the arches through the optical sensors in the centurion armor was more like a scan than an observation. The tiny maintenance droids buzzed around the structure, transmitting reports on completed and ongoing repairs, damage points that needed attention. Everything had to be ready.

An alarm sounded inside the helmet and triggered a visual display on the wrist monitor. It read 'Low power – 16%'. Lucas ignored it and walked over to a work surface toward the right hand side of the large open area.

At the base of the Viaduct was a large circular platform that measured exactly 150 meters across. At separate intervals around its circumference, there were three main energy deflectors, set back 20 meters from the base, towering up and over, curving toward the center at the top. Around the inner section, ten meters from the base, there were three smaller deflectors on a track than enabled them to orbit the center at high speed, stabilizing the warp field, or at least that is the way it was designed. Lucas had no time to test it, with only simulations to check systems were working before it was time to initiate.

Lucas had at first thought it humorous that the indigenous species had thought the Viaduct looked like a beautiful flower, even though the resemblance was obvious. The amusing part was that they thought of the Viaduct as a subject of worship or beauty, rather than the means of their destruction.

In the absence of original mankind, the remnants of humanity had adapted to this harsh environment. Their biology had fascinated his master, and their top scientists had used the research collection to develop their own cutting edge bio-armor. In a way, they understood these people better than themselves. Their beliefs were primitive. They had forgotten their true origin in their ignorance, forming their most prominent society around this gateway. They'd made it almost convenient to invade and take the planet; like animals, released from servitude, too stupid to stray from familiarity and run free.

Lucas smiled behind the mask of the Mk 3 Centurion Armor. Reactivating the Viaduct would act as a message to every citizen of the Omega faction that mankind had a future as the dominant spices on Earth once more. An overwhelming sensation of racial supremacy triggered the armor's internal sensors. Elevated heart rate—adrenaline spikes. Lucas clenched both fists. Time to report to Omega.

With a few commands entered into the underside of the left gauntlet, three of the droids stopped what they were doing and started to circle each other in the space four or so meters above the platform. Gradually, they got faster, emitting a strange mist-cloud onto which they projected an image. A large face began to appear, the three-dimensional image growing into a large head about five meters tall.

"Report!" demanded the head, with a booming voice that echoed around the structure.

"Repairs to the Viaduct will be completed on schedule," said Lucas. "I'm waiting on the replacement power source. Our benefactor has proved reliable so far."

"Have the drones succeeded in reaching the sub-sections of the Viaduct?"

"They have managed to navigate deep enough to perform an extensive diagnostic. I tracked back ten miles in each direction and readings showed that the old tunnels had collapsed over the years. They also indicated that the dampeners are still intact."

"I needn't remind you that interstellar teleportation on this scale is an exact science, everything must be aligned to function with precise synchronization." said the Face. "If the dampeners were to fail, the result would be catastrophic." As he tilted his head down, the Omega emblem became visible, indented in the skin of his forehead.

"Of course, my Lord." Lucas knew that the sheer force generated by the viaduct could tear it from the mountaintop without the subterranean dampeners. They acted like anchors, buried deep beneath the Earth's crust, magnetized to the planet's core.

Lucas knew the viaduct better than anyone else on the planet, even more than those who worshiped it. "The intelligence I gathered showed that these people still have no knowledge of how the machine functions, or that any of the surrounding locations are linked or related. The surface landscape has changed significantly from our archive maps, but every station or bunker I managed to find was either deserted or destroyed from the tectonic shifts."

There was a long pause before his response while Lord Omega decided whether or not he was satisfied with his agent's conclusion. "...And what of the locations you investigated? I trust any possible threat was neutralized? Any setback at this crucial stage would be unacceptable."

"The facility seemed to be used mainly to store old artifacts; relics from their war." Lucas knew that what was said next might suggest an ulterior intention away from the current part of the mission. "However, I recovered an item I thought you'd want to see."

Training a centurion relied on their unwavering ability to follow an order at any cost and Lucas knew deviating from the current objective was punishable by death. Omega had generals and lieutenants, whom he trusted to make decisions derived from their interpretation of events. A centurion was nothing more than an instrument with an objective. They were required to never second guess a command or make up their own mind on whether something other than their primary objective was relevant.

"You have your objective, Centurion. You are an instrument, a tool crafted for one particular task!"

"But, master…" interrupted Lucas. "If I could just show you…" Lucas removed the items from the case, throwing them in front of the large face. One of the droids adjusted its position to emit a thicker cloud of particles around items, suspending them in mid-air. As Lucas took more pieces out of the case, they assembled in an order around a circular space in the center. Lucas watched his master's facial expression change from one of anger, to intrigue before continuing.

"I recognized the designs from Omega development projects." Lucas pointed to the device integrated into the armor around his waist. "The device is similar to my own displacement iris. I found it…"

Lucas rummaged around in the case frantically all of a sudden, realizing there was a piece missing. While Omega studied the items another head materialized beside his.

The projection was half the size, appearing closer to the device as if to get a better look. "It can't be!" said the second head. "Where is the centerpiece?!"

Lucas looked up at the both of them, speechless for a second. Professor Brakus was a specialist in the tech department and one of Lucas's mentors. He'd actually designed the prototype Mk 3 armor worn by the Centurion, along with the integrated displacement iris.

"It's gone! It was in here!" Lucas threw the case to ground, clenching the armored fists again, this time in anger.

"Was there any description of its function in their records?! Do they know what it can do?" asked Brakus, sounding increasingly distraught.

Lucas studied the reaction of his Supreme Commander and one the faction's leading scientists. Lord Omega hadn't said a word, but his ever-stern expression and the fact that he remained silent hinted at its importance. The centerpiece must have been lost during the fight with the cop. The possibility that LEX or the FRA hadn't recovered it was slim, and Lucas remembered seeing the cop leaning over the case as it lay open.

"That damn enforcer! I should have killed him myself." Lucas looked up at the floating heads, and said in a calmer tone, "How is it possible that they have such technology?"

Omega's eyes shifted to the right for Brakus' response.

"I'd hate to speculate before I properly examine the device," said Brakus. "To think that technology such as this could exist on Earth is…"

Omega cut off the scientist who stopped talking immediately. "This line of conversation is irrelevant until the device is examined, as you said."

"You must retrieve the centerpiece," said Brakus. His face faded out to nothing while Omega remained.

"This will be your only objective once the final phase is underway," said Omega, the presence of his projected form loomed over the Centurion.

"Understood," answered Lucas, with a slight bow.

The transmission ended and the mist dispersed. All of the droids except one returned to continue repairs. The parts of the device remained suspended in the air.

Lucas stared at the items and circled the empty space where the iris should be. For a centurion to speak out to a superior officer was a serious offense, and to Overlord Omega it could have meant the death sentence. Whatever the function of the device, it must be of great importance.

Chapter 14

Joss tossed and turned, trying to sleep through the sound of his alarm. He felt around on the console by his bed, trying to hit the snooze button for the third time before finally giving in. The bright sunshine felt like a slap in the face as he opened his eyes and sat up. An afternoon nap never seemed to do him any good, even though he knew his body needed it. He ached worse than before and the idea of stepping into the cold shower in his cheap apartment was more that he could bear to think about in his current state.

He stumbled past the table and grabbed his jacket, throwing it on over his singlet vest. He took a prolonged look at the pigsty he called home, stepping over a pile of clothes and headed out the door. He had to get out of there now otherwise he was going to be late for the big reunion.

He hopped down the rickety steps, throwing a smoke into his mouth before realizing what was going on in the streets below. He scanned the scene with a detective's eye. The sky train station a block down was flooded with people. They seemed to be split into two main groups. On one side he recognized the 'Effigy's Hand' banners, and on the other a separate group had seemingly banded together to focus their aggression against the so-called fanatics.

"Fuck!" Joss muttered to himself, as his feet hit the street.

He saw a few cops standing around, monitoring the growing crowds and making sure everyone with a difference of opinion was keeping things civil.

He jogged over to one of the younger LEX cops he recognized. Zimmerman, he thought his name was, or Zimmer to his mates, "What's up, rookie?"

Zimmerman looked flustered and didn't recognize Joss at first, before pulling a double take, "...Akura? You picked a good time to take a vacation! This whole town's going to shit."

Joss scanned the crowd again, "So it seems."

"It's that damn Effigy bastard," said Zimm, with no attempt to hide his frustration. "Since they labeled him a terrorist, his followers have been acting out all over the city."

"Well, once you start blowing up government buildings you can forget about going back to peaceful protests," said Joss, taking a drag on his smoke.

"That's just it. They say they had nothing to do with it. It all kicked off after news of the attack this morning was made public."

"The feds?" asked Joss.

Zimm just nodded his head and moved off to direct a couple of civilians who were ducking under the barriers.

Joss walked a little closer as two of the Effigy's lackeys seemed to be about to make a speech. They were standing on the steps leading up to the station. They had drawn quite the crowd, totally blocking the way up to the train and the street below. The older man of the two held a megaphone to his mouth. It echoed loudly as he tested whether it was working beneath the sky train track, running 30 meters above them.

"The FRA has forced our leader into hiding with these horrific accusations of terrorism and war mongering!" said the Effigy's follower.

The second man took the megaphone, "This mockery of a government calls him a thief, a murderer! We will no longer stand for such heinous slander!"

It was the typical rant of anyone who might follow or sympathize with someone like the Effigy. Whether there was any truth to these accusations or not, people with this level of commitment would always be on his side. Joss tried to think subjectively, putting himself in their position. It was a method that had always aided his work as a detective, especially when working undercover. If there were this many members of the public who felt this way, he wondered what could have led them to feel such contempt for the government.

Joss shrugged to nobody in particular and took the last drag of his smoke, flicking it down a nearby drain on the ground. Fuck, if he really thought about it, he could think of 100 reasons the system didn't work. But it was better than war. Walter was right. The new generation didn't remember the hard times. Joss was only a small child himself when the war ended.

Joss wandered back over to Zimm, who stood there looking on edge. The protest looked like it was just getting warmed up, "Is the whole line down?" asked Joss.

"Everything up to the Protorium Interchange. Take the perimeter if you have a ride. Dispatch reports it all clear. These punks have been giving us trouble all morning," said Zimm, nodding in the direction of a group of glidebikers coming off the exit ramp and forcing their way through the crowd to get a look at what was going on. There were four of them, but they looked intimidating enough to send a few people hurrying off in the opposite direction. Another LEX cop stood in front of the group, sheepishly trying to wave them in the other direction.

Joss watched the altercation waiting to happen. The Leader got off his ride and walked over to the cop. The biker wasn't a small guy, likely carrying some kind of concealed weapon. The others thugs remained stationary for the moment. A couple of them sniggered, seeming amused by the impending situation. Joss couldn't hear exactly what the biker was saying, but saw when the thug grabbed the young cop by the collar of his uniform.

"You gonna get out of my fucking way?!" shouted the grizzly-looking man. Spit flew through his gritted teeth and past his handlebar mustache.

"N..now, sir. Step back! Or I'll have to use force!" spluttered the young officer.

Joss could see the poor bastard struggling and decided to take a casual stroll in that direction. He could see that the rookie was doing his best to keep the peace and couldn't make up his mind whether or not it was a good idea to draw his sidearm. Hesitation was his first mistake. "Time for a lesson," Joss said to himself.

"Hey, punk?" said Joss, walking calmly past the other bikers. "...A word."

Joss waited for the brute to get a good look at him, allowing him to take in exactly what was going to happen next. He could tell from the thug's size and body language that he could probably throw a heavy punch and could brawl. But the smell of booze in the air suggested he was intoxicated, which would slow his reaction time and limit his speed and accuracy.

The man turned to square up before Joss swung in with a right hook. The connection made a solid thump followed by the wet sound of his loose jaw. A tooth flew out with a shower of spit, bouncing off the speechless rookie's new uniform. The man was on his ass and wasn't showing signs of waking up anytime soon.

Joss heard movement behind him and turned to face the rest of the group. Another of the thugs, who he assumed was the 'number two' started to climb off his bike, and had produced a metal bar from somewhere on his ride.

"You're fucking dead, pretty boy!" growled the second scumbag.

Joss laughed at the joker's threat, watching as he clumsily dismounted his ride. This one looked more stupid than the last guy, if that was even possible. He also looked heavier, with the majority of his bulk around the midsection.

Joss accelerated to a double-timed trot toward the surprised-looking biker. "You're going to kick my ass from all the way over there? I've got a better idea."

Joss kicked the heavy bike with all his weight. "How about I hand you your ass, and you give me one of these bikes for the inconvenience!?"

The bike toppled over causing a domino effect, knocking over the other bikes behind it. Two of the men struggled, trapped under their rides while the last guy, a skinnier man, crawled out from beneath it. Joss watched as he attempted to pull a pistol from his leg holster.

Zimm had run over when the action started and had his weapon aimed firmly at the gaunt man's face. "Don't even fucking think about it!" commanded the young officer. The biker tossed the weapon to the side and sat with his hands behind his head.

Joss didn't wait for an answer to his question, walking by the thugs as they squirmed beneath their bikes. Joss glanced back at the young cop who just stood there, gob smacked. "You think you can take it from here, sport?"

"Erm..Yess, Sir!" said the cop.

Zimm wore a smile on his face that suggested the dust up just might have brightened up his day.

Joss snatched up the only bike not being currently used as a restraint and looked it over. It wasn't the nicest ride in the pile, but it was a ride nonetheless. He fired up the machine and gave it some power.

"Hey!" shouted Zimmer. "You can't take that. They've got to be impounded!"

Joss looked in his direction with a grin that said it all, but just in case his intentions weren't clear, "Tell the Chief, this punk gets his wheels back when I get my badge."

He gunned the engine, spinning the bike around in the right direction. The thing sounded like raw electricity as he hit the throttle, causing bystanders to move aside swiftly; even the Effigy's followers had been distracted by the commotion. Joss laughed to himself thinking about the Chief's expression when she read Zimm's report.

He hit the throttle again and headed for the perimeter road.

Chapter 15

The sound of footsteps approaching could be heard from inside the control room of FRA headquarters. Any agents present who looked to be slacking off, either sat up straight or hunched closer to their monitors. Word around the HQ was that the Inquisitor was pissed.

Darahk marched onto the observation platform of the large semi-circular room. His arms were placed firmly behind his back, his brow was low and lips tight, as if his whole body was struggling to contain his vexation. He spoke sharply, almost demanding a particular answer, or else, "You'd better have some good news for me."

The closest agent looked around waiting for the man next to him to speak before he realized Darahk was looking right at him. "Well...Sir..." replied the bumbling agent. "Nothing yet, but..."

"Nothing!" barked Darahk. "Where the hell is my missing corpse!? How can a body just disappear!?"

"I've isolated the transmission that hacked our communications. It's a Federal code, sir, but we're having trouble tracing the source," said an enthusiastic agent to the left of the other.

The first agent had almost turned back to his monitor before deciding to add one final comment. "We weren't the only team monitoring their systems," he said, instantly regretting it.

"I gathered that, you blithering idiot!" growled Darahk. "Just find out who it was."

"Yes, sir" he replied, his voice quivering with fear.

Darahk looked around the room. He had a great view over the city through the one-way, tinted windows. He thought of it as *his* office. He was in charge here: A team of no less than 50 agents at his disposal and more in reserve if he needed them. They were his eyes, ears, and fists, ready to strike if needed, awaiting his command. He hated it when something felt beyond his reach. He got a helpless feeling, as if everything he'd worked for since the war hadn't made a difference. The fact that the interference had come from somewhere in the agency made him grit his teeth.

Darahk noticed Lieutenant Rosair appear behind him. Her steps were lighter than his, with a calmer pace. She operated with an element of sleekness uncommon in the agency. The majority of field agents had a tendency to throw their weight around. Heavy boots and an imposing presence. Rosair could come down hard when she needed too, but in a way that you'd never see it coming.

"I've made contact with the informant, sir. We have to be ready to move tomorrow night," she said, waiting for her commander's response.

Darahk forced away his distractions, "You have the team standing by, Lieutenant?" He looked away from her toward the screen.

"Two teams forward and a third as back-up." She edged forward to stand beside him. "Any luck tracking down the intercept team?"

Darahk turned to face his subordinate. Rosair was the best he had and she knew that if there had been any real progress, he'd have told her already. Darahk knew this was her way of asking if everything was fine and he respected her for doing so while maintaining a professional attitude.

"Still nothing, Lieutenant," he muttered quietly so the agents on the lower levels wouldn't hear them. "A Federal code, as we suspected."

Rosair looked at the screen. "Interesting. Somebody high up enough in the agency to scramble our signal. Must have been the Commissar's staff," she said cracking the knuckles on one hand.

Darahk had observed this behavior before and recognized it as part of her thinking process.

"I should have been there, supervised the transportation of the corpse personally. I would have needed a damn good reason to hand it over, even to the Commissar's men." said Rosair, pausing for a few seconds before reverting back to their former line of conversation. "Sir, shall I go ahead and prep for the op?"

Rosair was ever calm in these matters. In fact, Darahk had only ever seen her riled up once; the day she found out her last partner was murdered. Rumor had it that their relationship had been more than professional before it happened. Her determination when it came to finding the killer was what got her promoted. Darahk promised her that if she applied that same determined attitude to every FRA case assigned to her he'd promote her to Lieutenant, and she could use the resources necessary to catch the thing that killed four FRA agents. She'd received the promotion almost three months ago and had taken to the job like she was born to it.

Darahk met the Lieutenant's eyes earnestly. "That bastard's slipped through our fingers for the last time..." said Darahk as the doors at the back of the room slid open.

Another agent appeared through the door and seemed to be in distress, "Inquisitor!" A few heads turned around. "A representative of the Order is here to see you!"

Darahk gritted his teeth again and felt them creak. He hated unwelcome interruptions.

"I tried to stop him, sir!" stressed the agent, panting from his sprint down the corridor. "He just barged through!"

Darahk saw the broad figure approaching from the other end of the corridor. He marched at a steady pace he recognized all too well.

"Akura! That's all I need..." he said, rubbing his brow with his fingers.

He turned around and faced the room of agents who'd all stopped what they were doing. He cleared his throat loudly, so everyone could hear. "Shut these screens off!" he ordered. "Anything from this morning's attack!"

The agents scurried around frantically as the Prefect of the Order reached the door. One last guard stepped in to block his path, in an attempt to buy them a few more seconds.

"My Lord," said the guard in a failed display of dominance. "This is a restricted area! You'll have to wait to be..."

Akura ushered the man aside with a firm yet non-threatening gesture, ignoring his words completely. He marched forward to stop a couple of meters from Darahk and Rosair. The guard Akura had pushed aside moved to follow him. He was about to place a hand on his Prefect's shoulder when Darahk raised a finger to stop him.

"Akura, this is highly irregular!" started Darahk. "You can't just barge into a restricted sector. As a Prefect of the Order, protocol states…"

"Don't lecture me on protocol, Darahk!" growled the Paladin, pointing his finger at the Inquisitor, cutting him off.

Rosair watched the two of them in a sort of stalemate. Akura said the Inquisitor's name like a dirty word. She'd never seen her commander hold back the way he was holding back now. The Paladin had an inch or two on him height wise and weighed a good deal more. He wore a cloak over an old, but ripped, stronger body. The kind of warrior's physique that looked like it came naturally with years of duty, and only strengthened with age.

His face was angled with lines that hinted at a life of hardship and conflict. The top of his head was bald, with longer hair tied up around the back in a tidy bun. Thick grey tufts extended down the sides of his face; adding to his grizzled, superior status. He stared at Darahk.

Darahk eyeballed the Paladin, sending the glare of that contempt right back at him. He certainly didn't fear the man and respected the Prefect to an extent. But this was his turf, and he was going to stand his ground. He held back and waited for Akura to say his piece.

Akura's voice boomed around the room, "I know all about the HGF you seized today, not to mention several other incidents involving fusion technology! The Order should have been notified the instant…"

Darahk cut him off mid-sentence, walking toward the Paladin to stand a meter away. It was important to display authority in front of his agents, "We would have informed the Patronas Council the instant we deemed it necessary."

"Necessary!?" yelled Akura! He lunged forward grabbing Darahk who looked both shocked and outraged. Akura's face was almost touching the Inquisitor's. "The last time I looked, I'd been in this fight a lot longer than you! This coalition means information goes both ways! I demand full disclosure!"

Akura's eyes shifted to the Lieutenant, a couple of meters away who had her hand over her weapon, like he'd triggered some kind of natural reaction in her when he grabbed her commanding officer.

Akura grinned at her. "Are you trying to be funny Lieutenant?!" he growled.

Darahk got over the initial shock and pushed Akura back. He thought that Akura sometimes forgot he'd fought the same war as him, even on the same side. He might have been younger by a few years but he'd seen his fair share of bloodshed.

"The war's over, Prefect! And I don't take orders from you! While you stand within these walls, I'm in command!"

Akura bobbed his head maintaining a slight grin. He'd gotten a rise out of the old stiff.

Darahk didn't find anything funny about the situation, but then again, he wasn't known for his sense of humor, "You want intel? I'll need to see clearance. Without the proper documentation, I can't permit this intrusion."

Akura gestured to someone who appeared to be standing behind him. The figure seemed to appear from out of nowhere, a much shorter man easily hidden by Akura's size and stature.

It was the first time either Darahk or Rosair had noticed the older man hidden behind the paladin. He looked up through thick circular glasses and handed a small scroll to Akura; two cylindrical pieces, about eight inches long, bearing the mark of the Order. The emblem was a dodecagon, with 12 triangular flags making up the sides, one for each of the paladin chapters pointing inwards towards a center.

Akura held the document in front of Darahk and the bottom cylinder lowered slowly. It was Gailan's time to dictate protocol.

"The mandate states that if the FRA has information on the illegal use of fusion technology, an Order representative must be notified," said Akura in his most serious voice.

Darahk read through the document even though he knew it'd be legitimate. It was handwritten on paper, nobody else produced official documentation in this way. It bugged Darahk. To him, it was just another primitive method that he thought was behind the times. When he joined the Agency, he did so because he thought their ideals were progressive. Having to report to the Order in these matters sometimes felt like a step backwards, despite the Council's public stature.

Darahk turned to walk from the room toward what looked like an elevator door. It read 'Level 7 clearance' on the top and had a palm and retinal scanner by the control pad. "If you're done throwing your weight around, you can follow me."

Chapter 16

Joss shifted down a gear as he approached his Father's house. As he reached the front entrance, he realized the gate was locked shut. Growing up, the gates were rarely closed. The compound looked unusually quiet, even derelict in the fading light.

All of a sudden two large floodlights lit up the area where Joss was standing.

"Who goes there?" boomed a voice from the watchtower left of the gate.

The light dazzled Joss for a second, forcing him to shield his eyes. He could make out the silhouettes of at least three guards, another irregularity. There was never more than a single tenderfoot initiate manning the front gate, and only to welcome guests. These sentries were on active lookout. *Maybe a little sarcasm would help diffuse the situation*, thought Joss. "The prodigal son returns," he said, unenthusiastically. "Get that light out of my face!"

As he coasted slowly past the main section of the house he tried not to think about the last time he was here, not that the apparently grim setting before him helped much. It was especially dark with all the lights off, everywhere except the practice hall at the back of the compound. He passed by several smaller buildings that looked like they were now sleeping quarters for the guards. He'd counted at least ten Paladin patrolling the grounds on the way in.

He remembered when this used to be living quarters for young initiates, and it was once in way better condition. It was the duty of the initiates to tidy and maintain their quarters. He remembered a fonder time from his youth when the entire area flourished with activity.

Lord Akura lectured in various studies and taught practical classes, advanced combat primarily. Young Paladin who required special attention would be sent here to train. Some of the initiates came because they were especially gifted, some because they were arrogant and unruly, or struggled with standard teaching methods. His father worked best with students that had an edge, 'An edge he'd rather see sharpened than dulled,' Joss had heard him say on more than one occasion.

In his early teenage years, Joss had fit nicely into that category, excelling in his studies. He'd found the training grueling, but fulfilling. He was also able to pick up the basics of coral manipulation quite naturally. His father had schooled him in Paladin martial arts to a certain extent too, without the Patronas Council's permission. He was only allowed to practice in private, behind closed doors, and almost always with his brother.

Joss pulled over and stopped by the training hall where the doors were open. It was pretty much the only building with the lights on in the whole compound, lit entirely by open flame. Two burning torches hung either side of the intricately carved arched entrance. The architectural design was similar to the coral designs he'd seen in the Patronas Templum, only made from wood, intentionally humbling the aesthetics.

Walking up to the entrance felt like retracing familiar footsteps, each wooden beam and surface carved by past initiates as part of their studies. A thousand candles enhanced the serenity of the hall, one for each soul that'd worked to rebuild the training ground after the area was devastated by battle. It represented the hardships every Paladin must endure, as well as the eventual reward.

This is where they had taken their first steps toward a life devoted to the Patronas Order. His Father often talked of how important it was for his students to understand the significance of their transition, an enlightened life in place of chaos and uncertainty.

Once Joss had finished taking in the nostalgia of his surroundings, he noticed Reagan ahead of him. His brother sat cross-legged, perfectly still, meditating in total silence. He'd seen his father do it many times before, sometimes for hours at a time, the practice was almost hypnotic to watch. He couldn't remember the last time he'd meditated, replacing it with more ambitious pursuits.

Joss watched as he got closer. Reagan had expelled the alloy from his body, suspending the meta-coral in its liquid form. The globules of metallic liquid seemed to orbit his torso in one constant, fluidic movement. The gentle flicker from the torches and candles reflected of the surface of the liquid around room, complementing the already tranquil surroundings.

"Where the hell is everyone?" boomed Joss. The volume of his voice disrupted the tranquility, enhanced by the acoustics of the great hall.

Reagan didn't budge, though he was obviously aware of his brother's presence the instant he entered the room. As well as the decorative aesthetics, the strategically placed meta-coral elements around the training hall helped sharpen ones senses and augmented symbiotic focus.

"I've been here a while," said Reagan, his eyes remaining closed. "The guards tell me the house has been empty all day."

Joss wandered across to the opposite side of the training circle. If his Farther was late it had to be work-related. The protests in town had made Joss over an hour late and he thought they might have started dinner without him. Punctuality was always expected with father, even enforced when they were younger. If you were ever late for a meeting with the Prefect there'd better be a damn good reason, and by good reason, he meant duty.

Joss admired the chandelier above him, hanging from the domed celling at the building's highest point. The extra time he'd had to reacquaint himself had lifted his mood. The improvement was evident in his tone. "I can't remember the last time we were both in here," said Joss.

"I can!" laughed Reagan, suddenly opening his eyes before standing up. The meta-coral moved around the surface of his skin for a second before he absorbed it within.

"If I remember correctly, you were on your ass," he stated, through a moderate grin.

"Is that right?" said Joss, while walking over toward the weapons rack on the opposite side of the room. On it, were three training staffs, each forged from meta-coral. He'd sparred with the weapons many times. They were designed to crumble with a potentially lethal strike, but that didn't mean they didn't pack a punch. He'd broken bones in these sessions before and had more that his share of cuts and bruises.

"I'd say we're overdue for a rematch!" exclaimed Joss, casually shaking off his leather jacket before grabbing one of the bow staffs. He spun the staff around in his hand and felt his ribs. He ached from his beating that morning, but he wasn't about to back down, especially from his brother.

"If you think you're up to it," taunted Reagan, retrieving his own staff that was leaning up against a nearby pillar.

"Please!" sniggered Joss, with a cocky expression. "I came all the way over here. The least I can do is mop the floor with your butt."

Joss took a firm stance and tried to concentrate, gesturing toward the center for the sparring area with his hand. His manipulation skills were a little rusty but you never forgot the basics. The coral rose up from the ground toward Joss' palm, transforming it into a perfect sphere. He turned to grin at his brother before realizing he'd already done the same.

Paladin had sparred in the training circle for centuries. It helped the tenderfoot learn the basics of maintaining balance during a fight, but could be a potentially grueling combat arena with two or more experienced warriors.

The platform they stood upon was actually a large half sphere, solid meta-coral, with the dome side underground and the flat side face up. The half-sphere was less dense than weapons-grade coral, and more malleable. It reacted to hard impacts and falls, becoming softer on collision. The density of the coral also made it easier to manipulate, more susceptible to symbiotic control, even for a novice.

Joss thought back to his previous training sessions. The process of the exercise was simple. You were to best your opponent using either staff or sphere. While sparring in the traditional sense you had to constantly be aware of your opponent's sphere, which could come at you from any direction. The exercise taught you to defend yourself from multiple attacks through distraction, while simultaneously concentrating to levitate the sphere, working you both mentally and physically. Even the higher-level Paladin sparred using this method. As well as using multiple spheres and a variety of weapons, they could also reconfigure the density of the half square beneath them to form more difficult terrain and obstacles.

Reagan practiced attacks with his staff while his meta-coral ball spun around him at a constant, controlled speed. "A hot-shot cop could lose his edge working the graveyard shift. I'll try and take it easy on you." Reagan locked eyes with Joss before stopping his sphere dead in front of him

"Keep talking, altar boy," Joss barked back, unfazed by the display. "I can't wait to see what prefect Le'san's been teaching you."

Reagan took a freestyle stance and moved toward Joss. "O'sar martial arts differ greatly from Suu'vitan."

Joss edged toward the center of the ring, suddenly feeling like he was being treated like one of the students at the temple. He noticed something in his brother's demeanor. He looked more confident and sure of himself. Josh pushed the thought aside and decided that he wasn't going to make it easy for him.

"Although alteration methods are similar," continued Reagan, "they stem from a difference in principles and beliefs."

"Sure!" said Joss. "Different enough to fight a war over. Why don't you show me?!"

Joss charged at his brother with a spiraling attack, followed closely by a tumbling sphere.

Reagan stepped aside effortlessly and hit the ball away with his staff!

The sphere deflected left a couple of meters before Joss regained control, bringing it back to hang in the air behind him. Joss made it sway side to side in an attempt to distract his opponent.

Reagan just looked right back at Joss, never breaking eye contact. He subtly suspended his own sphere out of sight behind him, making Joss focus his attention on the obvious threat in front of him. "O'sar elders believe that the coral is something sacred, a gift from nature. We see it as raw material to be harvested."

Reagan spun around, sending the coral ball speeding toward Joss who only just managed to dodge it before Reagan was on him. Their staffs clashed twice before Reagan stepped in with a shoulder barge, knocking his brother off balance.

"We call the art 'manipulation' and think of the coral as a resource or raw material. O'sar braves view their sacred 'bonding' methods as something far more spiritual."

"You favor the ancient O'sar methods over refined science and meta-physics? You have been out in the wastes too long!"

Joss leapt forward, striking his sphere with the end of his staff like a bat.

Reagan blocked the attack using his own sphere, sending Joss' flying. The loud, metallic thud made Joss flinch, and that's when Reagan countered, bringing his staff down hard. The brothers exchanged blows, each of them blocking the other's powerful attack.

Joss barely noticed the sphere as it flew by, narrowly missing his head. Joss reacted with a sloppy backhanded swipe, sending his sphere toward Reagan.

The erratic attack forced Reagan to drop and roll to the side before jumping hastily, back to his feet.

Joss brought the sphere around and attacked again.

Reagan saw the sluggish attempt early, dodging past it with a flying kick to Joss's torso, followed by a knee to the guts.

Joss sidestepped the attack, just managing to block it with both arms before stumbling backwards. He looked up to see Reagan's sphere hanging in the air behind him, as if he was beginning to tire, an obvious attempt at deception. Reagan would never give up that easily, or was he just holding back?

The thought of the latter angered Joss, but forced him to see the truth. He'd become the novice in comparison to this trained and travelled version of his brother. He was getting a practical lesson as well as a lecture. It reminded him of his sparring sessions with his Father as a child. Time to fight back.

His father had taught him to use his anger and frustration to his advantage, but always warned him of the cost of unchecked emotions during combat. Reagan wanted to play mind games, make him feel inferior. Joss knew how to aim for the sore spots.

"The O'sar blade suits you. You never really lived up to the old man's standards when it came to wielding a Suu'vitan blade. Father's skill with his claymore was legendary, on both sides."

"As was Le'san's," countered Reagan. "They were both masters of their art, derived from opposing foundations. Father is an expert at observing an opponent's weakness, and turning it into an advantage. I know now that this is why Father wanted Le'san assigned to me. He saw my potential to bridge the gap between our races."

"You mean he seized the opportunity?!" Joss attacked, almost catching Reagan with a roundhouse kick. He followed up with a backslash with his staff, which was deflected almost as fast.

Reagan sent his sphere flying toward his brother, hitting his fingers holding the bow staff.

Joss fumbled the weapon momentarily before readjusting and jumping in again.

Reagan ducked and weaved, parrying his brother's attacks, which he'd noticed were directed with a limited amount of accuracy, each one less powerful. His brother was tiring.

Reagan's time with the O'sar Prefect had taught him a lot about the 'bonding' and coral alteration. They lived a fulfilled, minimalistic way of life before the war. Choosing to wander nomadically, wherever their symbiotic connection guided them. With the discovery of the Lotus Ark and the rich meta-coral deposits around the area, they felt compelled to protect the land against those with an agenda that conflicted with their beliefs. It was argued that the O'sar had lost the most by the end, their culture decimated beyond repair. They'd made the choice to abandon traditions when measures were extreme and it had cost them everything.

Fighting his brother, it was clear to see how his own experiences had changed him. He no longer felt like the student. Before he left, they were evenly matched in combat. Joss could brawl with the best of them, and was a competent fighter, but in comparison he felt like it was hardly a challenge. Whatever Joss had been through, the skill was evident, but the spirit was lacking.

Reagan pushed forward kneeing Joss back and following up with a lazy roundhouse which Joss only just managed to block with his staff.

"To truly understand the bonding, you must study it in all aspects. Biologically, we're the same species, yet we fail to see the similarities that could make us stronger. Prejudice hinders progress…"

"The O'sar were the first to use an unorthodox method," said Joss. In that moment, they gave up everything they fought for. That decision sealed their fate."

"The Suu'vitan followed suit." said Reagan. "We are as much to blame for the millions that died. I never fully realized until I was out there, in the badlands."

Reagan attacked with a barrage of strikes that Joss struggled to block.

Joss took a couple of steps back, trying to catch his breath, " Did Le'san ever tell you stories of how they were enemies?"

"More about how they became friends," answered Reagan, edging forward, his expression without a tell. "Maybe he thought those stories were best left in the past. Our history is shrouded with hatred and regret. It is not my place to assign blame, nor should it be yours. All we can do is learn from the mistakes of our ancestors and focus on a united future."

Prefect Le'san had always fascinated Joss, his father's old enemy, turned closest friend. He'd always admired their unwavering respect for each other and found it hard to imagine them as generals on opposite sides.

"I wonder what it would have been like to see them fight?" gasped Joss as he attacked.

Reagan noticed his opponent's attention wavering. He watched Joss's staff come for him slowly. He kicked the feeble attack away easily.

"We've watched them spar many times before," he answered, breathing steadily.

"But never fight! Like the most hated of adversaries. That would have been something!" Joss flung himself around with the staff, throwing all of his weight into the attack.

Reagan fell back, but blocked the blow. It was time to end this. He crouched down and concentrated on the ground in front of Joss.

As Joss charged forward, the ground rose up to form a stump almost at knee height. He barely saw the ground move before he tripped, sending him flying. Joss landed in a heap on the ground, quickly jumping up with a surprised look on his face.

He charged again, stepping over the obstacle and sending his sphere flying fast toward Reagan!

Reagan altered the ground again, this time to form three steps in front of him as he ran ahead. Reagan bolted up the stairs as they hardened, jumping over Joss while striking the incoming sphere with his staff. The ball shattered into a cloud of dust as Reagan flew through the air. He landed on his feet, needing only a split second to compose himself.

Joss leapt into action, charging toward his brother. He was a meter away before something hit him hard in the side of the face.

Reagan's sphere shattered on impact, but sent his brother spinning out of control. He wasted no time, closing in on his stumbling opponent, sweeping his legs with his staff, putting Joss out of action.

Joss's lay on his back and looked up at the chandelier. His head was spinning and vision blurred. He noticed Reagan coming into view, holding out a blurred hand.

"Still lost in the past. You've not changed a bit," he said with a smile on his face.

Joss chuckled as his eyes adjusted, bringing his brother into focus, "You call that taking it easy?"

Reagan helped him up and Joss shook himself off. He was about to speak when he was distracted by the sound of clapping hands from above.

The observation balcony ran around the upper level of the building. Lord Akura and Le'san stood watching them.

Le'san was never without his large hawk on his shoulder. He'd had the mean bird for as long as the boys had known him. It squawked almost mockingly at the two young men.

"A split second lapse in concentration is more than enough time for an enemy to land a killing blow," said Lord Akura. His powerful voice echoed around the hall like he was lecturing his students.

Joss sighed, "Good to see you too, Dad."

Le'san bowed his head toward Reagan who had automatically stood to attention in the presence of his Preceptor.

"Prefect Le'san," said Reagan, returning the bow.

There was a pause while the four men warmed to each other's presence. It had been three years since they'd been in the same room as one another. It had seemed like an eternity. Everything felt different.

"Good to see you boys getting reacquainted," said Le'san, nodding his head and throwing a smile their way.

For the first time Joss saw a softer side to the old master. In the past, he'd always had an aura of rigid authority. It had always intimidated Joss, making him feel like a child. Not any more.

Joss switched his gaze to his father, who'd stepped forward to rest his hands on the railing around the edge of the balcony. He looked how he'd remembered, stern as ever. His expression suggested a more pressing matter was bothering him. Why did Joss get feeling that dinner was no longer on the agenda?

"It's been a long time since we've spoken…. to the both of you," said Akura. "I know you both came here under the pretense of celebration, but I'm afraid we have little time for pleasantries."

"I hate to say I told you so," Joss said, looking over at his brother with the familiar look of contempt Reagan was bound to recognize.

"Walk with us back to the house," said Le'san in more reasonable tone. " We have much to talk about."

Chapter 17

Reagan threw the Paladin's robe over his shoulders and followed the old masters down the hall. He looked over at his brother who looked unimpressed and had remained silent since they'd left the training hall. If Reagan was honest with himself, he too felt disappointed. If they weren't here for a family reunion what the hell were they walking into?

"Dad! We've not seen each other in years and that's all you have to say. What could be so important that you can overlook the importance of this occasion? Do you even know how hard it was for Joss to come here tonight? He was almost killed this morning and he still made the effort."

Akura continued on with no more than a sideways glance before pushing open the two large doors leading to the main living space.

Reagan scanned over the area that looked a lot different than he remembered. In their absence, the entire house seemed to have become his study. It was untidy with books and documents everywhere.

"I am aware of his involvement in this morning's attack," said Akura, as if nothing could surprise him. He'd always spoken this way.

They made their way into the living area and Le'san closed the doors behind them.

Lord Akura stood at the far aide of the room by the impressive stone fireplace.

"I've been following these latest attacks with great interest. I observed Darahk and his team as they left after your debriefing."

"What?!" erupted Joss. The words spilled out like he couldn't hold them back any longer. "You were there and you didn't think to step in?! It was more like an interrogation!"

"I couldn't risk alerting them to my presence," Akura said, raising the volume of his voice in response, then immediately regretting it. He paused and took a deep breath, raising a hand calmly in an attempt to bring the exchange down a notch.

He turned toward the roaring fireplace and hit a hidden lever behind one of the stone slabs. The large panel behind the fire slid back with the grinding sound of rock against rock. He turned back to look at his boys, gesturing toward the secret passage.

"Been doing some remodeling?" asked Reagan, staring down the staircase that had come into view. He looked over at Le'san who stood by with a passive expression. It was obviously no surprise to him.

Joss on the other hand looked as surprised as his brother, edging closer to the fireplace with a curious frown.

"This house was built shortly after the war," explained Akura. "I knew that in years to come I would need a place to operate, away from prying eyes."

Joss looked between his brother and the entrance to the secret hideout, "This goes way beyond taking your work home with you! Classic Paranoia." Joss stepped past his Father to peer down the spiral staircase.

"I've been watching the FRA closely," Akura continued. "They've been deliberately keeping information from the Patronas Order and I need to find out why."

"Does the Order know about this little side project?" said Reagan, sounding clearly shocked. He knew his Father didn't trust the FRA, as well as several members of the Patronas Council, but he would have never have suspected anything like this. All these years his father had been carrying out covert activities from the basement of his childhood home.

"I report to Patriarch Victus, like I would any other mission, only off the record. Some of the other Chapters are too close to the FRA."

"So you're keeping secrets from the rest of the council?" asked Reagan, rubbing his forehead. "Dad, I can't say that I totally agree with this course of action."

"I don't trust Wings either, but this is on another level. I didn't know the Order was in the secrets business," said Joss.

Le'san lifted a hand to rest on his student's shoulder. "I'm afraid this course of action was completely necessary, Reagan," he said, again with a conciliatory tone. "So far, your father's work has been strictly observational, gathering data. He updated me on his findings shortly after we returned from the badlands," Le'san looked over to his old friend to give him the chance to explain himself. "Tell them, Gailan."

"After I had something to go on, I headed straight to FRA headquarters to question the Inquisitor for myself," said Akura, turning to walk down the stairs.

The two brothers looked at each other before following him down the stairs. When it came to their Father, they thought they'd seen everything. His unwavering stubbornness over the years had led them to believe he would never change. This was something new.

Reagan looked to Le'san for one last nod of approval before he walked down the stairs.

Reagan had spent the last three years with this man, who he believed to be both rational and a devout disciple of the Order. These were the two men he looked up to and trusted the most. Whatever they were up to, it had to have some merit.

They came to a small door at the bottom of the stairs, which slid open on approach.

They stepped through into an open space far larger than Joss and Reagan expected. Joss recognized the state of the art surveillance equipment to the left side of the room. It was better than anything they had at LEX central. The other side was arranged like a laboratory, with forensics equipment set up all over the place. There was a large table in the center with holo-screen emitters suspended from the ceiling.

Joss nodded to himself, " I have to say, I'm impressed."

"This place is larger than the main level of the house," Reagan said.

"Lord Akura?" said a voice from behind a console.

The boys hadn't even noticed the small man at the far side of the room. His looked across at them through two thick lenses, approaching them with a small thin tablet.

"I've managed to break through the encryption, Prefect. You're going to want to see this!" said the man.

The holographic emitters came to life, projecting pictures and readouts that hung in the air over the workstation.

"Tasker and I became acquainted during the war." said Akura, moving over to the table and examining the data. "He poses as my scribe from time to time, but his real skill lies in the acquiring of information."

Chapter 18

The elevator seemed to descend for ages, with a tension in the air that made the tight space uncomfortable. Darahk and Rosair had chosen to remain silent, presumably thinking of ways to give the Paladin what he wanted without giving him everything they had.

Gailan thought the time would be better spent clarifying a few things. "I want to see everything…" he began

Darahk sighed, "Excuse me?"

"Everything," repeated Akura. "From the last six months: visual surveillance, ID on the perps, everything you recovered from the crime scene." Joss had his foot in the door and now he wanted to know what was inside.

Darahk didn't answer straight away. He glanced back for a moment before turning to look through the elevator window. They had reached the subterranean levels of the FRA HQ. "I'm afraid that's not possible," he muttered.

Rosair stepped forward to answer for her commander, "What the Inquisitor is saying is that the information is classified beyond your clearance," she said, in a smug tone, after giving him a wink, "Nice try though."

The pep in the female officer along with her 'balls out' attitude amused him, even though he saw through the smoke screen. She was good, but her lack of experience made her transparent.

Akura could see lights flicker lower down in the distance. They'd reached the end of the shaft and were moving down the sidewall of a large cave. The cavern looked like it was naturally formed, and high enough for three levels of what mostly looked like storage. This was probably where they stored all seized illegal tech. The Order had a good idea of where some of their facilities might be, but nothing like this.

He remained silent, looking down at his 'scribe', who'd been doing his best to keep a low profile over the course of their visit. Tasker had never fully trusted the institution after the treaty, even less than he did. It made him the perfect recruit.

Gailan glared at the back of Darahk's head, a man he'd known for over 20 years.

They had never liked each other, despite fighting on the same side during the war. He'd known about Darahk's black ops history, but only a few details that Akura was privy to. He knew him by reputation, and that he wasn't afraid to get his hands dirty to get the job done.

When they'd first met years ago he'd noticed a harshness to his character. He'd found Darahk to be emotionally objective and methodical, traits that had served him well during The Long War. Since he'd become the Inquisitor, he'd changed considerably, adapting impeccably to the Agency's set of rules and directives, becoming more pompous than harsh and more self-righteous than anything else.

Darahk turned to face the Prefect, as if he knew he was getting stared down. "I'm going to be honest with you, Akura, for what it's worth. I was acting on the orders of someone higher up in the chain of command when we intervened this morning. We don't even have the information."

Akura took a moment to read his expression before decided he was speaking the truth. "So... It's above your pay grade too," said the Prefect in a deep voice. "What about access to the corpse, or any of the weapons they were carrying?"

They came to a stop at the bottom of the cavern and the doors slid open. Darahk walked out into a room with a large rectangular window.

"The body wasn't recovered. My team was intercepted by another unit on its way back to HQ," Darahk said, avoiding eye contact with the Paladin.

"Every last thing was removed from the transport," added Lieutenant Rosair.

"The incompetence of this agency never seems to amaze me!" mocked Akura, with an abrasive laugh. "Just what kind of operation are you running Darahk?! Did you even know there were other teams operating in the area?"

"Nothing we were aware of at the time," answered the Lieutenant. "We were there working an entirely different operation.

Darahk turned to stand face to face with Lord Akura, the pleasure from the Agency's mistakes clear on the old Paladin's face, "We were there for a guy we've been chasing for almost a year now. He's responsible for butchering an entire FRA squad!"

Rosair opened the door from the observation room to the lab, "It looks like he's running with the Effigy now."

Akura squinted at the statement. He knew the Agency had publicly blamed the Effigy for the recent attacks, an accusation he found hard to swallow. He wondered if they actually had any evidence to back it up.

The Effigy spoke openly about corruption in the government, especially within the ranks of the FRA. He'd gone into hiding since the warrant was issued for his arrest.

"You're sure the Effigy is responsible for the attacks?" asked Akura.

"All the evidence points to his group. They wanted us to know it was them," said Rosair leading him into the lab.

"Or that's at least what they wanted you to think," Gailan said, with an air of suspicion in his tone. "It sounds like you were royally fucked out of your prize this morning. If you'd followed procedure, you'd have had a team of Paladin there to back you up."

The FRA had a habit of going with the most obvious solution when it came to investigative techniques. This time they knew they screwed up. Couldn't hurt to rub it in a little.

Darahk's eyes rolled back, " We had no idea HGFs were involved until we were on the scene! And, I don't need a lecture from you!" he said gesturing toward the center of the room.

Akura examined Darahk's frustrated expression. Pushing him a little had got him more answers and it was beginning to look like their intel was sloppy at best, despite what they preached publicly. It was likely they had no solid evidence that the Effigy was involved.

Gailan followed closely as the group gathered around the central examination table. The subject of attention seemed to be a gauntlet or prosthesis of some kind, heavily armored and abnormally large. Complete with five razor-sharp talons.

"We didn't come away totally empty handed. I recovered this item personally before everything else was seized," said the Lieutenant.

"We're still running tests, but we know it's pure meta-coral, no mechanics," explained Darahk. "These talons would cut though optimum grade armor like a knife through butter."

The agent running the tests watched the data from the test appear on the screen attached to the side of the table.

"At first it looked like a optimum construct, but after further examination we noticed distinct differences," he said.

A holographic diagram materialized above the claw. It showed the meta-coral in microscopic detail.

Akura examined the strange formation. It looked damaged or corroded. "Craft through unorthodox methods can be unstable," said Gailan, stroking his chin. "Weak points and imperfections are common in illegal weapons."

"It wasn't that we found imperfections," said the agent shaking his head. "We scanned the thing minutes after it arrived, and after the initial scan it was in perfect condition."

"Almost too perfect," added Rosair. "However a second scan an hour later showed that the structure had destabilized considerably."

Akura thought back to the war when fusion tech was in high demand. HGF weapons were being produced on a massive scale with limited regulation. Users lacked both discipline and training, causing abnormal symbiotic stress and strain on the tech. The weapons were lethal enough in combat, but were considered disposable with limited sustainability. Once the symbiotic connection was severed, the item would often breakdown in a matter of hours.

"Optimum-grade coral would normally take centuries to break down. I haven't seen anything like this since the war," said Akura. He looked down for any input from Tasker, but he'd managed to sneak off at some point during the conversation.

"Nobody could be producing this kind of tech on any kind of large scale without us knowing!" scoffed Darahk. "Coral distribution has been strictly regulated since the treaty was signed!"

Akura turned to look at him with a condescending stare. They'd seen the impossible before and it almost cost them everything. This resurgence of weapons grade technology was relatively small scale in comparison, but still nothing to be taken lightly.

"We were naive to think we'd destroyed every relic from the war and foolish for thinking we had complete control," muttered Akura.

"Come on!" Darahk continued. "Every coral deposit within 1000 miles is under heavy guard. We closely monitor any shipment coming in and out of the city. Black market suppliers could never get their hands on enough raw material to merit large-scale production!"

Akura sighed, "Despite the evidence to the contrary, who might have the means to produce such weapons, hypothetically?"

"The code insignia doesn't match anything we have in our archives. Looks like we're dealing with a new player," said the Lieutenant.

"Well someone's making the damn things!" barked Akura, suddenly noticing Tasker appearing in his peripherals. "There's no telling how many weapons could be on the streets."

Darahk moved to stand beside Akura. "If the Effigy and his followers have access to this kind of weaponry we could be looking at a major revolution."

Akura said nothing in response, looking back at the gauntlet. Darahk had nothing and was clutching at straws, trying to make it look significant. Fortunately, he had more information to go on.

....

"You don't think the Effigy has anything to do with the attacks?" asked Joss.

Akura looked up slowly, giving his sons a chance to process the information. "No, I believe his entire involvement in these circumstances has been fabricated."

"By the FRA?" said Reagan.

"Possibly," Akura answered.

Joss thought about what his father had said. "Whoever is behind the attacks, they may have deliberately intended to frame the Effigy to mislead authorities."

"Here it is," interrupted Tasker. The imp shuffled over to the main console he'd been working at. "I took the liberty of downloading their system files while they were distracted. This particular file was at the top of their classified list, extensive details on an upcoming operation."

Tasker brought up a life-size, holographic projection of an ape-like figure, fully armored and without a disguise.

"That's him!" shouted Joss. "That's definitely one of the guys I fought this morning!"

Joss recognized the creature's inhuman stance and unusual armor. This was the first time he'd seen its face, "It looks barely human."

"Look at its physique. You can see that it would move like an animal," said Reagan, pointing to the beast's ape-like arms and muscles. "Prefect Le'san and I encountered beasts like this during our time in the wastes, but nothing with this level of intelligence."

Le'san stepped closer to examine the thing's face, scanning over the details of the report, "A fully coherent, symbiotic possession. A mutation on this level is extremely rare.

"He's coherent alright!" added Joss. "This thing was taking orders."

Akura moved to interact with a nearby console, zooming in on what looked like scars around the ape's eyes, "Once a rogue synthiant takes a host it is usually driven mad by the mental conflict: a mindless beast," he said. "Any sort of intelligence would make for a lethal adversary."

Joss watched the others as they studied the hologram. He didn't care how smart the thing was. He looked at his Father, "The longer we wait, the less chance we have of catching him. The Lieutenant's got a hard on for this monster and she won't be wasting any time if it's slaughtered her men."

"We can't leave something this important in the hands of the FRA, especially if they're compromised from the inside." Said Gailan. "There are forces at work within their ranks that supersede Darahk's command."

Le'san rested his hands on his staff while his pet shuffled around on his shoulder. It seemed to resemble the old O'sar Prefect if that was possible, "Whether Darahk is lying to the Order or simply doesn't know, I agree with your Father on this."

Reagan's gaze switched between that of his Father and mentor, as if he was waiting for them to speak, "I think our next move is obvious. We need to take these findings to the council."

"And how long will that take?!" barked Joss. "This lead's fresh and exactly what I've been waiting for!"

"What?! You're going to beat them to it?" said Reagan, sarcastically. "They'll already have a team in place, maybe even boots on the ground looking for this guy."

Akura gave a nod to Tasker who proceeded to upload another projection, this time of an area of the city outside the wall. Joss and Reagan looked at other.

Tasker stepped forward, "An anonymous source has informed them of a rendezvous he'll be making later tonight. They plan to apprehend him before they make contact."

"We've had a short time to formulate a plan to beat them to it," said Akura confidently. "I've been waiting for two operatives who I can trust with the expertise to pull it off."

"What?!" said Reagan, shocked and in disbelief.

Joss retrieved a cigarette from his inside pocket and lit it, "I thought you'd never ask."

Chapter 19

Rosair stood waiting at the exit to the roof-landing pad. Patience had become one of her most valuable attributes as an FRA agent, much to her own surprise. Her father was with the FRA and she'd always known she wanted to follow in his footsteps. She'd been inspired by his respect for authority and his belief in the Agency.

He'd fought in the Suu'vitan military in the war, but never with prejudice for his enemy, eventually choosing a hot-tempered O'sar priestess as his wife. As a girl, she was headstrong much like her mother and not one to do as she was told. As the youngest of four and the only girl, she'd had to toughen up quickly, learning when to wait and when to act. Now was that time, and her patience had been pushed to its limit.

A door opened slowly in front of her and Darahk appeared. He rubbed his forehead with two fingers and looked strained by the cluster fuck of a morning they'd had.

"Who the hell did this guy say he was again?" asked Darahk, exhaling.

"He didn't. He contacted us with orders to 'stand by'," she said. The transmission matched the signal we've been chasing down all morning."

The two of them made their way outside and stood beside the large landing pad. Darahk squinted through the down draft as the hopper descended. He couldn't see anything through the heavily tinted windows, not even the pilot was visible.

The door opened the instant they touched down, revealing a tall thin figure. He was dressed entirely in black to match the unmarked hopper. His long black trench coat covered his lanky shoulders and his hands were set comfortably in his pockets.

The unfamiliar man stared at them through strange triangular sunglasses, which seemed unusual since it was dark. As he marched closer, they could make out some kind of hardware around his head, not bulky enough to be a helmet or offer any kind of real protection.

Darahk locked eyes with the man as soon as he got in range and maintained eye contact. He couldn't shake the feeling that everything was about to get turned upside down.

As the man got closer, his expressionless face turned into a smiling one and he extended a hand, a seemingly polite gesture that Darahk wasn't expecting.

Darahk's arms remained folded with only a slight nod to Rosair, ordering that she return the smile.

"You better have a good reason for fucking up my operation, mister?!" barked Darahk, but sounding as if his power had somewhat diminished.

"Relax, Inquisitor. We're all on the same team," said the man, raising his palms in a surrendering gesture. "I couldn't be sure if anyone else was monitoring the frequency when we intercepted. The organization we both serve has many levels, as I'm sure you're beginning to understand."

"Just what branch of the Agency are you actually with?" Darahk said, his arms still folded.

Malone pulled open one side of his coat to reveal his badge. A small hologram beamed from the device, listing his credentials.

"I see no name or title!" blurted Darahk, peering at the hologram. There was something at the top of the readout that looked familiar, a small symbol in the shape of a shield with a small star and a sword.

"My alpha level clearance should be all the credentials I need, but if it makes you feel any better you can call me Director Malone."

Malone looked over to the Lieutenant who hadn't said a word. "Any updates on the investigation?" he asked, as if he'd been in charge all along.

"You know it's hard to find something if you don't know exactly what you're looking for!" she said sarcastically. You could tell from the look on her face that her patience was wearing thin.

"I'm afraid I can't go into the finer details at this time," said Malone, pushing past them and marching toward the building. "I can tell you that the items stolen earlier were extremely dangerous. Pity you weren't able to retrieve them," he said dryly.

Darahk hurried to keep up with him with Rosair in tow, "Your men seized any evidence we did manage to save, without any explanation. Even if we had, do you think we'd have given it up easily?"

"All you've done is hinder our entire operation!" interrupted Rosair. "And you're still wasting our time."

Malone stopped at the next door and put out an arm to halt the group, "I already know that you're planning to move on the group tonight, or at least one of them. I'll be there to watch over the operation as it progresses."

"Now wait a damn minute!" she yelled, clenching her fists.

"Lieutenant!" said Darahk, looking her in the eye. He turned back to Malone. "What does the Commissar say about this?"

Malone stepped closer and got between them as if to alleviate the tension, "You are forbidden to discuss this with the Commissar, or anybody else," he said.

The two of them looked at each other, Rosair was about to speak before he beat her to it.

"That's an order," commanded Malone. "My authority supersedes his in this matter." He pushed the glasses down his nose to glare at them. "You're looking at the newest member of your team."

Chapter 20

Joss looked around his Father's secret command center and replayed the events that had led him to this point. He'd been out of it for so long he'd forgotten how quickly things could change; drawn together under the guise of a family reunion only to be recruited for an unsanctioned covert mission against the FRA. Just when you thought the day couldn't get any crazier.

Given the situation, Joss felt surprisingly at ease about the whole thing, even relieved to an extent that he knew his next course of action. His brother, on the other hand, wore a more concerned expression, and proceeded to pace up and down the large circular room. Joss put an arm on his brother's shoulder to draw him back to the group. Their Father was about to elaborate on his master plan, seemingly scrambled together at short notice with no other explanation than that they needed to act quickly.

"Over the past year, I have become aware of things that have shaken my trust in the FRA. and members of our governing hierarchy," said Gailan. "It all started with an anonymous tip. Initially, it just looked like random intel on various FRA. investigations and I failed to see the pattern at first."

Gailan brought up a map on the main view screens. Various locations were marked off with pictures of the facilities from the surveillance systems.

"There were also several recordings of public statements made by the Agency blaming the Effigy for the recent attacks. The investigations were scheduled impeccably close to the times of the attack and they were extremely thorough," said Akura.

"What exactly are you saying?" asked Reagan.

"I'm saying the evidence was flawless, and that was the problem," said Akura. "For all we know about the Effigy, he might be eccentric, but he's not an idiot. The evidence was too perfect. Whether he was involved or not, it was supposed to look like he did it."

"So the feds falsified the evidence. You know the identity of the informant?" asked Joss. "Maybe it's someone inside the agency?"

"The thought crossed my mind," said Gailan. "Next, I tried to arrange a meeting face to face, but heard nothing. The informant went dark for almost two months, no response at all...then one day he sent me this."

Akura turned to face the circular workstation where Tasker appeared to be setting up some kind of experiment. Three meta-coral appendages slowly extended from the table surface. They held an object carefully in place beneath the examination equipment. The item looked like a piece of something that was once circular, broken in half down the middle, leaving a jagged edge and heavily scarred surface.

Gailan drew back his cloak, pulling an old medallion from beneath his tunic. The item looked similar to the one on display. There was less damage to this medallion's surface, though it had a broken edge on the opposite side. "I've carried this thing around for 20 years, a keepsake from the war found amidst the rumble, or that's at least what I thought.

Akura held his half up against the new piece while a fourth appendage grew up from the surface to hold it in place. They fit perfectly, apart from a few worn areas, but clearly part of the same object. Now, the amulet was complete. You could make out the five indented triangles positioned at equal points around its circumference.

"The seal of the Acolytes," said Reagan, without missing a beat. He took a step closer to examine the pieces. "Has there ever been any other artifacts discovered to your knowledge? How come you never showed us this?"

"There is very little physical evidence that the Acolytes were ever here, only the accounts of those who fought alongside them and survived," explained Akura. "They disappeared after the final battle without a trace."

Le'san gestured toward their Father with his staff, " Your father found the first half after the battle that ended the War."

"I couldn't risk telling anyone else about it. Not even Patriarch Victus knows the truth. I couldn't put him, nor either of you in a position where you'd have to lie if it was ever discovered in my possession," said Gailan.

"Then why keep it at all?" asked Reagan. "Artifacts like these are supposed to be locked away in federal storage. You've been taking a great risk keeping this a secret for so long."

"I never had a choice as far as I could see. It was all I had left of them, along with their final words," said Gailan. "It's difficult to explain, but whoever sent me this had to know of the burden I've carried all this time, and precisely when to send me this message."

"The last time we spoke with the Acolytes, their leader confided in us, generals on both sides. He warned us that our struggle wasn't over," said Le'san, swallowing his emotion. "With the end of the long war in sight, his words were difficult to hear, and he spoke them as if they were riding to their death."

"It was only when they didn't return that I began to wonder," said Akura. " We were at peace, at long last, but as the years went by those words began to fester like a wound that wouldn't heal. It is only now that it's starting to make sense."

"We believe it's a warning," said Le'san. " The attacks, the civil unrest…"

"…This amulet bearing the mark, and the weapon I saw earlier today," added Akura. "This is only the beginning. We must act now to prepare ourselves for what is to come."

Joss looked over at Reagan who seemed to be taking it a little harder than he was. His Father had spoken of the Acolytes' return before; their naive young minds hadn't read into it too much. It was somewhat of a prophecy in underground religious circles and even among Paladin in certain chapters. They believed that the Acolytes would return when they were needed most, that not even their presumed death could stop them if the evil ever returned.

If anybody was tired of listening to his Father all these years, it was Joss, but something about this encounter and the timing of everything made it impossible for him to ignore. As a child he'd wanted to believe it, but like all fantasies, the legend faded with age, discredited further by his Father's paranoid delusions. Nobody ever wanted to imagine anything that catastrophic could happen again, nobody except the Lord Prefect.

He felt his hand reach in his pocket where he'd been keeping the item he'd found after the fight. If there was ever a time to mention the evidence he'd removed from an FRA crime scene, the time was now.

Joss stepped forward toward the round table. "Normally, I'd say you were overreacting and out of your mind, but this time it sounds like you're actually onto something."

Joss slowly removed the amulet from his pocket and placed it down gently on the table, "Maybe you should take a look at this."

Tasker slowly got up from his stool, and peered at the object over his dark glasses.

Le'san and Akura moved in for a closer look.

"I wouldn't touch that!" shouted Tasker. " You don't know how it'd react with a disciplined synthiant."

The two old Prefects snapped their hands back almost instantly.

Joss took a deep breath! "Whoa! It's safe...or at least I think it is. Reagan touched it and he still has both his hands," said Joss. I snatched this from the crime scene before the feds arrived. They had a case full of this stuff. We thought one of you old relics might know something about it."

Chapter 21

The Alliance tower was the tallest building in the city and the Commissar's official station. He'd made the decision to reside here permanently after an attempt on his life three years prior, and now enjoyed the comforts of round the clock security. From his office, he could see anywhere in the building as well as the grounds.

Commissar Fain stared out across the luminescent nightscape. The city looked blurred through his failing vision, but he found the warm glow alluring against the dark night sky. Looking down on the city from his safe haven helped calm his mood before turning in for the night. Maybe it was the sense of scale, everywhere else looked small and too far away to irritate him.

FRA HQ was visible from his office window, standing amidst surrounding buildings, exactly 20 km away. The final year of the war ravaged the city and it was agreed that the newly formed FRA would never have more than 20 km between outposts and checkpoints, in order to maintain a secure perimeter around the alliance tower. The original council building had been destroyed and the Alliance tower erected in its place.

He'd been the third Commissar in office after the war, serving for almost a decade. The strain of the job had aged him visually but mentally he'd never felt more powerful, with his objective clear. He'd turned 70, but there was still so much to put right in this city before he'd allow anyone to take away that power.

Fain heard the doors slide open behind him. Tailor was always punctual. He was the only one with permission to enter his space without an appointment.

The Commissar focused on where his legs used to be to engage his hover chair, making it pivot around to face the other direction. He had lost his legs in the war while actively protesting the violence. He was born of a Suu'vitan mother and and O'sar father and felt that he'd never really had a side to fight for. They'd been killed in a raid on a perimeter town early on in the war leaving him an orphan.

He'd grown up on the streets and managed to teach himself about the history of his people and each race's theory on the ancestors. The conflict that governed everyone's life around him never made sense to him and he developed a way of looking at the situation objectively, seeing flaws in both belief systems. His universal mandate and racially diverse origin, combined with a turbulent upbringing, had made him a popular candidate when he ran for the position.

Fain had never been a warrior and had always been an outcast, but since the end of the war he'd worked hard and achieved the power he believed he deserved. During the war, the idea of a crippled half-breed becoming the main figurehead of this society wouldn't have even been entertained. Now, he answered to no one but the Order, and they answered to him. The Order had their Paladin and he had the control of the FRA at his fingertips. He could control everything from that one room.

"Commissar?" said Tailor, standing to attention. "The Effigy's followers continue to riot through the streets, sir. LEX branch has their hands full with conflict zones all over the city. The sky trains are at a standstill."

Tailor was tall with a solid build, yet he had a look that would go unnoticed in a crowd. He looked like your basic FRA grunt, and knew when to keep his mouth shut so as not to draw any unnecessary attention to his presence. The Commissar handpicked every member of his personal security detachment, but Tailor was a specialist that could act as his eyes and ears in places he could not monitor. He'd had him tag along with Darahk's men in order to report back his findings.

"This menace continues to cause problems," said the Commissar, looking up at Tailor through eyes that were clouded over and surrounded by a weathered brow. "With the initiation ceremony tomorrow, our troops will be spread thin trying to control these outbursts. What about Inquisitor Darahk?"

"It was a coincidence that the criminal they were after this morning was a member of the team that carried out the raids," said Tailor.

"I see," answered the Commissar inquisitively. "

"Prefect Akura paid a visit to Wings HQ earlier," Tailor added.

An angry frown appeared on the Commissar's face and he brought his hands together, clenching them into fists.

"His Patriarch authorized the warrant," said Tailor. "Darahk was forced to share certain information with him. It was also a coincidence that his son happened to get involved in the pursuit. The Chief relieved him of duty as you commanded."

The Commissar took a deep breath and exhaled, "These 'coincidences'." he said, clearing his throat. "I've always prided myself on my ability to see a pattern when it's laid out in front of me. "These interfering factors are more a test of fate than mere coincidence. Akura and his spawn seem destined to be a thorn in my side whether they're directly aware of their actions or not. We must proceed with caution."

The Commissar turned the chair around to face the city once more. "Do you have it?" he croaked, with the voice of an aged man.

"The route schematic for the convoy," said Tailor." As requested, sir."

"Make the call," said the old man, turing to face the window once again. "Keep me up to date with the operation. The ceremony must go ahead as planned."

Tailor started to head for the exit before turning back to the Commissar.

"What if Darahk succeeds next time?" he asked.

The Commissar paused before he answered. He knew what he was really asking.

"We'll cross that bridge when we come to it," The Commissar muttered. "Right now he's acting as a better distraction than we could have hoped for."

Chapter 22

Tasker examined the object from behind a transparent meta-coral blast screen. The device hung suspended in mid-air at the workstation at the back that was separated from the others.

They all waited in silence to hear the verdict. Joss had seen a similar apparatus used for bomb disposal and examination of fusion weapons. "So, is it dangerous?" he asked.

"Not necessarily, not in its current condition. It seems to be part of a more complex mechanism," said Tasker, looking down through a microscopic lens. He sat back from the screen and gave Lord Akura a nod. "The forge signature of this device is an exact match with the amulet and I'd have to guess it's almost certainly from the same time and place."

"I see, " said Akura, rubbing his chin. "I've seen technology similar to this before, but not for a long time. I observed the Acolytes closely over the short period I fought by their side. The leader wore a device like this one. It looked somehow integrated into his armor."

"Did he ever tell you what it was for?" asked Reagan.

"The Acolytes made a point of avoiding contact with the general population as much as they could, and were especially discreet when it came to the weapons and equipment they used," said Akura.

Tasker looked at Joss, "You said that you managed to activate it?"

"Symbiotic stress could have triggered a reaction," said Akura, looking at Reagan and Le'san for their input.

"His senses were heightened; the adrenaline flowed from the fight," said Reagan.

"The Five possessed technology we couldn't begin to fathom," muttered Le'san, lighting his pipe."

Joss stood over the device. "It's safe to assume that this thing has the potential to do some serious damage, worst-case scenario, " he said.

"I'd say that's safe to assume," said Akura. "If the feds have been stockpiling illegal tech like this, they could be using their research to develop new weapons. If news of this were to go public, development off the books, on any level; it could ruin the FRA."

"It could destroy the alliance!" exclaimed Reagan. "This is much bigger than a simple dispute over procedure."

"So far, we're working purely on speculation, without any hard evidence," said Joss. "Apprehending this 'Sapian' creature might be our best shot at finding it."

He looked at Reagan, who had seemed to push past his initial shock of it all. The magnitude of the situation was hard to ignore, with their next course of action extremely time-sensitive if they were going to make a difference.

"Moving against the FRA could be viewed as an act of treason," said Reagan. "If they identify us, it's not going to be easy to talk our way out of it."

"Leave that to me," said Joss. "I have a few items I've been saving that we could put to good use." He looked up and noticed that his Father was staring at both of them with a stiff, yet proud twist to his expression.

Reagan turned to his father, "What exactly do you have in mind?"

Chapter 23

Two years earlier...

"What do you see, my boy?" asked Le'san, appearing as if out of nowhere.

Reagan had been surveying the area for 16 hours, with the last 4 through rain and harsh wind. He'd run out of the dry jerky the old lady from Bandahime had given him and was working on a foul-tasting mushroom he'd found. It was listed in his trial handbook as being quite nutritious, despite the flavor.

Bandahime was a small settlement they'd arrived at three days earlier, mostly populated by a segregated O'sar clan, content with living the simple life. Locals had been going missing over the last couple of weeks and Le'san had decided they should offer their assistance. Quadro was familiar with the community through trade and council and had decided to ride out to join us, rounding up a few of his warriors spread around the surrounding area. We had received a message informing us that he'd reached the town and was awaiting an update on our investigation.

" They've been coming and going all day, groups of three or four," said Reagan. "They appear to be scavenging groups, returning every two hours. However, the last left over three hours ago, shortly followed by another, and there's still no sign of them.

Le'san adjusted his telescope to focus on the camp, "This appears to be their main stronghold. While tracking them, I found two smaller camps, lightly guarded. One was situated around a well. I saw only two groups paying them a visit."

"Which means the others were headed elsewhere," Reagan said, lying in the dirt. He'd gotten used to the dampness by now, and had managed to find a spot beside a large boulder, which provided moderate shelter from the weather. He looked up at his preceptor, who remained silent, " Did you find any bodies?"

"None, which leads me to believe there's a place we missed...Wait!" he said, squatting down to steady his grip on the scope. "I see a group heading in this direction. I count 14 of them, 5 of which appear to be prisoners."

Reagan jumped up to a squat and grabbed his binoculars. "Shit! I'll fetch the horses..." he shouted, enthusiastically.

"Patience, tenderfoot! They still have some distance to clear before they're inside the perimeter. I've counted another four men guarding the fence and another two walking the camp. That's 15 armed assailants to neutralize before you even get close to the hostages. We have to send for help."

Reagan looked frustrated. He'd been waiting for some action all day, and he finally thought he'd get the chance to test his skills against worthy opponents. He suddenly realized that his excitement was making him act irrationally.

Le'san was crouched down behind the boulder now and was in the process of writing a message to Quadro. "Fly swiftly old friend, the wind is at your back," he whispered to the old hawk before turning to address Reagan. "Reinforcements should be here within the hour." He attached the tiny scroll to the bird's leg and released him into the air. It flew low to the ground at first to avoid detection before swooping up and disappearing into the cloudy sky.

Reagan was watching the bandits again. They were about two miles away from the camp now. "Wouldn't it be wise to intercept the group before they reach the rest of their men..?" enquired Reagan.

Le'san didn't respond right away, taking a minute to look over the camp and the road leading up to it. "I did consider the option," he said stroking his beard. "It looks like they're moving slowly, likely due to an injury. It'll take them as least 30 minutes to reach camp. By that time, we'll have the fading daylight to our advantage and reinforcements will be getting closer."

More waiting, Reagan thought. He stretched out his legs behind him and rubbed his hands together. The temperature had started to drop a little with the sun going down and he was starting to cramp up, "Master, permission to circle the camp one last time? I want to make sure I haven't missed anything, and I really need to get the blood flowing if there's going to be combat."

"So eager are you to prove yourself, young one? Have you even gone through the possibilities in your head? When Quadro gets here there will be enough warriors to handle the bandits. You'll have a much more important task: making sure the prisoners are escorted out of harm's way."

Reagan looked at his master's serious expression. He thought about questioning the order, but his better judgment prevailed. "I understand, Prefect," he said, producing his newly formed Vesica from his wrist. He admired the blade for a few seconds before absorbing it within.

Le'san placed his hand on the boy's shoulder and stooped down to Reagan's eye-level, "You'll soon be using that to defend your life, but not just yours. The lives of those prisoners will depend on your ability to protect them from danger. Bear this in mind when the time comes. Don't focus on who you will fight, but rather what you are fighting for."

Reagan pondered his master's words of wisdom and took a deep breath. He realized he'd been sizing up the bandits all day, which ones looked the strongest and who he should take down first. Any thought of reason had escaped him. He realized why Le'san had assigned him this task alone. One day, he wouldn't have his master there to tell him to think before acting. He'd have to make his own decisions.

"Hey!" said Le'san, snapping his student out of his trance. "You've done well today. I've yet to meet a tenderfoot who enjoyed reconnaissance. One last sweep of the area couldn't hurt," Le'san handed him a bundle of jerky to eat en route.

Reagan grinned and bowed his head slightly. "Thank you, Prefect," he said, turning to head toward the tree line.

He jumped down between the boulders for the first 20 feet. He barely touched the ground, trying his best not to make contact with the gravel. If he remained braced between the rock walls, he'd hardly make a sound. He got to the first tree and swung down from a branch, landing on the grass.

The instant he landed he thought he heard something, quickly dropping to his chest. The dry grass stood a good three feet high and provided the perfect cover. He waited a few seconds before peeking up to look into the woods. Nothing was there so he continued on.

He'd circled the area eight hours earlier, around mid-day. The bright sun made it difficult to evade the lookouts on the fence, but he'd found at least three points of entry other than the main gate. These bandits had obviously gotten used to operating unchallenged and become sloppy with security. At this point in the day, the light no longer penetrated the woodland, making for excellent cover.

He kept low and moved around the camp, keeping 50 or 60 meters of distance between him and the perimeter, when suddenly he heard that noise again. He dropped to ground level and waited. He held his breath until he heard it again. It sounded like a scratching coming from 20 meters closer to the camp. There'd been a group burning trash out there earlier when he'd arrived, so he'd kept his distance. Maybe he'd missed something important.

He took a few minutes to make sure there wasn't anyone around and moved in until he was less than 20 meters away from the perimeter. If he made any mistakes now, he'd risk alerting the guards. He found a hump in the earth where he could watch. He felt his stomach groan as he squished it against the ground and thought about the jerky. No time for eating now.

Suddenly, he heard the sound again, and this time he could see movement in the distance, about ten meters in front of him. He waited for the sound again, and watched to his surprise as the ground seemed to bulge up, before dropping back down suddenly. The next time it moved, he saw a hand reach out from what appeared to be a hole in the earth. As the grass covered top lifted, he could see that the hole was more of a pit, and there was someone inside.

Reagan felt his heart start pounding in his chest. How had he missed this for the last 16 hours? He looked at the smoldering fire that had been going for most of the day. Earlier it had been a real bonfire, at least six feet high. Maybe the smoke had blocked his vision, plus he'd been too far away to hear the sound over the rest of the activity.

Reagan tried to get a handle on the situation. He'd been gone probably 15 minutes. The rest of the group was getting closer and now there was a whole other variable. Time to signal Le-san. He looked up toward the spot he'd spent most of the day. Luckily, he could see it through a parting in the trees. He held up his wrist, concentrating to make the surface of his armor reflective, bouncing what was left of the sunlight to attract his master's attention. He waited a few seconds before trying again. He was just starting to worry something had happened when he saw him signal back. Reagan was about to reply when he heard shouting.

Reagan tucked in his arms behind the mound and carefully peeked over the fence. It seemed one of the patrolling guards had seen the flailing arm and had alerted another guard to assist in checking it out. He watched as the two guards wandered down casually to take a look.

As the guards got closer another arm stretched out, pushing what was obviously a hatch, open further. One of the guards started moving a little faster after seeing the door start to buckle. As soon as he got within range, he booted the unidentified prisoner as hard as he could in the general direction of where his face might be. Reagan heard the thud, followed by the door as it clattered shut.

Reagan watched as they secured the chains holding the door shut. One of the guards started yelling at the other while holding up what looked like some sort of padlock. It appeared the lock was not properly secured after their last visit to the hole. *Why the hell were they keeping prisoners down there?* he thought.

He was readjusting his position when he saw flashing in the distance. Le'san was calling him back, although he couldn't imagine why. He'd obviously seen what he'd just witnessed. Now this was a hostage situation, making a siege on the camp more complicated. Reagan was in the perfect position to set them free. He was about to signal back when he saw five more guards pile out of the side entrance. One of them was barking orders and gesturing in three different directions covering Reagan's path back to his previous look out position.

It had happened, and totally unexpectedly. He was on his own now, cut off from his master with a compromising and potentially lethal situation looming on the horizon. His mind suddenly started racing. How long had he been there now? Had the raiding party reached the camp? And why were the guards sweeping the perimeter? Maybe they suspected outside interference after inspecting the underground prison cell. Either way, it was on, and there were two guards heading in his general direction.

He made the decision to continue around the camp toward the northwest entrance, which was situated on relatively higher ground. The main gate was also facing north, meaning it would give him a better view of what was going on inside. He was cut off from communication with Le'san, but it didn't mean he couldn't be ready to attack when the reinforcements arrived.

It was getting darker and he made the decision to move at a crouched running pace to stay ahead of the guards. The trees where thick between them providing visual cover. All of a sudden, he heard screaming; nothing too close, maybe inside the camp. He saw the hill ahead, and scrambled up it to try and get a better look.

He could see the northeast entrance now, as well as above the fence in parts where it was lower. The bandits had a fire going inside and it illuminated the area nicely in the fading light. He could see shadows moving behind the tents, then even more as he got further around to face the entrance straight on. The raiding party was inside with more hostages. He could tell from the high-pitched screams that two of them were female. One of them was being dragged back to the group. Maybe she'd made a vain attempt to escape? He assumed that's why the guards were searching the woods.

Reagan weighed his options. How many hostiles were inside now? In the confusion, he'd lost count, maybe 15 - 20? None of them were guarding the entrance right in front of him. Should he take the opportunity while he had it? He could be inside when the reinforcements arrived. What would Le'san do? It's possible he was moving into position the same as he was. There was no way to be sure and the more he thought about it the more he felt the pull to act while he had the chance.

He was frozen in a standing position, hastily looking around to make sure the coast was clear. Suddenly, he heard the shouting get louder, then a high-pitched scream. The sound of the gunshot that followed echoed through the air, silencing the victim. His ears hadn't even stopped ringing before he realized he was bolting toward the entrance at full sprint!

Reagan came to his senses as he skidded through the opening, crouching down behind one of the tents. He looked between them at the gruesome scene, as one of the bandits seemed to be hacking off one of the arms of the recently executed girl. There were two men lying beaten on the ground, one looked unconscious. A girl wept on the ground beside her, staring at the body in shock. Reagan tried not to panic and concentrate on what the bandits were saying.

"This is what happens when you try and run. If you resist, you die like this bitch. If you're a little more cooperative then we'll keep you fed and give you a safe place to sleep," said a gravelly-voiced bandit. He had a strong build, but also a large gut hanging over his belt.

Reagan watched as one of the other bandits, a stout-looking female, examined one of the men on the ground.

"I think this one's dead too. You fucking beat him too much. I liked this one!" she said. She had a hand missing and a makeshift, hook-shaped prosthetic was attached to her stump.

"He's still good for eating," said the first bandit. "Looks like the beast gets a special treat tonight. Strip the good stuff and throw the scraps in the pit."

The Pit!? thought Reagan. They can't possibly be feeding the corpses to those prisoners. Le'san had told him that food was sometimes scarce out here. The two of them had gone without food for a day or two at a time, but there was always minimal vegetation to keep them going until they managed a successful hunt. The thought made him almost gag as he watched two of the other bandits hold up the man's lifeless body. The stout female walked over toward them and without hesitation sliced across the poor man's abdomen spilling his intestines. Reagan couldn't hold it together anymore and he vomited all over the ground beside him.

"Shit!" he whispered, aloud to himself. They'd heard that for sure. They'd stopped talking completely and he could hear footsteps closing on his location. The adrenaline was running through him, and just as he was about to produce his Vesica the blade was already there in his hand. The sensation he was feeling was like nothing he'd ever experienced before. There was fear, but balanced equally with excitement and an almost heightened sense of the battle to come.

The footsteps got closer and he felt his carapace thicken and extend to protect his abdomen, arms, and neck. The helmet closed in around his head; the face covering gave him a sense of security and fueled his confidence. He'd never felt more focused.

The first man stepped around the tent and met his blade! The strike felt effortless as it sliced through the man's torso. The enemy was faceless to him, dead before identified. He only felt the heat from the open chest cavity on his face as he moved to the next opponent.

The bandit fired off three rounds with his rifle, narrowly missing Reagan's torso as he moved within striking distance! Reagan countered; slicing off both his hands before lunging forward to knee him square in the face. He felt the precision of the impact against the shattering bone, sensing the vertebra at the base of the skull detach from the rest of the spine. He was filled with an unnatural hatred for the wrongdoers, and surprisingly felt no hesitation when it came to dispatching them.

He was in open ground now with three more opponents in his sights. The gravelly-voiced bandit raised his blunderbuss and before Reagan had heard the shot he'd formed a shield from his wrist blocking most of the buckshot. Two closed in while one reloaded. He had time to breathe. The battle seemed to slow to half-speed as he clashed with the stout woman wielding a club. It was no match for his Vesica as he sliced through the meager weapon, then into her shoulder, slicing off a chunk.

The gravelly-voiced bandit was next in his sights. Reagan took one step closer to him before he was grabbed from behind. Before he knew it, he was jolted backwards into a tight chokehold. Reagan cursed himself for not taking care of the closer assailant. As he struggled, he noticed two more men run around from the other side of the compound; the guards he'd seen earlier. One of them ran behind him toward one of the larger tents. The other came to aid the man choking him.

The bandit reloaded his weapon and started to laugh at him. The man grabbing him was way stronger than he'd looked and grasped his sword arm tightly. The chokehold was firm, but he adjusted his chin to hold off the full force of the squeeze. As the other man ran toward him lifting the butt of his rifle up high, Reagan found himself hoping for Le'san. He had to have been watching. Where was he?! Had he been killed or captured? What would he do in this situation?

All of a sudden his thoughts became clear. Only one arm was restrained, and he still had both legs, armored with an adjustable, second skin. His Vesica was an adjustable appendage, a part of him that can be visible one minute then gone the next. The only thing restraining him was his own self-doubt and the claustrophobic feeling of overwhelming odds. Le'san had taught him better than that.

With a simple thought the Vesica had been reabsorbed and reproduced in his left hand on his shield arm, driving between his head and shoulder into the bigger man's throat. He felt his grip loosen as the oncoming opponent's expression dropped to that of uncertainty. Reagan spun around slicing off his head and arms at both elbows. The remains stumbled past him before tumbling to the ground.

The bandit stood there taking aim with the blunderbuss, while the other guard squatted down behind him attending to something on the ground.

"Looks like we've got ourselves a lost pup," said the bandit in his distinctive gravelly voice. "Didn't they tell you that your laws don't count for shit out here?"

Reagan stood fast, holding his shield high while keeping an eye on both men. He watched the other guard as he hastily moved away from the larger tent he'd been standing by. The door was open and flapping with something moving in the darkness. Another hatch door hung open, considerably bigger than the one outside.

"What have you got back there!?" yelled Reagan, demanding an answer. The fear crept up inside him again and the men moved around him with their guns as if to force him toward the tent.

"You've interrupted feeding time and the beast gets cranky when he's hungry," said the bandit.

With a howling shriek, the thing came at him through the flapping tent doors. The feral creature moved quickly with its claws and teeth primed for attack. Reagan stumbled back and tried to get his guard up, when suddenly a spear flew in from the side. It knocked the creature thrashing across the ground less than a meter from where Reagan had fallen.

Everything else happened in what seemed like a blur of spectacular motion. Le'san swooped in as if in flight, followed by Hawk. He landed down hard with two feet on the bandit's chest sending him flying through the fire and the oil deposit beside it. He burst into flames, shrieking so loud it sounded more disturbing than the creature.

The Prefect moved with ease across the battlefield while his hawk ripped at the second man, causing him to drop his weapon. Le'san dispatched the panicked guard with the swipe of a blade across the throat, dropping him in a second.

Reagan was speechless as Le'san helped him to his feet.

"You ready to fight, my boy?!" he bellowed, without looking at him, but rather at the dark space where the creature had fled. "We must retrieve my spear, and I fear that beast won't give it up easily."

"Y...Yes," stuttered Reagan. " I'm ready, master! He composed himself and stood, sword at the ready. He could see nothing before him, nor hear a thing, then it charged again, this time from the side. He could see it better now, like some sort of wild boar, three times his size. It had an armored skeletal head that oozed black tar from gaping holes where there was no tissue.

The thing's roar sounded otherworldly, and like chilling death it pounced.

Le'san knocked Reagan left and rolled back to his feet, "You try and get behind it. I'll draw it toward me while you attack." He ran at the beast grabbing at his spear that stuck out in front of the thing's shoulder.

The beast writhed around, swiping at the old master, only inches out of reach.

Reagan wasted no time, jumping in and driving his Vesica into the thing's side. He stabbed it once, then again before it span around knocking him flying.

The beast flailed around while screeching even louder than before.

Le'san was still holding it fast, directing it toward the fire and the remains of the bandit. "Reagan!" he shouted. "See the oil, it seeps from the wounds.

Reagan had gotten to his feet and looked at where Le'san was gesturing. Where the thing's blood had gotten close to the fire, it had ignited. Without a second thought, he sliced off one of the flapping tent doors and wrapped it around his Vesica. He charged the beast, touching the fire as he passed to ignite his blade.

Le'san twisted the spear right, hard, to force the creature to face Reagan. When the frenzied creature had locked eyes on his student, he dived clear of its thrashing claws.

This time there was no hesitation when it came to the enemy before him, he charged the beast, screaming his loudest battle cry. He felt it again, the adrenaline and the supernatural rush of energy he'd felt when he first engaged the enemy, only this time it was more controlled. He focused on the thing as it leapt almost two meters in the air toward him, a mass of oozing flesh and bone. Reagan dropped to one knee, sliding beneath the beast, cutting open its rotting body. He rolled right under the thing's belly, not forgetting to retrieve Le'san's spear as he escaped to safety.

The monstrous boar burst into flames, before exploding in a ball of green fire, knocking the two Paladin back ten feet. Its final, dying shriek seemed to echo through the air after there was nothing left of the creature.

Silence again, but this time to Reagan's satisfaction. He'd spent all day waiting for action, and what he'd seen had been a lot different from what he'd expected and it had left him feeling different to how he'd imagined. It was a feeling of relief rather than glory. He felt no remorse for the villains, but was happy that the brutality was over. He looked around to see his master offering him a hand.

"So you've killed your enemy, boy," he said, with a most serious expression. "You've spilled their blood and from the look on your face, I'd say you got more than you bargained for." He nodded toward the disemboweled remains of one hostage and the dead girl.

Reagan suddenly noticed that reinforcements had arrived and were patrolling the camp. One of Quadro's men that he recognized was trying to console the distraught girl who was curled up on the ground. Reagan suddenly felt something hard and heavy crease up his stomach. He wasn't sure if he was going to throw up again, or if he was about to cry.

The adrenaline was starting to leave him. He realized he was cold all of a sudden and upon looking down, he discovered he was covered in the blood of his enemy. He looked around the battlefield at the men and woman he'd killed. Now, he had time to examine their faces. Their expressions looked frozen in time, as if they were still alive. They never knew what had hit them. It was only then when he came to the awful realization that it could have easily been him lying there, or Le'san. All it would have taken was one false move.

He felt his knees weaken under his weight and he buckled to the ground in tears. He'd tried to stop crying, but he felt powerless. All he could feel and taste were the tears and blood, his only comfort was Le'san's firm hand on his shoulder as he offered his counsel.

"It's always the hardest, to take a life for the first time; even if that life belongs to someone cruel and worthless. Just know that you succeeded today, my boy. This day has changed everything for you. The death here will forever haunt your memories and dreams, but you must always remember the glimmer of light in the darkness."

Reagan looked up to see the girl, no more than 20 feet away from him. He could see the other prisoners now, being helped over to the horses waiting at the far side of the camp.

Le'san met his eyes, "These people here today will never forget what you did. In relieving them of their suffering, it has in turn become yours, a pain you must always carry. This is what it means to be a Paladin of the Order."

Chapter 24

Jada had waited outside for as long as she could stand. She could see that he was watching the morning broadcast through the small window in the door, and yet he didn't seem fazed by the insanity. *That's long enough*, she thought and entered the Effigy's quarters.

The room was relatively large, with a domed ceiling, just down the hall from the observation chamber. To the left was a huge screen that took up almost the entire wall. The broadcast was grainy and distorted as always. The signal was weak this far away from the city.

The sound of the publicized riots boomed through the crackling audio output, a sound almost unbearable, but not to him. She waited patiently as her leader finished his morning routine. She'd seen it enough to know it was almost done. Tai Chi and yoga were two of his favorites, ancient Earth practices deciphered from decaying records found in this place.

She breathed a sigh of relief as the Effigy stood up and turned to face her.

"Mute sound," he commanded, and the infuriating noise was silenced. "I missed you this morning, you were up early."

Jada wanted to embrace him, but the subject of the broadcast had been getting to her all morning. She'd been unable to sleep as the days for action grew closer. The evidence was all around her. She nodded toward the screen with a distasteful expression. " We gave specific instructions to keep a low profile," she said. " They dishonor both you, and our cause. "

"They are free citizens doing what they believe is right. They feel antagonized, deceived by the authorities," answered the Effigy. "They have been left to act without my guidance since I was forced into hiding. I expected this."

She watched the screen in disgust as a group of rioters set fire to a vehicle and launched projectiles at the outnumbered LEX officers. They carried the Effigy's banner, "These acts of violence are being carried out in your name! Let me ride to the city. I will put a stop to this myself."

"Walk with me," said the Effigy. He threw on his tunic and cloak and headed for the stairs.

They walked down to the right-hand side of the briefing room to a control station on the lower level. This room was filled with more modern technology. Other followers were hard at work around the room.

"I need you here, Jada, and you can't risk showing your face in the city. I have to leave soon and you'll be in command while I'm gone. You know how important your part in our mission is."

The Effigy placed his arms around her waist, "We have one shot at this and it has to work, this is the only thing that matters, not our popularity."

Jada had been letting her emotions get the best of her more recently, especially when it came to him. The Effigy had taught them all that they had a responsibility to the people before anything else. Fulfilling that responsibility was top priority, even if it cost them their lives. They'd been preparing for this for a decade now, and lost people along the way, but the Effigy always reminded them that the real battle was yet to come. They all believed this, and believed in him

"I won't fail you," said Jada. "Your meeting is arranged, as you asked."

………………..

Ten Years Earlier...

"I have to admit," confessed Jada, "I had doubts that we would actually find it." Her voice sounded undeniably earnest as she led the man she'd come to know as 'the Effigy' down the ancient passage.

The Effigy's expression was that of patience and understanding, as usual. "Your instincts told you to trust me," he said firmly, but without harshness. "An individual with your experience learns to develop a sixth sense regarding such things. It let's you know when the path you walk is righteous. You had faith in me to lead you, and I'm glad to have finally gained your trust. That's all I ever wanted from you."

Jada had never once seen him angry, only devoutly committed to their cause. That's why she followed him. The two shared a passing look of mutual respect. A gentle nod from the Effigy made the gesture clear through his long hair and intriguing facial garment.

She squinted through the dull light at the mysterious mask that hid half of his face. It looked like it was crafted organically from meta-coral, and designed to give off a deliberately inquisitive, rather than intimidating look. The visible half of his face was heavily scarred, making it difficult to guess his age. She couldn't help but imagine what kind of horrible disfiguration he might be hiding under the disguise.

Just as Jada realized she was beginning to stare, The Effigy reached out from his cloak, lightly touching her shoulder with warm sincerity.

"We are nothing more than kindred spirits in the fight for our people," he said. "I simply told you where I believed this place was. You were the one who actually found it. It's because of your hard work and determination that any of this is possible."

"Thank you…sir," she said, awkwardly, trying to hide her overwhelming appreciation for his statement.

The walk together through this ancient sanctuary felt like they were sharing an awakening. She'd heard the Effigy's stories about this place, but she had to see it to believe it really existed. The Effigy had always known the truth, not that you would have guessed it to see his reaction. He seemed to find every step further through this labyrinth as intriguing as she did.

She tried to guess how much earth and rock was suspended above them. Most of the steel beams and cement foundations looked like she'd imagined they did the day they were constructed. The structure was over 1000 years old and still held strong for the most part.

A little further ahead, the rock had succeeded in overpowering the steel, pushing until the metal buckled, recoiling in submission. There was a team of devoted disciples working hard to stabilize the structure.

"This section of the corridor had almost fully collapsed," Jada said. "We've managed to reinforce it so that we could access this stairwell."

They moved through hastily toward a staircase visible at the end of the corridor, hopping around chunks of rock lying on the ground where the ceiling had given way. The stairs moaned and creaked as they descended, moving deeper underground.

The level below looked like it was more damaged than the one above it. A layer of muck a quarter inch thick covered every horizontal surface, and a stale musk smell hung in the air. You could see where nature had forcefully tried to take back the old passage. Roots were buried deep, poking through cracks in the roof of the tunnel. They hung down a meter or so as if they'd grown so far then given up.

The two of them stepped over a trickle of water that had managed to wear a channel through the thick floor. She noticed what looked like fungus and a strange algae growing sporadically in several locations. The freshness of flowing water combined with the damp scent of the vegetation gave life to an otherwise desolate environment.

She turned around and noticed that The Effigy had paused a moment, as if to admire the contrast between life and decay. He ran his fingers across the parts of the metal that were encrusted with rust while taking in the pungent aroma of the mushrooms. Without the presence of humanity, the environment was flourishing, reverting to a somewhat natural state.

Over to one side, another man was performing maintenance on one of the new beams in place to reinforce the structure. A woman beside him noticed the Effigy approaching and backed up to the wall, almost standing to attention. She looked like she was about to bow or salute before the Effigy raised his hand in a gesture that put her at ease.

"The passage was relatively clear beyond this section. The site is truly amazing," she continued, placing the torch in a makeshift sling on the wall.

The Effigy entered the room at the end of the passage. The other followers had been busy rigging up lamps in what looked like some kind of control room. Suddenly, his eyes were drawn to something at the far side of the room. He walked closer and was able to just make out a long-deceased figure, hunched over in a chair at one of the workstations.

Aside from the skeletal remains of the Progenitor, the room looked perfectly preserved in time. The Effigy wandered over to a console to the left of the corpse and blew the dust off the control panel. There were old gauges and dials everywhere. He wiped the thick film from one of the screens beside the controls.

"This was a monitoring station," stated the Effigy. "The schematic showed that the Viaduct was activated from ground level. The unfortunate ones below monitored system functions while the others escaped."

Jada stood at the mouth of another corridor waiting for her master. "We found very few remains until we reached this point. There are more of them in the main chamber. Most of the tunnels we found around the Viaduct lead to this point. We are still mapping the areas we can access."

The Effigy's hand hovered above the bony hand of the dead man. He noticed something on the floor, an ancient weapon of some sort. A revolver. He picked it up before noticing the hole in the back of the skull.

Jada watched the Effigy's actions, intrigued, "Maintenance work down here must have been left to the slaves, made to work while the cowards fled. From the scorch marks on the ground and walls, I'd say that many of them were vaporized."

The Effigy stood up, "Or maybe these people were remembered as saviors?" The question was rhetorical. "All those years ago, I don't think they were all that different from us. Maybe these workers remained behind knowing their loved ones had escaped their fate?"

He looked over at the wall at the other end of the room. A large emblem hung there, with the words 'United Factions', displayed beneath it in three languages. He recognized the English and Cantonese from the archives he'd studied and thought the other might be Russian. The once shiny, metallic finish looked dusty and tarnished.

The Effigy began to whisper, "They failed to realize the full extent of their self-destructive nature until it was to late, conflicted by petty differences. Only in the face of extinction did they unite behind a common goal. We can learn a lot from their hard lessons."

"The Progenitors destroyed our world! They fled! And now they want it back. They seem to have forgotten their lesson!" Jada was agitated by the Effigy's neutral opinion of their enemy.

"I understand your anger toward them. But you must also understand that they are desperate, just like they were all those years ago. When I stand in a place like this I see evidence of the great people they once were. I pity them more than anything."

Jada pondered the Effigy's words for a second or two, "Whatever mistakes they made in the past that led them to this point doesn't change the fact they intend to attack."

She looked down at the remains and the self-inflicted bullet wound. *Death by their own hand*, she thought. The idea conjured up a feeling of diminished hope. It reminded Jada of her own past, "It looked like they all took their own lives rather than endure what was to come. They embraced death."

"Maybe they welcomed it knowing their brethren would survive the apocalypse; that their children would survive. That humanity would survive." The Effigy looked back at Jada, waiting for her response.

The Effigy knew her history. In the old war, they'd fought on opposite sides. She'd been corrupted by unorthodox methods, brainwashed by what Synthatec had to offer. Her mind was once lost to the chaotic will of her corrupted synthiant. She had confessed to killing mothers with their children. When she committed these brutal acts, she had done so because she'd believed in what she fought for, until the real truth of it all became clear. Now, she hated the Progenitors for how they manipulated her people. Her hatred was a powerful incentive and the Effigy knew she would follow him to the end. That's why he'd chosen her.

Jada swallowed back the anger that was starting to boil inside her. Her lips tightened into a thin line. She took a deep breath to try and calm down, "You seem to empathize with them, while I fear I will never feel such emotion."

"When we find ourselves without empathy, especially for our enemies; that is when we have been truly overcome by conflict. When we no longer remember *why* we kill, but continue to fight on. When we've truly lost perspective and are without hope, there are no winners, only losers…only death."

The Effigy dusted off his hands; the gesture signaled to Jada that he was ready to move on, "They will call me a fanatic for my preaching, and you worse for listening to me. We will be called outlaws, and perceived as terrorists, but we will have a goal we know is for the greater good. The motives and actions of others are not always fathomable."

Jada thought about the Effigy's words, once again reassured by the man she was becoming proud to call her leader. She stepped to one side as if to let him walk ahead of her. "Your destiny awaits…master," she said with a smile.

The cave was higher and wider than could be seen beyond the reach of the artificial lighting. Three large claw-like constructs stretched out of the darkness. Where each one of the metallic talons had come into contact with the earth and rock, branches of the metal had stemmed off, growing and weaving throughout the cavern. At least 20 or so men and women worked on different levels of the rickety, old crosswalks, setting up all manner of equipment.

The Effigy stared up at the overwhelming structure as if to situate himself in the presence of this ancient artifact, "Witness the pinnacle of our enemy's achievements; the instrument that once ensured their survival."

Jada looked around the room at the others setting up equipment, "Ironic, that we now use it to ensure ours."

"The true irony is that their instrument of salvation has become a means to their end," said the Effigy, solemnly. "When the people of Porta Orbis witness all we have worked for, it will ignite the same hope as it did 1000 years ago. After that, our fate will be in the hands of the Acolytes."

"Every day our numbers grow," said Jada. "We will be ready to fight when the time comes.

The Effigy shifted his glare from the marvelous structure to his two most trusted comrades. "There is much to prepare before the prophecy is realized. The Viaduct will illuminate this valley once again. Of this I am certain."

Jada looked at him as if she wanted to say something, but decided to remain silent. She had rallied those in need when he offered them shelter and everything he'd said would happen had come true, so far. It must have pained him to know that his preemptive vision could never be fully understood by his disciples, but he'd taken them this far. It was as if he never had a doubt in his mind.

She smiled at her leader before turning to walk away. If he trusted her to carry out the task ahead, she must also be free of doubt. To question his teachings would be to betray him, and she could never betray this man that she was beginning to love.

Chapter 25

Sapian hung upside down above his bunk, swinging softly side-to-side with his eyes closed and arms crossed. This helped him focus before a job, and something just didn't feel right about the meeting. He had to go, he'd come too far to ignore this opportunity, despite the risk. Would he finally learn the truth of his past? He tried to think back to the last thing he could remember.

The blood rushed to his head, numbing reality, helping him delve deeper into his subconscious. He'd probed his mind for answers to the point of near death before. He'd tried hypnosis, meditation, and even an induced coma, almost suffocating. All of these methods took him to the same place. This was the safest one he'd found that enabled him to target that particular part of his consciousness. It was a place of fear and confusion, but also curiosity. His desire to unearth the truth was overwhelming.

He was almost there now. It always felt like an awakening, only within a dream. He could feel the breeze blowing off the small lake in front of him. He took a few steps forward to look at his reflection. There was something familiar about the eyes, but it was not his face. There were no scars and the bone structure had subtle differences, along with the growth of the fur around his face. He wore his armor but that also looked different, new and unmodified.

He touched the area around his eyes. The face looking back at him seemed more animalistic, but at the same time there was a less aggressive nature to his expression. He reached out to touch his reflection when a sudden shake disturbed the surface of the water. The hairs on the back of his neck stood on end and he felt a familiar swelling in his head.

Suddenly, he was compelled to turn around to face the forest. He tried to take a breath and something stopped him. He stared into the darkness of the forest at night. He wanted to close his eyes and turn away, but instead he moved closer! The breeze he felt from the lake now seemed like an unstoppable force, pushing him toward a terrible presence. Even with all the strength of his exo-suit, he couldn't struggle free, losing his footing and tumbling toward the shadows!

Unexpectedly, he found himself free, but his breathing had become erratic. He desperately tried to calm down. His eyes worked hard, trying to focus on his surroundings. He felt himself drop down to the ground, landing on his feet in a crunched position, safely back in his hideout. A welcoming feeling of security washed over him and the sensation of looming terror faded away.

Sapian dropped to his knees and rested his palms on the cool ground. Sweat dripped from his face onto the floor. After composing himself, he stood up and stretched his arms out, before walking toward his armor hanging in one corner of the room. A makeshift repair alcove surrounded the exo-suit, cobbled together from mismatched maintenance equipment.

The armor had been with him from the beginning and he'd often wondered where it had come from; the same place he did maybe? He seemed to know how it functioned and how to perform general maintenance. The armor acted like an exoskeleton, magnifying his strength and agility.

The bulkier sections were the large, interlocking shoulder plates. Between them was a moving part, which compensated for his own strength, giving him more power when required. The shoulder plates were connected to two shoulder blades, which were heavily armored and covered the majority of the electronics. From that, ten strong vertebrae connected the upper body section to the leg braces at the bottom. The mechanics of the suit compared more closely to some of the ancient technology he'd salvaged, rather than that of Meta-fusion tech.

These findings had initially led him to wild speculations, then to frustration as he struggled to remember his past. He was getting to the breaking point and this next lead had to take him somewhere. The FRA were getting closer to him every time he ventured anywhere close to their territory. At least this rendezvous was beyond the wall.

Sapian stepped into his suit and shuffled into the interface garment. It was made of a durable synthetic fabric with performance sensors positioned throughout. The servos buzzed with energy as the shoulders slid inward, adjusting to his size, each with a chest plate that extended down to connect in the middle. Once the leg braces clicked into place, he leapt from the corner.

He jumped ten feet across the room from a standing position, swinging around a steel roof support to land in front of his weapons. He picked up his sidearm, a custom-made energy weapon that could be used in a lethal or non-lethal capacity.

He realized it was necessary to carry a weapon early on in his criminal career, but killing everyone who crossed his path didn't sit well with him. There was no way he was ever going to clear his name by increasing his body count, not that the scumbag earlier didn't have it coming. He made sure the weapon was charged with back up cells to boot.

As he hopped toward the exit, he grabbed a ragged cloak and threw it over his shoulders. He didn't think the bandages or a mask were suitable attire for this particular meeting, but he wasn't about to walk out in the open without something to hide his features. He pulled the hood over his head and threw it back over his shoulder, hiding half of his face.

For the first time since he could remember, he felt like he was on the right path…but he'd been wrong before.

Chapter 26

The FRA hopper bounced over the ruins of the old city. The magnetic fields were choppy outside the wall and got weaker the further away you went from Porta Orbis. The vehicle jolted side to side before abruptly dropping a couple of meters!

"Sorry Ma'am! We're experiencing turbulence," said the pilot.

"Hold her steady! There's enough meta-coral in the ground here to keep us in the air," said Rosair, peering out of the windshield. The moon was bright tonight, illuminating the rooftops leading toward the dark horizon. Clusters of artificial lighting showed evidence of life scattered sporadically across the decaying cityscape.

The high risk of running ops with limited fusion-tech capabilities was usually enough to red flag a mission, but this one was worth it. As the pilot leveled out the craft, she patted him on the shoulder, before turning toward the main compartment.

"Listen up!" she shouted at the rest of the team, making their heads snap around. "Let's recap."

She looked over the troops she'd hand picked for the mission, as well as sizing up the late additions. Malone and his guards sat at the back of the craft and stood out from the rest. She recognized the state of the art armor they were packing, but as far as she knew it was still in the testing phase. They were equipped with an array of advanced gear that wasn't standard FRA issue. So far, he wasn't trying to call any of the shots and it was nice to have the extra backup, but the fact that he was wearing sunglasses when it was dark outside bugged the life out of her.

Malone peered at her over his shades, waiting for her briefing.

She took the hint and moved forward. "We're not expecting heavy resistance, but we've been here before," she hollered. "Our intel says our man will be alone, but he's been known to work with other shit-bag associates in the past."

A light started flashing along with the sound of an alarm, which got the team members fidgeting in their seats. They all checked over their equipment one more time, making sure they were locked and loaded.

Rosair hit a switch killing the alarm before checking her own unique weapons, a pair of matching automatic pistols. She'd had them crafted to be extra lightweight, balanced perfectly for accurate use with one hand. She'd had to go with a smaller round because of this, but the bullets had no trouble penetrating thinner optimum-grade armor, she just had to shoot with more precision at the more vulnerable locations. She took pride in the elegance of her weapons and her ability to use them proficiently, while others would struggle.

Malone watched her going over her pistols and felt a smirk creep up one side of his face.

She saw him looking and flashed him a scowl. "It's important that we make the arrest outside the facility," she said, addressing everyone. "This place is a known hangout for the scum of the outskirts and we're acting outside of our normal jurisdictional area. If the battle takes us inside, we have no idea what kind of arsenal they have waiting for us. Any questions?"

Rosair scanned their confident faces, "Good! Let's get this done quickly and quietly. With any luck, we'll be home for breakfast."

She walked to the back of the transport to find Malone examining his own strange- looking sidearm. It appeared to be energy-based, with a small screen that flicked out from the top before vanishing back inside. It had nothing you could call a barrel, just a wide, cylindrical charge output. The weapon seemed to be paired with a thick bracelet around his left arm, which he covered up as she approached. For a moment, she wondered if it was even a weapon, it looked more like some kind of scanning device.

She was about to enquire, but didn't want to give the impression that her mind was on anything but the mission. *The details were likely classified anyway,* she thought. *Maybe he needs reminding he's a spectator here, regardless of his clearance.*

"Just remember, we've both got our reasons for being here," she said, staring through the shades. "When we have him in custody, you can ask him all the questions you like, but until then he's all mine!" she glared at him with a stare that weighed in like a ton of bricks; she wore a frown to match.

He holstered his weapon casually and looked up at her, pushing down his specs so she could see the honesty in his eyes.

"I'm not here to step on anybody's toes, Lieutenant," he said.

His mannerisms oozed an awkward trustworthy appeal that surprised her at first, then made her feel at ease. He wasn't lying, but he wasn't telling her everything either. She wondered what it was she was missing.

The stalemate was abruptly interrupted.

"Rosair?!" said Darahk, over the communicator. "Are your men ready?"

Rosair glanced at her wrist monitor, "Yes, Inquisitor. We're 12 minutes from the location."

Chapter 27

Reagan looked over the equipment Joss had picked up from storage. He'd told him that he'd had these things hidden away for a rainy day. It wasn't raining yet, but it felt like a storm was coming. Joss had seized them from various undercover ops and illegal weapons depots; totally against the law, and not to mention, a federal crime.

Reagan pulled the large sniper rifle from the biggest case and walked over to his brother.

Joss was crouched down, scanning the area through night vision binoculars, which he'd also had in storage.

"Any sign of them?" asked Reagan, passing him the weapon.

They had a good view of the meeting point; an elevated position about 150 meters away in a distant tower. The top half had collapsed to the street below and they had a perfect line of sight through a gaping hole in the front of the building.

"Nothing yet, " said Joss, grabbing the rifle. "I forgot how much I hate stakeouts."

Reagan watched Joss set the rifle up on the tripod in seconds. Reagan wondered how many times he'd used this stuff, or pulled ops like this on his own time. At some point during his absence, his brother's career had taken a turn for the worst and he was starting to see why.

Joss lit up a cigarette and opened one of the smaller cases. Reagan took a look through the binoculars. The old city looked similar to destroyed settlements he'd passed through during the trials.

Meta-physics and fusion technology existed in the wastes, but in a much cruder form. Hoppers and other transports usually stopped working past a certain distance, due to the inconsistency of the coral formation. Reagan and Le'san had spent most of the three years traveling on foot.

"This reminds me of a time in the wastes," whispered Reagan. "We'd been tracking a group of bandits and sat there watching them for almost three days. We had to wait for them to move before we could intervene."

"Really?" asked Joss, making no attempt to keep his voice down. "I would have thought with being all that way from the city, I don't know…you could maybe bend a few rules."

"You can't 'bend' the code. It goes against everything you're taught as a Paladin," said Reagan. He remembered how Joss had stopped going to temple the instant he'd been denied his entry into the Order. "You can't just go around slaughtering any band of low lives you come across. A disciple of the Order lives by the scriptures. It must always be this way, especially operating beyond city boundaries." He instantly realized the irony given their current situation, but he'd already said it.

"What about what we're doing?" Joss asked, with a burst of mocking laughter. "What would the scriptures say about this?" He waited patiently for a response while checking on the location through the sight of his rifle.

Reagan stared into space for a moment before he spoke, "That question's been running through my mind over and over since we left the house. This could jeopardize everything I've worked toward my whole life."

Their activities were illegal in the eyes of the FRA, and they were acting without the support of the Patronas Order. He was acting on the orders of his Preceptor and a Prefect of his chapter, but something still didn't sit right. He thought about having to explain himself in front of a federal tribunal and he cringed. It was the truth, but the fact that the Order official happened to be his father, and a thorn in the side of the Agency, destroyed any merit their activities might have had.

Joss could see the conflict on his brother's face. He was obviously struggling with all this cloak and dagger stuff. "Man, you're so tightly wound! All those years on the righteous path have made you forget the harsh politics that really keep the wheels turning. If it's all as bad as Pops thinks it is, and the threat is real, all you're doing is what you signed up for." Joss recalled some of his Father's classes, "'A Paladin fights for the Acolytes and all that they stood for'. Exact words from the scriptures, if I'm not mistaken."

Reagan thought about his brother's words. If the Acolytes were coming and the prophecy was true, he was acting on the most basic part on his official mandate. This was the Patronas Order's main function, the very thing that had brought all the chapters together, O'sar and Suu'vitan alike. Joss was right in a roundabout way, even if his reasons for acting were self-serving.

"Dad really drilled that into our heads," said Reagan, before realizing the manipulation and his brother hypocrisy. "What about you? You were pretty quick to agree to all this too. The two of you soon put aside your differences."

"The old man turned out to be more useful than I thought," responded Joss with a sly glance.

Reagan knew that Joss seriously doubted many aspects of the so-called prophecy. To any rational person, peace can only last for so long before the powers that be shit the bed. Whether divine intention or a failure in democracy, the signs pointed to trouble on the horizon. "And it doesn't bother you at all that these are feds we're going up against?" Reagan asked.

Joss examined three of the tranquilizer rounds in one case while opening up another case beside it. He pulled out two cloak-like garments. The fabric shimmered in the moonlight. He handed one to Reagan and threw the other over his shoulders, covering his light body armor.

"I told Darahk he'd not heard the last of me," said Joss. "Besides, who am I to deny the prodigal return of the Five?"

Reagan threw him a look that called 'bullshit', and reminded Joss that he knew him better than that.

"Look, altar boy. All we are is cogs turning in the machine that's worked just fine for the last 20 years. What we're doing is protecting the best interests of the coalition government; an alliance founded solely on the Acolytes' legacy."

"That's what I keep telling myself," said Reagan, nodding his head, realizing all of a sudden that he couldn't carry out the mission wearing his standard Paladin armor.

He concentrated for a second and every marking and Order insignia disappeared from the armor. It became unrecognizable from that of a Paladin and even dulled in color and texture. After that, Reagan tried the cloak on for size then turned his attention to the rifle case where a small sidearm remained.

Joss had been watching through the riflescope, when his hand jolted up to alert Reagan, "We've got movement!"

Reagan dropped to a crouch behind the crumbling concrete wall in front of them, grabbing the binoculars and adjusting the focus.

"There's a team moving in from the east, and another one is coming from the south," said Reagan. "Wait… there's another team bringing up the rear."

The troops had a different look to them and the leader was dressed in formal attire rather than field uniform.

"Who's the suit?" asked Reagan.

"I don't recognize him, but his boys are certainly dressed for the occasion."

They watched the two heavily armored guards close on the location; mini guns, usually the kind you seen mounted, 6 barrels, 30 rounds a second. The things must have weighed a ton and by the pace they were moving at, their exo-suits likely gave them enhanced strength.

"Good luck getting tranq darts through that armor," said Reagan.

"You better get down there," said Joss. "The zero-light camo is good up to two meters, stay in the shadows and try to avoid hand-to-hand combat."

"I'm counting on you to take them out if any of them get anywhere near me."

Reagan lifted the hood over his head and pulled up the material over his face. When he stopped moving, you could hardly see him in the dull light.

Joss threw him an extra clip for the pistol, which he stowed under his cloak.

"These darts take effect instantly; they'll be out before they hit the ground," Joss said, holding the dart vertically in front of him. "You'll only need one."

Reagan climbed down through a hole in the floor before treading cautiously over a fallen section of wall onto the next building.

"Switch to closed field coms," said Joss. "Testing…testing."

"I hear you loud and clear," answered Reagan.

"I'll wait for you to hit the first team before I head for the target. Wait for the second to scatter and take out as many as you can."

"You got any plans for our party crashers? They're rolling without helmets, light headgear only."

"Well, we're just going to have to improvise," said Reagan darting silently over the rubble toward the action.

"You're approaching two feds patrolling the perimeter, two o'clock. Watch your back, " said Joss.

"That's why you're here!"

Joss switched his line of sight between his brother and the incoming feds. They moved in and out of light cover and didn't look to be expecting any interference to their flank; sloppy planning. He adjusted the weapon to check the north passage. He saw movement!

"I've got visual. Someone's moving in from the east, a block away," said Joss

He watched the figure walk toward them hesitantly, careful to remain close to potential cover. He zoomed in as far as he could before noticing something familiar in the figure's movements, something animal.

Joss kept watching, waiting for him to step out of cover, for even a split second. He watched as the figure approached a pile of rubble blocking his way, when he suddenly hopped over the heap, exposing his physique to the moonlight!

"It's the target. Here he comes," said Joss in his loudest whisper.

Reagan stopped dead in his tracks and held fast behind a fallen metal beam.

"You sure? Something feels off," said Reagan.

"I'm certain. Get ready to move on my mark…" said Joss.

He shifted the rifle to check on the FRA. The Lieutenant had eyes on the target and held up a fist instructing her men to hold. She opened her palm and fingers and the troops started to circle around to surround him.

"Be ready to drop him if he makes us," said Rosair, watching her prey from the shadows. She glared at him like a predator and felt her hand clench around her weapon.

Reagan moved a little closer until he was less than ten meters from the closest FRA agent. Now all he had to do was sit tight, stay out of view and wait for shit to get real. He played the scenario out in his head. He was pretty sure he could take out two before any of them noticed, two more before they got off a round. Then, it was anyone's guess once the bullets started flying.

Reagan was about to start moving around the perimeter to intercept when…

"Hold!" shouted Joss. "Hold!"

Reagan lowered his weapon and secured his hiding spot. He took a deep breath in an attempt to force back the adrenaline.

"Something's happening!" said Joss after a couple of seconds.

Reagan took a step back against a wall for cover, accidently knocking loose a piece of debris onto the ground.

The closest agents' heads snapped around toward the noise, looking right in Reagan's direction.

Rosair hadn't noticed because she was too busy watching the street as two large doors started to open. She eyeballed her sniper a moment before she saw the target duck for cover across from the entrance. "Shit!" she hissed.

Joss had lost sight of Reagan with all the commotion, quickly adjusting his line of sight between the feds and the large doors as they slid open. Just as he was about to shift his focus to scan for Sapian, he noticed another smaller door open above the main entrance. He could just make out the barrel of a heavy machine gun poking out from behind the armored turret. Whether they were expecting company or not, they were certainly prepared for it.

The large door finally ground to a halt with a loud clank and three men casually walked out. They were armed with large, retro looking shooters. One of them walked about ten feet ahead and stared out into the shadows in front of him, almost like he knew they were being watched. The men stood around for a few seconds before one of them gave a wave to someone inside.

The Lieutenant noticed the barrel of her sniper's gun start to shake to the left of her vision.

"Hold your fire!" she ordered, under her breath, while placing a firm hand on his shoulder.

Malone leaned forward to address the lieutenant, "They've not made us yet. Let's see what happens."

A few meters back the patrolling FRA officer surveyed the rear, and waved to another man to move in for back up.

Joss could feel a bead of sweat running down his face, and he remembered to take a breath. He looked for Reagan amidst the ruins. He could see two men now, wandering in his brother's general direction.

"Shit! They're spooked. Reagan, get back! One of them is heading your way. A welcoming party of goons just came out of the door to meet them. The ape looks as surprised as the feds do."

There was still no response from Reagan, which meant he was in a tight spot where he was either pinned or wasn't able to speak. Joss couldn't see where his brother was in relation to the patrolling feds, but it couldn't have been more than a few meters.

Back on the front line, the Lieutenant eyeballed the thug from the shadows. She knew he couldn't see her, but something told her he knew they were being watched.

One of the men gestured to Sapian, who was hiding behind an old door hanging from its hinges. "Come out, come out wherever you are, we're all friends here!" One of them said to the others, with a laugh.

Sapian stepped out from the cover of the door, and walked over to the thug waving him over. His hands remained hidden under his ragged cape, hiding the fact that he had his pistol at the ready. He walked until he was a few meters from the thug and then stopped.

"We've been expecting you," said the oversized man. He was smoking a cigar and blowing smoke through a thick, unkempt mustache. He was wearing light body armor over his regular clothing.

Sapian sized up the others. Each one was taller and heavier than he was. They looked like they could handle themselves, but that was the idea. He walked toward them, and they ushered him inside.

"Lieutenant!" said the sniper, sounding impatient. He was about to speak again, when Rosair snapped at him.

"Hold, damn it!"

The men started to make their way inside. They didn't appear to be in any kind of a rush. The gun turret above the door slowly moved from one side to the other.

Joss was frantically looking for Reagan now, switching between the door and the guard closing in on his brother.

The FRA agent was almost on top of Reagan when he jumped around to the space where the rubble fell, gun at the ready, but there was no one to be seen!

The guard lifted his weapon, looking puzzled, when suddenly there was another noise behind him. The agent whipped around and saw a large rodent dash out from the shadows and through his legs, almost knocking him over.

The other man standing watch nodded his head, and threw a shrug back at him. He took one last look around the dark cove and returned to his patrol.

"Reagan!?" whispered Joss, frantically. He wiped his dripping face and firmly gripped his rifle, finger on the trigger. "Where the fuck are you, Rea?!"

Below, Reagan lowered himself down through a hole in the ceiling above his previous position, just in time to see the agent returning to the group.

"Come in, Joss? What the hell's going on down there?!"

"Reagan! About time! Stand down! The target is moving inside."

Rosair had to fight everything inside her not to run out guns blazing. With the heavy weapon aimed right at them, the chances of snatching Sapian without casualties weren't good. They'd be lucky if half of them got out of there alive.

"Team two, circle the building; I want all possible exits covered." Rosair's voice, sounded almost threatening through her gritted teeth. "We'll get him when he comes out."

Joss felt his own breathing steady as he watched the feds bug out in several directions. "They've bottled it. They're going ape shit down there!" exclaimed Joss. "The guys inside must have known the place was being watched. The feds played it safe and missed their chance. Get back here!"

Chapter 28

The blast doors closed behind them with the sound of grinding metal. The mustached fellow in front of him turned to meet his eyes, glaring into his soul. He could see his hand still rested on his sidearm while the others seemed to have lowered their guard somewhat. If they were waiting until now to make their move, he was going to make sure he hurt them badly before they could overpower him. None of them seemed to want to say much and the anticipation was killing him. It was up to him to break the silence.

"Nice shooters, boys," he said, looking toward the smallest guy walking toward him, holding a blunderbuss. "You think they're big enough?"

"Check him." The mustached man grunted. He chewed on the cigar more than he actually smoked it.

Sapian lowered his guard automatically, sensing their demeanor as non-threatening. He could usually smell an attack from this close; the scent of apprehension or fear before an attack was unmistakable. These guys smelt like something, but it wasn't fear.

"He's armed," said another man. He was bald and had distinctive facial scars. "A shooter, blade too."

Sapian threw open his cloak, and pushed back his hood.

The big guy let out a long whistle. "That's some heavy duty dinner jacket you're wearing. Looks like you came geared up for a fight."

"You can't be too careful these days. The three of you are holding fucking cannons."

The smaller one spoke again, "You can keep the suit, but lose the rest. You'll get it back when you leave."

"Nobody carries in here except us," said the mustached brute, waving his cheap smelling cigar in Sapian's face. "Just a little safety precaution."

One of the thugs proceeded to collect all his weapons before pointing him to a small door at the back of the room.

"Anything else, last chance?" asked Sapian, pulling out a cigar and lighting it. It was clearly better quality.

The guard pointed across the room, "Just keep walking toward the chair in the far corner, the back room. You'll know the guy when you see him."

Sapian stepped through to the next room and the lights flickered on. The second he got through the door it closed behind him with a loud bang. He looked back through the small window to see the thugs chuckling and gesturing toward the other side of the room.

He forced any apprehension to the back of his mind and examined the small dingy unit. There was nothing really in it, a beaten up desk and a small chair over in the corner.

He didn't really know what he was expecting, but maybe something a little higher end for such a big time criminal. There was a loud humming in the room, like the sound of a generator close by. He started to walk slowly toward the small chair when something strange happened. As he got about halfway in, he seemed to break some kind of barrier, and part of his hand disappeared through the wall. He drew it back swiftly and looked around him. His heightened senses rushed to his aid. He could hear activity beyond the humming and he could smell people close by. He held still and felt his fur move. He could feel a warm breeze coming from the wall in front of him. He slowly put his hand through again before taking a big step forward!

The space in front of him became pixelated for a second. Then, he reappeared in a different room entirely. The dank room where he was before was an immensely convincing holographic projection. That's the kind of high-end tech he was expecting, along with the state of the art sonic emitter to block out the sound of the chattering punters. It was likely rare and expensive hardware and that was if you managed to make it past the gun turret and blast door.

The room before him was large and got wider toward the middle before narrowing out toward the back. The lower ceilings around the edge made the venue seem enclosed, with a thick fog hanging in the moist air.

Toward the middle, a tunnel ran vertically up through the center of the room. Chains hung down from above and moved side to side ever so slightly from the warm air that rose up from the below. He leaned on the railing and looked down the hole leading to nothingness.

"Classy place," Sapian said to himself.

He took another puff of his cigar, looking toward a group of the shady characters in a booth over to the right. The figures looked right back at him from the dimly lit corner, the lights of their eyes had an almost animal quality through the smoke screen.

As he got closer to opposite side of the room, an archway became visible and lead to a smaller circular chamber. Two guards were enjoying the company of an attractive girl. One of them raised his weapon when he noticed him approach. Before he could address the guard, a voice shouted from behind them, signaling them to lower their guns.

"Come on through," said one of the guards stepping aside.

The girl's smile turned to an expression of moderate disgust as Sapian passed by her. He was used to it, and he wasn't there looking for a woman. He looked down at the man sitting at the table in front of him. There were other tables in the room, but all of them were empty, like he'd arranged to have the section to himself.

Sapian watched as the masked man sipped on a drink from a small cup before getting up to welcome him. He was taller than he'd expected. He swept back a handful of dark hair, revealing the scarred parts of his face that the mask didn't cover.

"The 'creature' Sapian," he said with a husky voice, holding out his hand in a welcoming gesture.

Sapian decided not to return the expression, at least not until he'd heard what he had to say. "That's what it says on the wanted poster," he answered, taking a long toke on his stogie. "And what should I call you? You represent the Black Circle?"

"The 'Black Circle' is nothing more than a trail of breadcrumbs I left for you to follow. I needed to lead you to a place we could meet safely, face to face."

Sapian checked over his shoulder to look back at where he'd come from. There was something not quite right, but he couldn't put his finger on it. Maybe it was the lack of firepower in case the shit hit the fan or the fact there was only one way in or out of this place that he knew of.

"You look on edge, my friend. I mean you no harm," said the masked man, sitting back down. He'd pulled out a stool for his guest, in an effort to portray a relaxed, submissive attitude. Of course, the armed guards didn't help.

"It pays to be a little paranoid in my line of work," said Sapian, sitting down. "I was led to believe I was meeting with *a somebody*, not just somebody; somebody that can give me answers."

"Ah, indeed. Please, take a seat," he said, pushing back his long scruffy hair. "Like you, I have acquired a different name in recent years. You can call me the Effigy."

"I thought I recognized your face. You've been making the headlines a lot recently, but that's none of my business," said Sapian, putting his cigar out in the ashtray.

He seemed sincere enough, but Sapian couldn't shake the feeling of something looming, something waiting for him. He didn't want to be there any longer than he had too. "It's getting late. My associate tells me you have something for me."

"Yes, yes, Mr. Zed! You really should be more careful. That vile man knows an awful lot about you. And as for the news, well you shouldn't believe everything you hear. You know better than anyone that I'm not responsible for these recent attacks."

"Like I said, it's none of my business," stated Sapian. "I get all my work through Zed. For all I know, you could have been the guy who put out the contract."

Sapian pointed over his shoulder at the guards with his thumb. "Do I have you to thank for the escorts? I probably could have found the door myself."

"I wanted to give you a warm welcome. Besides, if I hadn't you'd likely be in the custody of the FRA right now," said the Effigy, finishing his drink. "They are surrounding the building as we speak."

Sapian cursed himself under his breath. He'd played along against his gut instinct and now he was trapped there. He'd already started to stand before the Effigy could put down his glass.

The Effigy started to laugh, signaling for another drink. The guards started to laugh too, in a sort of mocking symphony like he'd missed the big joke.

"Sit, my friend, no lawman would venture in here," the Effigy scoffed. "You are quite safe, but if you're in that much of a rush I'll get straight to the point. I do have something for you, something you've been searching for as long as you can remember."

Sapian stood fast, unsure of what to do. The Effigy rocked back on his chair. He was a federal criminal too, probably higher on the priority list than he was and he didn't seem fazed at all.

"What the hell's going on here?!" growled Sapian.

"Sapian, named by those that hunt you due to the category of synthiant possession. Wanted by the FRA for murderer and theft; specifically, the violent murder of six federal operatives. I have seen the evidence, truly savage, my friend."

"Watch your mouth!" he snapped

"No memory of his life before a year ago," continued the Effigy. "A desperate mercenary! A thug for hire!"

"That's enough!" yelled Sapian, smashing his fists down on the table, sending the empty glass flying across the room. "I'm no murderer!"

The Effigy jumped up from his seat to meet Sapian's eyes! There was less than a meter between the Effigy's eyes and a seriousness about them that commanded Sapian's attention.

"I know more about you than you know yourself. The visions you have, the nightmares? How you gaze across the water and wonder," the Effigy stood back with his arms wide open. "Images from the past you struggle to recall, The Lotus Arch!"

"How can you know that?" asked Sapian, looking bewildered and shaking his head. There was vulnerability in his eyes.

"All you remember is the violent re-birth, frenzied rage," barked the Effigy, sitting back down at the table.

"I did those things! They all seem so distant and unreal, fractured; yet the memories haunt me night after night!" Sapian dropped to the stool with one hand on his head. "We've never met. I don't know you!"

"But I know you. I know you all too well. I know the quest which you will endure, a journey of discovery and triumph."

Sapian listened to the increasingly fanatical tone in the Effigy's voice, but everything he was saying was true!

"This whole thing's crazy!" cried Sapian, his expression a conflicted mixture of anger and confusion.

"Crazier than the way you live, losing yourself further to crime? You don't even know your real name or where you came from. This is not living, my friend!"

Sapian looked down at his hands and remembered the sight of them covered in blood. He remembered the rage, and every day after that he'd fought to keep it contained. He felt the Effigy staring at him and raised his head to look at him face-to-face.

"Until now, all you have known is struggle, a fight, simply to exist," stated the Effigy. "I can help you!"

Chapter 29

Singleton tucked his jacket around his face to try and keep the sand out of his eyes. He'd never traveled to the east plains before, but had heard they were a nightmare to navigate in a high wind, and not to mention at night.

He'd been chasing a promotion for a year now and when the chief asked for volunteers he'd jumped at the chance. Their job was picking up the FRA's slack, transporting coralite from a refinery in the east valley. Usually, the feds would work their way north before moving east to Porta Orbis, but the increasing threat of ambush through the mountain pass had made it too risky, especially with only a light escort.

The intel had come straight from the top. The plan was to move out in the open. That way, they'd be able to see an attack coming a mile off and have time to call for backup. But in a sand storm like this you could barely see a mile or two ahead of you, and if they continued to move at this pace they wouldn't get to the city until morning.

"Any communication from Central yet?" yelled Singleton, bursting through the small door into the driver's cab.

"Nothing," said the haggard man driving. He was overweight from sitting day after day driving a truck, and looked about ten years older than he actually was. "I got a blip on the scanner so all we got to do is follow the marker."

The rig was 80 meters long including the two storage containers. It had four large tracks and could move over almost any terrain at a decent speed, but only if you could see where you were going.

There was just enough room for the five LEX officers and the driver, stuffed into the front cab, with space for two more guards to take shelter on the platform between the containers. The other four were on foot in the dirt. Singleton had ordered a rotation every hour to give the foot soldiers a break. It was coming up on that hour again and the men in the cab weren't looking to enthusiastic about going back outside.

"Come in, Jackson. How are things on the ground?" asked Singleton, waiting for a response. When he got nothing, he tried again, "Jackson, come in. Is anybody out there? Willis? Parker?"

"Sounds like the com system's down. The storm's interfering with the connection fields. Seen it before," said the driver, as if everything was going according to plan.

"I'm going out there. We can't see shit and now we can't even talk to each other. This just keeps getting better," said Singleton, pushing open the door into the strong winds.

He walked a few meters down the side walkway before he got to the ladder, sliding down to ground. He couldn't see more than a few meters in front of him and was careful not to stray too far from the vehicle.

He thought he could see a figure in the distance but as he got closer, it disappeared behind the back of the truck. Maybe they were huddled together toward the back. There was an overhang stretching back a few meters that might provide a little more shelter. He suddenly had an awful thought that they might have lost someone and jogged ahead in a panic until he could see the front of the second container.

As the transport moved steadily forward, he noticed the partition between the containers and decided to jump up to the platform. Maybe he could get a better look from the top if he could hold on to something to brace himself against the wind. He could see one of the other LEX officers leaning into the edge, tucked into the alcove.

"Hey! Where the hell is every…" He stopped mid-sentence once he saw the man wasn't leaning, but slumped dead against the console, impaled straight through to the metal, stapled against the hull. "Fuck, it's an ambush!"

He drew his sidearm and was about to duck around the other side when one of the LEX cops jumped on the ladder. He was clearly screaming something, but against the ripping wind he looked like a terrified mime making shapes with his mouth.

Singleton leapt forward to pull him up when another figure dashed by slicing the man clean in half. Singleton fell back, holding the man's torso on top of him. He watched the attacker over the dead man's shoulder as he turned his attention to him, closing in. Singleton managed to wriggle his gun arm free, firing off a couple of rounds in a panic. They were never going to hit anything, but maybe it was enough to make the attacker take cover around the other side.

He threw off the body and jumped up onto the ladder leading to the roof. He had to get back to the front cab to warn them! How many were they? How many LEX cops had they killed already?

He was up on top now, staying as low as he could while still gaining ground. He looked to the left in time to see the carnage below, at least three of his men cut down as he fled. He counted four attackers at least and prayed that that was all there was.

He was at the cab now, wasting no time before swinging down and cracking the lever, almost falling inside. Whatever relief he felt vanished when he saw what awaited him. He slipped on the blood that had flooded the floor. There were body parts everywhere, some killed while they rested in their seats, guns still in holsters. The driver lay slumped on the wheel, the same passive expression he'd had the whole trip.

A feeling of dread washed over him as he realized that he was likely the last man standing. All he could think about in that moment was how he hated himself for volunteering for this shit! He could have spent the weekend at home with his family enjoying the festivities.

He clutched his revolver and gritted his teeth. If he was going to go out like this, he wasn't going to make it easy. He snatched up one of the other men's service revolvers and made sure it was loaded.

The chaos of the storm whirled around him through the open doors and broken windows, before one of them burst through an opening. Singleton was ready, two shots at central mass then another through the head to make sure the job was done. He only had a moment to examine the body as he stepped over him. From the look of the gear they were packing, standard rounds wouldn't have penetrated their armor. Good job he'd requested an explosive tip upgrade as an extra precaution.

He decided he had the best chance of surviving from higher ground, scrambling back up the ladder onto the roof. As he got to the top, he saw that there were two more men waiting, and he didn't waste any time. Two more shots! They missed, but made the men scatter. One more shot hit one of them in the leg sending him tumbling.

He only had two shots left and he was going to wait for the next one to get close. He was about to take aim when he felt it, a strange, sharp sensation in his left shoulder. His arm dropped, along with the empty pistol. He could feel the warm blood on his hand before he saw the tip of the blade sticking through his chest.

He felt his body weaken, but he still had two shots left in the other pistol. The man ahead of him walked toward him slowly, as if he were already finished, and maybe he looked it. Singleton spat out a mouth full of blood onto the metal surface. For a second, he entertained the fact that the end was coming, but not before he emptied his gun.

His arm snapped up, faster than the attacker expected. Two shots, one after another, and two hits, sending the bastard flying off the edge onto the sand below. Singleton was about to let out a chuckle when he felt the blade run through him again, this time it felt deeper. It was a strange sensation; the feeling of precision surprised him more than the pain.

Singleton's body fell limp onto the metal and there was nothing left in him. As his vision faded, he saw his killer, standing steady against the wind. The figure's cloak flapped frantically around a strange suit of armor, holding the dripping blade. Whatever it was, it was a vision of death if he'd ever seen one; the tool of his demise.

Chapter 30

Joss pulled his face away from the riflescope for a second to rest his eyes. He squeezed them closed, blinking a few times before looking down the scope at the FRA troops. They'd been moving more frequently, circling the building and not staying in one spot for any length of time.

"These guys look like they're getting antsy," whispered Joss. "Any sign of movement round the back?"

Reagan was hanging back about 20 meters from the FRA patrol. He was used to spending hours stalking prey, a predator waiting for the time to strike, "The second team seems to be gathered around a small opening. It could be another exit."

"Let's hope they stay put. Our ride's waiting for us on the next street; any closer and we're made."

A block away, Tasker sat quietly in their getaway vehicle. They'd hastily thrown a plan together based on the FRA's objective to snatch the target at the main entrance, now they'd been left to improvise.

Prefect Le'san waited patiently back at the Akura compound. He'd been told to await their transmission, but had expected them to check in before now. Something wasn't right and if things had gone totally south they might have missed the opportunity to call for backup. He decided to attempt to contact them over the secure frequency. "What's taking so long?"

"They're holding," said Taker, as briefly as he could. "...Standing by." He couldn't risk any contact at this range without risking detection. The boys had to go it alone for the time being.

"I'm moving to shadow the team at the rear," said Reagan to Joss. "You just keep an eye on that front door."

The team at the rear seemed to have set up an ambush around what was possibly another way out. Reagan couldn't see any kind of door from his position, but he was close enough to be on them in seconds when they made a move. He had the higher ground and the team had no chance of spotting him facing the opposite direction.

"First team's holding fast," said Joss, following the troops dressed in the exo-suits. They were moving slowly between the two other teams, close enough for support if required. The one advantage to this formation was that they would be easy to avoid through cover while well camouflaged. "The rest of the troops are staggered between the locations. It shouldn't be too hard to reach one another if we need backup."

Joss slowly shifted between each member of the squad. The well-dressed agent seemed to be holding back while the Lieutenant ordered them around using only hand gestures. He could see the stress in her rigid movements. At least he wasn't the only one improvising. It'd be easy to get to his brother in theory. It was a short distance and he had stealth on his side. But anything could happen when the bullets started flying.

"Let me know when you see the first sign of movement," said Reagan, clearing his mind of any hint of panic. He took a deep breath and thought back to his training, reminding himself to be patient.

"When the penny drops," replied Joss, taking a breath. He tried to forget the fact that he was craving a smoke and needed to pee.

....

Sapian clenched his fist tight in front of him. This meeting wasn't exactly going to plan. He wasn't planning on having questions answered with more questions. The feeling that things were getting more complicated made him grit his teeth.

The Effigy had been elaborating on how he'd been working to expose the corruption in the government and how the Commissar is lying deceiving the people. He also mentioned how he'd been gathering likeminded individuals to stand against the government. This was starting to feel like he was being recruited for another job, only this time there wasn't any mention of pay.

"I didn't come here to join your rebellion, if that's why you sent this invitation!" Sapian barked, cutting the Effigy off mid-sentence, suddenly feeling like he was being groomed in some way. He'd been listening to the Effigy's rambling for a while and the answers he'd hoped for were sounding more like a forced agenda. "I don't give a shit about your idealistic crusade, or quest for power, or why ever it is you asked me to come here!"

"It is your 'quest' I speak of. Your destiny, and that of your companions has dominated my thoughts for more than a decade. The path that lies ahead, you cannot walk alone. You will need friends.

"I don't exactly have a busy social life, in case you haven't noticed!" said Sapian, sarcastically." He'd noticed that the conversation had turn into more of a monologue aimed in his direction. Nobody else seemed to be listening.

"You have met these would-be allies;" continued the Effigy, "I believe one of them owes you a favor."

Sapian had no idea what the hell the guy was talking about. Then, he thought back to the incident in the elevator from the last job.

"So, you've been spying on me too?!"

"More than you know! I've been watching you all for so long it's almost driven me insane." The Effigy leaned back in his chair, as if to give Sapian a moment to come to terms with his apparent significance.

"Almost!?" yelled Sapian, realizing the Effigy's apparent obsession with him. The lunatic was clearly devoted to this master plan and somehow believed that he was already a part of it, what ever that part was.

The Effigy leaned in towards Sapian once more, leaning on the table with a single elbow. "There's more you must hear, not that you'll fully understand everything just yet."

"Why stop now when everything was making so much sense!" said Sapian, crossing his arms.

"Your previous employer, the Stranger leading the raids. In saving his life, you have gained his trust. Once he thinks he has gained yours, he will present you with an offer."

"An offer? Doesn't sound much like the answers I'm looking for!" said Sapian, becoming fidgety.

"My job is simply to guide you in the right direction and you will discover the answers in time. You must walk the path for yourself."

"I'm getting sick of the games, scarface! So, you know some shit about me and I'm supposed to believe everything else you say? For all I know, you're working for this guy, trying to vouch for him in some fucked up, round about way!"

"There's truth in that statement. The Stranger is integral to the next stage of your journey, but I'm neither affiliated with them, nor involved in their mission. You could say that mine is that of a much higher ultimatum, the 'bigger picture' if you will."

Sapian despised this kind of guessing game when it came to business. Dealing with Zed was bad enough at times, but this guy was on another level. 'Cryptic' was an understatement.

"Now, listen very carefully," said the Effigy. "This is the important part. The second man is another you will reluctantly learn to trust. In a way you share an origin, and like you he has yet to discover the significance of his existence. "

"Oh really, is he a friend of yours, some other nut job with a messiah complex? This just keeps getting better."

The Effigy paused and leaned forward over the table. "He's a lawman!"

"A cop! Well, that's just perfect!" he said sarcastically.

"The one you fought at dawn today. You fought him for a treasure of which neither of you knew the value. Your employer had suspicions about its significance and likely knows the truth by now."

The Effigy suddenly had his attention, through all the insanity. He thought back to the raid and the case he'd retrieved for the Stranger. He had been employed to simply wreck the place, and the fact that that the attack had evolved into a robbery hadn't really concerned him until now.

The goods they'd stolen had led to the death of a cop, and ultimately the altercation in the elevator, which he'd been lucky to make it out of. The significance of the items in question hadn't been his prerogative and he hadn't given it a second thought.

Now, he found himself leaning over the table waiting for the Effigy to continue.

"It is the Coral Iris that binds you together. In time, you will meet face to face and you will be left with a choice."

"What kind of choice?" croaked Sapian.

"The only choice, my friend! The choice between good and evil! Surely you know the difference?!" said the Effigy, bursting into laughter.

Sapian rolled his eyes with frustration once again, "Get to the damn point, would you?!"

The Effigy hadn't budged from his seat, only raising his hand to the guards, signaling them to keep clear. "Make the right decision and everything will become clear."

The Effigy stood up suddenly and straightened out his cape as if he'd finished saying his piece.

"That's it? You've led me inside this death trap surrounded by feds to tell me what...to do the right thing?!" asked Sapian, with a tiresome expression.

"You didn't think this would be easy did you?" muttered the Effigy with a look intent to question his integrity and delve into his soul.

Sapian stared right back at him. He tried to decrypt the mysterious expression. The look made him ponder every crazy moment of their conversation. Was his insanity all an act? How did he know so much about him? He had to admit some of what he said intrigued him, but some of it sounded like madness. Whatever his true intention for bringing him here, they were clearly finished talking.

"Get me my weapons," said Sapian. " I didn't come here to listen to the rants of some freak show."

"Look who's talking? I know the knowledge you seek. If I told you everything I know, you couldn't even begin to comprehend," the Effigy reached into a pouch and threw something toward him. "Here's a little something to help you make the right decision."

Sapian caught the data-chip and clenched his fist around it. "....My gun. Enough riddles for tonight."

"Life is a riddle, my friend," said the Effigy, gesturing toward another door. "Careful on your way out."

Sapian thought about the meeting as he was ushered toward the exit. He appeared to have been led to a different door to that which he'd entered. The mustached man he'd met on his way in waited with his gear. He had helped himself to one of the cigars he'd had stashed in his utility pouch. He recognized the rich scent compared to the garbage stogie he was burning when they first met.

There was a smaller blast door at the end of the corridor. It must have been half a meter thick with a small rectangular window made from thick armored glass.

"Thanks for the cigar," said the meathead, wearing a dumb-looking smirk below the scruffy mustache.

Another one of the guards cranked the rusty lever to open the door. A gust of fresh air whooshed through as the airtight seal was broken.

The doors slammed shut behind him and he was back outside in the night. The tunnel ahead was some sort of service duct for the building above. By the look of the untamed growth of plant life disguising the passage, it was clear to Sapian that he was the first to use it in some time.

The vegetation provided visual cover, but the echoing wind down the tunnel carried the shuffling sounds of combat boots. He could smell that scent of apprehension; surging adrenalin glazed with fear. They knew he was coming.

"Great," Sapian muttered to himself. "Out of the frying pan...."

Around the other side Joss shuffled around on the spot to keep warm when he noticed movement below. Rosair stopped pacing around impatiently and signaled to her men who were watching the front door to move around the back.

"It looks like they're getting ready to make their move." said Joss. "Reagan?"

Reagan watched three FRA troops close on the opening. He noticed two more join the party from the alley to his left.

"I need to know the instant you have positive ID," Lieutenant Rosair barked down her communicator. Fifty meters back, the Lieutenant was crouched down behind a crumbling wall for cover, and had noticed Malone checking his wrist monitor once again. She'd observed the recurring habit passively and wondered what he could be waiting for, but Malone's agenda wasn't a priority at the moment.

"We've got movement at the other end of the passageway," said a skinny, dark haired agent. "It could be our target."

Malone looked up at the Lieutenant for her response as she drew her weapon. She was on her feet in a split second.

"I'm on my way!" shouted Rosair, making a run for their location followed by a three-man support team. "Malone, stay here and watch the main entrance."

Malone signaled to the heavy weapons to tighten up the perimeter before following her, ignoring the orders. He wasn't going to take over, but that didn't mean he had to do as he was told.

Reagan watched from the second floor of a wrecked building. The front had fallen down onto the street below, making him a perfect launch ramp toward the action. To the left there was an old fire escape, and the fastest way to the two guards on the left. They were in a staggered formation around sporadic cover.

He might be able to take down two with the darts at this range before the others noticed him, then he'd be a sitting duck. He was going to have to take them out at close range. *So much for keeping my distance,* thought Reagan. He still couldn't see what they were seeing, but he was close enough that he could move at them from the side and hit them before they even noticed.

"They've seen something down there," whispered the young Paladin. "Wait!" he readied his sidearm.

Without any sort of warning, something came hurtling out of the hole, narrowly missing one of the agents! The agent didn't even get a shot off before the grenade hit the ground! An explosion of smoke and a burning flash illuminated the dark setting! The loud bang echoed around the old ruins making the agents stagger back, dazzled.

Reagan only just managed to duck for cover before it went off. His ears rang from the explosion, but his vision was clear. It was time for his intervention. He moved out into the open in time to see the target take a running leap through the smoke intercepting the feds.

Sapian counted five of them before he landed, managing to get a shot off before they could lift their weapons! The energy bolt hit the skinny man's shoulder sending him spiraling round. He rolled on the ground, cradling his arm

The second man tried to take aim as Sapian grabbed the barrel of his rifle. With a twist, he flipped the agent on his back, knocking the wind out of him.

The third agent lifted her weapon and opened fire!

The Ape managed to stay ahead of the spray of bullets by a hair before smashing through a window into the half-demolished ground floor unit.

The three feds left standing closed in on the building. One of them threw a smoke grenade toward the window while another helped the winded man off the ground.

"We've got him trapped…" yelled the sergeant, before a dart hit him in the neck, cutting him off mid-sentence.

Less than a block away, the Lieutenant stepped it up from a jog to a sprint as her third team struggled to keep up with her.

"Keep him there! I want him alive!"

Joss tried to zero in on Reagan's location in the distance. "What's happening over there, Reagan? They're heading your way!" he said.

Reagan weaved between light cover as the feds tried to target him. "What are you waiting for?! Take 'em out! I'm moving to intercept!"

Sapian smashed through a crumbling wall to his left, into another room then out through a window to escape the smoke. The officer took a shot through the smoke, narrowly missing him.

Reagan used the perfectly timed distraction to make his move. He shot again, hitting one of them in the back with a tranquilizer, just above the belt line beneath her body armor. Her body jerked back in full spasm before she collapsed.

Another man turned around in time to see the camouflaged blur spin around and kick him in the face. A second kick knocked the third man's rifle off to the side as he squeezed off a shot. Reagan shot the fed in the sweat spot between the armor plates under his arm, sending him flying across the ground.

The man he'd kicked came to his senses and counter attacked. Reagan dodged him easily, hitting back with a hard uppercut! The punch knocked him back two meters. Bolts of electricity surged around his gauntlet as he made the strike.

The skinny agent shook off his aching shoulder and opened fire, shooting wildly at Sapian before Reagan puts his lights out; a well placed mercy dart in the left butt cheek. Now, he turned his attention to Sapian, just managing to get a shot off before he disappeared into the smoke.

Joss inhaled as he took aim. He knew he should take out the heavy weapons, but Lieutenant Rosair and her three men were closing on Reagan. He had the first man in his sights. He shot him.

The fed hit the dirt in a heap as Malone dropped to the ground, while signaling his men to scatter. "Sniper, take cover!"

The two heavy weapons scanned the area looking for the shooter.

The Lieutenant threw two smoke grenades into the open street, destroying Joss's line of sight.

Joss managed to get off one more shot, hitting another one of Rosair's men in the arm. There was just enough time to see him drop before the smoke engulfed Malone and the others taking cover.

The shot was worth it, but was not without a cost. Joss's heart sank as he looked down his scope at heavy troops below, miniguns zeroing in on his position. He had just enough time to grab his rifle as a barrage of heavy rounds annihilated his previous position. Chunks of rock and dust whirled around him as he made a dash for cover. "Reagan, report?" he coughed.

"I'm right on his tail," shouted Reagan, ducking under a low ceiling and swinging up a short staircase. He sprinted, but struggled to keep up. "This guy's fast!"

Beneath the smoke screen, Malone pulled the trooper to cover and checked his vitals.

"He's unconscious." he said, sounding surprised, "They're using tranqs."

"What the fuck?" Rosair growled, through the confusion. "Malone, you're with me. I won't lose him again!" she said, taking off.

Malone jumped up and jogged after her, signaling his men to guard the rear. "If he can't see us, there's a chance he'll move in to intercept. Don't let anything through the perimeter!"

Less than a block away, Reagan dodged between buildings, diving under a wooden archway in time to see his target duck around a corner.

Sapian slowed down and dropped to a crouched position. He was getting tired of being chased. *This guy just won't take a hint*, he thought. He took another flash bomb from under his cloak and pulled the pin.

He heard the footsteps getting closer. They were only a few meters away when he threw the flash bomb back down the alley!

Reagan barely had time to think about slowing down when they grenade went off, leaving him charging ahead blindly.

Sapian leaned out from the corner and extended his right arm.

The hard clothesline made contact with Reagan's jaw, sending him flying. He felt his body make a full rotation before eating dirt and losing consciousness.

Joss bounded down a staircase through the smoke at the other end of the combat zone. He could make out the outline of an agent and took a shot with the rifle.

The shot deflected off her thick armor and the fed opened fire, shooting wildly into the smoke destroying anything in her line of sight.

Joss managed to make it to cover. He was out of ammo so he ditched the rifle and pulled out his revolver. He knew he had to take them out without killing them, but he was out of tranqs and the thick armor covered everything but their faces.

He waited to hear the sound of the clip run empty. He could hear the agent frantically trying to reload as he made his move. The agent was still aiming the gun at his previous position and didn't even see him coming.

Joss jumped through the smoke kneeing the agent square in the face, knocking her to a pile on the ground. He didn't miss a beat as he saw another agent look around, trying to aim the clumsy weapon. His fist made contact with his jaw, knocking him over a wall backwards.

"That's for nearly wasting my ass," said Joss to himself.

Without wasting another second, he ran at full speed toward his brother. "Rea, what's your position?!"

Sapian flipped over Reagan's limp body. "You ain't no Wings agent," he said. He was about to crouch down for a closer look when he heard footsteps approaching, and took off down the alley.

Malone and Rosair reached the rear exit where their troops lay around in various states of consciousness. One of them tried to get to his feet. Malone tried to give him a hand.

"On your feet!" yelled Rosair. "There's a clearing 90 meters away. If he manages to reach the buildings beyond that, he's gone!

Joss could see the feds in the distance and decided that avoiding any further contact might be his best option if he was going to reach his brother. He noticed a stairwell leading up to the roof of the next block of buildings. He rushed up to the top, hoping to get a better look. His heart raced as he weighed his options. He'd given Reagan time to respond, and nothing. Time to try him again.

"Reagan, respond, damn it!" he noticed the worried edge to his voice. He knew Reagan could handle himself, but he'd fought the Ape himself. The thing was a killer.

He jumped a gap between two buildings and went around an old vent. He thought about what happened to Walt and tried to run faster. The mission was to bring the target in while avoiding been identified, but if Reagan was down it was only a matter of time before the feds found him. They were compromised either way. Time to call for backup.

"Tasker? You reading me?!" yelled Joss over the comm. "Dad!"

"It's about time," said the Lord Prefect. The old Paladin opened his eyes and stood up from a meditating position. He moved through the middle of the cramped transport vehicle. "What the hell's going on down there?"

"Reagan's gone dark. He was heading toward a clearing not far from our rendezvous."

"Move in toward the square. He could be in trouble," said Akura, giving Tasker a nod to get the thing started.

The stout man jumped up from his stool like lightning, sliding into the driver's seat. He fired up the engines, spinning the thing around and sending dust flying.

A block away, Rosair leapt over Reagan, barely giving him a second glance. She reached the end of the passage in time to see Sapian. The Ape was running across the large open area toward a fallen monument from a bygone age. He'd reach cover in seconds and rational thought overpowered her frenzy. She leaned against the closest wall to steady her aim before squeezing the trigger!

The armor-piercing slug tore through the back of Sapian's calf, shattering the left leg brace of his exoskeleton suit. He stumbled a few feet before falling into a controlled roll on the ground. He tried to move and felt pain shoot up his leg.

The Lieutenant approached cautiously. She could see the beast's pistol on the ground a few meters away, but couldn't be sure he didn't have any other surprises for her.

"I got you, you bastard!" Rosair said to herself.

Malone held his gun on Reagan who was starting to come around. "We need him alive!"

"He'll live!" she growled. She moved closer to the monster as he turned around to look her in the eyes.

On the roof above, Joss looked for a way down before seeing the remains of a staircase that jutted out a little over the square. The spot would provide adequate cover and a place to take aim. He could only see the two feds, but there were probably more on the way.

Sapian managed to stand to face his attacker. He couldn't escape in his current condition and he wasn't going to meet his end fleeing like a coward. Instead, he just grinned at the woman before him. He recognized the look of hatred in her eyes.

Rosair looked down her gun, scowling at the freak. "Freeze! Freeze or I'll blow that shit-eating grin right off your face!"

Joss stayed low and tried to stay hidden. He watched Rosair curiously and wondered if she'd shoot Sapian. He needed to speak with the Ape and there was no way he was getting any answers if he was dead or in custody. It was time to act now!

"Everybody, drop your weapons!" Joss yelled at the top of his voice. The sound echoed around the large open space.

Rosair jumped around with a start, drawing her second pistol and homing in on his location.

Malone kept his gun pointed at Reagan and tried to pull back his mask with his free hand.

"I wouldn't do that if I were you!" Joss hollered.

"You are interfering with an official FRA operation. Lower your weapon now," yelled Rosair.

"Everyone remain calm!" said Malone, trying to diffuse the situation

Across the clearing, the beat-up transport skidded onto the scene. Tasker hit a switch on the dash, flooding the square with light!

Rosair lowered her head, dazzled by the beams.

Sapian saw his opportunity and threw all his weight around on his good leg, kicking the pistol out of her right hand.

Malone took aim at Sapian, firing his strange pistol. The weapon discharged a pulse of energy, hitting Sapian.

The beast dropped to his knees, his armor smoldering and powerless.

Reagan was the next to seize the opportunity. He rolled over quickly, sweeping Malone's legs from under him. The moment he landed, he wrapped him up in an arm bar. The two of them tussled around on the ground.

Rosair was about to raise the pistol in her left hand when Joss fired. The slug ripped through the pistol, shattering it. He jumped down to the ground, his aim shifting between Sapian and the Lieutenant.

Joss picked up Rosair's pistol from the ground and held a gun on each of them.

Sapian tried to move but couldn't. He felt ten times as heavy as usual. Whatever hit him had shorted out his suit, causing it to seize up. He was trapped inside, helpless. He lifted his head, struggling to look at the Joss. His expression turned to a frown before it hit him. "You!" he mumbled

"Yeah me! Your buddy never got around to finishing the job. I've got some questions I need answered. You can start by telling me where to find that bastard who killed my partner."

"Sergeant Akura!" shouted Rosair. "Why the fuck am I not surprised?!"

"Shut up!" he barked, turning his attention back to Sapian. "It's my turn to ask the questions!"

Sapian started to laugh. "That's easy, chief. You just help me up and I can take you to him. He might not feel like saying much with his face fused to the wall."

Joss looked puzzled for a second before anger took over. He gritted his teeth and took a step closer. He was doing his best to resist ramming the gun down his throat. "What are you talking about?!"

"I'm telling you he's dead!" Sapian said, with a hoarse chuckle. "The rest of em', too!"

Joss could hear the sound of sirens from an approaching hopper. Time was running out!

"You're busted, Akura. You're done! Darahk will be here any minute. Who's in the truck?" she asked, nodding toward the vehicle in the background.

Joss ignored her and continued. He never considered the possibility that Walt's murderer wasn't still out there. The sound of the hopper was getting louder and he was wasting time.

"Who are you working for?" he screamed at Sapian. "What does the device do? Why were you after it?"

Sapian just shook his head submissively. "You're asking the wrong guy, pal. It was just a job!"

Reagan looked up to see the hopper move overhead. The side doors slid open and four agents rappelled down to secure the area. Two of the agents surrounded him and he raised his hands in surrender.

Joss watched the two of them pin his brother to the ground while the others moved in on his position, yelling at him to lay down his piece.

Malone watched as his men handcuffed their prisoner, but was suddenly distracted by the sound of a loud beeping noise coming for his wrist monitor. "He's here." he said, jumping to his feet.

Reagan tried to turn around as the two feds attempted to restrain him, "Who!? Who's here?!"

Malone looked at his wrist monitor again as it flashed, reading 'incoming power surge.'

All at once, the surrounding air seemed to rush towards a ball of green light that had appeared before them. Joss and Rosair were standing closest to the phenomenon and it knocked them off balance. As fast as it appeared, the vortex vanished, reveling an armored figure. Before they could react, the warrior struck, knocking Rosair out before grabbing Joss in a sleeper hold.

"We meet again!" said the distorted voice. "I believe you have something that belongs to me."

"What the fuck?" croaked Joss.

Gailan watched the event unfold through the windshield of the transport, pushing past Tasker to get out of the vehicle. With a casual gesture, he extended his right arm, producing his Vesica. The blade was twice the width of an average one, with the rest of his armor doubling in size around his body to form an imposing juggernaut. Without delay, he charged toward the center of the square!

From the sky above, Darahk looked down from the cockpit of the hopper. The pilot looked to him for some kind of explanation and got nothing.

"Who the hell is that?" barked Darahk. "Give me the speaker!"

"Whoever you are, this is an FRA operation. Put your hands behind your head and…"

"Sir!" interrupted the pilot, "He's locked onto us with some kind of weapon!"

Darahk looked as the figure turned to point the shoulder-mounted weapon right at them. The cannon seemed to materialize from within the armor, but different to that of a paladin's weapon. "Evasive maneuvers!"

Using Joss as a human shield, the attacker fired a powerful laser at the front of the FRA carrier. The laser grazed the hull, causing the pilot to swerve erratically. Alarms sounded throughout the inside of the hopper as the pilot tried to regain control.

The deflected laser sliced off the corner of the building below.

"The debris, it's disrupting the magnetic field!" said the co-pilot, his voice quivering.

"Bring her down over there!" screamed Darahk; pointing to the space between Akura and the mysterious attacker. "Land her right up that bastard's ass!"

The falling rubble provided enough of a distraction for Joss to make his move. He lunged backward, head-butting Lucas, knocking him back so he could make his escape.

The FRA agents took aim at the intruder and started to fire. Four or five shots whizzed by the armored head before he could grab Sapian, hitting the controls on his gauntlet. The burst of green light dazzled the incoming troops once again. And as fast as the armored figure appeared, he vanished, with Sapian.

Joss watched, stopped dead in his tracks by the spectacle. When the mystery man had appeared it had caught him off guard, but this time he had front row seats. He snapped out of his trance when he heard Reagan shout his name.

"Joss. Get the hell out of here!" he yelled.

Joss jolted back into action, disappearing inside the cloud of dusk kicked up by the hopper as it landed.

Malone stood motionless with his mouth gaping open, scanning over the data readout on the small screen attached to his wrist. "Amazing!" he gasped. "Isn't it?" Malone asked the grunts holding Reagan.

The two grunts just looked at each other and said nothing.

Across the square, Lord Akura marched toward the hopper. The ramp lowered and Darahk appeared. Two of the other feds watching the perimeter saw him coming and raised their weapons.

"Hold it right there, Paladin!" one shouted, while the other one looked intimidated and backed off slightly.

"Get that weapon out of my face!" growled the old Prefect. He looked through the two grunts at their commanding officer. "Darahk?!"

"Well, well, well! I was about to say 'the family's all here', but it seems we're missing one. Sweep the area!" ordered Darahk.

The two feds nodded with almost synchronized head movements and jogged off in separate directions.

A short distance away, Joss threw himself over a barbed wire fence onto a moldy wooden shack, which collapsed instantly under his weight. It took all he had to jump to his feet and continue. He scrambled over the next wall into what looked like an ancient burial ground. He'd seen them before—headstones as monuments. The engravings had become worn and unreadable from centuries of weathering.

Joss slowed down to catch his breathe. He could still hear activity in the distance, but was tired and dragging his feet. He felt like he didn't have anything left. He looked around at the unfamiliar terrain. "Where am I even going?" he gasped.

"You look out of breath, Sergeant!" said a voice behind him.

He whipped around to see yet another cloaked figure in the shadows. He was surprised he hadn't heard this guy coming. He whipped out his blade from its holster in a sluggish motion that gave away how tired he was feeling.

"Who goes there? I don't know who you are, but…" Joss spluttered.

The Effigy stepped into the moonlight in a non-threatening gesture. "Questions, questions, always questions," he said. "Your primate friend had many. Yet he didn't like to listen to the answers.

Joss squinted at the tall man before him. As he brushed back his long hair, he realized he recognized the face from the FRA broadcasts.

"The Effigy!?" Joss blurted out in disbelief. "That freak was meeting with you?!"

Joss used the last of his strength to lift his blade in a vain attempt at hand-to-hand combat when two men grabbed him from behind. Joss's eyelids became heavy all of a sudden as he felt a slight prick on the side of his neck.

"Sleep well, Joss," the Effigy said softly, with a slight smirk. "You've had a busy day."

100 or so meters away, Rosair forced her eyes open through her pounding headache. The lights from the hopper felt like bolts of electricity darting through her brain. The echo of muffled voices seemed far away at first, then closer and more abrasive as the volume increased. She tried to open her eyes again, this time seeing the blurred image of a face wearing sunglasses "What the…?" Her speech sounded slurred as she tried to find the words.

The blurred image began to sharpen until she was able to recognize it as Malone, extending a hand down to help her up. He rubbed his jaw with his other hand. He had a dry splash of blood that looked as if it had come from his lip.

"He got away, didn't he?" she groaned, getting to her feet. "Who the hell were those two fucks with him?!"

She cracked her stiff neck to the right to see a man she didn't recognize being handcuffed; Reagan. Lord Akura stood behind him, talking to Darahk. She'd already started to put the pieces together in her mind as she marched over toward them.

Darahk watched as the Lieutenant closed in with that look of ferocity she only let loose in the most extreme circumstances. She'd just failed again and got punched out for her troubles.

"What the fuck do we have here?!" barked Rosair.

Darahk raised a hand and placed it on her shoulder as if to command her silence, "Stand down, Lieutenant. I have everything under control."

"Is that what you call whatever that was?" scoffed Akura, with a discrediting look.

"Don't get me started with you Gailan!" said Darahk. "Now, one of you better be able to tell me what the hell we just witnessed?!"

Malone wandered over from a few meters away, still glued to his strange monitoring device. "Stabilized, trans-warp teleportation."

"Excuse me?" asked Rosair, rubbing the back of her neck.

"If you'd all stop bickering for a minute and be so kind as to accompany me to my transport," he said calmly, gesturing toward a futuristic looking hopper that was landing in the distance. "It's time I let you in on who the real enemy is."

Chapter 31

Where am I? thought Sapian. He seemed to no longer be able to feel his body. He could remember being in danger, and then he was gone; gone for an amount of time he was struggling to calculate. He tried to look down and realized he couldn't see his body. The only thing he could see was swirling light, spiraling toward a spot in the distance. Despite being apparently without form, he could feel a force pushing forwards, even accelerating. The feeling made him anxious. Suddenly, the spot in the distance started to approach at an unnatural speed. He wanted to cry out, but he couldn't make a sound.

In an instant, he was back in the real world. He felt the sensation of being dropped unexpectedly. His body felt cold inside but his skin was burning.

"Welcome," said a familiar, distorted voice. "You will feel better in a few moments. Your body isn't used to moving through the vortex."

"Vortex?" asked Sapian, before throwing up on the ground unexpectedly. He was struggling to take in the new surroundings with his throbbing leg and pounding head. It felt like he'd fallen asleep somewhere drunk and woken up somewhere else with a stinking hangover.

He clenched his fists tight, then extended his fingers; at least his suit was operational again, minus the damaged leg brace. He pulled out a med-kit from one of his pouches and sprayed a foam bandage around the wound. He still had 70% mobility operating with a single leg brace, but it'd needed fixing before he saw any more action. His mind started to clear once he'd patched the wound, giving him chance to examine his environment.

He was stood in the middle of a place he didn't recognize at first, but as he looked up higher it became obvious. He'd never seen it from this perspective before; the feeling sent shivers down his spine. The towering appendages of the Lotus Ark looked less like petals from this angle. They were actually huge arches set at various angles around the central platform. The structure was much larger than he expected up close, more marvelous than beautiful. Sapian couldn't help feeling insignificant in its presence.

He looked back at the Stranger. This time, he wasn't wearing a cloak and made no attempt to blend in or hide the unique armor. He just glared back at Sapain through the optical lenses encased in the sleek helmet, as if performing an examination in scrutinizing detail. He wondered how he appeared through the strange optical receptors.

The mask spoke again, "I think the words you're looking for is 'thank you'."

"I'm still searching for the words to describe what just happened. 'Unfathomable,' maybe? 'What the fuck!' might better describe the way I'm feeling?"

The Stranger revealed a bag from behind his back. He appeared to have been carrying it over his shoulder, but Sapian hadn't noticed it until now. The bottom was stained dark and looked kind of soggy. He pulled the drawstring open with a sharp tug and emptied out the contents. The flabby lump hit the ground with a squelching thud.

"A token of my good will." croaked the Mask.

Sapian looked down at the fat, ugly head. The face was covered in gore but he recognized it nonetheless. "Zed." He said without a hint of emotion. He looked even more repulsive in the flesh, if that was possible.

"This filth is the reason you've been having so much trouble of late. When an associate's problem becomes my problem, I believe it's in everyone's best interest to resolve the issue."

Sapian stared at the blubbery appendage, searching for an appropriate response. *Was this some kind of gift?* he wondered. He didn't get presents very often. In fact this was the first as far as he could remember. He wasn't particularly sorry to see Zed dead, but he certainly hadn't wished it. Sapian decided an honest response was the best option and said exactly what he was thinking.

"He looks even worse up close," said Sapian, with an awkward laugh. "Maybe it's the sliced jugular and blood running from the eyes, it forces you to overlook any redeeming features he might have had…" his voice trailed off.

"He's been informing the authorities on every move you've made for sometime now. I took the liberty of downloading the information from his database. His files on you are quite extensive."

The news didn't surprise Sapian, and it definitely explained all the extra attention he'd been getting lately. He'd never fully trusted the fat bastard. He'd only worked with him due to limited alternative options. He *had* led him to the Effigy, and although the visit turned from a few quiet drinks to an escape through a gauntlet of feds, at least he was finally getting somewhere.

At the time, the Effigy's words had seemed crazy, or random at best, yet here he was before a man repaying a debt, offering him a gesture of trust. However fucked up the situation was, he couldn't help thinking he was making progress.

He looked between the greasy head and his would-be 'ally', standing in front of him. Maybe that wasn't the best word to describe the Stranger, but it would do for now until he had time for further evaluation.

Chapter 32

Malone's customized hopper sped over the ruins with ease, much smoother than the standard transport used by the FRA. Rosair wondered what other equipment they might have been keeping to themselves. She couldn't believe she'd never heard anything about this secretive wing of the agency, not even a rumor. The Director seemed to be on the level, but something about Darahk's face as he sat across from her instructed her to keep her guard up for the time being.

Her expression told Darahk that she was reading him loud and clear. Her gaze shifted across to the Lord Prefect and the boy, and she wondered why they hadn't arrested them yet? How long had he been running operations against the Agency? She watched as one of the Director's men casually unlocked the Akura boy's cuffs.

"Do you think that's wise, Malone? This man just attacked my men," said Rosair, before correcting himself. "Our men."

"I think we've all concluded that everyone on board is on the same side. Of course, if you want to go a few more rounds I'll thank you to wait until we're back on the ground."

Akura looked between the two and realized they were waiting for his response, "I think we've seen enough action for one night," he growled.

Malone moved around the transport, checking various instruments and displays before halting to stand at the far end of the aisle, behind the cockpit where everyone could see him.

"I've had a team tracking the movements of this 'Warper' in and out of the city. He, assuming the suspect is male, is able to open passageways from one place to another, moving between them almost instantaneously."

One of the agents sitting by the comm station turned to address Malone, "The other team has reached the Akura residence."

"Thank you. Let them know we'll be landing there shortly," said Malone.

Akura spoke up, "Prefect Le'san has been briefed on the situation."

"You have my thanks, Lord Prefect. Your abode will provide an adequate space to set up a temporary base of operations."

"It's not like you gave me much choice in the matter, but I'm as eager as anyone here to get to the bottom of this," grumbled Akura. He threw a glance at Reagan that let him know he had everything under control. He wasn't sure if he could fully trust the Director, but his influence had kept his son out of shackles, not that he would have gone quietly. He grinned across at Rosair who'd been staring him down since they'd come aboard.

Reagan watched Malone adjust his unique wrist device. It was made up of three cylindrical pieces around his arm, which were all able to move independently.

Malone continued, "We've discovered a way to detect the energy signature generated by the portals, but haven't been able to hold a trace long enough to track him back to wherever he's hiding. We suspect it is far beyond the city boundaries or some place shielded from our scans."

Rosair decided to speak up, "Well, I for one have never seen anything like it!"

"Me, neither," said Reagan, throwing a look at his father as he moved over toward the communications station.

Gailan shook his head.

"Well I have," said Malone. "The item recovered by Sergeant Akura earlier today is believed to be a transportation device similar to the one we just witnessed." Malone had the attention of everyone on board.

"I wasn't aware that such technology was even in development, never mind in the field," Darahk said pompously, which indicated to everyone that he didn't like admitting it when he felt out of the loop.

"It isn't, nothing created by us anyway," said Akura.

Reagan moved down the hopper to sit beside his Father. "I still can't reach Joss on his communicator," he looked at Malone. "Could this guy have used this the trans-warp tech of his to snatch him too?"

"I don't believe so. I haven't detected another energy surge since he took the ape creature. Is it possible that he's returned to your Father's residence?"

"He won't return to my domicile, not if he thinks we've been captured," Akura said, looking back up at Malone. "He's smarter than that."

As they started to land, Akura turned to look out of the window and scanned the perimeter of his complex. Another one of Malone's hoppers had arrived ahead of them. Gailan could see Le'san waiting by the main entrance. He pushed passed the others and made sure he was on the ground first before causally approaching his friend as if it were business as usual.

Le'san spoke first, "The guards were a little reluctant to welcome our guests when they arrived. What's going on, Gailan? Are you sure these men can be trusted?" Malone's men walked by them carrying equipment inside the house.

"Well, they haven't arrested us yet," said Akura.

Tasker bolted past them, heading for the door. "They'll have to answer to me if they've moved any of my shit!" he barked, before disappearing inside.

Akura led them straight to his secret HQ. He observed his guests as they made their way through what had been his sanctuary for years. The existence of the sublevel didn't seem like much of a surprise to Malone. It made him wonder how long he'd been keeping tabs on him.

Darahk didn't say a word, while Rosier seemed to case out the facility. "This place is heavily fortified. Are you expecting some sort of attack?" she asked.

"This place shows up as a dark spot on our surveillance images," said Malone, sounding almost impressed. "It's invisible to sensors. Old school."

"He's right. It was constructed using ancient methods," Akura said, frowning and regarding Malone with a curious gaze.

Darahk had the exact opposite expression on his face. The inquisitor's lips remained tightly sealed until he decided he should say something. "You seem to know a thing or two about keeping off the grid," He turned to Malone. "I'm guessing you had the same idea when designing those fancy crafts you brought us in on."

"Guilty as charged. Zero percent meta-coral," boasted Malone. "All recycled titanium and a few other lightweight compounds salvaged from the wastes. Over the years, we've rediscovered ways to keep our operations secret. This branch of the agency is one of the government's best-kept secrets. Not even the Patronas Order knows of its existence."

"Where the hell do you operate from?" asked Darahk, his voice a decibel louder than before; loud enough to turn the heads of the rest of the group."

"We try to keep our HQ mobile most of the time, operating out of vehicles like the ones outside. We have a few low-key facilities like the one raided earlier today," Malone raised his eyebrows and looked specifically at Darahk and the Lieutenant. "Somebody's been onto us for awhile. We've been trying to discover the leak ever since these raids began."

"There was nothing about this in the rules of the treaty," said Akura.

"That's because the original team was set up before the treaty was signed," Malone said, looking at them over his shades. "In the dark days before peace, my predecessor feared the conflict would never end. She met other like-minded people, visionaries on both sides. They had grown tired of endless war-mongering and made a plan to safeguard what was left of their cultures before it was too late."

Le'san ran his fingers through his beard. "I remember hearing rumors of a secret faction. A number of O'sar clan chiefs were accused of conspiring with members of the Suu'vitan council. In those days, the general public rarely knew the truth behind such talk.

"Who do you report to?" barked Darahk. He looked frustrated by the whole situation. "You gave specific orders to keep the Commissar out of the loop."

"The Commissar controls the response unit of the agency. The FRA is our public front. We govern ourselves through an internal committee. Since the war, we've carried out operations specifically aimed at preserving the culture of our people. And, by that I mean O'sar and Suu'vitan alike.

"So, when the war ended..." said Akura

"Yes, much to my predecessor's surprise," said Malone. He looked over toward the rear section of the lab. "The committee made the decision to continue to work in secret, evolving into what has become known to its members as the Syndicate."

Akura looked across the room. Malone's men gathered around something they'd set up on the table. Tasker was trying to get a glimpse of what it was while two guards gestured to him to wait.

Reagan had been keeping quiet in the background, gently rubbing his sore neck, twisting it side to side. "If you guys are so off the radar, why tell us any of this?"

"I knew removing evidence from the crime scene earlier would attract Darahk's attention," explained Malone. "But it was crucial that I examined the body before the evidence started to degenerate.

"My missing corpse!" shouted Darahk.

"And the weapon we examined earlier today," added Gailan. "That's why the Director here has decided to let us in on his little game. He's lost control of the situation."

Malone let out a big sigh, "After what we all witnessed a moment ago, I think it's time I brought you up to speed on everything that's happened over recent months."

Malone walked away from them toward the back of the room. The two guards parted letting him through, he turned to them and waved at them to follow him.

The large table they had stood around hours earlier had been transformed into an examination table. On it laid the body of the perpetrator shot dead by Joss. They all found a place around the table. Reagan looked at his Father for some kind of insight, but he was studying the corpse, his arms inside the sleeves of his robe as if all of this was just as surprising to him.

The body they were looking at was actually half a body. Parts of the arms and everything below the knees looked like decayed meta-coral, even parts of the torso around the organs had partially dissolved, leaving large gaping holes in the cadaver. Gailan had read the report and knew the perp had died from a shot to the head. Aside from the exit wound, the head was the only thing that looked intact.

"If you'd pay particular attention to the head and face," said Malone, pulling an overhead lamp down so that they had more light. Malone pointed to scarring around the corpse's face.

Rosair leaned in for a closer look. "Deep symbiotic scarring around the eyes and ears; often the result of prolonged use of unorthodox techniques."

"You've already seen the new HGFs they're using," said Malone, looking at Gailan and Darahk.

"The grade of the coral was unique," said Gailan. "Its code structure was programmed to break down once severed from the host."

"Similar to our friend here…" continued Malone "After death, the remnants of the artificial tech accelerate the decay. We managed to identify him as a known terrorist with ties to the Brood. Our records show he was left severely handicapped in an explosion several years ago. The tech he was using seemed to have given him back everything he'd lost, possibly even enhanced his abilities."

Darahk had leaned in closer to examine the extensive scarring. "Unorthodox methods this extensive would have disrupted his neural pathways and seriously altered his brain and mental state. We have a good idea who might be recruiting such individuals, mercs with a grudge against the government. I'm sure you've read our reports. We believe the terrorist group led by the Effigy may have access to any number of these weapons."

"An alliance with the remnants of the Brood is a good way to build connections throughout the criminal underground," added Rosair.

Gailan struggled to hold back his contempt for their theory. "The Effigy protested the Brood's actions!" he shouted. "They even tried to have him killed when he first appeared on the scene!"

"Before he resorted to terror tactics himself," barked Darahk. "he pretty much stepped up and took their place as soon as they were out of the picture!"

"Or so we were supposed to think…" said Malone, shaking his finger.

"The Commissar's counter-terror unit examined each crime scene thoroughly." stated Darahk. "The evidence that they discovered was indisputable."

Gailan watched Darahk's face as it got redder. Darahk refused to believe that anyone could have a better grasp of current events than he did; his life's work for the last 20 years. The Inquisitor's attitude made him see fault in his own stubborn behavior. The evidence of internal conflict on his face was obvious.

"Did you ever visit the locations before his team arrived?" asked Malone, addressing the group. "The Commissar's special unit was first on the scene on every occasion, showing up seconds after the minimal response interval without fail."

Darahk glared at him, "Every member was hand-picked. They were chosen for their efficiency and special abilities."

"But this kind of preciseness in such an irregular pattern … something didn't add up.

I've had a team monitor all transmissions from the Commissar's office over the last month. I was alerted to the attack yesterday morning via a transmission between him and his major, one hour before it happened."

"I've suspected corruption in the agency for sometime now, " said Gailan, "But nothing this high up the chain of command. They were hand-picked all right; selected because of their loyalty to the Commissar."

"Wait!" said Rosair in a firm tone. "Just what the hell are you saying?!"

"Just over an hour ago a convoy transporting industry grade coralite was ambushed just outside of the city," said Malone. "If you'd be so kind as to bring up this morning's broadcast on the monitor."

"Why haven't we heard about this?!" asked Darahk, his expression shifting to one of confusion rather than anger.

Tasker activated the screen from the console, which he was sitting quietly at.

Malone nodded toward the screen playing the broadcast. "We intercepted a coded transmission on the Commissar's frequency earlier today, disclosing information on that shipment," said Malone.

The reporter proceeded to elaborate while they all watched, eager to find out what had happened, "According to reports, every LEX officer escorting the convoy was brutally murdered in what looks like another attack by the Effigy's followers."

LEX officials carried scorched bodies from the scene of the attack behind her. The wreck of a large hover transport burned in the background.

"Although no official statement has been released, word on the street is that the attack is retaliation after LEX offices pursued and killed members of the recently labeled 'terrorist' organization, led by the Effigy."

Gailan examined the details as the camera focused on one of the dead LEX agents on the ground, one of which was sliced in half. There were also scorch marks on the vehicle where they'd cut open the containers. He noticed the precision and couldn't help thinking about the energy weapon he saw the Warper use at the square. The focused beam of energy sliced the corner off of the building like a knife cutting through butter.

The reporter continued, "Sources report that LEX branch responded to the emergency call. Fusion response was said to be unavailable, due to the escalating situation of the extremists rioting throughout the city."

The footage changed to that of the Effigy's demonstrations over a year prior, old clashes with law enforcement and isolated violent outbreaks.

Gailan found himself scowling at the news broadcast. The Commissar had a lot of power over the media and this was a perfect example of everything he'd had reason to be concerned about. If there was truth to the Commissar's betrayal, he couldn't have done a better job of incriminating the Effigy. The public was already fearful, and would have jumped on the bandwagon, leaving anyone wiser open to protest. Either way, the situation would have escalated all by itself; a tinderbox waiting for a single spark.

Akura looked at Reagan for his opinion and his eyes said it all. The young Paladin was wise enough to see through such scandalous garbage, despite his years.

It was obvious what the Director was doing. Malone hadn't fully known whom to trust until moments ago. He'd already concluded that they were on the same page and that Darahk and his Lieutenant weren't a threat, just ignorant to the corruption within the agency. He was breaking him down slowly.

"This is preposterous! The Effigy's followers riot throughout the city at this very moment," screamed Darahk. "It all points to his group moving toward something big. You expect me to believe that the Commissar's behind all of this?!"

"Calm down, Darahk!" said Prefect Le'san. He raised a hand to keep the Inquisitor from getting any closer to Malone.

"I don't believe he's acting alone," said Malone. "But I have no doubt that it was him who leaked the information. He is the only other person with the clearance to access information on those locations, however limited. He knew they were FRA facilities, just not what their function was."

Akura stared Darahk down as if none of this surprised him at all. "The Commissar has many loyal to him. Politicians from the old days during the war, even Paladin," said Gailan in a calmer tone. "He was a member of the committee who originally voted for the use of unorthodox HGFs."

"That doesn't make him a traitor!" added Rosair.

"Thank you, Lieutenant! The Majority of the Patronas Council also backed that decision. We're not here for a history lesson, Akura! You seriously think the Commissar is trying to orchestrate some sort of coup?! He doesn't have the manpower to overthrow the Order!"

"Which leads me to my next concern, that the Commissar may have members high up on the council privy to whatever he's planning next. The Order is the only organization with the power to oppose him, and if he has allies within the council…"

Darahk cut him off mid-sentence, "Do you honestly think his men would side with him if he attempted such a move?"

"Nevertheless!" said Reagan raising his voice. "Everyone's had a chance to process the intel and I'll be damned if this is going to turn into a pissing contest. For argument's sake, let's say Malone's right. If he has allied himself with this, 'Warper'…with all of his technology and mercenaries at his disposal..."

"It could tip the scales in his favor," said Le'san, resting solemnly on his staff. "Tonight we witnessed the clash of the two major organizations charged with keeping peace in this city. We managed to fight amongst ourselves long enough for the real enemy to escape."

Rosair turned to Reagan, "Play us off against one another while the real threat hides in plain sight. I'm willing to give this theory the benefit of the doubt, but we're going to need proof."

"More like hard evidence," said Darahk. "And we'd better get to it quickly."

"Assuming it's not too late. What's their next move? Where will they strike?" asked Reagan, the voice of refreshing youth in the midst of old begrudging titans.

Malone pointed to the iris to his right turning everyone's attention to the artifact. It was still suspended in mid-air inside an examination chamber.

"When we tried to activate the teleportation device years ago, it was a disaster. An entire lab, the size of this room, disappeared without a trace."

"But this guy knows how to use this thing, right?" asked Rosair.

"But what I'm saying is that this thing drained an enormous amount of power. We had a blackout for ten blocks. If our man could somehow be using the coralite to enhance his device's capability…"

"He could use the device for something a lot bigger that one or two people…" muttered Reagan.

"…He could teleport a damned army right on top of us," barked Darahk "… Or at least a strike force big enough to do some serious damage. The majority of our government's leaders, if they were all gathered in one location!"

"The initiation ceremony!" exclaimed Reagan. "The patriarch of every chapter will be there tomorrow."

"Our assumptions and beliefs aside, this is a threat we can't afford to ignore, if even remotely possible. Le'san and I will report these findings to my Patriarch and request a meeting with the council immediately!"

"I will come with you," said Reagan.

His Father shot him a direct order. "No! I want you to head to the Velodrome as planned. Most of the Paladin will have left the temple to prepare for the festival. We still don't know whom we can trust and our absence may draw suspicion."

"…And you'll be our man on the inside." added Malone. "Keep your eyes peeled for any unusual activity."

Le'san nodded his head in agreement, "If people ask about our whereabouts you can stall them, but say nothing of the situation until we contact you. The last thing we need is the crowd in a state of panic."

"I will head for the Commissar's watchtower myself," said Darahk, his aged face as serious as ever. "If there's truth to these accusations, I promise I will find it!"

"I have a strike team I know is loyal to me," said Rosair. She looked at Malone. "If he's expecting resistance from within the organization, he might be ready for us. Can we count on you for back-up?"

Malone smiled at her, content with the renewed level of compliance. "You can count on my team and every resource we have at our disposal."

Chapter 33

Sapian admired the patina of the metal panels. They looked intact for the most part. Some areas were discolored and dirty from years of exposure to the elements.

Lucas surveyed the various areas of the Viaduct where repairs had been completed, before walking back over to talk with Sapian. "It's magnificent, isn't it? I was sent by my master to orchestrate the repair of this great machine."

"You must have had your work cut out for you," Sapian said with a smile. "I heard this thing was old. This whole area used to be some sort of ancient launch platform."

"You're not entirely misinformed. The beings who populate this land call it the Ark; an outdated religious reference. It amuses me that these people once chose to worship it, like some sort of sacred ground. The Viaduct was used as a means of escape from this planet long ago, but they weren't launched in any craft or shuttle."

The Stranger spoke as if he wasn't affiliated with any particular group inside the city. Sapian had heard stories of other groups spread out across the badlands, but the tales that were always told were about more primitive cultures, often stricken by poverty. This guy certainly wasn't poor and there was nothing primitive about the equipment he used.

The emotionless lenses focused in on him for a second before the mask turned away. Two drones hovered patiently behind him as if waiting for instructions. Whatever contact there was between them, Sapian heard no verbal exchange before they zoomed off in opposite directions around the site.

Lucas lifted open a large panel on the ground revealing a chamber beneath the surface. He waved over a couple of the mercs who were waiting by a large, cylindrical object covered with a tarp. As Sapian looked around the platform, he saw three more discarded tarps, and two other men were carefully placing the cover panel back over the chamber opposite to the one now open.

The two men hoisted it up onto their shoulders and slowly carried it across the platform. Whatever it was looked heavy. The two men looked strong, but not strong enough to carry something that size by them selves. Sapian remembered the clawed associate he'd seen dispatched earlier that day. These mercs must have all been enhanced by the Stranger's technology.

Lucas continued, "To reactivate the bridge between our two worlds is my primary objective. This place once bore witness to the end of an age and now it will serve as the means to the next."

Sapian's attention spiked. 'Worlds' is what he said. Did he mean figuratively or literally? One of the stories he'd heard was how the ancient races of Earth had fled the planet to the safety of space. He looked around the platform at the other characters and examined their weapons and equipment. They were mercs, not primitive earthlings or aliens. They looked equipped with similar tech to the Stranger, but they reeked of the badlands, literally. They were from here.

"Seems you've got a few people around willing to lend a hand," stated Sapian. There were at least 20 or so mercenaries loitering around the platform. Some worked away at various repairs while others seemed to be preparing weapons and ammunition.

"The first stage of my mission was to study my enemy, their strengths and weaknesses. I have had more than enough time to learn about the inhabitants of this city and the outcasts around it, even their flawed religions and fabricated history."

Sapian was listening to the Stranger, but found himself more interested in what he was doing while he spoke. Sapian had always been curious about unfamiliar technology and walked over to take a look at the machinery inside the chamber. He noticed similarities to some of the artifacts he'd discover in the old world below his hideout. Some of the tech looked like it had been retrofitted to the old systems, presumably to fit whatever they had under the tarp.

The two large mercs lowered the item into the chamber as a gust of wind blew the cover off. Sapian recognized the device immediately as a meta-fusion power battery. He'd never seen one that size before, not to mention the amount of coralite required to fuel it. However they'd gotten their hands on so much it was obvious they were connected.

Lucas saw Sapian staring, "During my time here, I found people still loyal to the true rulers. I have done my best to reestablish relations so that they will be spared."

He'd been distracted by the activity around him, so it took Sapian a moment to fully process the warrior's last statement before he realized what he had said. "Spared from what exactly?" he asked.

Lucas stopped what he was doing to address Sapian. "This world, all you see around you. This was never meant to be. They spread like a virus across the devastation they inflicted. This world will be cleansed so that my people can return to this place. They will yield to Omega, the true descendant of the ancestors, or perish by his hand."

He'd heard people speak of the ancestors, some in an almost reverent manner, and others who cursed them as some sort of oppressive overlords. He'd never once heard the name Omega. "Omega? So they believe that you're their gods...right, at least some of them?"

"What they believe is actually not that far from the truth. Some of them believe that their creators fled this land to explore the galaxy; some believe they were forced to leave. The latter is closer to the facts. To escape this cursed world was the only real choice they had."

Sapian thought about the words of this lone crusader. Whether his spin on the mythology of these people was true or false, the Stranger believed in what he was saying, sure enough. A hundred questions fought for priority in his mind. He looked over at the mercs again and remembered what the Stranger had said before.

"So you're trying to recruit me?" he asked. It was the only logical explanation.

"In just a few short hours I will re-open the Viaduct for my master. He will take his rightful place at the helm of this world, and the frail system before you will cease to exist. You will no longer have to live as vermin. There will be nobody left to hunt you."

The Warper walked off toward one of the small, automated droids, which he presumed were performing tests before the big game. A couple of the mercs sized him up from the other side of the platform. He wondered if they'd received the same treatment.

"You must have realized by now that you have no place in this world. You can die as one of them or you can fight by my side," Lucas' monotone voice implied the obvious ultimatum. "I brought you here with a specific job in mind, one to which you are most suited, given your part in our previous venture."

"We have crossed paths with an enforcer twice within the last cycle and I believe it is fate that our paths will cross once again. This time, I intend it to be the last. He has something my master requires. You have seen it before when I recovered it during the raid this morning. I want you to recover the item and put an end to this meddling anomaly once and for all. Consider it an induction into the house of Omega."

Sapian weighed his options. If Zed had been tipping off the feds, they'd have trouble tracking him down again; he could start from scratch. For the first time since he could remember, he was making progress. The Effigy's insane rambling was starting to make sense.

It sounded like the safer option if the Stranger was to succeed, but the thought of killing again, someone he knew was innocent, made him sick to his stomach and what the Stranger had planned out sounded a lot like genocide.

Whether his place in all this was in this world or a new order, it seemed he was to play the part of the assassin, the murderer. Maybe he would only find peace if he put the past behind him once and for all, get his hands dirty one more time in exchange for a place at the head of the table.

He turned away from the others to watch the rising sun. He felt around for the chip in the small pocket of his jumpsuit and wondered what kind of information could be on it, and what part it would play in the time ahead. He'd come face to face with both the men the Effigy spoke of. Only one of them had proposed any kind of reasonable venture so far. He'd hovered over the thin grey line between good and evil so long now he wasn't sure if he'd ever known the difference.

Sapian looked back at the Stranger who was waiting patiently, "Looks like I'm your man, so to speak."

The Stranger threw him a reassuring nod as the two mercs slid the last panel over the chamber. He typed a few commands into the tablet on his gauntlet and the drones formed a circle around the platform.

All at once there was a jolt and the whole place shook. Every piece of the Viaduct seemed to creak to life. Small lights lit up around every console and panel as energy streamed through the ancient circuits.

Lucas wandered over to the main panel, his attention shifting between the display on his wrist, the drones, and the console, "Begin preliminary system checks. I want to be sure everything's functioning at 100% before we initiate."

Lucas looked over at Sapian who was examining a display of one of the retrofitted monitors, "It has begun! The Viaduct was programmed to disrupt symbiotic energy, which their whole city requires to function. By the time they realize anything is wrong, they will have already lost the ability to communicate with one another."

Chapter 34

The shock of the cold water hitting his face made Joss jump up to a seated position. He was lying on some kind of ceramic examination table. He wiped the water from his eyes before realizing he was missing some clothes and was only wearing his pants and boots. There was a woman standing a few meters in front of him. She was so still his eyes almost failed to register her presence at first.

His equipment was on a table to the left, within arm's reach. His first instinct was to grab his revolver, but before his hand could reach the weapon his better judgment forced him to re-evaluate the situation. If they'd left his weapons with him, that probably meant he wasn't in any immediate danger.

He casually slid off the table and scanned over his equipment for his communicator. He had no idea how long he'd been out or what had happened to Reagan and his Father. The best-case scenario was that they'd evaded capture and were on the run. It was likely the feds had at least identified them by now, even if they'd gotten away.

"Your communicator will not work in here," said the woman in an almost angelic whisper.

He felt drawn to the melodic sound of her voice. It made her seem familiar in a way, even though he didn't recognize her face, half covered by flowing hair. He tried to think back to the last thing he did remember; an ambush by the Effigy and his thugs. The revelation suggested he should get straight to the point.

"What kind of terrorist kidnaps someone then leaves them their weapons in what I'm assuming is your hideout?"

"You've likely come to the assumption we intend you no harm, nor are our intentions to terrorize. Please forgive the rude awakening and the fact that the Effigy isn't here to greet you. He thought…"

Joss cut her off, "…That I'd react better to the sight of a woman? He's probably right, anyone else might have gotten a bullet." He threw on his shirt and gear, "I've never met a bunch of criminals so concerned with bedside manner. I *am* likely a federal fugitive by now. If this somehow makes me part of some kind of outlaws club, I would have appreciated a cigarette and coffee with my wakeup call."

Joss could read that she wasn't overly impressed with his sense of humor, but seemed to be putting up with him nevertheless.

"Strange that you should refer to this meeting as such," said the woman. She stared at him with a grin. She was beautiful, in a natural sense, but she seemed to be deliberately hiding part of her face. Her combat suit complimented her slender body in a way that looked comfortable, complete with a pistol up front on which she rested her hand.

"Follow me, please. We have a lot to talk about and haven't much time," she turned to walk out the door at the other side of the room.

Joss examined the bunker-like structure as he followed her through the winding corridors. He'd gathered that they were underground due to the lack of windows, and the musky smell in the air. The design of the place resembled architectural styles of other ancient buildings he'd seen in the wastes. Stone, steel, and concrete, no meta-coral, so he guessed he was still beyond the wall.

Each time they came to an intersection there was what looked like a map painted on the wall, with a red dot informing you of your current location. In the top right hand corner it read, 'Level 6' and below it there were words he didn't recognize, presumably different languages spoken by the ancients. Different sections were color-coded and painted lines ran off down different passageways, presumably to the designated locations. He scanned the maps for anything that looked like an exit. However, without any idea of the scale of the place, or what every dot on the map was, he'd probably get lost or captured ten times over before getting anywhere close to the exit.

As they continued through the complex, it became even more obvious he wasn't a prisoner. People that walked by in the corridor stared at him like they would any other stranger in their home, but there was no hostility at all and they certainly didn't fear him.

The woman quickened her pace, walking a few steps further in front of him before stopping beside a door. She held out her hand gesturing to him to enter. The wall around the entrance had cracked from water damage and the sign faded. Where there was once a door there was now an old curtain draped over the entrance. Joss pushed it aside and edged through.

The room ahead appeared to be a small amphitheater of sorts, a briefing room big enough for 40 or 50 people. The Effigy stood at the front with his back to him. His attention seemed to be divided between a console on the podium in the center of the floor and a wall of screens playing the morning news broadcast. The monitors that were powered up looked bright in the dull chamber. Joss' eyes ached, likely an after effect of whatever drug the Effigy used to render him unconscious.

As his vision adjusted to the brightness, he noticed that the signal looked a little rough, but it was clear enough that Joss could make out what was happening. The reporter was elaborating on an attack on a convoy outside the city and cross-referenced it with the past actions of the Effigy's followers.

Her voice sounded muffled through the old speakers. "The Effigy once made a name for himself as a powerful figure amongst certain left-wing public groups. His followers called him a spirit of hope for the future. Others called him a false idol, accusing him of undermining the alliance with unrealistic ideals for this post-war society."

"This turn toward urban terror tactics has led to further condemnation of the Effigy's cause, causing his followers to act out violently against authorities, striking fear into those who oppose them! It looks like the rioting will continue well into tomorrow."

"Good morning!" boomed a loud voice. The sound echoed around the room.

The Effigy switched off the broadcast, seemingly unfazed by the slander, "Do you think I could turn myself in and tell them I was with you the whole time."

Joss was careful to maintain a neutral tone, which was complemented by his casual stance, "I don't think that would do you much good. I'm probably a wanted man myself by now. Besides, kidnapping a city enforcer is hardly a justifiable alibi."

"You're probably right," said the Effigy, bobbing his head respectfully to the woman escorting Joss. "Thank you Jada." He added, in a softer tone, before watching her leave the room gracefully.

Joss noticed a passive, yet emotional connection between the two. The subtle display seemed to lighten the mood somewhat. One hand rested in his pocket while the other hung by his side, not too far away from his holstered pistol. If his years on the force had taught him anything, it was that you could never be too cautious. "I have to say it's a bit risky isn't it; bringing a cop inside your secret hideout?"

The Effigy turned to face Joss, "Bringing in any stranger to this place wouldn't be without risk, but I don't think of you as an outsider, Joss. You are more than welcome."

Joss raised his eyebrows at the unusual response. The Effigy knew him by name, a fact that made him wonder what he might want with him specifically. All he knew right now was that he felt moderately safe in an unfamiliar environment. He still had no idea where the nearest exit might be, so he'd have difficulty making a run for it. He scanned around the structure and wondered about its function. "Interesting place you have here," he said. The statement was as good an icebreaker as any.

"This location is just one of many terminals deserted by our ancestors and hidden from our kind. It was built as a hiding place, and an effective one at that. I had an idea of its general location and it still took years to find the entrance."

The Effigy turned to look at Joss over his shoulder. "The irony; a hiding place for humanity that remained hidden from people for 1000 years," the Effigy laughed to himself and turned all the way around to face Joss, "I know you must have many questions, but let me start by telling you that I brought you here for your own good."

Joss took a few steps forward. "You drugged and kidnapped me. On top of whatever federal charges…" Joss paused momentarily to examine his would-be captor. He noticed apprehension in the Effigy's behavior the instant he'd moved closer.

Joss had experience in reading body language. The years of grueling interrogations had taught him how to maintain a dominant demeanor. The Effigy looked vulnerable for a second and Joss decided to seize this opportunity. He started in on him like he would any other perp; by pushing his buttons.

"What else is there?" Joss continued. "Conspiring with a known murderer, not to mention assaulting an officer! To say that the horizon's looking a little grey for you would be an understatement!"

The Effigy laughed at him and moved closer, "My eyes have been fixated on the storm ahead for as long as I can remember. It is your future that concerns me. What lies ahead for you is far worse than you can imagine."

Joss' probing seemed to have had the reverse effect. The Effigy appeared to loosen up following his attempt to provoke an emotional reaction.

"This is the second time I've saved your ass today and yet you fail to see it," the Effigy's change in tone suggested he was now piloting the conversation.

He began watching Joss for the purpose of trying to gauge what he was thinking.

"I admit, my shooting's a little rusty," he said. The Effigy could almost see the cogs turning in the young officer's head. "I would have preferred to kill that savage, but who am I to argue with fate?"

Joss stood fast and frowned at the masked man and his disfigured features. The sudden feeling of confusion forced him to backtrack over the events of the day, trying to decipher what he was talking about.

The Effigy had been slowly edging closer and was now standing within a meter of Joss, invading his personal space. He lunged forward, grabbing his bruised ribs before Joss had the chance to move back.

Joss cried out, "What the fuck are you doing?!"

The Effigy let out a husky laugh muffled from behind his mask "Painful?" he boomed. "If it weren't for me, you'd have far less to worry about. Maybe I should have let him tear you apart like he did your partner."

Joss drew back and stared at him. The Effigy's right eye was hidden behind the mask and his left was surrounded by heavy scar tissue. Joss felt the seriousness of his stare through the disguise, forcing him to confront a startling reality.

"You're the sniper?" Joss looked away and replayed the events in his head. "Then, why the hell didn't you stick around? Why not take them all out?"

"If I'd held my position any longer I'd be inside a prison cell facing charges of terrorism. I couldn't risk a confrontation with the FRA."

It was a good enough reason, but didn't explain why he was there to start with. Joss' police mentality kicked back in and he moved on to the next line of questioning.

"Why were you even there in the first place? What's your interest in the ape?"

"Sapian is not your enemy, even if he doesn't know it yet," said the Effigy.

"Back at the square it sure looked like the two of them were working together. If you were there this morning, you know that was the guy leading the team. You could have saved us all a whole bunch of trouble if you'd just ended the bastard right there and then."

"This morning I was there for you. It was sheer coincidence that they happened to be there too, although I knew they would be. You could call the connection fate, if you believe in such a thing."

"What the hell's that supposed to mean? How the hell could you have known I'd be there, at that exact moment of time?" Joss realized his voice had got a couple of decibels louder.

"The knowledge I possess gives me the luxury of a unique perspective. Many of my disciples call it a pre-emptive vision, but in time you will discover the truth of how I know so much."

"I hope you didn't bring me all the way out here for one of your bullshit sermons! I take action based on the facts and evidence to back them up. I see two crooks running hand in hand, my gut tells me that they're working the same scam."

"You're not the only one struggling to find their place in this world. Believe me when I tell you that you can trust him. He is an ally within the ranks of our enemy and you will need his help in the hours to come. You must learn to trust the most unlikely of allies if we are to have any chance of stopping what is about to happen."

Joss took a few seconds to process the cryptic response. Again, his words suggested significance when referring to him. The ghostly figure glared at him in a manner that was almost penetrating, like he was waiting for something to show, something he knew about him, yet they had never met before. Joss felt the intrusion and it made his gun hand twitchy, despite the fact he seemed to be in no danger. The Effigy wanted something from him.

Joss straightened his body and adopted a more assertive pose, "You didn't just bring me here to tell me I owe you one. How about we get to the part where you tell me why you need me?"

The Effigy laughed at the reemergence of the no-nonsense cop he'd been hoping for. "Those detective instincts haven't dulled a bit," he said sarcastically.

The Effigy moved back over to the center console and powered up every screen on the wall in front of them. On the left monitor, a building plan appeared. Joss recognized the structure with the isometric image; it was the blueprints for the Velodrome, a place he'd visited at least once a year in his youth. The initiation ceremony was held there every year when the young Paladin returned from the badlands. The fact that today was the day of the event had totally slipped his mind with everything that was happening.

On the other side was a topographical map of the area surrounding the Velodrome. As the display rotated diagonally on its axis, what appeared to be a network of tunnels became visible, all leading in a different location outside of the city. One of the tunnels in particular was highlighted and led to what looked like a sizable structure not far from the wall. A familiar red dot flashed around the location. He wasn't as far from the city as he'd originally thought.

The Effigy raised both hands in the air and gestured toward the screens, "I brought you here to warn you of an attack planned for the ceremony this afternoon."

Joss' eyes narrowed as he tried to discover whether or not the Effigy was telling the truth. He reviewed what he knew about the man. He was a conspiracy theorist, viewed by the majority of the public to be a terrorist or a violent activist at best. He compared that with what he remembered his father had told him a day earlier; how he'd thought the Effigy was somehow being used as a scapegoat. He decided to play along for the time being.

"If what you say is true, why bring me all the way out here? I'm assuming we're still miles from the city. You could have gone through the proper channels. A bomb threat on the Velodrome wouldn't have being taken likely."

"I thought that it was important that you saw this place for yourself. I believed it was necessary to bring you here to prove to you once and for all that I can be trusted. You just witnessed a small display of our true enemy's power. Believe me when I tell you that this warrior is but the first soldier of many, and the Velodrome is where they will strike first."

"There are representatives from all 12 chapters of the Order inside the walls of that stadium! I'm just one man. We still have time to reach them on the long-range frequency."

"The enemy has taken precautions that inhibit us from communicating with each other. It was the first preliminary measure when the Viaduct was reactivated. Every aspect of the city's governing hierarchy has been compromised. I tried to warn your father of this, but the heat from the FRA forced me into hiding."

Joss had noticed the parallels between the Effigy's words and what his father had told him the day before, "You were the one feeding my father the information. You knew about all of this then and you backed off because of fear of being caught?!"

"I have my own part to play in the downfall of the enemy and I couldn't jeopardize the mission or risk them finding this place. The public had already begun to turn against us. I knew if he saw the amulet, it would act as a message he couldn't possibly ignore, even if it were the last time I was able to make contact with him."

"My money was on someone from the agency for the informant, someone who could have found the artifact after the war. The trick with the amulet might have worked better than you could have imagined. I think you've got the old man believing you were actually one of them, one of the Acolytes."

The Effigy hesitated in a manner that suggested he'd been waiting for Joss to come to this assumption or at least hoped he would. "And what do you believe?"

"My faith's actually not what it used to be and you don't exactly fit the description. If what you've said is true, your methods leave a lot to be desired," Joss paused and folded his arms. "That's just my opinion. And by my count, you're four saviors short of a prophecy."

"Is it in your nature to plead ignorance unless the evidence is right in front of you?" asked the Effigy. The question sounded more rhetorical.

Joss raised his eyebrows as if to tell the Effigy he was right.

The Effigy stepped forward and placed a hand on Joss' shoulder, "This narrow vision might have kept you alive over the years, but it's what's holding you back now." The Effigy's voice sounded deeper than before, his tone was almost identical to his father's.

"Your father and his associates have had time to put the pieces together themselves. Will you be able to put your differences aside when the time comes? Can you do what you must to get the job done?"

Joss thought about his options. He was starting to understand why so many followed the man before him. He had a way of giving you all the right answers before you even had chance to ask the questions. Something in his methods gave you the drive and desire to push forward through any comprehendible doubt.

Joss walked over to the screen to have a closer look at the map. "You said the tunnels run directly beneath the stadium? How long will it take me to get there on foot?"

"On foot, you would never reach the stadium in time. My people were good enough to double back and retrieve your glidecycle after the FRA had bugged out. It shouldn't take you longer than half an hour to reach the entrance beneath the Velodrome. It brings you out inside the outer wall. I have the plans and duty rosters for the FRA security detail inside the stadium. You won't know whom you can trust once inside. The FRA is compromised and it is likely every agent on duty is loyal to the Commissar and what he has planned.

"That's just great. I've dreamt about a 1000 different ways I could stick it to the Commissar, but all out war against his private army wasn't exactly at the top of my list."

"Try to think of the events about to happen as a pre-emptive strike." said the Effigy in a reasoning tone. "If we can pull this off, we can stop another war from happening and prevent more innocent people from dying."

"Before I go, you spoke briefly of your part in all this. Don't suppose you'd have time to fill me in?"

"Every disciple you see here has been preparing for what is to come for more than a decade. Trust me when I tell you, you will know when I have succeeded. Trust me as I have trusted you. Your brother waits for you inside the stadium. You are alone now, but you will you find your allies by your side when you need them the most."

Chapter 35

Akura tried a third time to communicate with the temple, and then again as they got closer, until he finally got through.

"Patriarch Victus, are you reading me?" asked Akura. The signal was riddled with interference. "We've been trying to reach you for half an hour."

"Gailan, my friend. What could be so urgent on the morn of your son's initiation? I thought you'd be at the Velodrome by now." He was dressed in the ceremonial garment of their chapter, a flowing robe with the intricately decorated chest plate. The chapter heirloom hung around his neck as always, complimenting the spectacular armor.

"My lord! Where are the other council members?"

"Most of the council was escorted to the ceremony early, as a precaution to avoid the riots. I was about to leave when I picked up your transmission on the emergency frequency."

Prefect Le'san moved into the frame on the view screen. "High Patriarch, please, if our suspicions are correct we may have very little time!"

"We have reason to believe the Commissar plans to overthrow the Order. He has allied himself with the menace responsible for the recent attacks."

Akura held up the two pieces of the broken amulet.

The old man attempted to squint through the distortion, "I don't believe it…the seal of the Acolytes!"

All of a sudden the Patriarch turned to look at something at the other side of the room, out of frame. It sounded like someone entering the room. As Patriarch Victus started to speak, the signal broke up again and the screen went blank.

"Something's not right," said Gailan.

"We must hurry to the temple. With most of the Paladin at the ceremony, it will be lightly guarded, vulnerable to attack."

Chapter 36

At the heart of the city, Darahk and his team closed in on Watch Tower. They had been monitoring the ground floor entrance for a while now and nothing seemed to be amiss.

There had been much debate on how to handle the situation. Storming the building from the top levels was Lord Akura's idea, but the Inquisitor had quickly shot down the plan, saying that it was a gung-ho response to purely circumstantial evidence.

"Scheduled reports indicate only the regular guard rotation. There's nothing to suggest that the Commissar might be holding up in there with an army waiting for us. Even if he is guilty, there's no reason for him to suspect we know anything."

"And you think he's guilty, Lieutenant?" asked Darahk.

She was his right hand and she'd never given him reason to doubt her counsel, but they were wading in dark waters. If they were wrong, they could be looking at life behind bars themselves.

"I think that there's a lot that needs explaining and our next logical move should be to confront him," Rosair knew Darahk was thinking the same thing, but it was her job to offer her opinion, even object if she saw fit. Ultimately, it would come down to his order.

Darahk held the binoculars up to his face again, scanning the area around the entrance. Surveillance of the upper levels would have been useful, but all federal buildings were shielded from external scans. All they had was the staff rota and how many troops were on duty.

"Lieutenant, we'll enter through the main entrance under light guard while the rest of the squad comes up from the sublevel parking. We can deactivate surveillance down there long enough for us to get inside the building."

"The advantages of breaking into a building with the same federal security systems," said Rosair. "I'll call to request an emergency audience with the man himself and inform them that we're minutes away."

"Make it so, Lieutenant," said Darahk.

Darahk watched Rosair return to the room next door where they'd been trying to establish communications for the last hour.

"Sir," Rosair began, "we weren't able to raise the tower on any frequency, even the short range transmitters are down and we're right across the street. Closed circuit systems only, at least we can talk to each other." She tapped the discreet receiver resting inside her ear.

Darahk rubbed his temple with his thumb and index finger, " If commutations are down all over the city the prognosis doesn't look good. I guess we're walking right into the lobby to ask to see the man. Did you try Malone?"

"I couldn't reach him either. Even the 'Director' didn't have a gadget on hand for this particular situation." she said derogatorily.

Darahk cracked a slight smirk before turning the face his team. He placed his hands behind his back and decided it was time to walk the line; ten of his best troops at the ready, including the Lieutenant and himself.

"You all know what we could be up against. Despite the accusations against the Commissar, I've got to give him the benefit of the doubt. However, I'd be a fool not to utilize any of the precautionary measures available to me."

Darahk turned to his third in command, a burly sergeant named Castle. His chin looked as hard as a rock. He wasn't as creative as Rosair, but he'd never disappointed him once in the three years under his command.

"Sergeant, I want this done quietly and without injury to fellow FRA personnel. If any of your men have any doubts about what we are about to do, they can consider themselves relieved."

"We will follow your orders to the letter, Inquisitor! We'll be using stun-charge rounds with regular ammo as emergency backup."

"Very good, Sergeant, let's hope it won't come to that," said Darahk. "Be ready to move in when we have an ETA from the Lieutenant."

Rosair stepped forward, "You heard the Inquisitors. Let's try and do this quietly. Those are fellow agents inside. We've got Plan B to fall back on if shit goes south. Be ready to move out in ten minutes!"

...

Eleven minutes later, Darahk and Rosair arrived outside FRA HQ with two armed troopers. Blackwell and Simmons kept back three meters and had their weapons lowered in a non-threatening manner.

With a thought, Darahk activated his closed circuit transmitter, "Beta team, prepare to enter the building in 20 seconds. Use caution. If they're onto us, they may be under orders to shoot us on sight."

"Yes, sir," whispered Castle over the comm, "We'll rendezvous on the operations level."

Darahk and the Alpha team moved through the peaceful lobby. Two guards made small talk ahead of them.

They hardly noticed them approaching until they were right in front of them. The smaller guard turned to acknowledge them

"Inquisitor Darahk," said the stout guard, "the Commissar awaits the report on your mission. He's expecting you in operations."

Darahk had his poker face well practiced. He was surprised that the Commissar was expecting a visit, but he didn't let it show.

"Yes, Sergeant, lead the way," he replied, throwing Rosair a look.

"This way, please." said the second guard.

As they walked toward the elevator, he tried to think of reasons why the Commissar might have been expecting him. The first one that came to mind was that they were busted. If so, they were ready for action.

The second was the communications breakdown. Darahk's mission reports were usually expected within 24 hours of carrying out an opp. There was a possibility that the Commissar had thought it was only a matter of time before the Inquisitor reported to him in person. It was the second reason that troubled him the most. A citywide communication failure was a major security issue, especially with the festivities.

Darahk thought he'd see what the guards had to say about it all.

"Hey!" he said, addressing the men. "Have you two heard anything about what's causing the communications interference?"

The two guards looked at each other, before the stout one spoke.

"It's nothing serious, sir. The Commissar's tech supervisor informed us of a few security tests they were running before the ceremony this afternoon."

"That so?" said Rosair. "We've been trying to reach you for the last two hours and even the FRA HQ has gone dark."

The guards looked at one another again. Their almost identical expression could have been mistaken for a distorted mirror image.

"Maybe FRA tech support was running the tests there too," said the stout guard again.

Out of the corner of his eye, Darahk saw Rosair's posture change. No way they were so stupid that they assumed he didn't know every single thing that went on in *his* building. They were definitely up to something.

"It's possible," she replied, playing along. "We've got so much going on right now it's easy to lose track of the maintenance schedule. "

Darahk's face looked like it was carved from stone. He just cleared his throat and said nothing. He watched as the Lieutenant examined them passively. It looked like shorty was the one in charge here and if they were heading toward a trap, he'd have to be the first to go. He hadn't decided whether the other one was just playing dumb or out of the loop completely.

…

Below, the Beta team had made it through the parking lot and waited for a patrolling guard to move away from the lower level entrance. Another guard manned a console behind a secure door and bulletproof glass.

They had to get past this single security point before they could make their way up through the fire escape. The remaining six agents had split into two teams. Castle and two others crouched behind a transport and waited for exactly the right moment. They had to wait until the other guard was out of sight before they hit him.

The three others waited behind a large pillar led by Jennings, a tall female officer with short-cropped hair. She welcomed the wandering guard by sweeping his legs out from under him and shooting him with the charge weapon before he could shout out.

Castle and the others made a dash for it. Willis and Gardner moved in without a sound, and crouched down below the bulletproof window. Gardner, the agent in front, took a few seconds to jack the locking mechanism.

The door slid open and the sitting guard shot to his feet and tried to grab his weapon. Willis fired his first, dropping the guard like a sack of spuds. The man slumped in his seat and rolled back behind the console.

"Checkpoint clear," said Castle, signaling to the others. He walked over to the unconscious guard and pushed his helmet down over his eyes. There was a shutter-blind that covered the majority of the window. He toggled the string on the right- hand side until it closed.

Gardner and Willis crouched by the console and entered a few commands.

"Beginning playback," said Willis in a monotone voice. "Standing by on level 5, level 6, 10. Confirm surveillance playback..."

Gardener waved his hand over the cam in the top right hand corner of the room. The corresponding screen showed an earlier recording of the unconscious guard going about his business. "That's affirmative," he said before addressing Castle. "We're all clear from here, sir."

"Well done," he said. "Check the stairs."

The three other agents headed for the entrance to the stairwell. Jennings opened the door a small amount before sticking a mirror through on a long pole.

"Looks clear. Quiet, too. I think we're good, sir."

"Move out!" ordered Castle.

...

Darahk felt the elevator slow down as they reached operations. The doors slid open with a hiss and the guards moved aside to let the Inquisitor and his people out first.

Rosair stepped out of the elevator ahead of Darahk. Blackwell and Simmons followed.

The Lieutenant quickly sized up four guards strategically placed around the room. They were wearing energy neutralizers and light armor designed for defense in close quarters. The stun rounds would be useless and only heavy rounds would penetrate that armor. Good job they were packing both. She could see the Commissar's chair at the other end of the room, facing away from them toward the window.

Two more of the Commissar's Elite guards appeared from elsewhere in the room as the chair turned around to face them. The man sitting there wasn't whom they expected.

Darahk couldn't hold back the look of surprise. In the Commissar's place was the guard he recognized from the interrogation room at LEX HQ a day earlier, the man posted to guard Joss Akura. On his chest were two wings, indicating he was a major. He'd been dressed in grunt gear when they'd last met.

Rosair knew an ambush when she saw one and took action accordingly, striking the stout guard with an elbow to the solar plexus, knocking the wind out of him. A low kick to the back of the legs dropped him to his knees.

Darahk was waiting for Rosair to act, and followed suit by grabbing the other guard's rifle, spinning him so he could act as a human shield. He aimed the rifle at the Commissar's men.

"What the hell is this?!" said the clueless guard. He really looked like he had no idea what was going on.

Blackwell and Simmons' weapons were up and they'd b-lined for the closest cover. Blackwell leaned behind a pillar to her right and Simmons crouched behind a large vase to the left of Darahk.

The stout guard looked up at Rosair as he slowly put his hands behind the back of his head.

The Major stood up from his seat and pointed his revolver at them.

"It appears that our suspicions are correct," he said. "We received a tip-off that the FRA had been compromised, and that the Inquisitor's loyalty was in question. Lower your weapons and we can avoid making a mess of the Commissar's office."

"We're not the traitors here! Where is he?" demanded Darahk.

"Far from here, Inquisitor," said the Major.

"Let the record show that I am here to arrest the Commissar and any members of his staff or Elite guard believed to be involved in conspiring against the coalition government."

The Major laughed in the background, "What do you think this is, you fool? The second you entered I hit the silent alarm. You have seconds before troops burst through those doors."

The transmitter feed between Darahk and the others had been open the whole time and Castle could hear everything going on in the room.

"Alarm systems deactivated, sir. We're about to join the party," he said over the closed circuit, his voice on edge.

"You don't know how right you are," growled the Lieutenant through gritted teeth.

"It's not to late to put a stop to all this. What is the Commissar planning with the Teleporter? yelled Darahk. "What is he going to do with the coralite? What's his next move?!"

Rosair noticed the closest of the Commissar's men edging closer. He pointed his weapon right at her, "Don't come any closer!" she commanded, with a look that promised repercussions. The penny was about to drop and she could feel the tension.

The stalemate was shattered as Castle and the others smashed through the two doors, one on either side of the elevator!

Darahk wasted no time giving the order, "Take 'em out!"

The room instantly erupted into a furious combat zone.

With Rosair distracted for a split second, the stout guard spun around before lunging at her!

She saw the sloppy attack a mile away, stepping back to bring the butt of the gun down on the ridge of his nose knocking him out. As he dropped, she noticed the Elite guard in front of her about to pull the trigger. Her finger squeezed all by itself. One to the head! She exhaled slowly, taking the time to find her next target.

The clueless guard made an attempt to run back to the elevator before being riddled with bullets, the barrage forcing Darahk to dive for cover.

Willis tried to push forward, but was taken down by a round to the chest.

Rosair scored a retaliatory shot to the head, cursing herself for being a moment too late.

Blackwell opened fire, forcing two more of the Elite guard to scramble for cover.

At the back of the office, the two guards worked hard to protect the Major, tipping over the large meta-coral crafted desk and taking cover behind it.

Darahk jumped up, coming face to face with an approaching guard. Too close to get off a shot, he barreled right at him taking him to the ground!

They exchanged a few punches before the guardsman drew his blade.

The cowards behind the desk fired wildly across the room, making everyone duck for cover, including their men.

Castle's eyes met the Lieutenant's. She gave him the signal that they could use a distraction. Castle snapped a smoker from his vest and threw it into the center of the room.

In a second, visibility was reduced to a meter or two in front of them. Darahk could see a knife poking through the smoke screen. He kicked it out of the hand holding it. He could see the outline of a chair to his right. He grabbed it, lifting it high before bringing it down on the unassuming bastard.

He crouched down again as a barrage of bullets hit the furniture around him. Once the smoke began to clear, he could see that his sidearm was within reach.

An Elite guard shuffled through the smoke meters away from Darahk. He noticed the Inquisitor to his left a moment before he took a bullet to the temple.

Darahk looked at the guardsman's frozen expression as he lay on the ground. Blood poured from his wound across the floor.

"Drop your weapons!" yelled Darahk as the gunfire eased up a little "No one's coming to help you and nobody else needs to die!"

"You're too late, Darahk. I am not the one who will decide whether your life will be spared. Only those loyal to Omega will survive the onslaught. Kill them…"

He was cut off mid-sentence as the windows were smashed in behind him, and a well-aimed shot struck his face.

Malone and his troops burst through the glass on ropes and start targeting the Elite guards. They scattered like roaches, desperately trying to find cover between the crossfire.

"Surrender! It's over!" Darahk said to the remaining three guards.

One was about to take a shot when Darahk put him down, shooting him twice in the chest at point blank range.

Malone engaged another in close combat, and managed to disarm him. Two of his men took him to the ground a second later. The last one threw his weapon down the instant he realized he the only one left standing.

"We've taken control of the lower levels. Is the combat area secure?" asked Malone.

Rosair looked around at all of the still bodies. The stout guard was starting to regain consciousness, so she rammed the barrel of her sidearm into the back of his neck.

"Area secure," she yelled back to Malone.

Darahk got to his feet and shuffled over to Blackwell who had taken a slug in the arm. "Is everybody all right?"

"Willis is down, sir," shouted Castle. One of the others checked his vitals and turned to Castle shaking his head.

Rosair and Castle exchanged glances. Another one of her men was slumped on the ground by the wall with the top half of his head missing.

"Willis and Paxton are dead, Inquisitor," she said mournfully.

"Damn it. The Commissar's not even here!" barked Darahk.

Malone holstered his weapon while the others saw to the casualties on the ground. "When I wasn't able to establish contact with anyone on the long range frequency, I suspected an ambush."

"The Commissar could already be at the Velodrome, or hiding out somewhere else entirely," said Darahk, pacing back and forth. "If he knew we were coming here, it's likely a similar ambush awaits Akura.

Rosair dragged the stout guard over from the elevator, throwing him in front of Malone and Darahk.

"Speak!" she ordered.

The agent spat a mouthful of blood out on the ground, "What is there to tell you? The Major told you himself, it's already too late."

Darahk crouched down so he was at the agent's eye-level. "He knew we'd come here, but he either didn't anticipate we'd come with reinforcements or he simply didn't care. Either way he has abandoned you."

"Just go ahead and arrest me already. When Omega takes control of this city, I'll have a place in the new Order."

Darahk looked up at Rosair as Castle dragged over one of the other Elite guards with a bullet wound to the gut. The traitor groaned and whimpered as the blood ran down his uniform.

"It seems to me that not every agent in the building is a traitor and I'm sure you've kept tabs on those you knew were loyal to the cause and those who weren't."

Castle threw the bleeding agent with the gut shot on the ground in front of them.

The stout agent laughed, sputtering through the blood behind his teeth. "You simply don't have the cell space for all of us," he said. "The Commissar has spent years preparing for Omega's return.'

Darahk drew a blade from the side of his boot. The edge looked sharp and the blade glistened as if it was likely cleaned and sharpened on a daily basis.

"Cages are for animals, boy," he said, removing a glove and touching the edge of the blade with his finger. "Since the end of the war I've dedicated my life to putting animals behind bars and this is where it has led me."

The rogue agent's smug grin started to droop as he witnessed the change in the Inquisitor. You could see the fear welling up inside him.

Darahk held the knife a couple of inches from the agent's face. Rosair and Castle look at one another.

The Inquisitor continued. "Since the end of the war, I have made it my business to stop those who threaten the peace I fought for. We cage them up away from society in the hope that incarceration will alter their way of thinking. When I look at you, you and your comrade here, I don't see animals. I see traitors. The ultimate threat to everything I fought and killed for. If there's anything I've learnt from my experience as a soldier, it's that there are no cages for traitors."

Then, Darahk grabbed the injured agent and pulled him close before driving the knife into his heart. The agent tried to cry out, but the breath was snatched from him. He flailed around for a few seconds, crying out before his voice turned hoarse.

Rosair's arms dropped from their folded position. She exchanged shocked glances with Castle. Malone didn't budge, only looked at the ground as if to give Darahk breathing room to work his angle.

Darahk wiped the knife clean on the dead agent's uniform and looked up at the quivering agent before him.

"A cold blade through the heart is a remedy I've found effective against traitors, long before your mother decided it was safe to bring you into this world."

The agent tried to crawl away before Castle grabbed him holding him firmly. It seemed as big a shock to him as to any of them, seeing this new side of the Inquisitor; a man who he believed to be 'by the book'.

"What?!... You can't just!...You can't let him."

"Quiet!" screamed Darahk. "You speak to me! They can't help you! You're going to tell me everything. Every shred of information you know or I'll make sure you see what your traitorous heart looks like before I drive my knife through it!"

Chapter 37

Reagan felt uncomfortable in full ceremonial attire. He'd returned from the badlands in the same robe and tunic he'd left in three years earlier. It was customary to wash and repair that one uniform whenever required throughout the trials. Upon your return, you were presented with the uniform of a fully-fledged Paladin.

He'd been looking forward to this day since he'd started his training, but with everything that was happening, the significance had escaped him. What he would face next would be the real test of duty. To overcome the conflict and find the strength within, the strength to make the hard decisions; this was what it truly meant to be a Paladin of the Order.

"Reagan," said a familiar voice. "I've been looking for you. The ceremony is about to start."

Reagan turned to address his superior. Ra'suun was about ten years older than him and was studying to be a Prefect. He'd trained at his father's dojo when he was a tenderfoot and had been one of the more ambitious of his father's students.

"Have you received word from my Father or Prefect Le'san? I've been waiting for a message from them for the last hour," said Reagan.

"I was about to ask you the same question. They couldn't be reached on the designated frequency or any other, for that matter. The FRA reports communications disruption, likely a result of the Effigy's meddling."

"That's not it. My father, he should be here by now. He wouldn't miss this, unless the circumstances were extraordinary," said Reagan.

"I'm sorry, Reagan," said Ra'suun. "The decision's been made to start without them."

"Which prefect is in charge of the parade?" asked Reagan.

"Well…Prefect Ravenclaw is next in the chain of command. He has been placed in charge in your father's absence."

"Take me to him immediately!" demanded Reagan.

....

Gailan watched Le'san's hawk as it soared overhead, surveying the scene. The temple grounds were quiet. With the sky train down, they had no choice but to approach from the rear through the mountain pass, less than an hour's ride from the Akura residence. He rode with every Paladin he could muster, 12 of his best plus Le'san and himself.

They entered the grounds through an area that was usually guarded. The silence was eerie because it was normally a bustling environment. Akura tugged on his steed's reigns to keep him steady. They hadn't seen a soul since they'd arrived.

Le'san's hawk banked right suddenly before swooping down to Le'san's hand. "Everywhere looks deserted," said Le'san. Even with the majority of the Paladin at the ceremony, there should be guards at the main security checkpoints."

"I don't like this," said Akura, in a low, suspicious tone.

Another Paladin mounted on horseback galloped back from one of the surrounding buildings.

"There's no sign of anyone and communications are still down," said the Paladin, as he rode alongside Akura.

Gailan could see that the Paladin needed to say something. "Speak now, my boy," boomed Akura. "We walk an uncertain path."

"That's just it, my lord. I'm having trouble believing that we're riding to our sanctuary expecting an ambush."

"We'll know soon enough. For all our sakes, I hope that you're right," muttered Akura. "Circle the grounds again and stay sharp. Meet us at the main entrance."

Akura approached the temple like he had 1000 times before, but never under these circumstances. Riding beside his best friend into uncertainty, he couldn't help but think back to the time the war had ended. After the 12 chapters signed the treaty, every one of them rode through the mountain pass in full ceremonial garments. Akura's chapter rode alongside its old enemies, led by Le'san. It wasn't until that moment that the idea of peace had really started to sink in.

He examined the expression on Le'san's face and wondered if he was thinking the same thing, but he'd always found the old shaman hard to read; a fact that continued to intrigue him. Now, they approached this monument of peace and unity with the fear that they'd be attacked by their own. The fear he was feeling wasn't the possibility of battle, but rather that everything they had fought for in the past would have been for nothing.

Even though he'd been warned of the future and even expected it to a degree, the truth that the prophecy was finally coming true was difficult to believe. *Had so little changed in 20 years?* The idea occurred to him that the old hatred had never been forgotten. It had just been relegated to the subconscious. Maybe he was just as ignorant as everyone else; blind to the fact that they were no better than they were back then.

They were almost at the entrance when Le'san saw a young rider approaching rapidly, tearing around the east corner of the temple at full speed. "Here he comes!..." said Le'san, pointing in that general direction. "He looks to be in distress!"

The rider was far enough away that his actions appeared muted in the distance. He waved his free arm frantically and seemed to be yelling something they couldn't hear or make out.

"Prepare yourself!" commanded Akura. He extended out his hand in an open palm, signaling to the men to spread out.

They adjusted their formation so they were staggered two or three meters apart.

He scanned between each of the small windows surrounding the huge door. Walkways ran around the structure on every level, nothing! No signs of life at all. He looked back at his rider in time to see him struck by an arrow, knocking him flying from his horse.

"Fall back!" shouted Akura, just as he noticed two small doors open out to the walkway on the second and third level. His reactions hadn't shown any sign of slowing over the years and he felt the fury of battle reemerge like a waking beast.

At least 20 Paladin wearing the uniforms of Glasrail's chapter spilled out of the doors to form two lines. Each carried a crossbow as their primary weapon; the signature item of Glasrail's Paladin. Their Vesicas were usually crafted as a secondary item, to be used for defense purposes in close quarters, if their enemy managed to get close.

"Surrender, Prefect, or my men will take your life," ordered Patriarch Glasrail, over the loud speaker. "Infidels to Omega's rule shall perish. This is what your master decrees."

Akura's eyes shifted back to the huge main doors as they started to creak open. They were barely open a meter when the harpoon turret of the Wraithclaw came into view. The hulking vehicle started to edge forward with the sound of the tank tracks tearing up the floor inside the temple.

The doors were almost fully open now with the armored vehicle visible in all its glory. The Wraithclaw was a relic left over from the war and the last of its kind. Until now, it had been stripped of all of its weapons, and for the last 20 years it had only been used for ceremonial purposes.

It appeared that Glasrail had remounted the harpoon turret for his little coup. He manned the gun himself, standing behind it surrounded by three guards.

At least ten more Paladin marched beside the Wraithclaw, with more behind the vehicle, using it as cover.

Akura clenched his teeth and looked around at his Paladin. There was nothing, but light cover in the area. Glasrail's entrance was a significant statement, but he wasn't going to intimidated by a peacock showing his feathers. He knew that Glasrail wasn't much for combat and imagined how he was going to make an example of him once he'd managed to close in.

Akura was about to turn to address his men when Glasrail stepped to one side, revealing the Commissar in a more compact version of his chair, accompanied by two of his bodyguards. Gailan did his best not to look surprised, although the appearance of the Commissar was the last thing he expected.

Akura waited for the chatter to die down before addressing the traitor, "I came here to warn you of the Commissar's betrayal. I didn't expect to find you on his leash, his loyal dog!"

Akura spat on the ground in front of him in disgust. His words shot through his gritted teeth like darts, "Where is Patriarch Victus? I refuse to believe he is a part of this treachery."

Just as he finished his sentence his attention was draw to the walkway above. Three Paladin struggled to carry something, it thrashed around violently in what looked like bundle of sheets. Gailan's expression changed from his battle face to that of despair as he realized the sheets were robes. He let out a gasp as he saw the familiar figure thrown from balcony, his mouth dropped open as the rope snapped tight around Victus' neck!

Glasrail gave Akura a few seconds to absorb the situation before he made him the offer, "There's a place for you, Gailan. You have always had a knack of choosing the right side when the time came. You're a survivor!"

Akura's fists clenched the hilt of his broad sword that had materialized as soon as the large doors had started to open.

Le'san watched his friend as if he knew exactly what his response would be. He took a few steps forward on his steed, awaiting his next move.

"What of the Paladin inside the Velodrome?" yelled Gailan. "Will they be graced with the same offer?"

A sinister smirk materialized on Glasrail's face as he stared down at the defiant Prefect. "After hearing of your betrayal and how you stormed the temple, not to mention your involvement with the Effigy? Those who make the wise choice not to fight will fall in line under my command."

Akura threw Le'san a look so determined that it said it all. He didn't say a word back to the traitor, only looked down at the ground at the emblem he was standing on; the emblem of the Patronas Order.

As he lifted his head to meet the enemy, he muttered one last thing under his breath, something only his men could hear, "I don't want to see a single one of his men left standing by the end, but Glasrail is mine. I want him to witness the magnitude of his failure before I relieve him of his traitorous existence."

Glasrail leaned forward to address the Prefect beside him who was patiently awaiting his order. "Prepare to fire," he said almost casually. "Let's finish this quickly."

The traitorous Prefect dropped his arm and the arrows ripped through the sky toward Akura and his Paladin.

Gailan saw a younger Paladin to his left begin to form a shield, "No! Keep your swords at the ready, await my word." Initially, Glasrail's posturing had caught him off guard, and it was time for a display of his own.

Akura walked out past his front line with arrows speeding directly toward him. With only seconds until impact, he leapt from him steed, driving his sword into the ground! He raised both arms above his head, commanding his armor to revert to its liquid form, before it grew into a beautifully crafted dome shielding his men. It stood strong, rooted deep in the ground as the barrage of arrows covered the outer surface.

The Paladin stared at their leader in amazement before his words snapped them back to action.

"Wait for it!" yelled Akura. He looked up at his construct hoping it would withstand the barrage.

Another volley hammered against the shield. A few of the coral-tipped arrows penetrated, sticking a few inches through. The Paladin tightened formation into two columns behind the shield.

Akura stood ready as ever, listening for the third volley. He'd fought against Glasrail's chapter in the war and by their side in the skirmishes against the brood. Their repeater crossbows could fire two shots before reloading, with the two lines firing consecutively above. He could see that the ground troops were holding back from beneath the shield, likely for the intermissive reloading. That would be the time for the charge, with at least limited cover to weave between until they could engage them, and if they remained staggered the Wraithclaw could only target a single rider. Only a few seconds were needed to launch a counter attack.

The third volley hit the shield making several more holes. Some of the thinner parts around the edge shattered as the arrows hit them. One of the riders took an arrow in the arm, and another ricocheted off a shoulder plate.

Akura prepared himself for the fourth and final volley. He knew they were only a threat at range. His own Paladin were unmatched in hand-to-hand combat and even more lethal on horseback. They just had to close the distance. "Get ready to attack! Make them pay for their betrayal!"

The final volley hit hard! An arrow narrowly missed Akura's head, while a Paladin at the front of the column took an arrow to the chest, falling from his horse. The right quarter of the shield cracked like thin ice.

The horses started to feel the tension and began to fidget. Akura grabbed the reigns on his beast, pulling it to him and remounting.

Akura lifted his sword and was about to give the order, when he was distracted by the sound of a hopper overhead. His first thought was that it was the Commissar's men moving to flank them, until he saw the transport and its distinguishing features! It was one of Malone's!

Glasrail threw a look at the Commissar who seemed as confused by the sound of the hopper as any of them.

As it descended, it turned around so that the open side with the mounted gun was facing the entrance of the temple.

Akura shielded his eyes from the dust kicked up by magnetic field. He could just make out the silhouette of a man before the air cleared, revealing Darahk manning the gatling gun.

The look on the Inquisitor's face was as determined as ever, a hunger Akura hadn't seen on Darahk's face since the war.

Darahk opened fire on the entrance, destroying the rogue Paladin on the balconies above, and sending the others desperately diving for cover! While the heavy caliber rounds ripped through the ranks, four of Darahk's agents rappelled down to join the rest of them.

"Ready your swords, Paladin! I refuse to stand here while Darahk takes all the glory!" Akura struck the remains of his shield with a swipe from his own sword, smashing it into a thousand pieces. As the pieces fell they became liquid again, gathering around his forearm to form an armored gauntlet and wrist guard.

"Charge!" ordered Akura, leading the assault. His horse quickly accelerated to a frenzied gallop, and Le'san and the others followed him.

Le'san's hawk took to the sky automatically, so it could monitor the battle from above.

Glasrail almost tumbled down the staircase at the rear of the tank as a barrage of bullets chased him from his command station.

The Commissar's chair had also been hit and his bodyguards carried him to safety down a side corridor away from the entrance.

"Somebody take it out, now!" screamed Glasrail! "Destroy it now!" he shouted.

The front cannon lifted on the Wraithclaw and fired the harpoon, measuring five meters long. The hurtling spear penetrated the armor effortlessly, scoring a direct hit on one of the front pulse manifolds. Black smoke erupted for a second before exploding into a ball of blue flame, sending the hopper into a spin.

The pilot managed to keep her airborne, but not before Darahk lost his footing!

The Inquisitor tried to hold onto the weapon's turret as the hopper leveled out. He felt his grip slowly loosening before he had to let go; falling almost 12 meters onto the body of one of the fallen horses. He rolled off of the corpse onto all fours and tried to catch his breath.

He looked up in time to see Akura chopping down one of the rogue Paladin that had strayed from the ranks. The Lord Prefect had seen him land, knocking away a couple of arrows with his sword that were heading in their general direction.

The rest of the rogue Paladin had charged out to meet the cavalry as they got closer and closer. The powerful steeds trampled them down like they were nothing more than long grass.

By this time, Le'san had reached the Wraithclaw and clambered up onto the top of it, slicing the barrel of the harpoon clean off.

The old Shaman looked the opposite of his usually calm and collected self. He spiraled around in a violent mixture of dance and combat.

Akura glanced over to check that Darahk was ok before addressing his paladin, "Move in to flank them. We can't let them escape into the compound…" He was interrupted by two of the rogues engaging him from both sides. With a step to the left and a single pivoting 360-degree motion he decapitated one and sliced the other across the chest.

He turned back to Darahk offering him a hand. "Are you just going to lay there and watch?" he said sarcastically with a grin.

"I gave you an opening, let's not waste the opportunity with needless small talk," Darahk drew his pistol, gunning down an approaching renegade as an arrow whizzed past him, missing him by less than a meter.

Akura looked across the battlefield at Le'san holding his own against at least three adversaries at any one time. The tank's main weapon might have been destroyed, but there were at least four archers taking cover inside, firing their repeater crossbows.

At least half the Paladin were on foot now, battling the retreating rogues as they slowly fell back to the compound. In a matter of minutes, Akura's warriors had almost halved the number of enemy troops, but not without sacrifice. He could see at least three of his fallen comrades, with another two struggling to hold off multiple combatants. They were outnumbered at least five to one when the battle started, and even though they'd done their best to even up the odds, they were still gravely outmanned.

Five more of the renegades closed in and opened fire. Darahk kept close to Akura as he knocked them aside with his broadsword, taking shots over his shoulder with each available opportunity. When it came to warfare, it was almost second nature.

By the time they got within range of Akura's sword, there were two left and he charged into them, smashing the closest one's jaw with the hilt before chopping the other in half at the waist.

As he started to calm down from his frenzy, he felt a chill creep up his spine that made him turn toward Le'san. His friend had taken an arrow to the right shoulder and another to the leg. He watched as the O'sar Prefect fought off one of them long enough for another Paladin to bring him his ride.

Akura was about to run toward the entrance when a rocket ripped through the sky above his head, striking the tank front and center. There was a split second before the thing erupted from the inside. Pieces of burning Wraithclaw flew in every direction.

Akura turned around to see no less than 50 men and women running to help them. At the front was their leader, a man he recognized instantly as "the Effigy"! He said the words out loud with a great sigh of relief.

Darahk watched the suspected criminal hastily ride toward them sporting a crudely assembled rocket launcher on one shoulder. He wasn't sure whether to raise his weapon or dive for cover.

Chapter 38

The dark tunnel seemed to go on forever. The time alone gave Joss a chance to go over everything the Effigy had told him, and he couldn't help feeling just a hint of doubt. The nav screen on the glidecycle showed he was entering the final stretch of the underground channel and he felt his body relax. The Effigy was crazy but he wouldn't have gone to all this just to send him to his death.

The feeling of claustrophobia started to subside and he kicked it down a gear and searched for anything that looked like a hatch or exit. A half mile on he noticed a few obstacles ahead. He stopped and dismounted, but as soon as his feet touched the ground his gut told him to draw his weapon. He'd not seen a single sign of life for the whole ride, but he wasn't moving now and was surrounded by darkness. He clipped a small lamp to the end of his barrel and flicked the switch.

He started with the wall to his left and worked his way up to the roof of the tunnel. He'd passed the center when something caught his eye. He backtracked a little and took a step to the side. Almost directly above him was what looked like a tower, only hanging upside down? One of the sides was missing with what looked like the remains of a ladder on the inside. However the ancients had designed it, there didn't look like there was any way to lower the ladder, and the hatch was a good 20 meters up.

The Effigy had loaded up the glider with gear, all contained within a rustic-looking satchel. He popped the lamp off the barrel and clipped it to the collar on his combat vest before proceeding to rummage through the bag.

The first thing he pulled out was a pair of thermoptic goggles. They were older and a little beat up, but when he flicked the switch they powered up. He peeked through the left eyepiece and scanned his palm, which displayed as various shades of red against the dark blue surroundings.

The next thing he pulled out was exactly what he needed. The Effigy knew everything that was required to get inside. He clutched the compact grapple gun. The thing was lighter than his pistol and it hugged his hand in a way that made him admire the ergonomics. He fastened up the bag and threw it over his shoulder.

He aimed the grappler up and flicked off the safety. A small holoscreen appeared above the sight and showed him a live, magnified image of where he was aiming. Two thin laser beams hit the desired target on the bottom section of the broken ladder. He felt two triggers under his finger, one of which was already pulled back. He pulled the other and the harpoon shot out with minimal kickback, burying deep into the surface of the concrete. A light on the hardware lit up green and the second trigger popped forward where the other had been.

He braced himself and squeezed the trigger. The weapon seemed to grip his whole wrist as it pulled him speeding toward the hatch. He slowed in time to grab the lowest strut that remained on the ladder. He directed the light upward and saw the hatch a few meters above him.

As he moved to open the hatch, the mechanism gave way easier than he expected, but he stopped. There was that same feeling of apprehension in his gut, again. He reached into the bag to grab the thermoptic goggles.

As he looked up through the hatch, he could see the heat signatures of two men at roughly 15 meters, directly above him. It took him a couple of minutes to examine the structure and work out that he was inside the stadium's outer wall, directly beneath the south-interior watchtower.

He opened the hatch cautiously and crept through it. He was literally less than two meters from the staircase leading to the inertia wall with only two guards standing in his way. There was a small vent at the foot of the hidden chamber. He was about to give it a good kick when he saw the thermal image of a figure approaching. He waited a minute or so for the figure to pass by before jimmying off the grill with his knife.

He snapped off the goggles so that they were around his neck. His next move was to take the tower, then the control room. From there, he could broadcast the evacuation order over the loud speaker.

....

"Prefect!" shouted Reagan, as he entered the Prefect's chambers.

Prefect Ravenclaw stood there patiently while two tenderfoots assisted him with his uniform. Out of all the chapters, the Mountain Guardians had the most elaborate traditional garments. At one time the most reclusive of the O'sar clans, they were now comfortably modernized as part of the Patronas Order.

The tall man turned around to address Reagan. He had an undeniably proud look to his character, with impeccably sculpted facial hair and jewelry. He adjusted the animal pelts around his shoulders. They were mountain wolves, killed by the Paladin as part of the chapter's initiation.

"What's this all about, Akura? It's not enough that I have to pick up your Father's slack. We have minutes before…"

Reagan barged into his space, cutting him off mid-sentence, "Master, if you'll just hear what I have to say! The Commissar! Earlier today, my father moved to apprehend him with the aid of Inquisitor Darahk…"

The Prefect looked confused at first, shaking his head in response to what he was hearing. He raised both hands to calm the boy down, almost knocking over one of the students helping him, "Just slow down! What is all this nonsense?"

"Hours ago, we learnt of the Commissar's plan to overthrow the Order. My Father hoped to resolve this at an emergency council meeting, but I fear he was too late. There's no time to explain, we must move quickly to neutralize those under his command."

Ravenclaw said nothing, taking a second to absorb Reagan's rant, "I won't lie to you, Reagan. I'd be a fool to fully believe everything you are saying without significant evidence, but even more so to ignore even the rumor of an attack."

The sound of loud trumpets interrupted the Prefect for the second time, signaling the start of the festivities. Ra'suun moved away from the window he'd been looking out of. "The Black Sea's march out onto the main platform as we speak! The festival has begun."

"Then we have to move quickly. Inform as many of the men as you can and tell them to warn the others!" He turned to Reagan, "Just what can we expect? Are we talking about some kind of explosive device?"

"No!" barked Reagan. "It's more complicated than that, but I expect that chapter patriarchs will be the primary targets. They think they have the element of surprise to their advantage, so we must be ready when they make their move. You will know it when you see it."

The stadium livened up with the sound of trumpets and cheers. Decorative trimmings and confetti blew up into the sky.

....

Rosair stared out through the windshield of the cockpit, eagerly awaiting the landing, "How long until we reach the Velodrome? The Commissar's men will be watching every entrance." She prepared herself mentally while loading her Gatling pistol.

"ETA, ten minutes," the pilot said, loudly enough so that everyone aboard could hear.

"Without communications and a valid code transmission, they might perceive us as a threat. If the Commissar has control of the defense towers he'll fire on us regardless. We'll have to come in hot, landing inside the complex. We've got to catch them with their pants down if we've any hope of pulling this off," she said."

Malone moved over to view the stadium in the distance. "That's why it's important we waste no time taking control of the observation level. With any luck, they won't be expecting an aerial assault. As far as they know we should have been detained or killed at Wings HQ."

Rosair remained silent, growing impatient. The approach felt like an eternity. They had no idea what kind of situation they were heading into and how deeply corrupted the rest of the Agency was. Best-case scenario was that Reagan had succeeded in spreading the word to those he could trust and they'd seized control of the rebels. She knew by now only to hope for the best, but expect the worst.

Chapter 39

The team of mercenaries assembled into a loose formation as the Stranger had ordered. The droids took a moment to align in order to receive the transmission. The mist filled the surrounding area before Lord Omega appeared before them, an imposing figure towering ten meters tall. A second later a three dimensional diagram of the stadium appeared in front of them below his looming presence.

Sapian stared at the projection as it glared down at them in what felt like an oppressive gesture of power, but not to the Stranger, who'd already dropped to one knee. It took a couple of seconds before Sapian realized the mercs were also on their knees, humbled by their would-be master.

"The Viaduct is ready for initiation, my lord," said Lucas. "Every test reports systems running at 100% efficiency."

"Excellent," he said. "Once you've eliminated your primary targets, leave our allies on the inside to neutralize any resistance."

Sapian could feel the vibration throughout his body. It made his fur stand on end.

He examined the old man's face. Since first meeting the Stranger, he'd been curious about where he came from and the people he served, not to mention their remarkable technology. But something about the aged face before him felt off and uninspiring.

He realized now that he'd been expecting something more grandiose, a godly figure even, like the stories he'd heard. What he saw before him was indeed ancient-looking, but with none of the divine traits he was expecting. The face looked familiar with a distinctive expression of contempt he recognized from people when they looked at him. As well as the obvious disgust, there was also a look of desperation. It was more predominant than all the other emotions his face conveyed. This was reinforced by the bitterness in his dictatorial tone.

Another face began to appear beside Omega's, almost a third of the size. It too, looked old and decrepit, yet softer beside the sinister-looking titan.

"After further analysis of the schematic you recovered, we've concluded that the device is of experiential importance," said the second head.

Omega spoke as the second head faded away, "It must be recovered at all costs. Prepare to receive the first company."

Lucas turned around to face Sapian who was listening carefully, "As you wish, Lord Omega. It won't take us long to secure the Velodrome."

Lucas marched over to the main console and powered up the systems to full capacity. The energy surged through the archaic machine. The sound was like a waking behemoth that had been left sleeping for an eternity.

Lucas swept his cloak aside and stood at attention, "We are ready to activate the Viaduct on my mark."

Omega waited for a second as if to treasure the moment, like everything that was about to happen was doing so by his will and at his command. "Begin the countdown."

Sapian watched as the looming presence faded to nothing and the drones took off to resume their maintenance checks. *That was the great Omega?* he thought. He looked like another weak man that hungered for control. He felt the natural push toward something of key significance in his life. For as long he could remember, he had been driven by his forgotten past, and now he was starting to see that it was this determination that had consumed him.

He'd failed to see the important part he would play in the future ahead. The Effigy's words were replaying clearly in his thoughts now. Perhaps they had always made sense, but he was too ignorant to see the truth before. He suddenly felt vulnerable. These soldiers around him weren't his comrades in arms, but just another team of masked delinquents. Was he to be nothing more than a hired thug, carrying out a job for a self-serving master? The Effigy had been right. He had a choice to make.

Chapter 40

Joss crouched down low beside the pillar and waited for the guard to walk to the opposite side of the tower. He noticed the emblem of the Commissar's guard on the uniform. For all he knew, this woman was innocent and played no part in her commander's plan. He crept closer and the crowd got even louder, drowning out any sound of boots on the ground, perfect cover. He swept her legs from under her. Then, he elbowed her in the face, knocking her out cold. He scrapped her communicator and took her ammo before gagging her and cuffing her to the railings.

He surveyed the area and plotted his next course of action. The Velodrome resembled a huge rhombus-shaped bowl with a tower at each point around the edge of the outer wall, two at the northern point. From each tower there were walkways that extended down to the inner wall and there were three levels where the crowd would sit. The control room was between the north towers, above the main entrance. On each side was a large platform. The north was reserved as a landing spot and the south was designated as the place where the Paladin had to line up before their march beneath the banners that hung over the wide channel between the two sides.

From this location, he could see the rest of the FRA patrolling the wall. They seemed to be setting up ammunition dumps at sections on the walkway while snipers set up around the higher guard points where they would have a better line of sight. They were turning the stadium into a killing bowl. There were civilians scattered around the public stands, but they were nowhere near at full capacity yet. At least the rioting had helped to delay the arrival of the public in its majority.

There was no way the Commissar could get away with a massacre without some kind of explanation. There would be at least a handful of witnesses that could testify as to what actually happened. He'd need a scapegoat, some kind of distraction.

Joss screwed the silencer to his pistol and looked at the unconscious woman. The thought of putting a bullet in her for what she was about to do entered his mind and vanished just as fast. He wasn't about to kill an unarmed opponent, but he wouldn't be as forgiving of the next traitor he encountered.

He kept low and took his time. From what the Effigy had told him, he didn't have any time to waste, but it would all be over if he got sloppy and was detected. He ducked around a corner and squeezed the trigger. The bullet silently tore through the agent's chest, as the ceremonial music of the orchestra played on. The man crouched beside the sniper rifle clambered frantically to take aim.

Joss reacted and sent a precision round through his head knocking the body tumbling down the spiral staircase to the control room. He hesitated and thought about grabbing the rifle. He noticed the scope, not standard issue for a fed, and then an idea occurred to him. Once the Warper teleported in and started shooting there'd be mass hysteria. The FRA would open fire under the guise of protecting the crowd when they'd actually be targeting the Paladin. Nobody in the crowd would be able to prove otherwise.

After the massacre, the Commissar would fabricate evidence tying the Effigy to the attack while his followers rioted through the city. A perfect scapegoat, while the conniving bastard would take charge of the situation like the hero, putting him in control of the whole city.

Another agent emerged from the control room, seemingly alerted by the sound of his squad mate's descent down the stairs. Joss put two bullets in his chest and charged down the stairs, grabbing the dead man's shotgun instead of taking the time to reload.

As he reached the entrance, there was another moving target to intercept. He lifted the shotgun and brought the stock of the weapon down hard, sending the fed to the ground with a shattered upper mandible.

A second man jumped up from his chair and tried to draw his sidearm. Joss took two steps forward and opened fire, sending him flying through a nearby window down to the landing platform below. The time for stealth was over.

Joss composed himself and grabbed the microphone. The sound of the glass breaking and the sight of a falling corpse had turned a few heads. He noticed a couple of agents heading his way from the perimeter wall above.

"Can I have your attention please?!" he said. The feed echoed around the stadium thanks to the perfect acoustics. The orchestra faded into silence and the roar of the crowd started to subside.

"This is Sergeant Akura of LEX Branch. The Commissar is wanted for treason against the Allied Government. Lead members of the Patronas Council are taking action to apprehend the traitor as you hear this. The festivities are hereby postponed until further notice. Please remain calm and make your way to the nearest exit."

Across the stadium, Reagan recognized his brother's voice and stopped what he was doing. He ran outside so that he could see the control room.

Josh scanned over the crowd, as the majority remained static. They looked at each other not quite knowing what to make of the situation. At least they weren't panicking, but then they weren't exactly fleeing to the exits either.

Reagan pushed his way through onto the floor, through the chapter of Paladin parading around the circuit. He reached the podium and pushed the tenderfoot waiting to give a speech out of the way.

"It is true!" yelled Reagan. "At this moment, Paladin are securing the exits and relieving any FRA agents in collusion. We are taking control of the Velodrome."

Joss could see his brother was about to add something further when the FRA snipers opened fire! He took cover as the barrage hit, dropping the rifle from his shoulder and making sure it was loaded. He peeped out briefly as three more shots whizzed past his head and ricocheted around the control room.

Now, he knew their position. He shuffled over a few feet and leaned out, aiming his rifle. He fired two shots, hitting the first sniper in the head and the other in the shoulder. As he ducked for cover, he noticed two more agents climbing aboard the east gun turret and another heading over toward the west platform.

He was about to take aim when he heard the sound of the incoming hopper.

"That's Akura down there!" Rosair screamed, hanging out the open side door of the hopper.

Malone stepped up to see for himself, "Looks like the party's started without us."

They watched from above as Joss gunned down the agents attempting to operate the turret. Malone gave the order to open fire on the surrounding turrets. The armor-piercing rounds turned the turrets to scrap.

Malone grabbed the receiver to make an announcement as the hopper descended hastily inside the stadium, "To anyone loyal to the Commissar, this is you first and only warning. Surrender your weapons to the nearest Paladin or LEX official or be dealt with accordingly."

As they touched down, Joss walked out onto the platform, careful to keep within cover. The first person he saw was the Lieutenant marching toward him. "Are you here to arrest me Lieutenant?" he said with a grin.

"Not today, Sergeant. Any sign of the teleporter or Sapian?"

"Nothing. What about my father?" asked Joss. "It looks like my brother has been making some progress here."

Malone stepped off of the hopper, followed by six of his men. They split into groups of two and proceeded to round up the renegades around the platform that had surrendered.

Malone approached Joss. "Darahk took a hopper to rendezvous with your Father. The enemy has found a way to disrupt our long range..." he paused as the ground beneath him started to shift.

It felt like a small earthquake, the earth shuddered, but in short bursts rather than in a constant rumble. All of a sudden there was a flash of light and the sound of the loudest thunder any of them had ever heard. The whole stadium went silent before the entire area was flooded with blinding light. Shrieks of confusion could be heard in unison. They shielded their eyes and tried to refocus as the light subsided.

Joss looked over at the only structure visible over the high walls of the Velodrome. The panels of the Viaduct moved so fast they were a flickering blur against the huge beam of light. It erupted like a volcano toward a swirling vortex high in the sky.

255

Chapter 41

The intense flash and surge of energy made Sapian shield his eyes at first, before embracing the sight. The mercs beside him seemed just as impressed, and not without reason. You could actually see another world in the distance. It spiraled toward him, reminding him of his experience teleporting with the Stranger. Sapian experienced a slight feeling of vertigo before steadying himself with one hand on the ground.

As he started to stand up, he noticed the Stranger a few feet away. Lucas looked up through the portal, as if mesmerized by its beauty. His proud posture was clear beneath the armored battle suit, demonstrating a sense of accomplishment after all the hard work.

All of a sudden there was a loud swooshing sound at a volume that nearly made everyone cower, except the Stranger. In a split second, they were joined by at least 100 soldiers, an entire platoon of heavily armed troops. The officers stood front and center.

One of them checked the tablet attached to his gauntlet, "Rematerialization confirmed, teleportation successful, General."

The lower part of the General's face was the only thing visible, "Secure a perimeter around the Viaduct. Prepare to receive more troops at ten-minute intervals." He took a few steps toward Lucas, who bowed in his presence. "Your primary objective is complete, Centurion. You are to proceed with the second phase."

"Yes, General," said the distorted voice, turning to face Sapian. "You all have your objectives. Prepare to move on my command."

....

Akura looked over his shoulder at what the Effigy was looking at. The Viaduct could be seen between the two mountains and the light was visible for miles as it penetrated the cloudy skies. It was from this point that the Acolytes had originally discovered the Ark, eventually erecting the temple to mark the occasion.

The battling Paladin stopped fighting almost simultaneously, turning to behold the phenomenon that lit up the darkening skies. The clouds had started to drop off over the peaks and the rain was starting to come down hard.

The Effigy's army had evened the odds against the rogue chapter, forcing them to retreat inside the temple. Akura looked back at the Effigy who watched without saying a word.

"I suppose you have an explanation for all of this," said Akura.

"I believe you were told to expect trouble," replied the Effigy, looking back at him. "I don't have all the answers, but I can tell you that the attack will be in vain. I have been planning for this day for 20 years."

Darahk wandered over from helping one of his wounded agents. "So what's next? You show up here to save the day then it's business as usual?"

"My job is done here. You fight side-by-side, united against a common enemy," said the Effigy. "My disciples have surrounded the temple. Glasrail and the Commissar have nowhere to run. I believe you have a traitor to dispatch."

"You talk as if you knew this would happen, like you expected all of this," said Darahk

"Our roles in this part of our history were already set. It was our destiny, if you will. For what seems like a lifetime I have known the path that lies ahead, yet witnessing the events unfold always comes with a sense of relief."

"You're one of them, aren't you? One of the Acolytes?" asked Gailan. "But, I don't recognize you from the five I met all those years ago."

The Effigy stowed his rocket launcher and drew his sword from its sheath. He took a few steps past Darahk and Gailan before turning to face them. "You got the amulet, didn't you?" the Effigy didn't wait to hear an answer before taking off to follow his riders, heading around the other side of the temple.

"What the hell was that supposed to mean?" said Darahk, loading his pistol. He looked over at the entrance, picking off a rogue Paladin who was scrambling to his feet.

Some of the rogues were starting to surrender and the Effigy's followers were helping to secure the main entrance.

Akura shook the blood from his blade with one sharp flick of his broadsword. He couldn't find the right words to respond to Darahk before a quote from the scriptures came into his head. He knew Darahk wasn't exactly a fan of the Order, but he was familiar somewhat with their doctrine.

Akura cleared his throat as the two of them marched in unison toward the temple to claim their victory. "To try and fully comprehend the words of the Acolytes is nothing more than folly, given our limited knowledge of unexplainable events; but trust in their words we must, as they gave themselves to serve our future."

Darahk shook his head with a sarcastic look of contempt, "Normally I'd take such a response as an insult to my character, but the statement appears to fit the circumstance."

....

Around the north side of the temple the Effigy watched the Viaduct and waited for the signal. More than ten of his men stood around in anticipation before the light subsided and the panels slowed their rotation. There was still a bright beam of blue light that illuminated the clouds above. He couldn't help but admire its beauty, but it wasn't the fireworks he was hoping for.

He could sense his men waiting for some kind of explanation, "The interstellar portal it still open. Has anyone heard from Jada?!"

"The signal from the Viaduct is still jamming communications. Our plan seems to have had little effect on the Viaduct's function."

"That's not it. My calculations couldn't have been incorrect. Something has gone wrong down there."

....

Jada pushed her way past the people as they fled from the cloud of dust that filled the passage in front of her. A woman stumbled blindly over a pile of rubble. She caught her the moment before she fell, propping her up against the wall, "The readings show the gate still functions. Tell me what happened!"

She coughed violently, trying to wipe the dust from her eyes, "One of the inverters failed when the gate powered up. The whole tunnel came down on top of them. They're all dead!"

"We must repair the malfunction!" she waved over a group of able disciples who'd followed her down to the scene of the accident. Jada saw another survivor materialize from the cloud, carrying a toolbox. The dust was beginning to settle, but she could smell smoke in the distance. Jada snatched the equipment from the other man and pointed him in the direction of the exit.

"The whole chamber's on fire!" said the woman in her loudest croak of a voice. "You can't…"

"The Viaduct must be destroyed. If we fail now then everything we've been working toward was for nothing! I need volunteers. Everybody else get out and help the others to safety."

The three able-bodied disciples looked at each other in apprehension before reluctantly following her into the smoke.

Chapter 42

Reagan observed the crowd as their frantic screams got louder. Many of the civilians looked frozen, staring up at the unbelievable sight, while others ran around in a state of panic that was quickly becoming contagious. As he scanned across one of the walkways above, he almost missed a dark figure that appeared in a blink of an eye. Another 30 meters or so down the gangway, another figure became visible. This time, he noticed the vortex, like the one he'd seen the previous night. It looked somehow less spectacular against the backdrop of the phenomenon atop the black mountain.

  Reagan had already scrambled up the walkway, and proceeded to charge at the closest of the assassins. He sliced through one, decapitating the bastard, and then moved on to the next. The second assassin saw him coming and swung around to fire. He couldn't be sure how his armor or shield would fair against such a weapon so he decided agility was the best defense. He rolled beneath the blast a moment before it reached him. He was on his feet in a split second, slicing off the end of the barrel. As his opponent fell back, he followed up with a single slice down through the mercenary's shoulder, cutting half the way through his torso.

  He watched the slaughter down below. The Paladin fought hard to protect their Patriarchs, hastily escorting them inside to safety. He counted at least 20 of the attackers remaining on the lower levels, and watched as a group of Paladin moved to engage the assassins at close range. Some of the Commissar's men had rallied against them, but they were no match for the Paladin up close.

  Other Paladin on the ground level did their best to round up the civilians and find them cover. Reagan watched as one the invaders sliced through three advancing Paladin, their armor seemed defenseless against the laser weapons. The scene looked like total chaos from where Reagan was standing. The bodies of at least a dozen more fallen Paladin littered the ground.

...

At the other side of the stadium, Rosair slid across the landing platform to reach Malone, who'd been yelling something at her that she couldn't make out. The light show from the Viaduct was accompanied by a strange sound that was becoming higher pitched. The tone seemed to mute any sound outside close proximity. Suddenly, it was as if the screaming crowds were running around silently, with only their fearful expressions left to explain their actions.

Malone's gaze shifted from the screen on his wrist tablet to different points around the surrounding area. He snapped out of it when he felt Rosair barge into him. "They're here!" he screamed.

Up above, Joss couldn't hear the others, but watched as six figures materialized a few meters away around the platform. The closest had barely become visible before Joss aimed and fired. The slugs hit the bastard twice in the chest, sending him stumbling toward one of the others.

The next man opened fire with the familiar laser weapon! Joss leapt halfway down a staircase to the next level before the turret he was standing beside was sliced to pieces. He peeked out from his cover to see the two feds he recognized. He was about to run straight for them when another laser beam ripped across the ground in front of him, narrowly missing his legs.

Rosair singled out Sapian amongst the others the instant he'd appeared on the other side of the landing platform. He had the Warper with him, with two other goons between her and her prey. She stood up, as if blinded by her hunger for revenge.

She was about to fire when Malone barged into her, knocking her clear of incoming fire. He dragged her to safety as the hopper, along with one of his men, was reduced to smoldering rumble behind them. He shook her violently, his face a few inches from her, "Get your fucking head in the game, Lieutenant. You want to…."

He was interrupted mid-sentence as Rosair opened fire with her Gatling pistol, shredding the man in front of Sapian, sending him diving for cover.

Joss saw the opportunity and wasn't about to waste it. He honed in on the second goon, charging up from beside them before squeezing the trigger. The armor was tough, so he made a point of emptying his magazine to ensure the job was done. A stray shot ricocheted off Warper's armor, attracting his attention.

Lucas turned and fired in Joss's general direction, only realizing who he was after he'd ducked for cover. Lucas hesitated and was about to pursue him before a barrage of bullets made him drop to the ground.

Malone's men advanced cautiously with heavy weapons, forcing the Warper to take cover out of immediate danger.

Malone targeted one of the mercs with his special weapon and fired. The pulse struck hard, causing the man to drop to ground in a heap. Malone watched as the mercenary started to cough up black tar and blood while his armor crumbled and broke down. He flashed a glance over to Rosair as he darted back behind cover. She looked as surprised at the effect as he was.

"You got any more of those things handy?" yelled Rosair.

"I'm afraid it's only a prototype and requires time to charge between blasts." he responded. " move around the platform and maybe we can close in from all sides."

Rosair attempted to move around to flank the invaders, with Malone following closely behind. They used the smoldering wreck of the hopper as cover while she exchanged shots with Warper. Each shot from the laser left them with less cover to hide behind.

One of Malone's men saw that the Director was pinned down and moved out of cover to throw a grenade. He'd already pulled the pin when he noticed the Warper had seen him coming. The sizzling beam sliced up through the right side of the agent's torso and arm, causing the grenade to explode. He was killed instantly by the blast while the other agent was sent flying across the platform.

...

The sound of the explosion broke Sapian from his trance. He watched as his comrades carried out their mission. The brave Paladin charged them, putting themselves between the lethal blasts and the civilians. He looked down at his weapon, held tightly in his hand and realized he'd still not fired a shot.

He looked back at two of the other mercenaries as they opened fire into the crowd of women and children. A female Paladin ducked and weaved through the burning energy blast, and was left burned and half naked. She threw her sword through the neck of the one merc before falling to her knees four meters from the next.

Sapian watched in slow motion as the merc lifted his weapon. He was a second away from shooting the defenseless Paladin when three bullets ripped through him. Two shells tore through his masked helmet and face, and the last through the laser causing it to explode. It took a moment before he noticed the shots had come from his hand cannon. He looked down at the sight of the Paladin as she stared up at him.

One of the other mercs further down the stands witnessed his treachery and moved to fire in his direction. Before he could take a shot, he saw a familiar Paladin swoop down from the rafters above, striking down hard with both feet. Reagan glared at Sapian and noticed the look of recognition. They maintained eye contact for a moment before Reagan turned his attention to another assailant.

Sapian looked back at the Stranger closing in on Joss and the two FRA Agents. They were quickly running out of cover. The cop scored a hit with each shot he fired, but the rounds from his revolver seemed to have no effect on the Stranger's armor.

Another blast from the laser cannon ripped across the rear wall behind the platform catching Malone in the back, as he was about to fire his weapon. He wasted the shot, discharging the weapon into the air before dropping it. Rosair darted back to drag him to cover as Warper closed on their position.

Lucas looked around for his men before noticing Sapian, "I have them pinned down! Do what you were brought here to do!"

Sapian could see all three of them caught between diminishing cover and he knew they were likely running low on ammunition.

Rosair watched Sapian moving in from behind Warper and took aim with her pistol. She pulled the trigger, but got nothing; out of ammo! She could see Malone's weapon meters away and risked moving out of cover to grab it! Another blast from the laser ripped past her almost slicing off her arm, but she got it. She was about to take aim when she saw that the display on the weapon read 'empty'!

"Shit!" she shouted out loud. She knew she had nothing left. Only a knife at close range if it even got to that. There was the previously mounted weapon from the hopper lying on the ground about ten meters away, but she'd be fried at least three times before she could reach it.

She looked at Malone who lay immobilized, breathing heavily, then back at the weapon in the distance lying on the ground. She looked right as she heard another shot come from Joss. He leapt over the remains of the back wall to meet them.

Malone struggled to reach inside his jacket, as Joss got closer, "Akura…" He mumbled as blood ran from the side of his mouth. "Take the iris, get it as far away from them as you can. Maybe it wasn't such a good idea bringing it here after all," he said, forcing a smile.

Joss grabbed the device and it seemed to shimmer in his hand. He felt the symbiotic energy tingle through his fingertips. "Maybe…" he said, in response to Malone's statement. "But maybe it's the only thing that's going to get us out of this."

Without another word, Joss stepped out of cover with his hands up, one hand was holding his pistol and the device was in the other. Joss watched the Warper as he appeared hesitant to fire his weapon, assumingly because he was holding the device.

They seemed to be stuck in momentary stalemate. The Warper's prize was in front of him and what would be his next move? A few steps behind the Warper he could see Sapian closing in. Ordinarily he would have thought as back up, until he noticed the particular look of intent, an unmistakable look that he would have never expected.

Sapian lunged at the Stranger grabbing the laser cannon and aiming it into the air. The two of them wrestled back and forth before the Stranger got in a knee to the chest. Sapian recoiled with an instinctual backflip that evolved into a spinning roundhouse. The kick spun the Stranger around before Sapain grabbed him, rolling backwards and throwing him several meters away.

Lucas landed right on the edge of the platform, the laser cannon just out of arm's reach.

Sapian watched **cautiously** as the Stranger got to his feet.

Joss darted forward toward the cannon, realizing there was a slim chance he would get to it first.

Rosair had been waiting for her opportunity since she first saw the 50 caliber lying on the ground. She jumped to her feet and swiped up the heavy machine gun faster than she'd thought possible. She had only a second to check that it was loaded before they opened fire. The sounds of the heavy rounds demanded the attention of the others.

Joss and Sapian jumped for cover in opposite directions.

The thick slugs tore into the Warper's armor, knocking him back until there was no more ground beneath his feet.

Sapian jumped up to a standing position in time to see the Stranger fall a good 70 meters to the ground level.

…

Reagan chopped down another two of the Commissar's troops as he saw Warper fall out of the corner of his vision. His instincts told him that he'd survive the drop and he began to make his way down to intercept.

As he navigated his way down, he passed a patriarch from one of the Suu'vitan chapters. The man was in his late 60s and fighting side by side with two female O'sar Paladin. The patriarch had altered the texture of his shield to be more reflective and was using it to partially deflect the laser blasts while the faster O'sar braves flanked them from the sides.

Reagan altered his own shield to be more reflective and continued on his path. He was almost at the sublevel now and was careful not to trip over the dead bodies, more than he could count.

They'd suffered heavy casualties, but the sight of the survivors fighting side by side motivated him to find his target amidst the chaos. If he could stop Warper before he escaped, maybe they could put an end to all this.

Reagan crouched to peer through the crowd before a familiar shimmer caught his eye. The partially scorched banners hung in tatters, blocking his field of vision. He squinted through the smoke until he saw a familiar shimmer in the distance.

Reagan could see the Warper getting to his feet at the end of the narrow channel down the center of the arena. As he got closer he could see him examining the damage to his armor. It seemed to be self-repairing rapidly before his eyes, each plate regenerating and clicking into place. Reagan slowed his pace as the Warper turned to face him, as if sensing his approach.

"You think you have a chance of stopping me all by yourself," said the distorted voice.

A large banner ahead of him swept to the side, wrapped in a curling cloud of smoke. It hung on by a thread for a second before the fire severed the material from the flagpole. The banner floated to the ground in a display of atmospheric slow motion, landing in front of the Warper and bursting into flames. The dark warrior approached slowly through the fire, as if the flames were of little concern.

Reagan secured his shield around his left arm and held his sword by his side. He'd earned a moment's rest before the end game, "I thought I'd try and find you before you pulled your disappearing act. I'm thinking you're the kind of dishonorable filth that has your minions do your fighting for you."

Lucas threw back the ragged cloak and extended each arm, each holding a surgically lethal blade, "How wrong you are."

The sound of the Viaduct in the distance got louder again with the surge of energy. The sky above ground became saturated light. The screams of the crowd followed seconds later.

Lucas relaxed for a moment to bask in the success of the mission. "Your rule of this planet is over. For you, death will come quickly, but for the others, they will come to understand the necessity of their demise as they are systematically exterminated."

Reagan stared down his opponent, ignorant to the Warper's maniacal rant. "Do you always drone on and on like this, or can you fight?!" shouted Reagan, before charging toward his enemy.

Chapter 43

Jada braced herself against the closest beam as the supports creaked and loose rock crumbled to the ground. The Viaduct had opened twice now and her heart raced as she scrambled through the collapsing passage.

She made note of the time between the power surges; 15-minute intervals. She wasn't far from the next chamber and could tell from the fire damage that she was getting closer to the source of the explosion.

The thick smoke was almost overwhelming. She couldn't shake the thought of the enemy's army increasing in size every time the Viaduct was activated. But more than that, how she was failing her leader, the man who had given her purpose and a reason to live. She felt her body surge forward as if driven by a force she couldn't hold back even if she wanted too.

She saw fire ahead, but she didn't even slow down before charging through it, leaving the other two men waiting. She felt the melted fibers of her over garment stick to her flesh, but the adrenalin seemed to hold back the agonizing sensation long enough for her to maintain a clear chain of thought.

She noticed a fire extinguisher to her right and snatched it up, aiming it at the flames, dowsing them enough for the other two men to scramble through.

She could see where the fire had started now; the three thick cables hung from the rafters, disconnected from the power inverter. "Come and help me with this," she shouted to the others.

Each of the cables weighed a good 50 pounds and they were strapped together. Only one of the inverters looked to have malfunctioned. "The coralite cylinder must have ignited with the surge: bad insulator!" Jada yelled to the bigger man. "The woven strands of the cable that was connected to it were scorched and melted. The entire part will have to be replaced and the cable stripped and reattached."

Jada despaired as her injuries started to sting beneath her armor. She shuck off the sensation, and grabbed the large satchel from one of the men. He was a thinner looking fellow with a fearful expression on his face. Jada unraveled the spare piece of cable and looked up at them both, " I need you two to strip and replace this section. You have ten minutes while I replace the inverter!"

The thinner man looked at the other man; a taller, stronger figure who was holding up the cable, "I can do it, as long as he can hold it steady enough."

Jada opened the toolbox and started to pull away the scorched remains of the inverter. "Then, let's not waste any more time."

………………………………..

Akura stared at the three fallen FRA agents on the ground by his feet. One of them was still alive. He'd caught the woman across the chest with his backswing just before she'd gotten a shot off.

Darahk walked over to the dead body of one of the rogue Paladin and peered up at the wide staircase leading to the platform, "What are you waiting for, Akura?"

Akura looked up at Darahk, "They have nowhere else to run."

Darahk looked at the dying traitor at the Prefect's feet. He quickly aimed his pistol and fired two shots at her chest.

Akura looked back in time to witness her last dying breath before her eyes became lifeless. "Then let us finish this, Inquisitor," he said, and led the way up to the roof level.

Gailan lifted his sword to a defensive position. They'd killed the few remaining troops in their vain attempt to protect their traitorous masters. He'd noticed the look of confidence in some of the rebels he'd fought, while others seemed more hesitant, even confused as to why they were fighting against men and women they'd called allies. The old Paladin felt a distaste for battle that he'd never had in his youth. The feeling of victory wasn't what it used to be.

They got to the top of the stairs to see the Commissar staring out over toward the Viaduct. Gailan wondered what use a blind man had for such a view; maybe he sensed his defeat below and yearned to be far from here.

Glasrail aimed his crossbow at the approaching men, "You fools think you've won?!"

Akura and Darahk separated, giving him two targets to shoot at. He'd only get one shot off before someone put him down.

Gailan looked at the disgraced Patriarch, "Your Paladin lie dead on the ground, their loyalty to your misguided beliefs has cost them their lives."

"They died in service to the true rulers of Orbis, the world we have claimed as our own… I am simply their servant, loyal to the true gods."

Glasrail raised his repeater an inch before Darahk shot him in the left knee, dropping him back to the ground.

The Patriarch rolled around in agony as Gailan kicked the weapon far from his reach.

Darahk got a few meters away from the Commissar before the old man spoke.

"You had to interfere. You couldn't have just…My plan with the Effigy was perfect. He would have gotten the blame for the attack on the ceremony. The city would have rejoiced at the return of the ancestors as they helped us bring order to chaos."

"And what of the Order? They would have never let themselves be slaughtered so easily," said Darahk.

The Effigy appeared at the top of the stairs behind them, "They would have fabricated evidence connecting me with various members of the council.

Akura looked down at Glasrail as he squirmed on the ground, "You knew I'd made contact with the Effigy, even before I knew that he was the one giving me the information."

"We were looking for ways to incriminate members of the council that we knew would cause problems," continued the commissar, " The fact that the Effigy was feeding you the intel was inconvenient, but it gave us the evidence we needed."

Glasrail threw his head around to face the Commissar, "Hold your tongue, you old fool!"

"Can't you see? It is over for us, Glasrail. At least I succeeded in paving the way for the ancestors' return."

....

Jada hurried to fit the inverter in place, with less than five minutes left on her wrist tablet.

The two men lifted the cable in place as Jada fired up the soldering device. She'd soldered the connection a quarter of the way around when the torch failed. Jada made sure that everything was connected and tried again. Nothing. She'd seen it was almost full when he'd grabbed it. She furiously slung the pack from her shoulders and checked the levels. It read empty.

Jada examined the bottom of the tank and there was a hairline crack where the coralite-bonding agent had leaked out. She tried not to throw it down in anger before frantically rummaging through the toolbox. She knew there wasn't a spare in there, but she had to look just in case. She scanned the surrounding area, but could find nothing amidst the scorched remains.

The thin man looked down at Jada's tablet, "The power levels are rising! Less than two minutes!"

"It's not going to hold if I let go of this!" said the bigger man.

....

Reagan took two steps back as he parried the Warper's spiraling combo. He'd never felt strength like it. He countered back with a kick to the sternum followed by a strike across the shoulder.

His blade sliced through the first layer of armor, but at a cost. It dulled his blade considerably. Reagan could feel the inconsistency in his weapon's edge and concentrated to perfect the construct.

Warper attacked again, striking three blows against Reagan's shield. The third strike sliced through the shield, chopping a piece clean off.

Reagan was caught off guard by the effect of his opponent's weapon and was distracted enough to succumb to a kick to the side of his knee. He recovered quickly, striking Warper's groin with his hilt before landing an uppercut from a crouching position, sending him sliding across the ground.

Lucas harnessed the momentum, rolling back to a standing position as the light from the Viaduct swelled across the sky once more.

Reagan prepared himself for the ear piercing sounds and the vibrations through the ground when the light started to flicker.

Lucas checked the power levels on the small screen encased in the gauntlet, "No! It can't…"

The two of them looked up as the light got brighter, brighter than before. The sound made Reagan cover his ears and drop to the ground.

In an instant, Reagan felt an overpowering feeling of weightlessness, combined with the unrelenting volume and blinding light. He felt his rib cage vibrate so hard he almost had to vomit. He tried to gain control of his limbs and curl into a ball, and then suddenly everything was quiet, but the silence only lasted for a fragment of a second before the deafening explosion!

Reagan composed himself in time to see his opponent disappear before him.

....

Even from miles away the flash was bright enough to make Darahk shield his eyes. Seconds later, the shockwave rolled over the temple and everyone on the roof went silent.

Glasrail cracked his neck around to see the cloud of dust and smoke bellowing from the ruined Viaduct. He tried to clamber to his knees as Akura grabbed his arm, twisting it in way that forced him to look.

Darahk could hear the whimpering sound coming from the old man in front of him, "I'm guessing that wasn't part of the plan?"

The Commissar clutched his face with both hands and started to cry pathetically.

"My people appear to have succeeded, if not a little behind schedule," the Effigy said, walking to stand level with Gailan and Glasrail.

Glasrail turned slowly to face him. "You. You did this?" he squirmed, and made a vain attempt to lunge at the Effigy.

Akura threw him back on the ground.

The masked man looked back at him with a half smile visible even through his scars. "You may have been plotting this little coup for a while, Patriarch, but I always knew you would fail."

Darahk moved another step closer to the Commissar. Once he'd confirmed he'd been unarmed, he lowered his weapon and removed the cuffs from his belt. He thought about putting two in the back of the old man's head, but something about his former commander's pathetic demeanor made him feel pity, despite the hatred welling up inside him. Maybe such a quick death was better than he deserved. The people had to know that all of this was his doing by now, and he should be around to realize his failure and face his punishment.

The Commissar had heard Darahk approaching and turned to face him. His blind eyes managed to find Darahk's face somehow, with nothing but the look of loss and sorrow. He looked like he was about to say something, when his lips started to quiver. His chair jerked forward with a start, tumbling off the edge of the launch platform.

Darahk jumped ahead in time to see the old man hit the ground, the chair smashing to pieces on top of him.

He turned around to look at the others, and was just in time to see the Effigy execute Glasrail. His gesture was almost passive as he shot him in the head at point blank range.

Akura jumped back in shock, despite his own plans to kill the patriarch. The old man's death had brought satisfaction but more so by the fact he didn't have to be his executioner. *Had his taste for the death of his enemy dwindled so much with age?* He wondered.

"What the hell was that?!" yelled Darahk. "He might have had more to tell us, maybe shed some light on the situation!"

The Effigy threw the rifle back on his shoulder and turned to head back down from the platform, "There will be no light in the near future. We have succeeded in destroying the interstellar Viaduct, but I fear it may be too late. An invasion force numbering in the hundreds could be marching toward the city gates as we speak."

Chapter 44

Joss looked over to see a familiar enforcer running toward him.

Simmons looked around at the wreck of the hopper and then over at Sapian standing a few meters away. "Looks like you have everything under control up here. We got long-range communications back shortly after the thing went up. Most of the Commissar's guards are either in custody or…dead."

"Nicely done, Sergeant," said Joss. "Call the Chief and fill her in on what went on here. Tell her to send as many people as she can spare. We have to regain control of the streets. There's going to be a lot of scared people asking questions. This is just the beginning."

Reagan appeared at the top of the stairs a few steps behind the cop, "Fancy meeting you here. I hope you have some kind of explanation as to what we just saw take place here. What can we expect next?"

"An army is my first guess," said Joss. "He said that this Warper we fought was just the first of many."

"Who said?" barked Reagan.

"The Effigy," answered Joss. "He's been trying to help us piece things together from the beginning. Where's Dad? Is he here with you?"

"Father went to meet with Victus, hoping he could prevent all this. Even with the intel we had, they still managed to catch us off guard," said Reagan. "Many Paladin died today, including three patriarchs. The prefects are doing what they can to hold the chapters together."

Rosair walked over from where she'd been sitting with Malone. She waited until they'd noticed her before she spoke "Malone's dead," she said.

She looked over to see two LEX officers covering up his body and carrying him to another hopper that had landed, "Any reports on the leader?"

"I fought him below, but he escaped," said Reagan, regretfully. "When the Ark exploded, he activated his device and hightailed it out of here."

"It appears that reactivating the Ark was his objective," said Joss. This elaborate scheme with the Effigy was all a distraction to keep us in the dark."

"That wasn't his only objective," said Rosair. "He wants the iris, the one you're carrying." She pointed at the satchel Joss had around his shoulder.

"He already possesses the means to teleport," Joss said. Why would he need another? With the gate destroyed, do you think he'll still come after it?"

"Maybe his objective is to keep the technology out of our hands, for fear that it could be used against them." said Reagan.

"Whatever the reason, I believe he'll do all he can to retrieve it," said Sapian, who'd remained silent while the others had been speaking.

"Please enlighten us," said Rosair, with an element of disgust in her voice. "You seem familiar with his entire operation."

"Because it's all he has left," said Sapian. "I was there when his master gave the order to retrieve this thing and it sounded important. This kind of screw-up's not going to go down too well. He'll do everything possible to make up for a failure of this magnitude. If nothing else, he'll want revenge. I betrayed him."

Rosair took a couple of steps closer to the ape, waving a finger in his face, "Your sudden change of heart doesn't change the fact that you're a terrorist and a murderer. Do you expect us to trust you?"

"Not me exactly…" Sapian slowly removed the data chip from his utility belt. "The Effigy. He gave me this and told me that I could trust you."

"That's it? Did he tell you what's on it?" asked Reagan.

"You've obviously never spoken to the guy," said Sapian, with a nervous laugh.

"It sounds like him," said Joss, raising a hand to the Lieutenant who had a hand resting on her gun. "He's not always the clearest when it comes to filling you in on significant life-changing events.'

Rosair nodded toward another hopper perched on the edge of the platform. "Bring it on board. Make sure that thing's not armed," she said, gesturing toward Sapian. "If he so much as fidgets awkwardly, he gets a bullet."

Reagan interrupted, "I think we get the picture, Lieutenant. I'll need to make contact with my father once we're aboard."

....

Lucas surveyed the destruction of all their hard work, ignorant to the screams of the injured Omega troops at the foot of what used to be the Viaduct. It was damaged beyond repair. Every panel was left twisted and deformed by the explosion. The center console was a melted ruin next to the scorch marks left by the incinerated soldiers.

The General had survived the blast and was yelling in Lucas' face, repeating himself for the third time, "Can you hear me in there, you insolent failure?! Remove your damn helmet, for the last time. You will have to answer to Lord Omega for this. We need to re-establish commutations with Omega command immediately!"

Lucas ignored him and walked over to an injured scientist who was performing diagnostics, "Do basic systems function enough to run a diagnostic? I want to know who's responsible for this. There may have been more than one traitor in our midst."

"Centurion!? I demand your obedience!" the General interrupted again. He gestured to the two soldiers who stood there watching. "You are relieve of duty, Centurion. "

Lucas grabbed the General by the throat, cutting him off in mid-sentence. The troops looked surprise, but only one moved in an attempt to intervene. Lucas snatched his rifle before knocking him unconscious with it.

"You have no idea what this failure has cost me," said Lucas. "This was my mission. I have trained for it my entire life. I won't deny Lord Omega's rule over this planet, and that means everybody has to do their job.

Lucas released the General, shoving him into one of the other soldiers. "You will assemble all the survivors and march on the city, take it before they rebuild their defenses."

The General took a few seconds to speak, "But my army…"

"You still have over 200 able-bodied soldiers, with superior firepower. Do you think repairing this archaic machine was my only task here?!" Lucas didn't wait for a response. "I've spent a year orchestrating the destabilization of their regime from within. They are weak! They are broken! I won't let all I've worked for go to waste!"

Another science officer ran over, accompanied by one of the drones, "The diagnostic shows a malfunction in the stabilization system beneath the structure. It caused the gate to overload. We've discovered a network of tunnels that runs for miles underground, they weren't on our schematic."

Lucas turned away from the quivering General to examine his wrist display. It read low power again, and without the energy field generated from the Viaduct, he was back running on reserve energy, "Did any of the others make it back here? The traitor should have tranz-warped back here the same time as me."

"It seems he was able to remove the failsafe before dematerialization, but the tracking device you planted on him was undetected. We're picking up a signal heading north of the Velodrome."

Lucas raised a hand as if to signal the drones into action, "Only three of the drones survived. I'll need all of them! Whether he's aligned himself with the other troublemakers or they've arrested him, he will lead me to the iris.

Lucas pointed at the General, without doing him the honor of facing him, "I need any men you can spare. I have enough energy for several jumps. When I have retrieved the device, I will report to Lord Omega personally."

Chapter 45

Reagan had tried to raise communications with the Temple twice before Le'san answered. The old Prefect looked a little worse for wear, but he could read from his expression that they had been victorious in their endeavor. He saw his father appear behind Le'san on the screen, followed by Darahk.

"Father, are you receiving audio?" asked Reagan.

"Receiving loud and clear," said Gailan. "It's good to see you both unharmed."

Joss ducked in from behind his brother, "Likewise."

Reagan shrugged off his brother's cocky attitude, "We managed to stop the attack and then regain control, for the most part, but not without sacrifice. When Rosair informed us of the suspected ambush at the temple, we feared the worst."

"Patriarch Victus is dead," said Gailan. "Glasrail and his Paladin were in collusion with the Commissar. They'd been conspiring to pave the way for this invasion force. With the FRA compromised and the Order out of picture it would have been easy for them to take the city."

"We were greatly outnumbered," said Le'san. "I doubt we would have succeeded without the help of our mysterious friend here," Le'san pointed over at the Effigy who was talking to his troops behind them.

The Effigy was alerted to the fact that they were talking about him and moved into frame.

Joss pushed his way forward, "I don't believe it. You seem to make a habit of showing up in the most relevant of places. We were about to head over to pick you guys up, before our furry friend here showed us the data-chip. He's told us that it came from you."

"It is the next breadcrumb you mush follow on your path," said the Effigy, cryptically. "You will need each other for what lies ahead. The Stranger will stop at nothing to retrieve the iris. You can only beat the Centurion if you work together."

Akura waited for the Effigy to finish before continuing, "We will regroup with the survivors to the east. We have spotted a sizable force advancing across the channel. It appears that a considerable amount of the invasion force survived the explosion."

Darahk stepped forward, "I'll be taking command of the FRA for the time being."

"I suspected as much," said Joss. "I sent word ahead to LEX HQ, filled Flint in on everything that happened."

Gailan leaned forward as the others dispersed behind him, all but the Effigy, "When this is over, it will be a tale of victory that we will have shared together. I am proud of you both."

Joss felt a peculiar feeling wash over him as he heard his Father's words. He looked at Reagan who didn't seem to be affected in the same way. "Good luck," he said. He saw the Effigy place a hand on his father's shoulder before the transmission terminated.

....

"This is unbelievable," said Reagan, bringing up a 3D holographic display in the cockpit of Malone's hopper. " The blueprints enclosed in the file show a bunker, some kind of silo deep beneath the surface…"

Sapian moved forward from the rear seat he'd been designated, beside Joss. Rosair was piloting the vessel with Reagan in the co-pilot's seat.

"Yeah, according to the Effigy, there's a number of these ancient compounds hidden around the area," said Joss, leaning down to examine the display.

"…And that's not all they're hiding down there," Reagan continued, just as the lower part of the hologram was revealed, peaking Sapian's interests.

"It looks like a shuttle of some sort…?" said Sapian, staring at the screen as if he recognized it. He suddenly noticed the others were staring at him.

"You know what that thing is?" asked Joss

Sapian looked around at all of them, trying to ignore the Lieutenant's suspicious glare. "Not exactly, I remember images, from before I became, what I..." he corrected himself. "…who I am today. For years I have searched for the answers to my past."

Reagan zoomed in and enhanced the display.

Sapian squinted at the familiar, yet undeniably foreign aircraft, "The Effigy knew this would trigger something from the depths of my addled brain. He knew it! He somehow knew this information would help me make the right choice."

"Come on!" erupted Rosair. "Am I the only one questioning the motives of this lunatic? Why entrust this kind of intel to this killer? Why not give you the information?" she yelled, gesturing toward Joss.

"It seems he wanted us to work together," answered Joss. " He told me that Sapian wasn't my enemy, called him my ally! The Effigy knew he would help us, even before he'd made the decision."

The two brothers seemed to trust him enough to at least entertain what he was telling them, but Sapian could literally smell Rosair's hatred for him. He tried to catch her eyes in the reflection of the windshield, "At first I thought the guy was nuts, talking in riddles. Yet, he somehow knew things, things about me that nobody does."

"We all know what you are," she seemed angered further at his attempt to form an explanation or make peace. She kept her eyes on the landscape ahead, deliberately avoiding the gaze of the creature.

Sapian decided to give it a break and sat back in his chair. Winning the Lieutenant over wasn't something that was going to happen overnight. He took a cigar from his pocket and lit it up before noticing Joss looking his direction.

"Do you mind if I...?" Joss asked with a smirk, pointing to the pack of cigars.

"Help yourself," answered Sapain, while offering him one from the pack and continuing to tell them his story, "He told me that we were bound in our destiny and that this device had something to do with it."

"If he'd told me my destiny involved smoking cigars with a talking monkey I wouldn't have believed anything else the guy said." Joss said, flashing Sapian a smart-ass grin.

Sapain looked at him sharply at first, as if he'd taken offence. He wasn't exactly used to light hearted humor, and it caught him off guard initially. Before he'd realized what was happening he found himself laughing out loud. Reagan and Rosair looked as surprised as he was. This kind of laid-back exchange was a refreshing change; despite the fact it was at his expense, and given the impending circumstances.

Reagan shook his head with the hint of a smile at his brother's seemingly undeniable charm. "All right you two," he said, peering over the console from the copilot's seat. "We're closing on the location," he said.

Rosair looked over the console to the area below the hopper. "What exactly am I looking for? I don't see anything."

"You will," said Joss. "These ancient bunkers are designed to be hidden from detection, especially when it comes to our technology."

'And you know this, how?" asked Rosair.

"The Effigy," said Joss as if that answer explained it all. "Yet another of one of the cryptic explanations he's best known for."

"I'm starting to feel privileged that I never had to deal with that freak on a one-on-one basis," she said, bringing the hopper to a halt in mid-air. She started a steady descent between two jagged peaks.

Reagan pivoted his chair to man the nav station "The cavern stops ten meters down…"

"And then what?" said Rosair.

Joss reached over her and pointed at another dome-like structure. This one looked smaller than the Effigy's hideout, and was partially covered with vegetation. "It won't show up on our systems. Take her in manually."

…

From the complex below, Lucas watched their descent and couldn't help but feel the apparent significance of the unfolding events. As an Omega centurion, duty had always been black and white, but over the last few days, things had happened that had awakened a feeling of doubt and uncertainty. With communications severed from high command, there was an almost irresistible urge to take control of the person that existed before there was only the 'Instrument.'

Lucas had access to the Omega archives and had had a chance to scan over the relevant details concerning the function of this particular iris. Its potential power was intriguing, tempting almost.

With a single hand gesture, the troops under Lucas's command scattered, spreading out around the facility in preparation for the ambush, "Prepare to fire. Let's give them a warm welcome."

The Omega troops opened fire on the hopper; the energy blasts hit their target, one after another. The first shot broke through the dome; the second one grazed the hull, and the third and fourth sliced off pieces of the hopper, devastating crucial systems.

"I'm not going to be able to keep this thing in the air much longer!" yelled Rosair. She struggled to avoid the incoming blasts between the narrow peaks of the valley.

"Look for a place to land this…" shouted Reagan.

"Are you fucking kidding? Land where?!" answered Rosair. "We've got to get out of here or we're toast." She cranked her neck around to face Sapian. "That bastard led us directly into an ambush!"

"Enough all ready!" shouted Sapian, kicking out the heavily buckled side hatch. He secured a couple of ropes and threw them out." Rappel down and find cover!"

He jumped over to the cockpit, "That means you too, Lieutenant. I'll keep her steady until you're clear. I can make the jump without a rope!"

Rosair jumped up from the pilot's chair and gave him a hard stare as she passed.

Reagan went first, smashing through one of the few remaining panels with his shield before landing on a rickety walkway around the top of the complex. He pressed against the wall and watched the next barrage take out the last remaining engine.

Rosair landed on the platform below, followed closely by Joss. One of the energy blasts burned through his rope sending him into a free-fall. He managed to grab hold of the railing and hang on until Rosair pulled him up.

Sapian let the hopper spin around once before leaping out, dropping almost 40 feet before grabbing a rafter to slow him down. He felt the exo-suit strain with the pressure, swinging down to the platform below Joss and Rosair, where the first of the Omega guards stood. The grunt didn't even see him coming as he kicked him over the edge.

Rosair watched the enemy soldier as he fell, firing wildly in all directions and taking chunks out of the surrounding walkways. She jumped for cover as the hopper exploded above.

Joss waited for the debris to fall past them before drawing his weapon and helping Rosair to her feet, " I guess that means he's on our side!" he said, to no response.

They split up, running in opposite directions. Rosair headed for a spiral staircase that ran down the left hand side of the cylindrical structure. She almost fell as she reached the top, dodging under two stray shots so close they singed her hair.

Sapian took aim with his pistol and shot the man that had her pinned down.

She returned the favor by gunning down two more that darted from one side to the other. They had the advantage of the higher ground and the light from their rifles made them easy to spot. Just as she was starting to feel impressed with herself, two shots hit the central beam destabilizing the stairs. She fell forward over the side, rolling down to the next level and smashing through a console before hitting the ground.

Sapian landed a few meters in front of her. He looked up at the craft before him. It was around 15 meters tall and 5 across. There was a platform leading up to what looked like the main hatch. He was about to make a run for it when something rushed past overhead, slicing through the barrels of his pistol.

He ducked and rolled to get clear before realizing it was one of the drones that he'd seen performing the repairs on the Viaduct. It fired again, sending him running back beneath the cover of the platform above.

Meanwhile, Rosair had gotten to her feet and was trying to get a lock on the robot. It weaved side to side erratically. She fired once and missed, fired again and hit the shuttle behind it.

"Stop!" shouted Sapian.

"Well, what the hell do you want me do?!" screamed Rosair. "It's got us pinned down!"

Joss could see Warper waiting, looking at him from a lower platform around the tip of the rocket. He leapt over to the ladder at the far side of the gangway, sliding down to meet him. He opened fire as Warper charged. Every round bounced right off of his armor.

Lucas slowed to stop a few meters in front of him. "You might as well give me the iris. Give it to me now and I might decide to spare you the torturous demise I've been planning. Your pitiful revolver has no effect against my armor."

Joss looked over at the platform running parallel and tried to estimate the distance between them. He looked back at the Centurion, and pulled something from behind his back. "That's why I brought this!" he said, rolling a grenade between his opponent's legs before leaping over to the next platform.

It exploded, taking Warper by surprise and knocking him back over the railing to the platform below.

Joss looked down through the smoke at his opponent. Energy surged around the Stranger's armor, but didn't seem to have any serious effect.

It only took the Lucas a few seconds to scale the ladder to where Joss was standing.

Joss looked over at the masked figure approaching and thought about what his next move should be.

...

Sapian ducked and weaved, practically throwing himself around the underside of a platform before snatching up one of the droids. He landed, smashing it hard on the ground, right beside one of the laser-wielding minions.

The soldier fired, narrowly missing him before Rosair took him out. There was one more between him and what looked like the entrance to the shuttle.

Sapian watched as the second man fired back at the Lieutenant. She'd found cover behind a rock-face built into the structure. He darted beneath the platform where the second gunman was planted, surprising him from the side. He disarmed him with his left foot as he went to pull the trigger, before breaking his neck with his two free hands.

The entrance to the shuttle was in sight. He knew the rational course of action was to help the others and make sure the area was cleared, but his eyes were fixated on the shuttle. Before he could make a conscious decision on what to do next, he found himself right outside the entry hatch. He looked around for a lever or switch, before noticing the palm-sized panel on the right hand side.

He placed his hand on the scanner. The door opened.

...

Reagan had pinpointed five targets the second he landed and was systematically moving through them. The laser weapons were easier to evade at longer distances but he was beginning to see the flaw in their function at close range.

A moment before they fired, he felt a tremor from his synthiant, almost like the magnetic interference from the energy generated by the weapon warned him of the shot's trajectory.

The Omega guard fired twice. Reagan stepped between the blasts and sliced off both the man's arms before kicking him over the edge. Another guard opened fire. He dodged one bullet, and then attempted to deflect the other with his reflective shield. He deflected the blast somewhat, but it knocked him back and he felt his armor weaken.

He looked at the shield and saw that it was almost destroyed. It took a second's concentration to re-form it before he moved in to counter. He made a mental note to rely more on his agility, rather than trying to block the blast.

He could see Joss on the platform below. His brother had retrieved a fallen weapon from one of his enemies and had aimed it at Warper.

Joss fired once. The round hit the Stranger's armor and energy circulated around each panel. He fired again, but the effect was the same.

Lucas looked up at him through the optical sensors, "Your mind is too primitive to understand our energy-phase technology. Why would we create armor vulnerable to our own weapons?"

Lucas stopped suddenly as Reagan's Vesica landed a few meters in front of him.

Joss looked at the weapon, which was within arm's reach, just as Reagan landed at the other side of the platform behind Warper. The sleek warrior looked confident in his composure; double-bladed staff at the ready. They had him surrounded but he wasn't showing any signs of backing down.

Reagan formed another Vesica in its place. His left shin-guard broke down and was reabsorbed to compensate, "Optimum-grade coral will damage his armor!"

Joss didn't waste a second before snatching up the sword and charging in. Their weapons clashed. It had been years since Joss had wielded such a weapon, but it felt natural in his hands. Joss brought the blade down hard and the swords clashed.

Josh was surprised by Warper's unnatural strength combined with his speed and agility. He dodged a strike from the right, before parrying one from the left. Josh countered with a slice across his opponent's shoulder. Sparks flew from the spectacular armor as two of the smaller plates flew off in opposite directions.

Lucas recoiled, feeling the damage. He could see Reagan waiting behind, and with a subtle twist of the weapon, the staff became two short swords.

Joss barely managed to block one of the blades as it came flying toward his head. He knocked it away just in time, but not before it caught his face, leaving a gash across his cheek.

Lucas attacked with the second blade knocking Joss's aside before landing a roundhouse kick across his face.

Reagan was about to charge in to flank him before one of the drones appeared from below, getting between them. It fired one shot that he managed to deflect with his shield, then another whizzed past his head as if to stop him from interfering. The drone's laser weapons were powerful, but nowhere near as devastating as the foot soldier's canons.

Joss was lying on his side. He could hear the Warper's approaching steps and adjusted his grasp on the Vesica. *Just one step closer*, he thought as he waited, then he attacked, swiping furiously behind him before jumping to his feet. He sliced his opponent across the knee, making the Centurion stumble. Joss followed up, quickly knocking the blade from his left hand, followed by a well-placed front kick.

Lucas blocked his next strike with his gauntlet; hanging onto Joss' blade as he tugged at it, metal grinding against metal.

As Joss tried to pry it loose, he inspected the effects of his attack as it sliced through the gauntlet. He saw blood begin to run down Warper's armor.

Lucus twisted the blade, making him let go of it before following with an upper cut. It knocked Joss on his ass and left him in a daze, "You looked almost surprised to see blood, like you were fighting something more, something beyond human. It pleases me that you'll meet your end knowing that I'm nothing more than flesh and blood. It was my superiority that defeated you, a millennia's worth of superior knowledge and power."

...

Reagan waited for the right moment to move past the drone. He tried to make a move and it fired a shot by his feet, just enough of a warning shot to keep him at bay. The Stranger must have been controlling it somehow. It was the bastard's intention for him to watch Joss suffer.

Reagan watched as Lucas grabbed Joss, and then decided it was time to take action. He pulled the iris from inside his robe and held it up for the drone to scan.

Lucas turned around instantly to see the iris.

"Is this what you're looking for?" shouted Reagan. "Why don't you let him go and I'll think about giving it to you," Reagan had that feeling again. The drone was about to fire.

He charged a few steps forward before launching his shield at the flying robot. The shield hit it, sending the robot spinning. It fired back at full power in several directions. The shield bounced back to Reagan in time for him to deflect one of the stray blasts toward the platform! The laser sliced clean through the ancient steel.

Reagan fell forward as the platform collapsed, only just managing to grab onto the other side. He looked down at the ground below. It was a good drop to the bottom. He might have survived it, but not without severe injuries. Both his arms rested on the platform, one clasped part of the railing to the side while the other held the iris.

Lucas bent down with one foot on Reagan's fingers. He released the iris to grab onto it with the other hand, sliding a few inches further down. Lucas snatched up the device without a second's hesitation, so preoccupied with the prize that Joss' stealthy approach from behind went unnoticed.

Joss took his time and was careful not to make a sound.

Lucas looked down at the dangling Paladin and was about to input the teleportation command to HQ when the tip of the blade became visible through the chest plate of the armor.

Lucas flailed around to face Joss, both hands clasped on the iris. Josh had let go of the blade and was trying his hardest to pry it from the armored gauntlets.

Bolts of energy started to surge between them, compromising the Centurion's armor. The plates of the mask slid back and forth involuntarily as energy tore through the shimmering metal.

Joss tried to make out the face of his enemy through the bright light. He felt every hair on his body stand up with the surge of energy, as well as an overwhelming pulling sensation.

Reagan could only watch, as the vortex grew around them, this time slower than before. There was a familiar high-pitched noise for an instant, and then there was nothing! They were gone.

Chapter 46

Reagan crawled up onto the platform where his brother had been standing seconds earlier. He looked around for any sign that he was near. The first thing he noticed was the silence, no more gunfire. "Rosair!" he hollered down the cylindrical structure.

Instead of a response from either Sapian or Rosair, the platform beneath his feet started to vibrate and rattle, followed by a quiet hum that was slowly getting louder. He might have guessed it was the shuttle before the headlights came on, dazzling him for a moment.

The hum turned to a rumble, rattling the unstable platforms. Sections had sustained heavy damage and he wasn't even sure he could get down without risking injury.

He ran to the other side to look for a way down before he heard the Lieutenant's voice.

"Akura! You better get down here…" she said from below.

Reagan cursed under his breath and decided to make his move. He jumped onto large beam leading to a small staircase. The beam held but the stairs it was supporting gave way, falling three stories and hitting the ground. The falling staircase had taken the surrounding plumbing and cable with it, bringing everything attached tumbling down. He could just about reach a dangling length of wire that was caught around the railing above. He jumped and grabbed hold of it, before sliding down 30 meters. It snapped several meters from the bottom, leaving him to drop awkwardly to the ground before rolling to one knee.

He heard her voice again. "Akura! Reagan!" she shouted.

It was coming from the open hatch, accessible from a raised platform at the other side of the hanger. He had a good view of the shuttle now and it looked like it had been tipped on its back end to face upwards toward the sky.

Reagan ran up the short staircase and went inside, making his way to what looked like the cockpit. There he found Rosair, with her gun pointed at Sapian, who was approaching what could only be the pilot's chair.

It looked to be a one-man vessel with the operations station situated inside a transparent sphere, front and center. There was a chair inside the orb, accessible from both sides through two round portholes a few meters wide. The chair was surrounded by what looked like relatively basic controls as far as he could tell. There were other consoles and workstations around the room, but only the systems inside the orb appeared to be booting up. He took a few cautious steps toward them.

"Tell him to get away from there, would you?!" demanded Rosair, glancing back quickly to see Reagan standing beside her. "I'm finding it real hard to think of a reason not to shoot him!"

"Hey! She's right. We've got no idea what this thing is. The bastard got away with iris and he took Joss with him," he paused for a second. "The mission's over."

Right after Reagan finished speaking, an alarm started to go off from inside the orb. Sapian hopped right into the pilot's chair without hesitating.

"Get the hell out of there!" shouted Rosair, before addressing Reagan. "I say we shoot the ape before he pushes anymore buttons."

Reagan raised a hand again in an attempt to diffuse the situation. "Everyone just calm down," He took a few steps closer to the control station. "What is it you're doing exactly?" he asked Sapian.

"I'm tracking this new signal. Or at least I think I am," said Sapian, scratching his head. I know these systems! I know them like I was trained to use them."

Reagan looked at where he was pointing on the 3D display of what looked like Orbis, or at least an older version he recognized from ancient scriptures. Another planet was visible on the display with what looked like a long tunnel between them.

"What do you mean 'trained to use them'?" asked Reagan.

"The Effigy led me to this location. He wanted me to find this place. I've been here before."

"If you've been here before, why the hell would he need to give you the damn coordinates?" shouted Rosair, taking a step closer.

"Not in the bunker, this fucking shuttle. This was my shuttle!"

Rosair and Reagan looked at each other, unconvinced.

Sapian slowly gestured to the 3D display. "I'm guessing the Centurion pulled his usual disappearing act? The systems came online as soon as we heard the vortex appear above. Its been monitoring the signal ever since."

"You saying we could use this thing to track them?" asked Reagan.

"I'm saying this thing's locked on to the signal," Sapian nodded toward Rosair. " I'd love to investigate further but it's hard to concentrate with a gun to my head!"

Reagan turned and looked at Rosair, "Let's hear him out. Someone's going to have to examine this thing anyway. He says he knows how it works."

"And you believe him?!" yelled Rosair. "Get a fucking grip!"

The two of them were silenced suddenly by the sound of the hatch sliding shut. They stared for a moment before simultaneously turning to face Sapian.

Sapian grinned at them before placing a slightly bent cigar in his mouth. He rummaged around frantically, trying to find his lighter.

Rosair marched right up to the other side of the orb and pressed her pistol right against the apes left temple. "You're going to open that hatch on the count of three."

Reagan had already moved over to the exit and was trying to force the electronically sealed door.

"You can't open it," said Sapian, with a smirk. "All the controls here are synchronized to my DNA. He found his lighter and lit up the stogie. "Like I said, this is my ship, and if I were you, I'd find something to hold onto."

Reagan started to hear sounds coming from outside the shuttle. He looked at the Lieutenant who had her gun against Sapian's forehead now, as he'd turned to face her. He watched as they stared each other down, Sapian casually exhaled smoke as if everything was going according to plan; Rosair clenched her teeth with her finger on the trigger.

Rosair suddenly turned her weapon to point it at the control terminal. " Shut this thing down or I put one in the controls! Even if this thing gets off the ground you won't be able to fly it. You might be a savage, but you're not crazy."

Sapian reached down calmly and securely fastened his harness. "I said grab hold of something. A couple of days ago this might have seemed crazy to me, but right now nothing has ever made more sense."

Rosair jumped around as Reagan placed a hand on her shoulder, "Move to the back of the craft. I can breakdown my carapace and construct a protective shell around us. It won't be indestructible, but it'll be better than nothing.

The whole thing started to shake around them as they hobbled to the rear. Reagan tugged on her arm so that she was behind him and crouched down on one knee. He placed his left hand on the ground and his armor reverted to its liquid form.

Rosair watched as the fluid coral bonded to the surroundings, hardening around angles to anchor in place. It started to reach up in sort of a crisscrossed weave around them, over her legs and around their waists. It grew out around the floor beneath them, securing them to the hull in sort of a makeshift harness.

Reagan felt the craft leave the ground with a force that pressed him to the back of the ship. He managed to turn his head enough to look out of the small window as they rushed past the ruined battleground where they had fought.

Rosair looked over his shoulder at the sky through the windshield as they shot up into the clouds. She still had her weapon clasped firmly in hand and thought about how she could have shot the ape there and then, ending it right now. Instead, she was being launched off the planet as far as she could tell, to who knows where. She suddenly felt panicked at the thought before remembering she was still within reach of her goal. If they made it through this and wherever they made it through to, she was going to make him pay for what he'd done. She wouldn't hesitate a second time.

Chapter 47

Gailan stood in front of the Templum Patrona, looking down the long staircase toward the station. The Effigy had been expecting transmissions to resume once the Viaduct was destroyed and had hijacked every broadcast screen around the city.

His speech had rallied the protestors to aid the authorities in keeping the peace. Chief Flint had reported that the situation at the Velodrome was under control and that the surrounding area was secured. She'd also explained that the Effigy's disciples had been surprisingly cooperative and had actually been helping the enforcers with the wounded.

Gailan felt the Effigy's presence behind him. There was something familiar about the mysterious entity. His significance in all of this was still unknown. He'd noticed him speaking closely with Le'san while the old Prefect lay on a stretcher. He appeared to have been comforting him, but as far as he knew the two of them had never met. What words would he have for a dying stranger?

Le'san's wound had turned out to be more serious than the he'd originally let on, and still he managed to fight until the threat was overpowered. The shaman initially appeared to lie down as if to rest after a hard days work, until he'd informed all around him that he believed his wound to be fatal. Still, the certainty of his fate seemed not to bother him.

He turned to walk toward Le'san, passing by the Effigy without saying anything. The Effigy didn't seem to be expecting any exchange of words. He only stared toward the west. Gailan realized he was tired after their victory and decided he wasn't in any kind of mood to start deciphering the man's actions.

Akura stopped beside the stretcher, the old hawk shrieked and shuffled closer to her master. He'd seen the bird aid the old shaman in battle many times, and had even been so unfortunate as to feel the huge talons tear into his own flesh. She had been his eyes and ears beyond the reach of his own senses.

Le'san lay almost directly under the coral trunk stretching the full length of the temple. One hand clutched his staff over his heart and he held out the other to feel the first few drops of rain as they fell through the opening at the top.

Akura always admired the O'sar people's connection with nature, a trait Gailan's people never fully comprehended, all except Reagan, according Le'san's reports. Gailan lowered to one knee and examined his friend.

He'd turned his head as he noticed Gailan approaching, "You'd waste time watching an old man die, when war is upon us?"

Gailan rested a hand on his friend's shoulder, "You fought like the young brave I remembered from the old days. You've earned a good death."

"Fighting against brothers, Paladin, which we shared peace with for a generation? I feel glad to die, if only to escape fighting yet another pointless war," Le'san's eyes closed as he reached up to hold Gailan's hand.

Akura nodded his head and looked at the old hawk as it fidgeted around beside him. "I suppose you want me to keep an eye on this old turkey? He's almost as stubborn as I am," he looked down at his old friend and waited for a response before realizing he was gone.

He gazed at the old shaman and the peaceful smile on his face. *Maybe he really was happy to die*, Gailan thought. He looked back at the old bird. "Looks like it's just you and me now," said Akura.

As soon as he'd finished his sentence, the thing took off narrowly missing him as it flew overhead.

Akura stood up and was about to curse out loud before he realized it was heading outside. It swooped up through the open doorway before landing on the shoulder of the Effigy, who was still standing in the exact same spot outside the main entrance.

Gailan removed his cloak, covering his friend before making his way back outside.

As he approached the Effigy, he noticed the bird cozying up to his masked face, a gesture of affection he'd never seen from the animal.

"That old bird seems to like you," said Gailan. "Just when I'd thought I'd seen everything."

"She senses the loneliness we share," said the Effigy. "We have both lost loved ones in the battle, and this is only the beginning."

"There's still no word from my sons. We're putting a team together to track them to the hopper's last know position."

"Look no further," said the Effigy, slowing raising his arm to point at a light visible on the horizon. "I've been expecting them."

The shuttle ascended rapidly towards the stratosphere, the thrusters illuminated the overcast skies.

Akura stepped forward and stared off into the distance. "What…what is that thing?" he said, looking to the Effigy who remained silent. "Are you saying that my boys are on that thing?!" his voice became more of an agitated growl.

"What you are seeing is destiny, my friend, and the beginning of a chain of events that our fate as a species revolves around," the Effigy turned to put a hand on the Prefect's shoulder.

"Where are they heading?!" demanded Gailan, in a panic. He watched as they reached far up into the sky and disappeared out of sight.

"Don't worry, my friend. You will see your boys again, but for now Joss has a head start and the others have some catching up to do.

………………..

Joss forced his eyes open to let in the light. It felt unwelcome at first, stabbing at his eyeballs like needles. He squeezed them together tightly once more, feeling them water before opening them.

The surroundings looked unfamiliar, but he appeared to be on some kind of landing platform. He looked around at the red cliffs surrounding him, and the red sky above. It looked like the sun was about to set. He tried to move his arms and legs, but they felt too weak. He attempted to roll over, noticing a large wall around what looked like some kind of base. Just when he thought that nobody else was around, he heard a murmur behind him.

He tried again to move his body. He flexed his core muscles and used every ounce of strength he had to try and turn over, throwing himself backwards to see Warper.

His opponent was lying on the ground a few meters away, the once impressive armor ruined and smoldering. Parts were melted and fused together. The bastard had his back to him and lay curled in the fetal position. Joss looked around for a weapon to finish the job, but found nothing other than a rock, twice the size of his fist.

He felt stronger now, the pure adrenalin reminding him of the fight a moment ago. He scrambled over to Warper and pulled the body over to face him. He was about to bring the rock down when the face became visible—*her* face.

He paused, holding the rock in the air. He wasn't expecting the soft feminine features beneath that cold, ferocious mask. She was so pale she was almost transparent, and she had no hair at all on her head and face. The chest plates hung off the armor partially revealing her breasts through her scorched jumpsuit.

He could have finished her off easily. She was barely conscious, with both eyes shut tight. She was truly vulnerable. Yet, all he could think about was how he should remove one of his own garments to cover her up. She was beautiful in an alien sort of way. Her skin almost looked like it had been preserved within the armor, aside from a few cosmetic wounds.

He was brought back to reality as he heard noises coming from over the towering wall. The blast door opened slowly in the distance revealing four more figures. They wore similar armor to Warper, only with subtle variations in design.

He wiped his eyes, hoping to clear up his vision, just in time to see one of them lift his weapon. A moment later, Joss felt a cold sensation rush through his neck and into his bloodstream.

He managed to raise his hand to feel the dart in his neck before he collapsed. Falling painlessly onto the hard surface of the landing platform, he felt his eyes get heavy once again and the last thing he saw was the blurred figures as they approached.

Chapter 48

The way home…

Reagan felt like he'd being away from home for an eternity, even though the 3 years had gone by quickly. Despite been excited to see his family again, leaving the badlands had left him with an unexpected feeling of sadness. He felt like a part of him would never return home, like he'd left the naive boy he was back in the wastes, forever lost. Reagan had seen things that had changed him and he tried to imagine his life if he never went back, drawn to the challenge of the untamed world rather than the comforts of home.

Le'san had noticed him daydreaming and gave him a firm nudge. "You don't want to spend your days wandering the wastes, you'll end up looking like Quadro." he said.

Reagan looked up at the old man he'd come to know so well. Le'san always seemed to know what he was thinking. "I feel like everything's somehow simpler out here, not easier, but not as complicated as life in the city."

"To experience the natural order of things is good for the mind. You wake when the sun rises. You find food. You seek shelter and eat as the sun sets. Your survival depends on what nature has to offer and whether you're worthy of the prize. This way of life can be a hard thing to leave behind."

Does every tenderfoot feel this way when making the journey back?" asked Reagan.

"Not all," said Le'san, "only those who fully embrace the opportunity. You have taken to this environment naturally, like you were born to it. It is familiar to you now, and will be forever a part of who you are."

Le'san packed his pipe and lit it up. They were walking through a narrow channel between two lush green mountains. Storm clouds hung in the air above the thick canopy of the trees that offered them shelter. The sound of the pounding rain combined with the leaves rustling in the wind created a clamorous tranquility.

"The reason you feel this way is because you have also witnessed the hardships many face living out here, suffering at the hands of those who choose to oppress." said Le'san. "You understand that the intervention in the fate of others can reap a significant reward, but can also come with great sacrifice to ones self, even if you survive the endeavor."

"Helping those people was the only time I didn't have to worry about food or shelter, there was only those in danger and the evil that threatened them. Making the decision to act was easy and I never even thought about failure or whether I might be killed."

"That's exactly my point," said Le'san, taking another toke on his pipe and chuckling to himself, "evil is not always as easy to spot in a place like Porta Orbis. The enemy hides behind masks of deceit and lies, their agendas disguised through complex politics that govern their actions."

Reagan looked ahead and could see where the plant life was starting to appear more sparsely in certain places, replaced by the coral-rich ground. As he looked closely he noticed the familiar shimmer beneath the surface; they were getting close to Reprataas, the place where he'd felt like his journey had really began. Le'san had taken them a different route to the way they came, and when Reagan had asked where they'd be setting up camp he hadn't given a clear answer.

"Wonder what's for dinner tonight?" He said to his master with a comical smirk. He could almost taste the hallucinogenic fungal broth and he wondered if he'd be partaking in the ritual one more time before they headed home.

Le'san laughed out loud before answering, "I'd been waiting to see if you'd catch on. I wasn't initially intending to pass through Reprataas, but Quadro has extended us an invitation to a special ceremony this evening. I thought it would be the perfect way to end our journey."

"I knew you were up to something when you wouldn't let me read the last message Talon delivered." said Reagan. "I can almost feel my stomach churning thinking about it. It almost seems worse knowing what to expect."

"Well you don't need to worry about that this time around. This time they'll be feasting and drinking; a celebration dedicated to Piesus' great sacrifice."

"Sacrifice? What do you mean?" Reagan looked at the old Prefect trying to get a read on his expression. He'd been keeping these details secret from him for some reason, but wasn't quite sure why.

"Piesus has expressed his desire to leave this life and give himself to the eternal bond." explained Le'san, while puffing away on his pipe.

Reagan knew what that meant from his teachings. The eternal bond was when you sacrificed your physical form to be one with the coral. It was how the Acolytes were able to form the Templum Patrona and inspire a whole civilization. He'd heard of Prefects attempting the practice before, usually when ailed with terminal illness or old age. The dying Paladin would forge meta-coral tombs around their bodies. There were at least 10 of these tombs around the gardens of the temple and there had been sightings of others found high up in the mountains, some suspected to be hundreds of years old.

"Is he sick," asked Reagan, but somehow he knew that wasn't the reason.

Le'san paused for a moment as if he was trying to find the right words, " To make a statement such as this, it requires the individual to have such a belief in the necessity of the act, that others can rarely understand."

"Is it true that he was the first to come here to study the phenomenon at Reprataas?"

"Not too far from the truth. He was part of the first group, a party of at least 20 devoted souls. He is the only one still living." said Le'san. "The others succumbed to the serum and lost themselves to indulgence. Some died due to self-neglect and starvation, while others became paranoid and delusional, eventually turning on one another."

"You're saying it sent them crazy?" said Reagan, looking a little surprised. These people were supposedly all Paladin, high-ranking members of the order. Reagan had heard stories from Quadro's men and some of them sounded a little far-fetched.

"You've walked in the dream world. Is it really that hard to believe?" asked Le'san.

Reagan knew the question didn't require an answer. The dream-state was as terrifying as it was fulfilling. You might become obsessed with the reward once you'd managed to control the fear that came with it.

"Piesus proved to be mentally strong enough to find a happy medium," continued Le'san, "He pushed the boundaries, trying to find out what led to the most beneficial experience without taking more than it was safe to consume. He was the first person, to our knowledge, able to visit another's dream sequence. It's a task that he always found extremely draining. He's tried to teach the practice to others over the years with limited success."

"Quadro told me that he rarely left the ruins of Sythatech, and never strayed too far from the living coral." said Reagan. "He's definitely like nobody else I've ever met; distant in a social sense, but his presence was eminent within the dream-state." They had met up with Quadro on more than one occasion over the 3 years and he'd taken the opportunity to inquire about the old man who'd shared his vision.

"You have told me what you saw during your experience," said Le'san, " I wasn't the only one surprised by the events you witnesses. You saw the conflict and death that haunts our past, as most do, but you were also allowed a glimpse of the future. To see both in the same vision, and from someone so young, it's unheard of. Piesus was apparently deeply unsettled."

Reagan wore a frown on his face and thought back to past conversations with his master. They had spoken about his dream-state vision a number of times, but Le'san had never suggested that his experience was anything out of the ordinary, and certainly not negative.

"You make it sound like I'm somehow responsible for what he's about to do." said Reagan, stopping dead in his tracks. He was about to enquire further when Le'san cut him off.

"Look ahead." He said, gesturing in front of them.

They'd reached the end of the passage where it opened up to look out over the clearing. He could see what used to be old ruins below, but it wasn't the decaying factory they'd visited before. It bared some resemblance in various sections but what was there now was nothing short of spectacular.

The structure looked to have doubled in height, with the once crooked spires twisting together to form a tower that stretched up toward the sky. The color and texture was also different. The bottom part was dull as lead like before but as it grew upwards the surface got lighter, looking more metallic and shiny. The surface at the top where it appeared the most reflective sparkled like a homing beacon, drawing them in.

Reagan turned back to his master for some sort of explanation. " What has he done? He can't be the one doing that, can he?" Reagan had never seen anything quite so amazing.

Le'san looked as astounded as his apprentice. "I've never seen anything like this before. We have to get down there. If we step up our pace we can be there within the hour."

As they hurried as fast as they could toward the newly formed tower, Reagan began to feel giddy with excitement. He looked at his master who seemed to be trying his best to suppress an overwhelming urge to laugh. "You feel that?" said Reagan, clenching his fist in response to an unusual feeling of euphoria.

"It is most unusual. If it is indeed Piesus' doing this, his dedication to the practice seems to have been worthwhile." Le'san stepped up his steady trot to an enthusiastic sprint, with Reagan close behind. The run felt almost effortless as they hastily approached the site, with only a slight feeling of frustration that they weren't getting there fast enough.

As they got closer to the tower, they could see Quadro standing outside, but not alone. He had another 10 of his warriors either side of him, standing in line. He couldn't help compare the questionable welcome to his initial visit to the location. *What was going on in there?* Reagan thought to himself.

As they approached the armed rank of men and women, they noticed that they were all standing perfectly still with their eyes closed. They had their hands rested on their swords but not in a way that looked threatening. Le'san slowed down, signaling to Reagan to do the same. He was about to say something when Quadro opened his eyes.

" You must wait here Le'san." said Quadro, with an unusually serious tone to his voice. " He has requested the presence of your student first, and him alone. There will be time for you to pay your respects at the ceremony afterwards."

Le'san looked a little confused by the strange request but understood that Quadro always meant what he said, even when in one of his more eccentric moods. He looked over at Reagan and gave him a nod.

Reagan felt that euphoric feeling start to fade away, replaced by hesitation and uncertainty. He looked back at Quadro's warriors and realized that all of them were now staring at him. He'd come to know some of them quite well, and others were strangers, yet all of them looked at him like refusal couldn't possibly be an option.

Reagan shook off the backpack he'd been carrying and removed his poncho. He tried to think of something to say before deciding that silence was the only response needed. What ever was about happen was of great significance and he wasn't going to ruin it with unnecessary questions. There was only one thing left to do. He nodded and walked forward.

To be continued…

Afterword - 10 years in the making

It feels like it's been a long road getting the first installment of this series competed. I came up with the initial concept a decade ago in 2009 after a year of travelling around the world. A few years before that in 2006, I'd finished my illustration degree in Manchester, England and was presented with the same challenge every postgraduate faces; actually finding a job!

I'd worked in various minimum wage jobs while trying to explore different artistic ventures, but the monotonous everyday grind seemed to be taking up all of my time and was holding me back creatively. I'd been working since I was 16 in bars and restaurants, not to mention a short stint in retail, as well as factory production, which was by far the worst. And even then I knew that doing that kind of thing for the rest of my life just wasn't an option.

Like a lot of people in my position, I just didn't know exactly what I wanted to do; only that I wanted to do something art related. I'd become interested in tattooing as well as thinking about writing a comic book, but didn't really know where to start with either.

In the meantime I'd also had a couple of friends return from backpacking around Asia. After hearing their stories and how awesome it was, I decided that it was something I had to do before getting into anything serious. If I limited my leisure activities and tried to save money, maybe I could go for a whole year! I thought I'd start in South America and work my way around, passing through Australia and New Zealand before finishing the trip in Asia. Now I had an attainable goal to work towards, which seemed to relieve the pressure somewhat. It felt like the first year of University again, a plan I could focus on for the foreseeable future.

I feel like my time abroad was a real character defining moment for me. Getting away from it all gave me the opportunity to take a step back and think about my life while simultaneously immersing myself in the different cultures of the world. It also gave me the chance to really get the partying out of my system, something I think back on as a distraction from productivity throughout and after university. It's not that I regret any of the amazing times I had and meeting the people I shared them with, but everyone has to grow up eventually.

While travelling, I really had the chance to think about a story I wanted to write. I'd been sketching out the characters and scribbling down notes, but it wasn't until about 6 months into my trip, that I came across something that really inspired me to get the ball rolling.

I was in a mall somewhere in Malaysia looking for an English language comic to read on the beach, when I stumbled upon 'The Resonator', and 'The making of a graphic novel'. This rare find was a two-in-one flipbook. After reading the story, you flipped it over to the reverse cover where there was another book. In this second book, the writer/illustrator explained the production from concept to finished product. This book is still readily available, but back then Internet shopping wasn't what it is now, and I was backpacking in Southeast Asia. It would have been the last place I would have expected to find it, in a pile beneath a bunch of other random books.

This book gave me guidelines to work from as well as helpful pointers regarding character development and plot structure. At that time I'd never really written anything other than essays at school and had no idea where to start. I loved movies more than any other media, so I tended to imagine stories that followed a similar pace and structure.

I thought I knew a good story from a bad one and often wondered how such obvious plot holes and sloppy writing made it into major productions. It wasn't until I started writing for myself that I found out how easy it was to overlook certain things; crucial details that are obvious when you watch a movie or read a book that somebody else has written.

Fast-forward to the end of my trip, and I'd met a nice Canadian girl in Laos (later to be the mother of my children) who was somewhat ahead of me in adulting and yet another major factor that made me re-evaluate where my life was going. She already had started a career in nursing, with a house she was renting out to pay for her trip. She was a little older than me, but it still made me feel like I had to get my shit together.

After travelling together for a few months we decided to settle in Bangkok, Thailand for a while to have a bash at teaching. I had a friend who was doing the expat thing and it looked like fun. Again, it was obvious to me that I wasn't going to do this for the rest of my life, but it gave me a job with a steady paycheck and time to write the script for my graphic novel.

Every shred of time I wasn't teaching in the classroom or occasionally socializing, I was working on my script. As well as writing I had taken on a few low paid (no paid) comic book illustration jobs to give me some practice working within the media. It was clear that I had had a long way to go, despite being what I considered to be a competent artist at the time.

Shortly after this is where I made my first crucial mistake, which I have since repeated, at least once more after. I was impatient. Having done a couple of small web comics I thought I was ready for a bigger project and jumped the gun.

I hadn't really finished the story, but had enough of a script for a first issue. I had a mate read it over and point out some undeniably laughable literary mistakes, and I thought I was good to go. I did have some solid character designs and a good idea of the environment, but thought I'd just work it out as I went along, totally ignoring the advice from 'The making of a graphic novel'.

One of my major character flaws is my lack of patience and wanting to rush to get as many things done as I can. It is literally the bane of my existence when it comes to people I'm close to and any project I undertake that you just CANT rush, like writing or art. If you rush it, it'll most likely be crap, meaning you'll have to redo it, meaning you'll waste more time, meaning you'll likely rush it again…and it goes on and on like this until you take a step back and give the project the time that is required. So if there's any advice I'd give an aspiring writer attempting a sprawling science fiction series, it's BE PATIENT!

On the flip side of the coin, it's good to be as productive as possible. Finding the time to write while in a relationship and working a day job can be challenging and there never seems to be enough time in the day. I'd say I've always been reasonably productive, or at least since my mid 20s. But now I'm in my mid thirties, with a wife (or rather, common law partner), two kids and a tattoo business to run, I really understand the value of time and how little spare you seem to have with everything that's going on.

So, back to Bangkok 2009, I've finished a 15-page issue of my comic. I know it's not done, but I'm relatively happy with it and I'm thinking I can use it in my portfolio to scout for future work. I wasted a lot of time redrawing, re-inking, and reediting the script; things I should have worked out when drafting the initial script, if I'd only been more patient.

I let a few co-workers read it, along with my parents, to most likely bias reviews. My dad was quick to point out that it was only action and barely an introduction to a story, a fact of which I knew but likely needed to be reminded of. When you have the story in your head, you can look at the pages within context, but that doesn't mean everyone else can. It just wasn't up to standard, and it was going to take a lot more work to turn it into a finished product. The more I read it over and over, the more I knew I needed to develop it further.

Now we were half way through 2010 and we were planning to move to Canada. I'd decided not to return to England, meaning everything had to be put on hold as far as writing was concerned. The comic went through further redrafting over the years after I moved. By the time the first part was finished, it ended up been a double issue, 50 pages in length. Now I felt like I had a fully finished issue of a comic book setting up the reader for the rest of the series.

My next step was publication, *how hard can that be,* I thought. For whatever reason at the time, I decided to contact Arcana in Vancouver with my book that was then titled 'Children of Terra'. I'd googled the title and found that there was also a Christian band under that name, but that didn't bother me. At the time I was really attached to the title for some reason, and wouldn't even entertain the idea of changing it.

It probably goes without saying that getting a comic published wasnt as easy as I thought it would be. Most companies don't want your whole book; they want you to submit a few pages of sequential artwork with a one page brief. I found this immensely difficult with my own story, as it seemed so grand in my mind. I still don't really know why I struggle so much to do this for my own work. I'd taken a job ghost writing for another author in between writing drafts of my novel, and found summarizing their project in a single page relatively easy, even quite enjoyable.

After waiting for a few weeks, the comic got turned down and I was about to look for alternatives when I had a worrying thought. What if it did get picked up? How would I find the time to do the following issues? I'd read great comics that got behind with production and release, only to die out and never be completed. That's the last thing wanted to happen to mine.

I thought this part in the development was worth mentioning since it was where I repeated the same mistake again. I'd been working on the script for the second and third issues and thought the second was ready to go. Again, I rushed through the illustration process and came out with a comic that looked completely different to the first. At this point it was 2013, 3 years after competing the last. My art style had totally changed; likely due to the fact I was spending most of my time designing tattoos rather that paneling comic books.

It was sometime shortly after that, in between home renovations and having my second child that I realized I would never have time to illustrate the whole series. A few years earlier, this would have been a thought that would have gotten me all depressed, but this time all I felt was a great sense of relief.

I was now a professional tattoo artist, and in relatively high demand. It was a day job that I loved (still love) and I'd been making plans to open my own shop in the near future. I knew I had to dedicate 100% on my focus on that until everything was set up, but I still knew that I wanted to tell the story.

Family and friends would ask me if I was still working on the comic and when I thought about it, the idea of tackling the workload didn't sound very appealing. To my surprise, I realized that it was the illustrating part of it that I wasn't looking forward to. I love drawing, but drawing all day, only to go home and draw all evening became less fun and more of a chore.

I'd taken on writing jobs on the side that I found enjoyable and challenging, and a nice change of pace from tattooing all day. At the same time I'd started reading the Ex-Heros series by Peter Clines, and was really inspired by the fast paced style of writing.

At the end of 2016 I decided I was going to convert my comic series into a written novel, writing the first draft in less than a year, then the second draft the following year. Almost two years later I finally have a finished product.

I've always found the creative process of others interesting and inspiring, and hearing other people's stories usually gives me the push I need to continue when I really need it. I hope to produce my own ' making of' book titled 'Children of Orbis : Ten years in the making', in the near future.

Thanks for reading! Keep an eye out for the next installment.

Paul James Thompson – mailto:pj@darkspacemedia.net

You can keep up to date with future projects at
https://www.darkspacemedia.net/

You can also follow me on social media

Instagram https://www.instagram.com/darkspacemedia/

Twitter https://twitter.com/darkspacemedia

Facebook.
https://www.facebook.com/darkspacemedia/?ref=bookmarks

Paul James Thompson - 2018

Acknowledgments

As I mentioned before this thing has taken me ages, and writing in various formats has been a massive learning curve for me. I managed to stay motivated by surrounding my self with the right people.

I have been lucky enough to have a fantastic upbringing. My mother had that affectionate approach to parenting a younger person often needs, and always told us to make sure we took the time to pursue the things we loved, so that we wouldn't regret it in the future. Dad was always, and still is a hard worker, which provided the perfect counter balance. He constantly reminded us that you have to work hard for a living if you're going to succeed, and that you need money if you want to take advantage of the many things life has to offer. They've always been there to provide advice and opportunity, whether it is higher education or financial assistance.

Now I have a family of my own, with a patient, loving woman (you know who you are). She has always supported what I wanted to do, despite having little interest in tattooing or science fiction herself. She was never afraid to offer her honest opinion or criticism, constructive or otherwise. Tracy has also given me two fantastic daughters that have taught me that time is an ever-dwindling commodity, and that you have to be the most productive version of yourself in order to be a worthy father figure while simultaneously achieving your personal goals.

Cheers to all my friends and family who have offered their support and have tolerated my ramblings over the years as I have tried to explain my story. Also, thanks to those who read those early iterations in script and comic book format. They were littered with mistakes and tarnished with shabby dialogue. Thanks again.

Thanks to my meta-readers and secondary editors Elizabeth Thompson and Geoff Thompson, (Mum and Dad). Thanks for your hard work and your opinions are always appreciated, bias or otherwise.

Thanks to my editor Rebecca Saloustros. https://twitter.com/Rsaloust. Her technical input assisted me greatly in reworking my novel to a professional standard.

Made in the USA
Middletown, DE
09 December 2020